Tainted Obsessions

Azreay'l

Gotham Books

30 N Gould St.
Ste. 20820, Sheridan, WY 82801
https://gothambooksinc.com/

Phone: 1 (307) 464-7800

© 2023 Azreay'l. All rights reserved.

No part of this book may be reproduced, stored in a retrieval system, or transmitted by any means without the written permission of the author.

Published by Gotham Books (September 13, 2023)

ISBN: 979-8-88775-522-9 (H)
ISBN: 979-8-88775-520-5 (P)
ISBN: 979-8-88775-521-2 (E)

Because of the dynamic nature of the Internet, any web addresses or links contained in this book may have changed since publication and may no longer be valid.

The views expressed in this work are solely those of the author and do not necessarily reflect the views of the publisher, and the publisher hereby disclaims any responsibility for them.

TABLE OF CONTENTS

Special Acknowledgment And Commitment vii

Dedication xi

Meet The Author xii

Plan Of Action And Milestones xiv

Disclaimer xv

Prologue 1

Chapter One: The Deceitful Security Breach 15

Chapter Two: U.S. Missile Strike Platform (USMSP) Departure 45

Chapter Three: The Passionate Underway 75

Chapter Four: The Covert Landing 107

Chapter Five: Island Of Ecstacy 135

Chapter Six: The Island Of Terror 167

Chapter Seven: The Joining Forces 199

Chapter Eight: The Cuban Massacre 229

Chapter Nine: A Traitor's Way 259

Chapter Ten: A Revengeful Quest 289

Terminology 323

SPECIAL ACKNOWLEDGMENT AND COMMITMENT

A momentous toast to my developmental stage fans who previously previewed *Tainted Obsessions* in its rarest form, in various online excerpts. Thanks to the generous strangers who pulled no punches in critiques. Your welcomed comments, appraisals, and constructive criticisms have helped bring *Tainted Obsessions* to its pinnacle.

Cover illustration: Dmitriy Shironosov
My hat goes off to my photographer, Dmitriy Shironosov, and his great staff at Photo Studio PressFoto.

https://www.gothambooksinc.com
Gotham & all major booksellers, the official sites
for Tainted Obsessions!

A special thanks to my previous editing team and those who previously supported editing and fine tuning of this novel. Bravo Zulu! Thanks for your quality time and endless efforts that have gone into making *Tainted Obsessions* a delightful read. With your help, *Tainted Obsessions* has received professional reviews, constructive criticism, and the required polishing before production.

For new authors: You never can do it all with just spell and grammar check alone. ~smile~

My learning experience is that you write one way, proof another, and go to production another. Of course, there seems like there are a gazillion other little gadgets with which to contend..., LOL. Just enjoy what you do, and have fun doing it!

For future fans: Thanks in advance for your eager eyes, which first caught *Tainted Obsession's* beautiful cover, drawing you near and sparking your curiosity. Your excellent taste has not gone unnoticed, my dear friends.

Look around...,

The world is full of followers and needs more leaders! Are you a follower or leader? If a leader, why allow others to deceive you into things that are an abomination.

DEDICATION

In loving commemoration of my grandfather(s): Mr. Randy Alston and Mr. Leonard Peterson, who inspired me to go the distance and stay focused on the prayers and dream.

MEET THE AUTHOR

Who is Azreay'l? He is a: freelance, amateur author, inventor, poet, business developer, songwriter, business planner, and visionary. He lives in Newport News, Virginia, with his lovely wife, Mary. His greatest gifts are those revealed from the North, encompassed through extraordinarily vivid imaginations, dreams, daydreams, and nightmares. Spiritual interventions are his creative blessings for his talents and works.

He joined the U.S. Armed Forces in 1980, served in the Army and Navy, retiring from the Navy in June 2001. He served 20 years of faithful and honorable military service and retired as a highly decorated Chief Petty Officer - Enlisted Surface Warfare Specialist (ESWS).

He concentrates his authoring towards the success of being a mixed genre author. His first four novels are under copyright with the Library of Congress (LOC).

He is ecstatic about the release of his first three patented inventions – GRID-LOCX (a new strategic board game), the Viral Shield (VS-2000), clear-shield face mask, Personal Protective Equipment (PPE), and CLICK! (a new strategic board game). He works diligently on his mega-billion-dollar valuation business plans for his future, global-enterprise venture(s): Dynamic Dimenzions, LLC, STITCHUZ, LLC, and JVINCO, LLC, which ties all of his current projects together. His business plan aids new investors in increasing the Return on Investment (ROI) for these start-up portfolios while assisting entrepreneurs in launching their businesses with lower overheads.

His authoring learning experiences are writing one way to perfect a style, proofing a hundred times if needed; only to search the production product, realizing you are not perfect! Of course, it seems like there are a gazillion gadgets with which to contend for proofing…, LOL. You can never do it all with just spell and grammar check.

Advice to new authors: Regardless of the world; full of critics, those jealous of your accomplishments, and those envious because they can never reach the goals you are trying to achieve, so they try to discourage you. Forget about em', as my old Italian buddy would say! Just go for it, and enjoy what you do, and have fun doing it! Nothing hurts a failure but a try…, some knowledgeable person once quoted.

To future fans: Thanks for your eager eyes, which caught MadUsoul's Crossing's enticing cover, drawing you near and sparking your curiosity. Your excellent taste has not gone unnoticed, my dear friends.

As for Azreay'l, if he's not working the 9-5 IT Security or sky-lighting in intelligence operations; he's drafting that next new invention, detailing a prototype, detailing an intense plot for the next novel, or working on that subsequent inclusion or expansion for his enterprise business model.

Azreay'l's hobbies:

Mixed-genre writing
Inventing
Drafting leading company business plans
Developing strong business models

PLAN OF ACTION AND MILESTONES

NOVELS

Other novels by Azreay'l. Now Showing!!!
"MadUsoul's Crossing" – Horror
"Liberty Call... Port of Spain" – Hilariously funny, Comical
"STITCHES" – Gut-bustlingly, Comical

Other novels by Azreay'l in the makings!!!
"The Mirror in the Mirror" – Bone-chilling, Horror
"To... Nowhere" – Suspense, Inspiration
"Forgotten Sorrows" – Heart and mind-melting, Deep Inspiration
"Drugged" - Heart and mind-melting, Deep inspiration

GOALS

Short-term: To be an established, well-known mixed-genre author, inventor, invention-publisher financier, and chairman of the board of directors for my future businesses.

Long-term goals: Become a business planner, developer for several new companies and develop into a thriving, generous venture capitalist and philanthropist.

DISCLAIMER

Tainted Obsessions... What's *Tainted Obsessions*? Merely a compilation of words pulled together from a vision, the author's. These words are thoughts that have crossed the minds of many generations gone on before us, those with us, and those to come. They're words written to express actions meshed with a part of our life cycle, our reproductive system, yet playfully scripted.

This novel is written for pleasure. *Tainted Obsessions* is a novel for entertainment purposes only! Please, don't get it twisted! This novel's written with an adult and mature audience in mind. When you purchase this novel, please keep it under lock and key, and away from minors or those with minor-like tendencies.

With my most sincere thanks, I present to you, *Tainted Obsessions.*

-smile-

Freedom of speech. . ., there is nothing like it, so enjoy!

PROLOGUE

In a rural community, a dimly-lit moon peeps from behind thick clouds. A torrential downpour heavily beats upon the earth. Strong winds slightly tear through a rural community, knocking over things not fastened securely for the forecasted, severe weather.

Not a creature is stalking on dark streets because even wildlife has retreated in the hopes of safely riding out the perceived devastating storm.

Days prior, Tricia, a beautiful, thirty-two-year-old, sun-tanned, five-foot-eleven, thirty-eight-twenty-thirty-eight measure, fit babe with long, black hair, a slender body, and curvy hips, sits at work polishing her nails. Out of nowhere comes a startling outburst of laughter. Unhesitant, she eavesdrops on coworkers and overhears them mentioning a new author, Azreay'l. Curious, Tricia patiently waits for the next outburst when the cubicle next to her draws to a gentle whisper. Three women and a gay male closely huddle around the computer monitor. They continually browse over more hot, juicy excerpts, and more laughter rises. The furor and laughter grow so loud that Tricia misses the author's title but quickly thumbs through several significant websites searching until eventually finding it: 'Tainted Obsessions.'

"Mmm..., there you are!" she whispers, cringing until rising and peeping up along the cubicle's ledge.

Quiet yet tensed, she gazes over a few heated excerpts. Her heart races faster until her warm flesh begins perspiring slightly. In a daze, she gently sways from side to side. Tricia's mind goes into a whirlwind, and she's mesmerized by the continual flow of sensual and seductive words. Her daydream draws her deeper until having thoughts of having sex. Immediately, flashes of previous heart-pounding sensual scenes rush through her mind like a tidal wave. She draws deeper into the first few pages until finally recognizing the mellow jazz from her iPod's headset rising in her ears. She twitches back and forth in her plush, leather swivel chair with one foot slightly pressing hard into the carpet as she rocks back and forth until feeling sexier and palpably in a sensual mood.

She thumbs through a few more pages, roaming over several more paragraphs. She twitches so much that her nylon G-string snuggly tightens, cupping her wide, round pelvis more firmly. Her soft hands rub over her soft thighs until slightly clawing before moving to her knees. Her fingernails slightly claw at her firm thighs once more until slowly pulling the bottom hem of her dress to her upper thigh. Her moist fingers caress the warmth of her soft thighs, warming them more. Instantly, she feels something stirring deep inside her lower belly, just below her belly piercing, and slowly working its way down to just above her wide, raised pelvis when her hips unconsciously begin grinding. Beads of perspiration begin forming on her forehead. Her collarbones became tingly when quickly releasing the mouse, fanning her blushing face. She reaches for her refreshing drink, taking light sips of iced tea before fanning more. She grows hotter under her collar, with hands unconsciously rubbing back and forth over her chest. She feels a slight resistance against her soft, moist fingers. Her eyes slowly lower as she sticks out her chest, finding nickel-size impressions protruding through the thin, sheer material. She gently closes her eyes and takes deep breaths for a brief second.

Something bumps against the cubicle, and she tenses. Within seconds, her body begins swaying to soft medley music, which her mind instantly grows focused on again. A smile quickly grows on her face. Without hesitation, she immediately pull out a credit card, figuring out her bills until quickly realizing money is too scarce this pay period to make the purchase. Without a second thought, she grips the phone tightly and calls her boyfriend to have him make the online purchase and ship the novel directly to her house.

From that evening forward, Tricia rushes home daily, growing impatient after not receiving the novel on its expected delivery date.

On the evening of the storm, she pulls into the driveway, finding a package neatly tucked away behind the rocking chair. She dashes from the car in a mad rush, swiftly running onto the porch. She brings the package to her chest, cuddling with it until slowly easing it away while staring at its decorative mailing wrapper. With an even tighter grip, she pulls the package into her bosom, mildly rocking from side to side in excitement. Her fast-beating heart begins racing faster.

The key turns, and she pushes the door open, rushing inside. With one firm grip on the wrapper, she tears the package and stares at the beautiful cover until snappily flipping it over. A smile instantly grows on with eyes slowly cast down the back cover. Her mind grasps each intriguing word, holding on before excitingly moving to the next word.

The room's natural light reflects through the skylight ceiling, dimming as clouds suddenly darken. For a second, Tricia squints to finish reading the last few sentences.

A sudden thunder crack roars following severe lightning flashes, startling her. She nervously jumps, catching a second bright flash through an open window. More loud, thunderous thrashes come, almost simultaneously, slightly vibrating the house. Her feet begin to shuffle across the floor as she rushes to the door. She peels the sheer curtains apart and stands, watching thicker clouds expressly approach. More distant thunder and mild flashes of lightning make the storm appear as if drifting away and then seemingly moving closer.

The soothing sound of rain picks up its momentum.

Her mind drifts, and she focuses on the gentle poundings of rain upon the roof.

In a daze, she soon finds herself looking into the mirror, staring deeper into it until subconsciously unraveling the bow on the back of her dress. Her eyes move up and down her curvaceous body until staring back, admiring her perfect, somewhat made-up face.

She seductively walks closer to the mirror, taking her time while swaying her hips harder with each step until she giggles senselessly. Her eyes ramble over black, silky curls and sandy blonde streaks. Her hair dangles about her face until slightly shaking her head and playfully smiling. Without a doubt, she knows she's a knockout, a total bombshell. Her concentration breaks, and she smiles in a playful mood, pretending to be the supermodel she had always dreamed of.

Her fingers run through her long, soft hair. She brings a handful up and over her shoulders and holds it in a pinned-up fashion, blowing kisses and winking. She slowly turns her head from side to side, with her hair slightly swinging back and forth before a few more poses. She dims her eyes to look even sexier, puckering her full lips and then slightly licking them.

She feels a little sexier, so she strikes another vogue pose, but with eyes dimming a little more. Her index finger slightly runs over the curvature of her face and then soft lips, until parting her perfect, full lips.

One hand slowly caresses her hourglass body and then moves to her shoulder. She softly grasps a shoulder strap, gently pulling it to one side until one smooth shoulder seductively slips out, then the other, while her hips sway just a little harder.

Finally, she drops her dress; down to nothing but pink satin panties and a matching bra. Her eyes rove over her pretty, unblemished, soft skin. She leans forward, grasping the edge of the dresser, and then turns to one side. Before she knows it, she sticks out one double-jointed, perfectly-curved hip and the other. Her sexy body unconsciously begins snaking in a wanton Egyptian-style dance. Her eyes wander up and down her perfect body, admiring her gorgeous body for minutes while performing a few dances, even more seductive. Without delay, her body moves on to other erotic dances that she's perfected over the years, from nude dances or stripteases for boys or men who had come and gone in her life.

In the heat of passion, a gently perspiring hand eases deep between her thighs, clenching tightly as her head gently eases backward, with her eyes closed tightly. A glossy, well-manicured fingernail finds its way to the rim of her panties, stroking back and forth along the elastic band before slightly pulling it from her soft flesh. She allows the band to slap gently against her tender flesh a few times. The continual playing with her waistband drives her wild as her mind wanders through past sexual scenes of men in her past. With one more tug against the waistband, her glossy-nail-covered index finger slips inside, her hand dipping further down until stretching her panties.

Her body turns slightly, easing back against the dresser. Her hands move up and down a few more times until she appears frozen, with eyes clenched tight while licking her beautiful lips. She gently grasps the dresser's edge with both hands, rebalancing until slightly standing with a sensual yet devilish look.

Amid deep seduction, and before she knows it, she's almost nude and striking a few more poses. She reaches for her phone when naked, snapping a few sexy pictures, and instantly emails them to her boyfriend. With one last snap, she eases the camera back on the dresser and stares deep into the mirror once more before turning her back to the mirror, pinning her hair over her head, and looking over her shoulder with eyes roving over her lovely backside. "Mmm..., Mmm..., Mmm!" she barely whispers.

Her round apple bottom gently eases back until she feels the coolness of the firm oak. She rises on tiptoes with a cheek in each hand, easing one cheek at a time on the dresser while rocking from side to side to absorb the coolness of her warm flesh. Her eyes rove back over her shoulder, wandering down the mirror until gazing upon what looks like a perfectly-shaped heart made of smooth flesh. Her head slightly turns forward and shakes as if in disbelief that something could be so perfectly formed and so beautiful. A smile grows with her eyes looking back once more while slowly grinding her hips and then moving them, sensually. Her hands caress her body at her hips, and both cheeks rock back and forth until fully turned on.

Her weight shifts as one foot draw further from the other until they spread as wide as they can while still supporting her firm bottom. Her long hair sways from side to side while plots the next position for what she's conceived in her mind. An index finger pierces her lips, and she slightly sucks on the tip, deep in thought.

Her back eases into the cool mirror.

"Sss!" she barely whispers as her back slowly warming while tensing for seconds. Her fingers run across washboard abs, circling her belly button for seconds before running along the top of her imaginary hairline. "Mmm..., damn, babe..., Mmm," she moans with her eyes closed while thinking about her boyfriend and their last encounter.

Within seconds, she closes her eyes tightly. She continually licks and sucks her lips. She slightly bites her bottom lip a few times in pure ecstasy. Her moan grows louder, and she controls it and slightly muffles it for minutes.

The storm begins pressing harder upon the community, interrupting her from time to time. The thunder grows louder, and lightning flashes are even brighter, yet both still seem somewhat distant.

Over ten minutes later, she's well overheated and deeply pleasured.

The too familiar yet pleasant smell of her fragrantly sweet nectar gently creeps into her nostrils.

Suddenly, a loud crack of thunder comes, causing her to tense. Another thunderous crack follows but sounds more distant. She quietly stands, listening for minutes.

Out of nowhere, golf-ball-sized raindrops begin pounding heavily on the old tin roof.

She drifts into a daze and soon is heavily thinking of another romantic encounter with her boyfriend. Tricia's mind instantly drifts again, and she focuses on how horny she is when her mind draws back to the novel. She freezes in an instant, thinking of what to do next, realizing she wants to shower and get comfortable before the long-awaited read.

In even deeper thought, she stares into the mirror at her beautiful body and grows hypnotized. One soft hand slowly runs down over her thigh and deep between luscious thighs. Her other hand glides alongside her thin waistline; fingers twirling small, gentle circles against warm, tender flesh again.

Within seconds, both hands meet, gently rubbing over tight-abdominal muscles until slowly inching upward while still twirling but barely touching flesh.

She turns in a sexy sway and eases on her tiptoes. She sits, slightly hung off the edge of the bed. Her sensual back-and-forth motion against the edge of the mattress makes her sensitive until her spine tingles. She becomes tenser than at work a few days ago.

Overly turned on, she leans back as far as she can go until against the throw pillows. Her long hair drifts off her shoulder, strand after strand. One hand runs up and down each smooth thigh, slowly stroking just above her imaginary hairline. Her hand cups the curvature of her wide, raised pelvis as she strokes deep in her thighs until palming the curvature. She leans forward, looking at the new tattoo just above her pelvis, which reads, 'LICKABLE.' She gently and playfully pats her pelvis a few times until a smile grows and eyes wander toward the ceiling in a devious stare. "Mmm!" she moans with a mischievous smile.

Within minutes, she's breathing even heavily and moaning lightly until it too, grows heavier. The delays in single, soft moans grow louder when she lets out a deep moan and then screams. She seductively shakes her head; her face frowning while in a deeply pleasurable transformation. With tension brewing, she grabs a handful of long hair in both hands, lightly tugging at it in a heated passion. She spins out of control, with eyes rolling slightly in sheer pleasure and ecstasy. Her toes tightly curl with cheeks tightly flexing tighter before repeatedly clenching and releasing for minutes.

Her legs flex until spreading them wide and stopping only when they're as wide as they can open and still support her awkward position. She grows weak, not wanting to surrender to massive pleasure. She grows even tenser until letting out a scream when cringing with her face torn up, trembling like a leaf, for minutes. She grows greedy for more pleasure, so she tries once more, covered in sweat and breathing heavily, when one loud and uncontrollable scream parts her lips. She freezes in place with her hand covering her mouth in disbelief, listening until the sound of the clock rises.

A sudden, sharp knock comes between a few heavy breaths, followed by a few heavy poundings, which make Tricia jump, nervously. She freezes, growing quiet when trying to hold her breath and laugh. Her room remains remarkably silent as she listens closely for the pounding, soon realizing it's from a broom handle tightly held in the hand of the old woman from upstairs, a familiar sound, especially with her boyfriend's weekend visits when accustomed to hearing it. The bang came again, then a few more robust whacks, until it abruptly stopped.

Tricia is exceedingly exhausted and breaks out with a smile. Her hands uncover and then cover her mouth when giggling and trying to hold her loud outburst of laughter. Her hands ease from her mouth and then hurriedly cover it again in pure embarrassment. She takes a few quiet steps, limping over to the couch and falling into a deep but muted laughter. She's unable to hold her laugh, still very tense, when it escapes. Her tightly-balled fist begins pounding the back of her squishy cushion chair to get most of her laughter out.

With a frown, the old woman finally reclines upon her sofa. Her eyes wander to and over the hardwood floor. She sits, pissed, but can't help but listen to the uncontrollable, loud laughter, which grows louder by the second. Unable to hold back the heavy laughter brewing deep inside, the old woman grasps a paisley-covered sofa pillow, covering her mouth. Her belly jiggles for minutes until a gentle outburst of laughter comes as she joins Tricia in a burst of silent but forceful laughter.

Tricia's laughter finally tapers off, and she drapes a towel over her sexy body and smiles again. She stares at the ceiling, shaking her head in disbelief, and then goes into a mild trance. Her mind drifts into a slight meditation. A vision of the old woman's sweet face materializes in her mind. Tricia wonders how she will conduct herself the next time she sees the old woman and grows deeper in thought. Her mind finally clears, and she gathers her clothing and heads for the bathroom. Inside, she cracks open the window and listens to the fading rain.

She immediately refocuses and adjusts the shower head to her desired setting. She climbs inside, tense from the hot water, until her body welcomes the intense heat. Freshly bathed and perfumed, she slips into her ruffled, dark-blue bra and matching panties. She cuts off the lights except for the one near the bed, which gives the room a cozy, romantic setting.

She slowly moves about the bed until comfortable and relaxing upon soft pillows gently pressing against the headboard. She reaches for the lamp, dimming the light just enough for reading.

Out of nowhere, she acquires a strong thirst and sudden desire for a nightcap when opening the bottom of the nightstand. Her hand slides inside, pulling out the fifth of Sekif's Gin, pouring half a glass, and leaving the bottle on the floor next to the bed.

She briefly glances back to find the novel slightly extending from under the pink satin pillow. She settles on her back, slightly reclining before downing her first shot. She pours another, takes a sip, and stares at the ceiling again. Her mind drifts to seeing her boyfriend over the upcoming weekend. Still not satisfied with the effects of the drink, she sits, taking yet another stiff shot, and then reclines, riding high on the pillows.

Minutes later, she finds herself bent halfway off the side of the bed, pouring yet another. She balances to sit up, and her eyes glaze over her shoulder at the clock on the dresser.

Within seconds, and like clockwork, the phone rings on the hour.

After clocking out of work, Darius, her boyfriend, calls as accustomed. Daily, he would call and talk to Tricia on his short journey home. Most of the time, he would call just to be sexually worked up. He especially enjoys when Tricia meshes her London accent with other foreign languages when talking sexy. Her toying in different languages while talking naughty would have him ready to pleasure himself either on the side of the road or in his parent's driveway.

The two are accustomed to talking for over thirty minutes or more before ending the call with soft kisses and heavy breathing while saying their goodbyes.

Tricia always says she loves him in her sexy, native tongue just to get him even hotter and more bothered.

After a longer-than-thirty-minutes session of naughty talk and sexy play, Tricia is well-pleasured and exceptionally weak when hanging up. She remains in one spot for minutes, on her stomach, half-naked. She lye tangled in soft, red satin sheets; one thigh and cheek exposed fully. Her breast presses hard into the mattress. Her eyes barely crack open, yet they're stale from total exhaustion. Her warm, gin-scented breath slightly overpowers the room when her soft whisper turns into a mild but gentle snore.

Later, she's tipsy, and over-relaxed. Her hand eventually falls lifelessly toward the floor, accidentally knocking over a half-empty bottle that collides with the half-filled glass of gin, spilling both.

The phone's irritating alarm slowly brings her out of a pleasurable dream of her and Darius in the heat of passion.

She stares slightly at the ceiling for minutes with her mind plotting how she would love for the dream to continue, then advances to how she would have had it end.

She slightly turns over on one side. Her bone-straight hair drapes slightly over her blushing face, predominantly covering her eyes, which are still frozen sluggishly. With eyes barely open, she gazes along her arm and down to glossy fingers when her mind drifts back to how delightful she felt before and during her call.

She lies there longer until she is irritated and finally fed up with the phone's ringing. She struggles to reach for the phone, accidentally knocking it to the floor. One foot slips to the floor as she staggers to stand. With the receiver finally in hand, she listens to the manly voice, which speaks in French, followed by a few sentences in her foreign language. She stands in a trance, looks down at her wristwatch, and hangs up. Her eyes drift back to the bed and then over at the novel. She leans forward, picks it up, and then stumbles over to the loveseat, dropping down and easing back.

By now, she's slightly pissed at not having cracked the novel open, and she's eager to get to a hot and juicy scene. The cover opens quickly, and her hands anxiously flip through a few pages. Her eyes sift through keywords in search of one word that would stop her cold in her tracks.

"Mmm…, there you are," Tricia whispers, smiling while running her fingers deep between warm, soft thighs and patting her wide, raised pelvis a few times.

She feels even more sluggish but reads several more pages and then stops on the page where the main character, Demetrius had just gotten wild buck while at sea with a woman character named Valencia Novella. She sits daydreaming and visualizing for minutes what she just read. Erotic scenes take her body on an emotional roller-coaster ride until breaking her concentration. She tensely reads more, trying to put the novel down, but well-connected scenes soon have her consumed and in the mood. Before long, she yawns a few times, fighting off her sleep. She makes it through a few more pages when she stops and grabs a bookmark. She wants to read more but desires to be wide awake, so she misses nothing.

Her mind rapidly shifts, immediately drifting to a deep conversation held days earlier with a battered, longtime friend, Kelley. The play-by-play graphic details Kelley conveyed about finding her kid's father in bed with another woman some time ago rush wildly through Tricia's mind. A gut-wrenching feeling rises in her stomach until her heart is heavy, and she's deeply saddened.

Deep down inside, Tricia wants to do something memorable to bring joy to Kelley's world, so she allows her mind to run freely.

A car door slams outside and breaks her gentle thoughts. She sits for a while, with a clearer mind, and then stands and walks over to the bed. She climbs beneath the soft sheets, snuggling up next to her pillow. After blowing car horns from a few passing cars past, she hears rain finally tapering off. Through her window, she sees the half-moon when a few porch lights come on, and the small community begins to come back to life just as she's nodding off.

Upon waking hours later, Tricia receives a call from her father, a foreign ambassador, who informs her of a prominent family investment meeting in London that she needs to attend. He goes into minor details, constantly stressing the importance of her being there, seeing how this will be a tremendous payout for her family.

During the call, Kelley is still heavy on Tricia's mind, so she tells her father about Kelley's ordeal and the hard times Kelley's been through.

He listens closely, then grows quiet, and then silently listens more but in a trance. Tricia's voice changes to a sweeter tone when she asks if it's all right to bring Kelley.

There is total silence as he thinks hard and a little longer. He leans forward and puts out his cigar. "Business is more important than bonding," he whispers, puffing when declining to have Kelley accompany her there.

After Tricia hangs up, she sits meditating for minutes. She walks around even longer until finding herself standing in the middle of the room. With little time to schedule the short-notice trip, she begins packing. She ensures the novel is the first item in her carry-on so she can enjoy it on her eight-hour flight. When she's almost packed, she makes a call to her supervisor and puts in an emergency leave of absence.

Months later, in Virginia, Tricia's boyfriend, Darius, introduces his cousin, Tom, to Kelley when Tricia and Darius manage to pull off their first blind date ever.

Based on Kelley's rough past relationships, when asked, she's particularly reluctant, but loneliness, and her wish for a new companion, is too overwhelming.

After Kelley and Tom meet, they're quick to realize that they're compatible and believe its love at first sight.

Later, Kelley gains total trust in Tom.

Due to Kelley's father and uncle's rambunctious lifestyles, she made it her business to refrain from bonding with her family.

In fear of Tom being judgmental at times, she keeps him in the dark concerning her father and uncle. Something inside has her feeling that disclosure could be dangerous, had Tom gotten too close to her father or known more than he needed to know about her family's lifestyle.

Advancing a year forward and in the present day, Tom Powells, chief of Strike Force One, has been engaged to Kelley Rice for a few years.

Their love is in full bloom. Over the course of a remarkably short time, they have become even more in love. They are accustomed to doing anything at the drop of a hat to keep the flame in their relationship strong. They prioritize remaining persistent in making each day meaningful, so they eagerly seek and explore new ideas to keep life remarkably straightforward.

Tom is seventeen years into his career as a Special Forces Senior Enlisted Advisor. Two of the four years with Kelley have been long-distance due to the world's crisis, operational commitments, and challenging Special Forces missions.

Kelley is a receptionist for a dentist. She's a single mother of two.

Tom is without children but treats Kelley's as if they are his own.

Kelley was born and raised in a small country region north of the Great Virginian Mountains. At twenty, she leaves the States by her parent's force to live with her father and uncle in London for five years. Though Kelley never liked jokes about being country, deep down inside, she's proud to be country.

With a desire to keep her past just that, she never tells anyone, not even her closest friends, about her devastating life in London. Without a say, she has a forcibly up rearing under her father's gangster and corrupt lifestyle.

Kelley's father is a successful businessman, and a corporate lawyer, before getting mixed up in his brother's criminal lifestyle. He has gained his illegal status from secret, illegal dealings, executed in the company of her mobster-type uncle. Kelley's mother and father separated when she was eight, around the time that her father moved to London with his oldest brother, a drug lord heavy into drugs and human trafficking.

Kelley's father had her trained by the best in karate and self-defense, due to the corrupt environment in which she lived with him. He felt he would not always be around to protect her. He also knew that as beautiful as she was, she was a prime target for the sex trade, a trade he too was heavily into, business-wise. Kelley's radiant beauty, lush figure, and provocative sandy-streaked hair made her a target of nearly every man's lust. Kelley attended the most prestigious colleges in London, including Cambridge. She was basking in wealth; her father had her tutored by the best scholars money could buy.

Kelley, a virgin then, went into her first sexual heat, five years too soon.

One day, Kelley is targeted and intentionally kidnapped. During a plotted city blackout, her captors place her body for sale to the highest, wealthiest bidder at a private slave auction outside the city.

Unwilling to give up her body to hoodlums and remain in bondage, she takes desperate measures, executing her skills in tactical and combat training, and it pays off.

In her first forced, pre-sexual transaction, she's able to subdue the drunken, wealthy patron and escape while he's undressing. Without a doubt, she knows she can't outrun the inevitable: the rich man's two athletic bodyguards. When recaptured, she takes desperate measures and kills both armed men with her strong hands and stealth black-belt tactics.

Safe in her home a day later, she makes a promise seeing how her uncle and father did not know about the kidnapping because they were traveling in France for a week. She fears her father and uncle's retaliation and punishment, so in fear for her bodyguard's safety, Kelley requests that they keep her kidnapping a secret. She even swore the household of her father's security staff to secrecy because of their fear of what her uncle and father would do to them.

The captivity and killing haunt Kelley nightly as she relives the men's brutal screams and cries, which play like a broken record in her mind. Deep inside, she knew she would always have to keep the capture and deaths well-hidden out of fear that they would retaliate and possibly start a small civil war, one they were highly capable of carrying out in an orderly fashion.

Tom was from a little town in Kestrel, North Carolina, and he considers his hometown monumental compared to where Kelley was born.

Kelley is extraordinarily soft in her demeanor and always keeps to herself. Her life before the States focused only on education, though she's forced to live around drugs, human trafficking, and prostitution. The crime she'd seen living with her father and uncle could have made even the cruelest of the cruelest blood boil.

During the last year or two of her stay in London, the pain she endures turns her cold and callous. She drops down into a deep state of depression after seeing her male companion's execution in broad daylight while they sit outside a restaurant in the heat of the day. Back then, visuals of her friend's execution would flash through her mind nightly in sweat-drenching nightmares. She occasionally would wake in cold sweats three or four times a night.

Shortly thereafter, her father would force her into psychiatric counseling. He demands that she block out everything from her first day in London until that day. His fears were that the things she had encountered would come back to haunt her. Deep in her mind, she knows its best that she accepts his demands, and she knows he's only making the demands in her best interest, so she accepts.

Upon Kelley's return to the States, she's quick to adapt to a less stressful society and a more settled life before exposed to more drama from the first man she's ever loved, Jeff. She's become self-coping without further counseling and was doing well with putting her days in London behind. Her relationship with Jeff eventually turns her world upside-down, and she spirals into a deep depression from the things Jeff takes her through when he decides to show his hidden, womanizing, and abusive traits.

Kelley's life before Tom focuses on and around the kids after ending a long, dead-end relationship with their deadbeat dad, Jeff.

Jeff is exceedingly selfish, abusive, and a roadrunner who never has made time for Kelley or their children. At every given opportunity, Jeff would go out of his way to do anything to bring Kelley down to nothing just to keep her unhappy.

Kelley, now thirty-five, was deeply in love with Jeff at one time but over the years, she has become resistant to his physical and verbal abuse. However, deep inside, there's something emotionally attaching her to Jeff, though she keeps her feelings weighted deep inside. Jeff is her first true love, so it was a constant battle, fighting off deep feelings for the first love she once knew.

On two occasions, there were incidents of physical abuse stemming from Jeff staying out all night or not coming home for several weeks.

Too often, Jeff would spend bill money on booze and women, forcing Kelley to borrow from friends and relatives just to make ends meet.

During hard times, life was difficult, forcing Kelley to take on odd jobs. She even entertained thoughts of stripping at the Magic Castle just to make ends meet with the little extra money she was receiving from public assistance.

On several occasions, Kelley has found herself struggling to keep her head above water with property owners and creditors. Throughout life, Kelley knows her blessings, coming and going, and she's always able to pull through any situation with a little prayer and faith.

Something inside makes her feel like she's always on the run from her past, so she sometimes remains distant from friends. She lived a somewhat sheltered life when with Jeff. When things got bad between them, Kelley was devastated before the incident that broke them apart. She came home from work one day to find that Jeff had managed to block her department store and credit cards. In his devilish ways, he had figured out a way to gain access to her personal banking accounts, even her cell phone, in an attempt to exert what he thought was his manly power over her life. She was quick to grow tiresome and was dead set on not giving in to his childish games.

With her father, she knew that untold wealth was at the tip of her fingertips, but after short periods of meditation, she always seemed to come to her senses. She didn't want to make the grave mistake of rekindling a relationship with her father.

On several occasions, her father would send huge certified checks for her and the kids, but she would burn or tear them up.

Kelley's immensely attractive and has a compassionate heart.

Finally able to put her past behind her, or so she thinks, Kelley has become one with a very loving spirit. She is one who truly loves sharing. She would give a stranger the clothes off her back and has a genuine concern for people, always willing to lend a hand to friends in need. She's exceedingly secretive, and when with Jeff, she never wanted anyone to see what she was sanctioning in her abusive relationship, afraid of rejection or ridicule.

Tom and Kelley's life together made them realize they had endured their share of deadbeats.

Some time ago, Jeff, lost in his own little world, had not realized Kelley had outgrown him and his crap.

Kelley ended her relationship with Jeff after coming home early from an out-of-town casino trip with the girls. She catches Jeff with her best friend, fast asleep in their king-sized bed. She's stunned and in disbelief. Kelley stands at the bedroom door, furious after finding them cuddled, naked, in her new, unused satin sheets. So many murderous thoughts run through her fierce mind, but her pain won't allow her to act immediately upon her anger. She stood in silent tears for what seemed like hours, a total mess and consumed for the moment, staring into the face of the man she loved and friend who betrayed her. Her old lifestyle, which she vowed to keep locked away, flashed through her mind, and her friend's execution in London plays through in slow motion. Repeat sessions, recommendations, and self-therapy from counseling soon rush in as she gains control of her murderous thoughts, just enough to calm down.

Soon, visions from the front door to the bedroom flash through her mind. Her temperature rises, and the room begins spinning slightly. She sniffs, crying while backing from the door with her foot accidentally coming down on one of her son's toys, slightly smashing and breaking the plastic.

The loud noise instantly wakes Jeff and the woman with them, nervously jumping up, tipsy-eyed. They looked around, quickly easing off the plush mattress and scrambling for clothes. In fear, they dressed speedily, bumping into one another while running around looking for other clothing previously flung all over the place in the heat of passion.

One thing for sure, it's not quite clear what might have set Kelley off; it could have been the rose petals leading from the front door to the bedroom, the two empty champagne glasses on the mantle, or empty, dinner plates for two left on the dining room table with her new, unused, lipstick-stained, long-stemmed glasses. Then again, it could have been the clothes strewn from the dining room to the bedroom or the stained panties hung on the bedroom's doorknob, all the scenes Kelley had only dreamed of and never experienced.

On the other hand, there is one story for sure that is not just a rumor, and that is; Kelley almost killed that poor girl. In her furor, she put a permanent, deep scar across Jeff's upper thighs while trying to dismantle the manhood he had always bragged about the whole time she had known him.

On the brighter side, Tom, on the other hand, is terribly civilized. He's well-mannered and liked by everyone, and he knows how to naturally sweep women off their feet with his Southern accent, charm, and hospitality.

Tom's worst relationship was with an immensely wealthy and spoiled brat who cheated on him with her ex-boyfriend, months into their going steady.

Her secret escapade resulted in pregnancy, so she's quick to try to pin it on Tom. She and her family are one hundred percent certain that it's not Tom's baby. She suddenly wanted to give up the other person and make her relationship work with Tom simply because the other person was a lowlife and deadbeat.

Through DNA, it's determined that Tom is not the daddy; nevertheless, her parents try to buy Tom's hand in marriage. Their little angel had finally gotten a wake-up call and realized her Mr. Right had come and gone.

Immediately after the breakup, his ex becomes pissed when constantly rejected. She's on a war path and determined to make Tom's life a living hell, even across remote states, and she's not one to give up or in so easily.

With Kelley now Tom's top priority, he's no longer willing to jeopardize his love by putting up with his ex's sporadic little games. He becomes immune to her foul play and plots. He is at a point in his life where he wants to end his ex's little masquerade forever.

At some point, his ex-fiancé finally realizes it is over. In her most cunning and feeble attempts to undermine him, out of spite, she descends as low as to have him arrested for assault and battery. She knows Tom doesn't have an abusive bone in his body but wants to project him differently before friends and family. She's deep in her scheme to make the charges stick, but as fate would have it her girlfriend refuses to lie in the end, afraid of making fraudulent statements.

Over the years, distance and high expenses from her mischief ultimately lead her to find others closer and more focused on her childishness. Those other men soon realize that her childish behavior is too expensive and emotionally draining to endure, so she now constantly moves in and out of more short-term sexual escapades.

Jeff, on the other hand, is different. He's brilliant at using the kids to harass Kelley whenever he's bored and decides to show up without notice. Kelley rarely heard from him until she initiated a child support order for seven-hundred-and-ninety dollars a month. To him, this outrageous high court order was much higher than the zero child support money he had grown accustomed to paying. To Jeff, the injustice of having to pay the high settlement gave him a reason to call more often, just for the hell of it. He would make contact just to piss her off or upset her, especially after paydays, when he would find himself tense while opening the white sealed envelope with his depressing paycheck after two hard weeks of labor in construction.

Kelley's acceptance of Jeff's inappropriate behavior eventually becomes a serious problem for her and Tom.

Tom soon grows convinced that Kelley still has a peculiar spot in her heart for Jeff though his hidden curiosity is not strong enough to support his theory which is drawn out of a little jealousy. Regardless, Tom always manages to ignore his thoughts because deep inside, he loves Kelley with all his heart and feels she's the perfect partner to keep him happy and grounded.

Out of Kelley's genuine concern for others grows natural resources in loving a man deeply and sensually. She's instrumental in keeping Tom's spirits high because she supports his goals and aspirations. She's passionate about accepting his little likes and dislikes, which makes him complete.

Reared by a tight-knit family, Tom is decidedly family-oriented, and he's a perfect gentleman and scholar. He is ready to settle down and wants a family fully assured that Kelley is the only woman he wants to secure in his dreams of family and happiness. Tom knows that Kelley's spiritual and outer beauty, with her special and loving characteristics combined with talent, is hard to find in many women.

Tom would schedule his regular duty tours aboard ships during the summer months, when able, to be with Kelley and the kids during the winter. Tom and Kelley consider themselves outdoor enthusiasts, so it's only natural for them to look forward to a vacation in the Great Tennessee Mountains at Lake Patina, an exclusive skiing resort, in the dead of winter.

CHAPTER ONE:
THE DECEITFUL SECURITY BREACH

In Washington, D.C., a dark, gloomy sky sends tiny ping-pong-sized raindrops heavily pounding upon the earth for hours before subsiding. The full moon moves northwesterly at a moderate pace, shining through various openings in thick clouds.

What appears to be a twinkling star grows scarcely seen with the naked eye, continually fading behind various clouds and reappearing at intervals. Finally, the Mach speed of the star-like object slows. The undetected malicious XV11 satellite terminates its intensive search for the unmapped, undisclosed Command Center. The satellite stands still for minutes and then slowly spins on its large spindle. It waits patiently for the right moment to transport its illegal signal in an unauthorized download.

Inside the Command Center, two hours remain during maintenance downtime before deep-space, satellite, and intelligence operations resume. Staff stands around in dressed-down military uniforms, talking amongst one another, but some return to their workstations after their last evening break.

After some time, a side door opens, and Captain Wright enters, dressed decoratively with medals dangling about his chest. "I have the CONN and DECK!" he shouts over moderately whispering voices.

Outside the Command Center, satellite antennas maneuver, synchronizing with outer space satellites. Red, yellow, and green lights flash and alarm in tandem.

Without warning, a red threat radius changes into a bright blue circle around the Command Center, and its assets begin illuminating bright red until in a pulsating glow.

Inside the center, large monitors flicker as if on the brink of blacking out.

"Damn! What now?" the captain shouts, slamming his headset to the floor.

"Sir, we're being jammed!" Commander Dukes shouts, surprised.

"What! What the hell?" the captain responds, springing from his high chair.

"Good evening," a deep, somewhat-familiar voice resonates throughout the control room, bringing most in fear when instantly realizing the breech. "No need to adjust your monitors; I'll have my technicians do it for you." The distorted screen slowly clears with the man's image zooming in and out at intervals. "You may not know who I am, but that's irrelevant at this point but know this..., many nations will view this video I'm about to download if you do not meet our demands within the prescribed times," the unknown man says, passing a disc to one of his men.

"This is absurd! Who the hell are you?" Captain Wright shouts, gazing over the Cuban major's uniform, his insignia, and then his gold nametag before looking over others neatly dressed down in dress uniforms.

"No need for hostility, captain! What I need for you to do is prepare to record this broadcast."

"Wait!" the captain shouts in rage. "I'll record your damn footage, but only over secure circuits." Finally, the captain recognizes the man from a previous U.N. mission briefing by the deep scar on his face. The captain motions to Mr. Villan (Mr. Vee), the communications officer, when meeting him in the back of the room.

"Colonel Shaw…, assumes the CONN and DECK!" The captain yells when exiting with Mr. Vee hot on his trail while rushing through long corridors until bursting through the conference room door.

The captain turns on the recorder, which automatically disables the screen in the main control center.

Instantly, the major appears on the big screen but seems somewhat distracted before looking up again.

An unusual top-secret trademark flashes immediately across the screen, followed by indirect footage of several camouflage men viciously running through a dense forest and then the bushy woods.

Instantly, the captain realizes the filming is that of Strike Force Two when a uniform patch comes clearly in view when a man passes.

They closely watch the team maneuver around a tropical-like island. Soon, close-up and remote footage captures the team sweeping through villages and killing men, women, and children. The footage soon transposes to a relaxed military camp, where the men seem drunk while partying. The final scene ends with half-naked, beautiful women strip dancing before the men to a piece of Jamaican-style music, which softly plays in the background. The screen blinks a few times when white lights illuminate the conference room, and the Cuban major's war-torn face reemerges.

"As you can see, the team is well, sir. They are captives, heavily sedated for their safety but they know that the women take excellent care of them while in captivity," the major says in a deep Cuban accent. The major mischievously smiles while reaching for the disc and case, which one of his men passes back to him.

"This can't be!" Captain Wright shouts, slamming the bottom of his balled fist against the shiny mahogany table with tears welling until dropping from his cheeks.

"Stop kidding yourself; you damn old fool! Listen! You will receive an express package in two days with further instructions. You just tell your government that they had better pull their heads out of their four corner contacts and deposit one-point-four billion into the Jewels' Bahamian bank account if they don't want this film aired before the U.N., other countries, and American people!"

The man signals one of his technicians when the screen goes blank.

The satellite stands still until it increases its rotation. It rotates a few turns backward, reverses directions, and begins slowly spinning until it reaches a very high-speed rate and zooms across the dark sky until vanishing.

"Call Admiral Kitts!" Mr. Vee says, handing the captain the preprogrammed secure uplink phone.

The captain drops down in the plush leather chair. He presses a button, which automatically dials, and waits for the answering machine message to end. "Sir, its Captain Wright..., sorry for calling so late, but we have had a code-one alert requiring your immediate attention. Sir..., can you please return my call without delay..., thank you."

After some time, the main control room door swiftly opens, lightly slamming into the wall before retracting. "This is Captain Wright resuming the CONN and DECK! Make your reports..., Chief, switch to dead reckoning and satellite tracking. Let's try reacquiring that satellite's signal, and if not, reacquire our intelligence image outside of Kuwait."

The noise level drops to a dull roar when the team begins the intensive and extensive search for the unknown satellite for over thirty minutes without success.

Commander Dukes stares over the huge screen, quickly assessing the threat indicators. "Nothing but the ballistic missile tanks are still on Route 31. I'll transmit the images to our area commanders via the Persian Gulf Commander," Commander Dukes says, still aggressively staring into the satellite's monitoring screen directly overhead.

When a red light blinks near the monitor, everyone continually stares at the screen, observing several camouflage tanks taking cover under trees.

A steady buzzer sounds off when the satellite acquires an active lock on the tank's position.

"Captain Wright..., you have an outside, secure call, sir," the female communications officer says in a mild tone while adjusting her headset.

"Very well..., patch it to the conference room," he says, exiting through the double doors after relinquishing the CONN and DECK again. He enters the conference room and finds the phone in an unsecured mode; when switching to secure and starts in on his initial pre-brief and mentions recognizing the Cuban major. When the call ends, the captain drifts into deep thought of the victim's screams, which plays vividly and continuously in his mind.

Within the hour, Lieutenant Smith, a very tall gentleman, and Admiral Kitts, five-foot-eight and medium build, arrive, dressed remarkably casually and almost identically: hats, trench coats, and shiny, black dress shoes.

"Evening, sir..., since you've been pre-briefed, I'll move straight to the footage," Captain Wright says, dimming the sconce-type wall lighting and overhead lights.

The unfamiliar logo reappears, and the video plays in its entirety, with the projector automatically activating the bright lights thirty minutes later when the video stops.

"Well, that's all, sir, but as mentioned, further instructions are forthcoming in days concerning the transfer of one-point-four billion into a Jewels' Bahamian account, so we don't have long before they scramble our network's signals."

"So..., 1.4 billion dollars and more info in weeks, huh? Hell, man..., it will take weeks just to get approval, more or less transferred." The admiral cuts his eyes over at the lieutenant, who seems to be in a daze. "Lieutenant..., here, take this and burn off a copy of the disk for Strike Force One's initial briefing," the admiral says, handing over the gold, classified-stamped disk.

"Strike Force One?" the captain anxiously responds, shocked and in deep thought.

"Well, of course! Who else can handle such a task swiftly and knows these Cuban operations areas better than any other strike force unit?"

The captain gapes at the floor in disbelief. "Who would oversee such a huge, untrained, unplanned mission, sir?" the captain nervously asks.

"The lieutenant's here's been anxious to get back into special warfare and tactics," the admiral says, cackling while looking at the lieutenant, who mischievously smiles back.

"Wouldn't miss it for the world, sir," the muscular lieutenant says with his eyes softly roving over at the admiral.

"Captain Carrington's their C.O., so I will order in Lieutenant Smith here as the Executive Officer (X.O.)..., so there..., that was easy. Well, gentlemen, have a great one! I have a busy day at the White House tomorrow morning, so I had better be going," the admiral says, walking over and reaching for the doorknob.

When Admiral Kitts opens the door, he sees the back of a man's head as the man is about to turn at the next corridor. "Admiral Michaels?" he calls out in a moderate tone. He picks up his pace, swiftly coming up on the corner, but doesn't find him anywhere in sight.

The captain and lieutenant eventually walk out and find Admiral Kitts approaching.

"You must have forgotten they closed off the back exit, huh, sir?" the captain says, smiling when hearing the lieutenant giggle and seeing the admiral smiling.

"No..., not really..., I thought I saw Admiral Michaels," he says with a somewhat puzzled look when looking back in the direction he had just come from again.

"Maybe it was Sergeant Williams..., because most people think they look like brothers. I don't know why Admiral Michaels would be here this late unless there was a hot intelligence mission underway," the captain says.

Captain Wright escorts the two of them to the side exit and closes the security door when the admiral and lieutenant reach the bottom level, where they continue in conversation.

The following day, at an early morning meeting, Admiral Kitts unknowingly presents the deceptive intelligence information. He obtains endorsements for launching the covert operation later that afternoon and immediately phones Captain Wright via secure communications at the Command Center.

When the captain receives the mission's details, he feels giddy when the conversation transitions into matters that are more sensitive, and the admiral discloses highly-classified information, even beyond top secret, unknowingly.

"USMSP R. L. Peterson is the transport vessel," he goes on to say. "She's refueling in Norfolk, Virginia, as we speak. Strike Force One needs to be onboard no later than midnight the day after tomorrow. Authentication time, one-six..., I'm prepared to authenticate!"

Captain Wright's eyes scroll over the aluminum authentication device. "Roger, sir, authenticate C4574," the captain responds, rapidly flipping through the electronic decoder token hung on a lanyard around his neck.

"This is Admiral Kitts; I authenticate A78568, out!"

The captain hangs up and instantly motions Mr. Vee to the back of the room. "Commander Dukes, bring me the strike authentication booklet!" the captain says in a confident yet commanding tone.

Everyone looks around, amazed at hearing the commander open the triple-digit safe, which is not common. The commander reaches inside with trembling hands, dragging out the second authenticator.

Bystanders instantly hear keys clanging together from the commander's hands nervously trembling after the authenticator is free and lifted from the safe.

"Chief Jones has the CONN and DECK!" the captain yells, holding the door and waiting for the commander and Mr. Vee to exit.

The door in the corridor swings open, and the three men approach the security vault.

Inside, the commander affixes the keys to the secure phone when a light but pleasant automated woman's voice speaks. "Strike Force One is active; please remove the Sky-Tel keys..., thank you."

Strike Force One's recall pagers sound simultaneous.

Specialist Ogwin is sitting in a dark theater with his girlfriend and his girlfriend's two kids.

Specialists Antonio and Bobby are at a BBQ at their parent's house. Ensign Terry, who's married, is at his girlfriend's, frolicking with her in front of the fireplace.

Specialist Johns and his wife, who are expecting their first child, are at the local supermarket.

Captain Carrington is at home, lying on the floor, playing the game, 'TOP COMMANDO' with his three-year-old son while his wife sits in the recliner, quietly crocheting.

The three of them continue staring at the de-energizing lights on the panel. "That completes the automatic callbacks with the exception of Chief Powells," the commander says, still looking at the one un-lit callback button next to the chief's name. With his fingers swiftly scrolling down the phone roster for Tom's home number, the commander's hand moves forward. He furiously dials with eyes still locked on the row of numbers.

The phone rings a few times and then stops.

He starts dialing again when hearing the door swing open.

"Afternoon, gents," Admiral Kitts says, walking in behind the lieutenant, who's forcing the door open against his back. "Lieutenant," he says, turning and passing the lieutenant a large, brown envelope containing the battle orders. "Captain, report on the team's activation," the admiral says, sitting at the head of the table.

"Activation's complete with one unaccounted for, but it'll immediately be taken care of, sir."

The admiral nods and paces around, fidgety for a bit before exiting. He comes up to the intelligence briefing room, where he finds Admiral Michaels and another junior officer in deep conversation. He stands to the side, with Michaels nodding, twisting his long waxed mustache ends, and acknowledging his presence. He stands waiting to talk with Michaels but soon walks off and leaves after feeling Michaels will never end his long-winded conversation.

Hours later, Admiral Michaels sticks his head inside the operations control room and motions Captain Wright into the hallway, asking him to provide a detailed synopsis of the approved operation while nervously twisting his long waxed mustache ends.

Captain Wright frowns as he questions in his mind why Admiral Michaels would ask about the operation, seeing how he's the targeting officer, and not directly involved in that particular mission, which is a violation of the new 'You sure as hell don't need to know policy'.

"With all due respect, Admiral, under what authority are you asking for this covert operational information?" Captain Wright finally blurts out nervously.

"Now, you look here, damnait! My division will supply targeting information should these guys require inland intelligence and targeting with SAS missiles."

"Well, sir, as far as I'm concerned, and with all due respect, I'm not sure you have the clearance, but I know for sure you don't have the need to know."

"You listen here, you little dipshit! Damn you..., you just report to my damn office in the morning, and I'll show you who has damn authority. For the life of me! Moreover..., to think that I was recommending you for a promotion to line officer! What the hell was I thinking, an?" the admiral shouts with wandering eyes, turning briskly and walking away while looking back a few times.

The admiral enters his office, slamming the door. He stands looking over his desk until laying down an electronic recording device, which he switches off when a smirk grows on his face. He cuts his eyes back over to one side, quietly listening when the door squeaks a little and then swings open swiftly. He reaches down, secretly and anxiously, flipping on the electronic device again.

Captain Wright enters quickly, apologizing when expressly spilling his guts about the whole operation. He rattles on about the mission fabricating some of the undisclosed information to make it more interesting. When the last word leaves his mouth, his eyes drift down to the floor, and he immediately becomes embarrassed by his unethical behavior.

"Now, was that hard? Look, Captain, you can trust that I'm certified and cleared for this operation. Actually, I'll be Admiral Kitt's relief because he will be on leave by the time the team reaches the operation area. Admiral Kensington advised me of his plans for this mission this morning but was in a rush; so really, all I needed was a heads-up to be abreast of what was going on. Hell, who wants to walk into a meeting half-assed and unprepared? Well..., thanks, captain, and oh yeah, you can bank on that promotion because I'm up for promotion to the chairman of the board," Admiral Kensington says, standing and extending his hand to receive the captain's weak handshake, which he sturdily shakes vigorously and with confidence.

At the end of Captain Wright's shift, he arrives home. He rushes to the door, deactivates the security alarm, and then undresses. He grabs sweatpants from the chair, zipping his hooded sweat suit when lacing his sneakers. He dashes from the top step and runs to the door, activating the alarm. He steps onto the porch just in time to observe the sunset. With slight bends and twists, he stretches his calves, looks around, and jumps from the porch with brute force. His sneakers sink deeply into the thick sod grass connected with the long, neat landscape and concrete jogging trail.

A third of the way into his jog, the trail rapidly darkens in areas heavily overhung with towering Oak, Weeping Willows, and other long-hanging branches. Halfway through the course, he turns, running three-fourths back, as accustomed when slowing and then walking. He stops near a concrete bench, where he takes a few deep breaths.

Instantly, the sound of fresh, wet, crunchy leaves grows in his ears. He focuses on a few careening branches deep in the woods until spotting what looks like the silhouette of a tall, athletic-built person kneeling. "Hello! Hello! Who's there?" he shouts, expressly backing with his heart pounding faster.

Small bush bow gently forward with a masculine figure, suited in black spandex and knit mask advancing, extremely fast, and almost as if transparent.

Captain Wright launches in a twist and then fast sprints when a sharp slap comes against the side of his chest cavity, just behind his arm. "Oh..., ho, ho, ho!" he screams in a weak and dwindling voice with a hand touching the tip of the sharp metal object, yanking on it, and immediately losing consciousness.

The assassin peers from outside the bushes, looking up and down the dark, grim trail when he runs over and removes the dart, then fleeing into the thick brush.

Hours later, a young couple takes a shortcut through the woods and walks onto the now well-lit concrete trail. They're amazed at the new, brightly illuminated streetlights as they proceed up a slight incline.

The girl notices colorful lying off in the tall grass when lightly advancing in a trot and backing down even faster. "Ahh!" the young girl screams, finally recognizing the somewhat-mangled body when in a sharp turn and slamming into her lover's arms. She screams again, abruptly loosening her tight grip from around his waist. "Ahh!" she screams even louder in horror, a third time expressly backing away from her lover and the corpse.

"Get help!" he screams, gently shoving her off when running and dropping down on his knees. He quickly turns the body over to administer CPR, clearing the airway quickly and going into chest compressions.

The girl runs up the steep trail's incline at top speed, then down the slope, screaming at the top of her lungs. Her feet quickly shuffle up the steps and onto the porch of the first house, frantically knocking and then heavily banging on the door with a few good tight-fisted whacks.

Within seconds, the door quickly flies open with an old couple standing startled and holding their pounding chests, with eyes wide open.

"Call an ambulance! Call an ambulance! There's a man's body lying in the grass along the jogging trail!" she frantically says, almost out of breath.

The old man vanishes around the wall and sprints for the phone in the back bedroom.

"Calm down, child! He's calling the ambulance and the police," his wife says, fearfully holding her chest while staring back into the girls bulging, teary eyes.

The young girl nervously shivers and cries harder until the old woman pulls her into her arms, embracing and comforting her. She rocks the girl from side to side a little longer, comforting her more when feeling her calming and less tense.

The old man reappears seconds later. "They're on the way! Hell..., let's get down there and see what the heck is going on and see if there's anything we can do!" He grabs his and his wife's overcoats, flinging his halfway on, and then helps his wife into hers.

The young girl nervously leads the way, leaning slightly against the old woman and crying harder.

On the other side of town, Mr. Villan has just arrived home. He jumps from his dull, primed jeep, leaning over and grabbing a few grocery bags, when a few bushes gently tilt back and forth, unnoticed, over against the front of the house.

The assassin patiently waits in the thick bushes aligned with the front of Mr. Vee's house. He loads yet another poisonous dart and quietly cocks the weapon when taking a steady aim at Mr. Vee's head as he's making his way up the sidewalk with arms full of groceries.

From a distance, Mr. Vee hears a few deep barks from his neighbor's dog, which catches his attention.

"What's going on, Pat?" Mr. Vee's neighbor yells, fighting to gain control of his vicious pit bull, Rex.

"Hey, Jonathan..., let him go..., he just wants to play," Mr. Vee says, placing the bags on the wet sidewalk.

Jonathan releases the thick, shiny chain, and Rex takes off at full speed like a low-riding, heat-seeking missile, with grass springing high and upward from his hind legs with each pounce as they dig deep in the fresh sod.

The pit's growl grows more vicious and louder until his bark comes again and loudly echoes.

The assassin's eyes widen, seeing the dog inbound when springing upward, screaming, and then redirecting his aim. The long barrel aligns with Rex's body as he rushes in, in stealth mode, like an even faster, low-riding, heat-seeking cruise missile until pouncing high and seeming to be in slow motion.

With a steady aim, the dart invisibly plunges forward, hitting Rex dead center in his chest.

The poison instantly sinks deep while he's still four feet off the ground until falling lifelessly onto the wet grass, sliding several feet before stopping yards from the assassin's feet. The poison abruptly stops Rex's heartbeat.

"What the...!" Mr. Vee shouts, startled and frozen.

"Rex!" Jonathan screams, frozen as well until taking off in a stride, sliding a foot or so from Rex, when dropping down over him with both hands clenching long blades of grass while rocking back and forth, balancing.

Mr. Vee leans forward to launch toward the assassin but freezes when the man trains his gun between them in a fast, sweeping motion.

"Back the hell up, or I'll shoot!" the assassin shouts nervously while slowly waving the gun.

Mr. Vee moves back, and Jonathan looks at the man and then back at Rex, staring at his dog until his face transforms from confusion to pure anger and evil.

The assassin lowers the gun to Mr. Vee's chest. "I said, move the hell back!"

Mr. Vee and Jonathan keep their eyes pinned on the assassin but slowly separate, creating distance between themselves in hopes of an advantage.

Jonathan stays crouched until out of the line of fire, and without warning, he expressly launches upward, screaming until silenced when the gun slaps in his face hard, dropping in midair ad knocking him unconscious.

"Turn around! I said turn around! Now, get on your freakin' knees and put your hands behind your damn head!" the assassin shouts to Mr. Vee.

Mr. Vee does as asked, slowly with teary eyes, while thinking about his fiancé and daughter.

"Please, you can have anything; just spare our lives, please!" he cries. For seconds, Mr. Vee feels the man slowly closing, and then suddenly feels the heat from the man's warm breath running along the back of his neck.

Across town, the two dispatched and misdirected emergency vehicles come to the other side of the trail, where chains block the entrance. Soon, sirens fade then grow louder when closing in fast on a crowd of folks gathered around Captain Wright's body.

The two emergency response vehicles slow down, vectoring tires into the steep curb.

The ambulance and police cars rock, side to side while climbing an even steeper sidewalk and when almost side by side, the police car swiftly speeds past the ambulance.

The policeman slams on the brakes, sliding sideways a few feet in the damp grass and luckily stops inches from pedestrians standing with wide eyes and fast-racing hearts.

Two officers jump out, pushing everyone back while the paramedics immediately make their way behind the officers.

The paramedics drop down to their knees, checking the captain's vital signs. Afterward, they cover him and dispatch a detective and coroner.

Two women rush on the scene, peeping over folks' shoulders until the taller woman spots the too-familiar-looking expensive jogging sneakers when her mouth drops open. She anxiously pats her daughter's shoulder when two loud feminine screams come from out of nowhere. The women thrust forward, pushing their way to the front, and knocking over a few people when falling forward into one officer's wide-receiver-looking shoulders.

The officer pulls them together and holds them back until the other officer rushes over and assists with getting the women under control.

The officers divert the women off to the side and over to their cruiser.

Thirty minutes later, the assassin shows up outside Admiral Kitts' home, where he sits watching neighboring houses before placing the dart gun in his waistband. He backs up a few feet into the woods, lighting a cigarette. He soon hears a car's engine when backing deeper into the woods, kneeling until the car's headlights slowly pass and the taillights fade around the corner. He stands, pulling out his cell phone and dialing a number as a second car swiftly passes.

"Bear, this is Range Rover, I've put one down, had a problem with the second, and now I'm on station; standing by to carry out plan Bravo," he says.

"Down? What the hell do you mean down? I specifically told you to rough them up and nothing else. You damn idiot! You're going to mess around and screw up this whole damn operation! Hold one!"

The assassin eases up, still fumbling around with the dart case until counting indentations of the missing poisonous chrome-and-silver darts. The assassin's fingers gently run inside the blue velvet case's liner, gripping the next-to-last dart, bringing it to eye level, gazing over the fine, surgical needlepoint and milky-looking poison, which forms into a teardrop at the end. He presses the back-end rubber-boot seal, removing the excess air bubbles.

The phone bumbles around a bit until there is slightly some soft breathing. "Next time, you follow my damn orders to the letter..., do you hear me?" the deep voice screams.

"Roger Bear, this is Range Rover, out," the assassin responds, taking a few more puffs on the short cigarette butt before flicking it to the sandy ground and leaving it burning.

Admiral Kitts flips through television channels with the phone still pressed tightly to his ear. His head bobs up and down in deep thought, listening to the person on the other end until finally, he hangs up. He continues sitting in his dark office, watching television a little longer while sipping cognac until finally standing and turning out the lights.

The doorbell rings, and he takes off in a little stride, slowly putting his glass on the lamp-lit podium. He turns the knob, and the door bursts open. His eyes widen with excitement, and his mouth instantly drops open.

"Hi honey!" his dingy, frail-looking wife says in excitement. "I lost my keys again," she says, kissing, embracing, pulling away quickly, and rushing for the kitchen.

He eases back into the drink and a chair, soon hearing rattling pots and pans.

In Hampton Roads, Virginia, Tom stands at the back door wearing his favorite tight-muscle shirt and loose-fitting, checkered boxers. He is focused on something at work until his mind shifts when reminiscing about last summer's fun with Kelley and the kids.

Finally, he refocuses and looks around the room when suddenly the central heating fan blows warm air across the back of his neck, causing fine hairs to spike. He takes another sip of cognac and fades into more deep thoughts of his early-morning, passionate lovemaking session, which eventually has him in even deeper thought until fully aroused.

The aroma of fried pork chops instantly grows, breaking his intense concentration. Minutes later, a faint hint of onions and gravy lingers about the room until all the mingling flavors consume the room.

Kelley stands off in the corner in a trance. A smile grows with her eyes browsing over the keepsake bracelet Tom and her kids had given her a few years earlier as a birthday gift.

He finally finds Kelley standing near the bar with a single glimpse over his shoulder.

Kelley stares back, smirking until winking and looking so sexy, wearing her thin, red, silk, body-conforming shorts, cut about a quarter of an inch below the curvature of her pretty, wide, raised pelvis.

Tom grows excited, staring at her raised pelvis, cupped, stretched, and curved in the tight material, dropping off deep between luscious thighs.

In a sexy stance, she stares at him for seconds, playfully batting her lovely eyes and giving this sultry to arouse him more.

Tom's eyes roam over her perfect, cupped breasts, down to her thin waist and curvy hips again. He gazes down at her pretty, wide, raised pelvis again, which forms a perfect, round cup from a different angle as she twitches from side to side in a slow turn. He grows more anxious. He takes his last sip, placing the decorative cognac glass on the glass table when passing. He comes within inches of her, leaning forward and gently pressing against her soft but firm body. His arms slide around her waist, pulling her closer when her perfume's strong fragrance suddenly rises.

Her lovely scent arouses him even more until, with another deep breath, he inhales her like a fresh breath of air. He squeezes her tighter and then releases a little, with one hand moving up and down her firm body.

Tension grows until she's beginning to move around sensually, continually, and seductively, careening from side to side.

The faint fragrance of her apple body spray from her morning bath rises and lingers until overpowering the food.

She eases into him, placing her head against his massive chest when her apple-fragranced hair lotion swiftly releases an even stronger sensual scent, which lingers. She leans forward slightly, and her lips begin nibbling at his neck and chest. Her long, bone-straight, sandy-brown hair slowly drapes across his arms at intervals. "Ooh, babe!" she moans. "Mmm, ooh, Tom!" she whispers.

Tom guides her into the living room with a hand bracing the couch's arm when lowering onto the black leather sofa. His hands caress her hips, manipulating her body until she's on top and easing one foot onto the couch, straddling her thick, smooth, lightly-tanned thighs across his firm body.

She lowers onto him with their bodies clinging together like a fist in a tightly-woven glove. She settles firmly, gently rocking back and forth in a playful spirit, and instantly feels him pressing hard against her bottom as she moves around more until finally comforted.

They begin kissing harder and fondling more until they're frantically breathing.

"Ooh, yes!" she cries. "Mmm, yes..., ooh yes, Tom!" she moans until somewhat refocused and breaks her concentration, staring deeply into his beautiful eyes. "Mmm..., excuse me while I go check on dinner," she says, lifting a little but still playfully grinding until stopping when almost to her feet when Tom reaches to caress her. She speedily pulls away, smiling and bursting into laughter until her soft laughter turns into a silly little giggle.

Minutes later, he eases up, pouring another straight drink, then stands staring at the kitchen doorway until he slowly approaches, light-footed. He peeps inside, finding Kelley with her back to him while placing the meat in crystal dishware.

"Mmm..., so, where were we?" he whispers, sitting his glass on the granite counter, aligning his raging bulge with the crease of her round cheeks and stroking her gently. He slightly presses harder into her, stretching the thin material, and she feels his firmness as he moves in a teasing spirit.

"Babe, your hands...; they're so cool," she says, tensing and then quickly warming up to him while leaning back and grinding against him. She grips the counter's edge with hands, leaning forward and seductively twisting a few times until feeling him lean deeper until freezing.

Tom's tongue runs up and down the back of her neck, and he begins kissing the nape.

"Babe, your mouth..., it's so cold," she says, tensing and then smiling.

"Better to eat you with, babe," he playfully says, looking deep into her eyes as they make eye contact.

She turns away and then looks back again, batting her long eyelashes.

"I could eat you right here where you're standing," he says, lifting and plopping her gently on the cool marble countertop.

"Hey..., let's not start something you can't finish," she says, staring into his beautiful eyes while winking.

"Babe, you know I can handle mine," he replies, stroking her soft thighs a few times and then gently holding on to them until massaging them.

Her head falls back with hair slowly drifting from her shoulder, strand after strand, until perfectly dangling in midair. "Babe, that feels so freakin' good," she softly moans. "Ooh, ooh..., mmm..., ahh," she continuously moans, with moans growing louder as her breathing increases. She moans longer this time, whining until her fist slightly pounds his firm chest.

She balls in a knot, in minutes, tenses, and tries shaking off the sensation for minutes, but it consumes her. It takes her a while to get herself back together while smiling with her eyes closed until abruptly opening them. "Babe, the food!" she shouts, mildly pushing him away.

He takes a few steps back and stands back, laughing. "Hmm..., had you burned it..., the Chinese restaurant doesn't close until late," he laughs aloud.

She looks over the buttery, shiny rolls and then slowly closes the oven with seductive eyes roving over his hot body again. She leans back against the counter, staring once more with a big smile. "I love you so much. Babe, you know you mean the world to me..., right, sweetie?"

"I love you more," he replies, looking even deeper into her sexy eyes.

"I doubt that..., sweetie," she says in a deep thought. " Well, what I should have said was I love you to no end..., I love you to death, yeah, that kind of love," she says, drifting into deeper thought of what she wanted to do to him right then and there until breaking her concentration. "So, do you want to eat or play first, mister?" she asks, leaning over and removing the rolls. She leans again, turns off the oven, and then turns, batting her sexy eyes again with eyes slowly drifting down when noticing her hard nipples protruding, her top fully conforming to the curvature of her perfectly round breasts.

"It depends on what I'm eating or playing with," he says, licking his tongue out and then slowly twirling it around. He moistens his lips a few times to look more seductive and even naughtier.

"You and your feeble mind..., food, silly!" she responds, pretending to be clueless when shaking her head in a slight daze before turning off the exhaust fan. She feels a little heated from his gentle strokes, which barely touch her skin in continual yet gentle foreplay.

Tom kisses her lips and slightly breaks away, reaching and pouring wine and then arranging long-stemmed candles on the table. He proceeds to create the most romantic atmosphere, dimming the lights. He gazes over at her as she walks into the dining room and goes into a daze, amazed at her radiant beauty and dangerously curved body.

Kelley makes several trips, laying out the meal and arranging the table as she sees fit, and with the last dish positioned upon the plate coaster, he pulls her chair out. She slithers into her seat and looks up at him with glistening eyes.

With love and a little lust, he kisses her slightly raised collarbone right up to her slender neck and then sensually dips his tongue deep into her earlobe, leaning her trembling.

Kelley grows overheated and sits, twitching with hands grasping each side of the soft-cushion edge of the chair and holding it for seconds. She tries breaking the slow chill running up and down her spine, and within minutes, she's finally able to shake the chill when caressing his hand and taking one finger deep inside her soft lips, with him lightly moaning when pulling back.

He smiles at her, grabs her hand, and begins to thank her for the beautiful meal.

"Oh! Tom! That verse was so sweet, babe," she says, in awe when staring deep into his eyes, smiling.

Well into their romantic dinner, the phone rings, but she motions for him not to answer.

"What..., that could've been Martha or your father calling from London," he says, slightly straddling his chair to see if he can read the caller's I.D. He eases back a little as if to sit up when her hand grips his upper thigh.

Her fingers make their way up and down his inseam until he's firm to her touch, gently forcing him back to his seat in a playful gesture while laughing.

Martha..., well Martha is Kelley's best friend and an old friend of Kelley's mother.

Kelley's mother passed away years ago when she was walking and hit by a drunk driver.

Martha was their regular sitter on exceptional occasions or when they wanted or needed time alone from the kids.

Tom and Kelley love the kids dearly but cherish every quiet, sensual moment they can capture, not having to be quiet in the bedroom with them there.

Martha finds joy in keeping Brandon, four, and Ashley, five, every chance she gets. She is particularly fond of Kelley and always treats her as if she's the one who had given Kelley birth, even when her mother was alive.

Martha knew of the things Kelley was allowing Jeff to take her through, from frequent updates, from inquisitive neighbors. Back then, knowing these things made Martha even more attentive to Kelley's needs, but she always kept Kelley's mess from Kelley's mother.

With genuine love and concern for Kelley, Martha would never hesitate to guide Kelley through the difficult situations she came to know about. It seemed like it would bring angelic spirits just to have womanly talks with Kelley from time to time, or vice versa, when Martha sat talking about how lovely her husband had been to her.

Martha had become Kelley's support system when Kelley finally had gotten enough nerve to dump Jeff's sorry behind. Martha's was extremely elated when Tom and Kelley met. She was almost as radiant as Kelley was because she was so happy for Kelley.

Martha's an older, gray-haired woman who more or less looks remarkably young for her age. She exercises regularly and takes excellent care of her body. She's without children, so the lack of them only makes her love Kelley's kids dearly.

Martha's husband, Bill, died several years earlier from a stroke while gardening in the backyard on one of the hottest days that summer. The tragedy happened on Martha's birthday because he wanted to surprise her when she got home from visiting relatives, who plotted with him by keeping her away longer than usual.

Well invested, Bill's wealth came from insurance policies, investments, and ventures he had dabbled around in over the years.

Still deeply in love, Martha never wants another man to take Bill's place, so she always keeps to herself, rejecting many men on a quest for courtship.

The kids hate Jeff, but Tom always preaches forgiveness, even though he despises Jeff from the stories of abuse and negligence Kelley had endured.

Tom and Kelley continue in conversation before Kelley breaks her concentration. "Hey..., are you going to change so we can go over to Kelvin and Julie's?"

"Sure, babe," he says, running his fingers along the shaft of her neck.

She smiles and pulls away when turned on by his touch and stands before he stands.

They go back and forth carrying dishes until the dining room is clean.

Kelley drifts back into the dining room for one final look when Tom pulls her close in his arms, kissing her collarbone and neck right up to her perfect lips.

He reaches for her hand, pulling her across the living room, and she resists his tug and goes to the stereo, flipping off the switch, and upstairs they go.

Things get heated once more in the bedroom, where they striptease until they are down to panties and boxers.

She kills the mood when backing him away with firm hands. "Babe, hurry; we're supposed to be at Kelvin and Julie's in an hour," she says, breaking her concentration.

Tom kneels on both knees, snuggly wrapping both arms around her waist and slowly lowering his hands below her waist until burying his face deep in her thighs. He instantly smells her perfume-sprayed body when the scent rushes higher.

She grows overheated and unable to bear any more pleasure when grabbing his massive arms, pushing him away, and bursting into great laughter. "Tom! We'll have plenty of time for this later, babe," she says, blushing with thoughts of canceling the visit.

He stands, walking off and leaning toward the shower's faucet with hands slipping inside and turning the lever to massage.

"Can I get in with you handsome?"

"Huh..., no way..., you'll only start something and complain about how I made us late."

"Well, I'm getting in anyway," she says, making her usual funny face with eyes crossed to get a good laugh out of him. Her hands rest on her perfectly curved hips when making more silly faces, and finally causing him to chuckle, then burst into a peal of great laughter.

"Can I bite one of those apples?" he asks, staring at her fit, round, smooth-skinned bottom as she slips out of her panties, dropping them.

She stops and looks over her shoulder. "No, but you can kiss these lovely apples," she says, smacking her right cheek and pulling on the roundness of it. She releases the other cheek in a way that firmly makes it jiggle back in place, and then looks back again, smirking, until slightly vanishing into mild streams of steam.

Tom drops his briefs, climbs in behind her, pulls the door shut, and turns, accidentally brushing against her.

"Who's irresistible now?" she asks, smiling and pulling her long hair to one side to keep it from getting soaked.

He turns his back to her. "Hey..., let me know when you're ready to switch sides," he says, keeping his distance and yet peeping and lusting over her gorgeous body.

Minutes later, they switch under hot, thrashing water.

He washes her body, standing from behind until playfully grasping for her thigh; with soapy hands browsing upward along her curvy hips to her hard abs and then upward. He presses his chest into her back as his hands gently massage her until her eyes close and her light moans grow heavier.

When it's Kelley's turn, she strokes her soft hands across his back, presses against him, and plays around a while longer until she reminds him of the time again.

After drying off, they rush through closets naked, looking for something warm, casual, and ironed. In an attempt to break their record, they dress in less than twenty minutes tops, minus Kelley's additional thirty minutes, for hair, nails, and face.

"How do I look?"

"I like you better naked," he replies, laughing as she returns, smiles, and then winks.

With a minimal delay, they leave the house, and Tom manages to cut down the drive by speeding a little more than usual.

They soon exit the off-ramp, and Kelley squints through the light fog noticing that her brother's car is not out front where he normally parks.

"See, I told you, you shouldn't have played around so much!"

"Who was playing? I'm strictly business, babe..., and no-nonsense at all times," he says, looking deep into her lovely face, glistening from the indigo dashboard lights.

They sit quietly until suddenly a pair of headlights emerges but before the car reaches them it turns down a side street and vanishes.

Tom strikes up a conversation, which leads to a discussion of her father, but she quickly ends it, playing it down and moving on to something more pleasant.

"I guess we can pick up a couple of DVDs on the way home," she says, in deep thought as to how rude it was, cutting him off. "Mmm..., I know..., we can go home and cuddle in front of the fireplace and get our drink on," she responds with naughty thoughts while looking over at him, smiling.

"You must have read my mind," he says, quickly forgetting how she rudely played him off when smiling, placing his hand upon her knee, and slowly moving his hand up her inner thigh, gently stroking.

"Are you ever not horny as hell?" she asks, giggling and bursting into laughter.

"Sure, when I'm fast asleep," he says, bursting into laughter again.

"Well, I know that's a lie because I mess around with you when you're asleep sometimes, and man..., damn, you get so freakin'..., man, umm," she says as if she is feeling him right then and there.

They leave and make a few runs, arriving home an hour and a half later.

Tom lights the fireplace while Kelley turns off the main light in the foyer.

They caress with added kisses and then playfully start in a slow dance to a couple of songs they had danced to months earlier at Kelley's co-worker's wedding.

The third song concludes, and Tom spreads the comforter out near the fireplace. He pops the champagne open, filling their glasses, and passes her a glass with his glass still held out in a toast.

"So, what shall we toast to?" she asks, winking.

"With you, sweetie, I can think of a thousand things, but let's make this a special one by toasting to that thang I'm about to get up in," he says, gently tapping her glass while trying to keep a straight face. His lips slightly parts, revealing his bright, white teeth when he immediately breaks out in laughter, spilling a sip on his shirt and brushing off the slight overspray.

Kelley takes another sip, placing both glasses near the fireplace.

They undress until they are down to panties, bra, and boxers.

He grasps her hand, kneeling with her on the thick, padded, paisley comforter.

They cuddle and talk for a while until caressing each other, and before they know it, they're fast asleep and warm in each other's arms.

Tom awakens first from soft, mellow music that played throughout the night, and with a rock-hard, pee hard-on, he eases out from underneath the covers, trying not to wake her when rushing to the bathroom.

Afterward, he peeps out to ensure she's still asleep when he turns and stares into the partially-open medicine cabinet, pulling out the small sewing kit's scissors from a leather pouch.

Tom eases back into the living room, placing the scissors near the fireplace when climbing back under the comforter. He giggles, holding the scissors in hand and reaching for the side of her panty's band, slightly pulling the thin material from her body and releasing it from guffawing so hard. Once again, he tries to slide the material between the scissors when he cuts one side and then the other. Tom moves closer once more, unsnapping and removing her bra, without waking her. He rests on his side and goes into deep thoughts when mischievously smiling. He fondles her, gently massaging her until she moans and grinds her hips seductively and subconsciously.

He stops and turns his head with eyes peering at her chest as it rises and falls with each timed breath. He stares, admiring her smooth skin when gently leaning forward, kissing her arm while working his way down until awakening her.

"You left me hanging last night," she says, yawning in a mellow tone.

Tom smiles while lying back, then places his hands behind his head "Kelley..., Kelley..., Kelley! You were so good, babe," he replies, licking his lips.

She quickly dresses under the comforter and then stands and backs over to the CD player, which she turns off. She switches from CD to radio, facing him again. "Now, what was it you did?" she asks, cheesing.

Tom looks over at her and then does a double take, leaning forward with eyes slightly bucked and surprised to see part of her panties dangling from the front of her waistband. He turns a bright pink and then red as he tries hard to fight off his laughter, which bursts loudly and uncontrollably.

Her eyes drop, and she pushes her hips forward, surprised to find the colored material when her hands grasp the panties, pulling slowly and then yanking when they no longer pull tightly between her thighs. "What the...?" she says, slightly bent over and unable to stop hee-hawing. She points at the long, stretched material, which swings freely, and can't stop laughing.

Tom chuckles so hard that his stomach muscles ache.

"Ok, you got me, babe..., that's ok, but the big payback will be hell, mister," she says with a big grin, laughing even heavier when plotting several ways to pay him back. She picks up a rose from the mantle, trying to imagine what he could have done to her when sniffing it before walking out of sight.

Within minutes, Tom hears water running from the upstairs shower.

Kelley dresses, and afterward, she enters the office, looking for hairpins, when hearing an unfamiliar noise. She looks around and then lifts his jacket to find his pager flashing and vibrating inches from the edge of the desk. She grasps it in her balled fist and makes a mad dash downstairs, breathing heavily and excitedly.

Tom notices her stealthy movement and excited eyes when spotting the pager; when his heart drops; when finally seeing the blinking red light when springing up to meet her, and he instantly hears his heart beating. 'I must have accidentally turned it on vibrate,' he thinks when pressing the recall button, but he doesn't get a response.

Tom sprints upstairs at top speed, bumping into walls and then gaining his footing when expressly moving forward. He rushes into the office, leaning over the desk, and presses the green, flashing button to activate the phone's secure option when the secure screen flashes across the LED and the automated voice speaks in a clear and distinctive tone.

Tom eases in the desk, correctly authenticating near the end of the message when a series of beeps sound off. "Yes..., Chief Powells, Strike Force One, ID 127589, I'm prepared to authenticate."

"Access verified..., you're to report to the Norfolk, Pier 5 Depot, no later than 2400 hours, on 22 March. The commanding officer is Captain Ronald Carrington, the executive officer, as assigned. The Officer-in-Charge is Ensign Terry, and the boarding vessel is the United States Missile Strike Platform—R. L. Peterson (USMSP—493). The mission's briefing will be held onboard, and the length of the mission is unknown."

After a final series of beeps, Tom enters his secure passcode, acknowledging the receipt of verbal and official orders. He hangs up and eases into the office chair when his mind goes haywire, trying to figure out what could have happened to cause the team's sudden activation.

Kelley unnoticeably enters and places his boxer briefs and shirt on the edge of the desk.

Tom comes out of the daze, finally realizing she's there when he reaches for his clothes half-dazed. "They just activated us, so it looks like I'll be leaving for a while, but I'm not sure for how long. I'd better stock up on some personal hygiene items."

"No need...; you're good. I just restocked your stash, and I never unpacked your bag from last month's trip, so you have plenty," she says in a daze and drifts into fear. "Oh yeah, speaking of the devil, I've been meaning to tell you that my father called in the wee hours of the morning. He wants us to fly the kids over for a visit; it would be a good time for you two to meet since you're always asking about him finally," she says, dazed as to whether she was ready to see her father again, introduce him to Tom, or let him see the kids. So many thoughts run through her mind as she continually stares off into space while rethinking the lie.

Tom's distracted in his thoughts also and doesn't give the comment any more thought.

The following morning, Kelley awakens first, and she's sad but in thought for some time while thinking of Tom leaving. Her mind drifts on thoughts of her past dealings with her father and lifestyle overseas, and then on to her close friend's death when her mind draws blank and then swiftly shifts back to Tom's little prank. She grows eager in her plot and thinks a little longer about how to repay him when easing back from under the covers. She lies there thinking longer, then eases out, quietly entering the bathroom. She reaches for the shelf, pulls out a soft cloth that she wets, and then soaps with warm water. She stirs around in the medicine cabinet for seconds, then removes a tingly lubricant and slides it into her panty's waistband.

The door cracks open, and she peeps out, looking until she is sure that he's still in a deep sleep when tiptoeing out and slipping under the covers. She over-lubricates her fingers, fondling him, and he subconsciously grows fast from excitement.

Somewhat fully aroused, he begins drifting back into a sweet dream.

Kelley plays around a little longer until the dream of making passionate love to Kelley grows with him, finally coming out of his erotic dream to find himself on the edge of losing it. She goes eye-to-eye, giggling until he blurts out with some silly tone, then soft moans with toes curling tighter when tenser and gripping some of the comforter when it rises and falls in a jerk. "Ba, ba, ba, boom!" she screams, jokingly in an exciting gesture. "See..., I told you payback would be hell, buddy," she says, bursting into a loud, crazy laughter. "I've always told you not to underestimate the power of a woman..., no, the power of this woman!" she grins.

Tom just lays there with covers slowly pulled over his face, totally embarrassed by her constant teasing of his ugly facial expressions. After some time, he gets up enough nerve and goes upstairs and showers. Afterward, they dress, load the car, and come back inside, but they're not satisfied with the quick packing.

Tom feels they may have missed something, so they make one final round to make sure. He strays through his closet and then digs around in her closet for the belt he had seen her throw inside a few days earlier. He fumbles around with things on the shelf until stumbling across a black box that he pulls out, staring at it for minutes. His eyes swarm over several clothes, missing the military style uniform neatly tucked away with the shiny high ranking insignia on the collar. He finally shakes it and is about to open it when hearing Kelley's heels clicking, so he quickly slips it back under the clothing, covers it, and eases the door shut.

Kelley walks in and notices her purse hanging from her closet door is still swinging. She looks over her dresser, pretending to be looking for something, and then grabs her eyeliner, gazing over at him to find him staring and a little fidgety. She walks out and stops at the end of the hall, stepping out of her heels.

Tom steps back inside her closet, lifting the clothes higher and still curious about what's in the box when opening it to find a sealed handgun box. He pulls out the heavy box, walks to the bed, and places it in plain view.

When he looks up, he finds her standing there and looks up again as if surprised.

They stare eye-to-eye, in silence, for seconds.

"Care to explain?" he says in disbelief.

"Sure thing…, my father asked me to pick it up and ship it to him, so I got it as a gift for my father, ok?" she says, in disbelief that he would go through her personal belongings and in a tone of disappointment. She stares at him longer, then rolls her eyes and walks out.

She eases into the car, and Tom looks back at her with curious eyes when locking the door.

He walks up seconds later in deep thought when climbing behind the steering wheel with her snuggling and kissing him.

A tear rolls down one side of her cheek and then the other, and he soon hears continual sniffling.

The ride to the depot seems like forever, with Kelley's constant crying until she falls asleep, still cuddling, and miles from the base.

Tom slows and dims the lights when closing in on the main gate, with the guard silently motioning for him not to wake her when only checking Tom's I.D. He makes a few turns and reaches the pier, with the car coming to a slow roll with Kelley sitting up, rubbing swollen, puffy, pink eyes. Tom climbs out, straightening his dress uniform.

Kelley climbs out, and they meet at the trunk, embracing, hugging, and kissing.

Tom pulls her tight in his arms. "Babe…, I love you, and I'm going to miss you so much. Please kiss the kids for me and tell them I'll miss them dearly and that I love them."

"I love you so much, babe, and I'll miss you even more," she says, almost staring through him when an endless river of tears trails down her cool, rosy cheeks.

Tom kisses her once more, wiping her cool cheeks with the back of his index finger.

"You know, instead of going to see my father, we could invite him here," she says in deep thought, meditating more when realizing it's best for her to leave her past overseas and not endanger her kids or Tom by the dangerous reunion. She meditates more until realizing her biggest fear is someone identifying her as a killer.

"Really, babe? That would be great, honey. I'm not sure what happened with you and your father, and I'm not going to pry, but I think you will tell me all about it when you're ready to open up. Whatever it is, you need to settle those differences and move on because life is too short to be distant from family.

Just think about it, Kelley; the kids need to meet and spend time with their only grandparent, and it happens to be on your side of the family. Besides, babe..., you're struggling..., we're struggling..., so why not let your father help?" he says with one last embrace and a deep, sensual French kiss that seems to last for minutes before releasing her and walking away. He looks back several times while crossing the four lanes and approaching the guard shack. Tom reaches into his coat pocket, looking back once more to find the car's last taillight steady with her still sitting there.

"Chief...," the sentry says, stepping out of the shack and looking at the rank insignia on his headgear, leaning forward, checking Tom's I.D., and motioning him through the gate. "How's it going, Chief?"

"Evening, shipmate," Tom responds, nodding and then looking back to find the car's taillights vanishing around a building.

A black car pulls up out of nowhere, shining its bright headlights against the shack.

Tom looks over his shoulder and stares at the car until realizing its Cryptologist Technician Specialist First-Class Antonio (Tony) Reeves.

Tony leans, kissing his wife and daughter, then climbs out on the passenger side. He snatches his duffle bag from the backseat and walks up to the driver's window, kissing his wife and his little daughter, who climbs into her mother's lap.

Out of nowhere, strong winds pick up, intermittently gusting.

Tom looks back once more at Tony when thinking about his brother.

Now, Antonio and his younger brother Bobby joined the team under the buddy system. They shared and enjoyed the pleasure of working and being stationed on missions together, and fresh out of Special Forces Training (SFT), their first assignment was with Tom.

"Good morning..., top of the morning, Chief!" Antonio's wife loudly yells over another sudden gust that drifts by when Tom's eyes peel back toward the car.

"How are you, Mrs. Reeves?" Tom yells, waving to his wife and daughter as she pulls away.

Antonio walks up smiling and flashing his badge when greeted and motioned through the gate.

The two take off down the dark pier and come to the second gate, approaching the guard shack, and motioned to proceed after flashing I.D.s.

Out of nowhere, a heavy and somewhat torrential downpour comes, and they walk swiftly, quickly hugging the overhand of the long warehouse building. They stop at an indentation that provides no coverage when standing for minutes awaiting a break in the rain, and it comes minutes later and slightly tapering off.

Tom leans out, looking up at the light drizzle dusting against the bright lights. "There's not a better time than now," he says when they step off, heading down the dark pier and looking up as far as they can, but barely seeing the ship.

The heavy rain comes again and without warning, with strong winds blowing sideways with sudden, stronger gusts of winds when hugging the building again and walking faster.

They come up on the ship's bow and stop at a steep overhang and the warehouse's entrance, where they are shielded from the heavy rain for well over ten minutes until the rain begins trickling. They take off once more and finally approach the brow, adjust their bags for the steep climb, and then readjust their bags again when approaching the well-lit quarterdeck (ship's entrance).

They show their I.D.s and salute the Officer of the Deck (OOD).

"Request permission to come aboard, sir?" they simultaneously shout over the heavy downpour, which bangs heavily on the ship's steel decks.

"Permission granted," the OOD says, saluting Tom and looking at Tony as he steps up when looking at his watch and saluting again.

The OOD motions them to one side and then stands a few feet behind them, gazing over the sailboard. "We've been delayed due to another shipment of your team's classified equipment being en route."

Tom and Tony's escort shows up and escorts them to the berthing area (sleeping quarters).

Tom and Tony drop off their things and climb several decks, heading to the wardroom. They enter the last quiet deck and rush up to the wardroom's door; where Tom reaches for the door handle when the door flies open with a beautiful female ensign walking out.

"Thank you, ma'am," Tony and Tom say almost simultaneously.

"Welcome," she responds, batting her longer-than-human, model-like eyelashes and smirking.

They hold the door and stay focused on the brunette's fine, curved apple bottom in her tighter-than-regulation uniform as she struts and sways her hips more than usual. She shyly looks back, then steps off again, realizing her hourglass figure has them admiring her beauty. She stops and stands, briefly looking back, finding them stuck in a stupor with their mouths dropped open, not realizing she's even looking at them until she waves, breaking their stare when vanishing around the corner.

Busted and finally realizing it, they scramble inside the packed wardroom.

"Man, she's doing some serious trawling!" Tom whispers, heel-to-toe with Tony when shuffling further inside.

Tom and Tony walk forward with hands coming expressly to their shoulder massaging. "What's up, fellas?" Bobby asks, releasing them and vigorously shaking Tony's hand. "Sup, Chief?" he asks, extending his hand to Tom.

Tom's eyes swarm over the room, quickly acknowledging his men's presence with precision eye contact and well-rehearsed nods. "Not much," Tom says, backing up a few steps to let another female officer pass.

The first to make contact was Radioman Specialist First-Class Jeff Ogwin (Oggie, or Gee): Oggie's from Louisiana, a homegrown country boy, six feet tall, solid build, and baldheaded. He's single and never married, but he'd give the world for his girlfriend's two kids.

Next: Electronic Technician, Specialist First-Class Robert Johns, five-eleven, a complete nervous wreck, and a stone nerd who's practically afraid of his own shadow. Johns made the team simply because of his stellar ability to troubleshoot the team's diverse Special Forces equipment. Johns and his wife are at the end of their seventh month of pregnancy with their first child. John's a problem child, always needing guidance in basic decision-making and simple directions. Unsure of Johns' ability to function in hostile environments, Tom previously requested that he be transferred to a less active unit after he froze up on a shoot-out, which almost cost a civilian hostage her life.

Next: Ensign Michael Terry, five-foot-eight and a real softy; he's married with no children. Terry is a frail individual; any attractive woman can easily get Terry's attention without effort. Terry had serious family problems when first joining the team, especially when his wife caught him cheating several times with women in their small military housing complex.

Tom continually pans the room and looks off into empty space when his visual role brings a flood of memories of Radioman Specialist First-Class (RM1) Ronnie Swiss, who died during the team's last mission. Tom's mind wonders over the last few deadly hours of Swiss' life, breaking his concentration when the door springs open and slams shut.

Now, the two pretty boys who Tom turns to after his last acknowledgment are Cryptologist Technicians Specialists First-Class Antonio and Bobby Reeves.

Jointly, these are the outstanding men of Strike Force One, standing tall to the beckoning call of national security, life, liberty, and the pursuit of everlasting freedom.

Tom is always exceptionally professional. He's six-one, about two-hundred-fifty pounds of solid steel. He sets the tone for stellar military appearance, standards, and core values. Tom is a model example for his men and those around him, in and out of uniform.

Strike Force One has coordinated over five successful close-range combat tactic encounters with the enemy and, in most cases, in close coordination with their sister team, Strike Force Two.

Both teams have received several meritorious awards for stellar combatant performances as joint forces and were awarded even more medals when operating with Coalition forces.

The only unfortunate mission was the team's previous mission, which claimed the lives of seven of their comrades, including RM1 Swiss.

With the sudden tragedy still fresh in their minds and as if it were yesterday, they continually try not to remember but simultaneously respect the memories of RM1 Swiss.

Meanwhile, the government's statement to the press is that there was abundant evidence indicating a security breach.

The Command Center, in the presence of congressional hearings and investigative boards, had blamed RM1 Swiss for negligence and improper watch standing.

Everyone on the team knew Ronnie was not responsible but upheld the code of Special Forces silence, one deceptively set by their superiors.

Suddenly, the phone rings over loud voices twice before Lieutenant Smith answers.

"Sir..., OOD..., I just received word that the Connecticut shipment is at the main gate, awaiting clearance by customs," the OOD says as if excited.

Lieutenant Smith looks around, and then cuts his eyes over at Tom. "Chief, come with me," the lieutenant whispers, rudely slamming the phone down.

Tom exits the wardroom and comes up behind the lieutenant at a near jog.

They rush down narrow passageways and ladder wells until slowing when walking into the open hanger bay.

The lieutenant approaches the OOD promptly, coming to an abrupt halt. "May I have the invoices?"

"Why..., yes sir," the OOD says, reaching deep into his coat pocket. "Here you are!" he responds with attitude from the lieutenant's rude phone mannerisms.

"Thank you..., Chief..., please come with me," the lieutenant says, sharply saluting. "I have permission to leave the ship!"

"Very well," the OOD says, sharply returning his salute.

"Request permission to leave the ship," Tom says, saluting.

"Very well," the OOD says, sharply returning his salute.

Tom follows the lieutenant down the brow and aft of the ship, where they approach a white government sedan.

The lieutenant slings the driver's side door open and jumps in, slamming it shut.

Tom jumps in with the passenger door halfway open when the lieutenant peels off, burning rubber.

Halfway down the pier, the lieutenant alternates the high and low beams, crazily honking like a crazed man until rolling the electronic passenger side windows down. "Next time, I want this damn gate open before I pull up to it..., do you hear me?" he shouts. He speeds toward the slow-opening gate, swerving hard to one side and barely missing the sentry when swerving back in his lane. He briefly halts the vehicle at the crossroad and then takes off fast again.

He reaches the first intersection, stops for a passing car, and then races through side streets, running a few stop signs when rounding the corner, where he comes within a hundred yards of the main gate. He increases speed once more, slamming on brakes and skidding about six feet or more on the wet asphalt before stopping. He jumps out and slams the door with brute force and feet quickly shuffling against the asphalt as he rushes up to the security guard, making eye contact without blinking. His eyes wander over the man's low rank on his security badge until anxiously looking around the shack.

Tom finally eases out, running his fingers inside the rim of his trouser and tightening his shirt to reestablish his sharp uniform appearance.

"Who's in charge here?" the lieutenant harshly asks.

The sentry points across the walkway and presses a wall buzzer twice when the door slowly opens, and the Chief of Security and Customs Officer walks out and over to the guard shack.

The Chief of Security reaches for the documents extended outward in the lieutenant's hand and begins checking the invoice. He thumbs through longer until near the back; where he finds the document seal at about the same time the customs officer points to it.

The two continually scan over the shipping credential statements and then look at each other with surprised eyes, realizing they have no authority to conduct a thorough search or even open the container. They stand motioning the guard over to the back of the trailer so he can check and ensure the seal is not broken.

"Come on through," the Chief of Security says, waving to the long-distance truck driver who is sitting, cleaning his nails, and gazing at the shack from time to time.

Lieutenant Smith grasps the documents when handed to him and thanks both of them when he and Tom climb back in and slam the doors almost simultaneously. He floors the engine and speeds off, swerving in front of the eighteen-wheeler while frantically waving to get the truck driver's attention.

A mild, then fast-growing and blowing horn sound off, and the sentry does not hear it but soon turns, seeing alternating lights when finally registering the blaring horn. He shoots up fast, nervously springing from the shack, and slips, almost falling into a puddle of water.

The lieutenant rolls up fast with the driver's window coming down. "The long-distance truck is cleared!" the lieutenant shouts, stopping and pointing to the rear when speeding off. He proceeds to the end of the pier and pulls over, parallel parking against the warehouse, when jumping out and waving the truck past the sedan.

The equipment arrived at 0215, but due to the piss poor planning and the unavailability of the Port Service's cranes, backup plans were in place for loading the shipment using the truck and ship's crane, which was an even longer, riskier, and more challenging operation.

Minutes later, a Senior Supply Specialist (SSS) walks onto the pier with a clipboard in hand while other supply personnel converge on the quarterdeck looking around. He spots the lieutenant and walks under the brow. "Sir, there's information I need from the invoices before we start unloading," the SSS says, hesitant to take a few steps under the brow after seeing the lieutenant's mean face.

"Here," the lieutenant says, rudely thrusting the documents into his hand.

The tall, overweight driver, dressed in coveralls, climbs out of the cab after filling out his delivery paperwork. He walks to the back of the trailer and opens one door, then the other, securing the doors to the side of the trailer, backing away, and looking around.

The SSS walks up to the driver, grasping his clipboard under his arm. "If you don't mind, sir, I can compare documents while you're talking to the lieutenant," he says, pointing to the lieutenant, who stares back with attitude.

Tom meanders over to the rear of the trailer and stands on tiptoes, looking inside the cold, dark trailer with minutes passing.

"Ok, Lieutenant, I'm ready to start off-loading," the supply specialist says, walking toward the lieutenant and driver, who are deep in conversation.

The driver puts his cigarette out in the mangled sand bucket and walks over to the back of the trailer, struggling to climb, and then hook the cables to the boat's pad eye. He operates the truck's winch until looking around with bright eyes. "Ok..., Take it off!" the driver shouts.

After the equipment is unloaded, an older and heavy-set supply specialist soon wobbles over, checking for serial numbers and any apparent damages.

Minutes pass when the supply specialist walks from the truck.

"Everything checks out well, sir," the supply specialist says, passing the clipboard to the lieutenant, who snatches it, sloppily scribbling in the authorization block. He turns, politely passing the clipboard to the driver, who signs the delivery time sheet.

"That's it..., I'm out of here," the driver says, shaking the lieutenant's hand while screaming over the loud noise of a few low-flying surveillance U.S. Secret Service aircraft. His eyes follow the plane until it vanishes over the trailer while he's shutting the last door.

The driver climbs up, easing away from alongside the warehouse when picking up speed. He slows, flashing headlights a few times until spotting the guard rushing over to the gate and swings one door open, latching it, and then the other.

After the first boat is loaded and secured on the ship, Tom salutes the OOD and makes his way across the hanger, heading toward the conning station. Minutes later, he steps inside the cool, dark room, slowly adjusting his sight when noticing a woman's figure approaching.

The female ensign extends a welcoming hand. "Hi..., I'm the ship's navigator, Ensign Tamara Haun," she says softly.

Tom takes a few steps back, and she reaches around him, stroking her soft hand across his muscular back, stopping him from backing into the bulky, hot coffee maker.

"Thanks, gator," he says, looking back into the light streams of steam.

A loud announcement blares through the speakers above Tom's head for him to report to the wardroom.

"Well, as you were saying, ma'am!"

"Oh, never mind, you'd better get going, Chief," she says, giggling.

"It's been a pleasure though short," he says, shaking her warm, soft hand.

"Same here," she responds, hesitant to let go of his soft but firm touch.

Tom walks into the wardroom minute later to find everyone standing at attention when snapping to attention.

"At ease!" Ensign Terry shouts.

Everyone takes their seats and looks toward Captain Carrington, who is standing at the head of the table with his eyes rolling about the room, smiling, nodding, and gazing back into many of their faces. "Good evening, ladies and gentlemen, I'm Captain Carrington, Commanding Officer of Strike Force One."

Now, Captain Ronald Carrington has been in the Special Forces ranks for fourteen years before taking command of Strike Force One. He's very professional and looks remarkably honorable in his military appearance, as he is tall (six-foot-two) and slender.

Captain Carrington's eyes swarm over the room, spotting his XO peeping out from behind another officer. "This is Lieutenant Smith, acting Executive Officer from the Washington Command Center..., welcome aboard, lieutenant," he says, acknowledging the six-foot-one X.O. by gesturing to his left while he's walking up.

The captain's eyes roam again until finding Tamara, who is entering through the back door. He stares into her lovely eyes, quickly focusing on others so it doesn't seem too obvious when noticing a few heads turning to look back at her. "I'm sure most of you have introduced yourselves by now, so I'd like to take a few minutes to welcome everyone. As you all know, everyone involved in this mission will be using this makeshift wardroom, both officers and enlisted, and vice officers, which is forward due to confidentiality reasons."

He pauses, hearing a hatch slammed in the passageway before continuing. "I don't expect my men to mingle with the ship's crew, unless necessary, to accomplish their daily routine. So, now that I've got that out of the way, I want all of you to know this will be a unique but challenging operation in the Western Caribbean. I'm not at liberty to reveal the entire operation due to its sensitivity in nature, but the name of the mission is Operation Golden Seal. The operation's plans and orders are under review with the Admiral, ship's Commanding Officer, and Operations Officer. We set sail soon, so everyone should try to get a good night's rest. Now..., as Bugs Bunny would say it..., ah..., that..., tha..., tha..., that's all, folks!" he comically says, almost sounding like the fuzzy character with laughter breaking out.

His hand instantly goes high, trying to regain their attention. "One more thing!" the lieutenant goes on to say. "I need Strike Force One immediately assembled in the flight conference room..., thank you."

"Attention on deck!" Ensign Terry shouts as everyone snaps to attention. "Dismissed!" the ensign shouts after the captain and lieutenant exit.

Everyone disperses except Tom and his men, who stand fast with confused looks.

"Let's get up to the conference room ASAP!" Ensign Terry, their team leader, says when turning, then continuing his conversation with the female officer until turning again, finding his men still there.

"You heard the ensign!" Tom says, being nosey and then playfully jumping into his karate stance to put his men's minds at ease when they all get a good laugh.

They single-file through passageways and finally up two sets of ladders, mumbling under their breath until entering the conference room, where they fumble around for seats. They grow quiet when the lights dim and sit watching the podium as Captain Carrington fades away from it into pure darkness. His sandy white hair and the white in his eyes and eyebrows look florescent when he fades back into the dimly-lit room. "Well, men," the captain says, in his deep, scratchy voice. "This is Lieutenant Smith..., XO, as mentioned earlier.

Now, I know I've been promising a debriefing from the last mission, but I'm still not in receipt of the investigative reports from the Joint Forces Investigative Field Office. Oh..., one other detail, unrelated to the previous mission: The ship will not be carrying helicopters, so the aft, starboard side of the ship is available to us. Furthermore . . ." he rambles on before rudely interrupted.

"That's all, gentlemen," Lieutenant Smith says, pissed that the captain hadn't told them he'd be running things and for them to report directly to him instead of the captain. "Dismissed..., get some sleep," the lieutenant says rudely.

The men look at one another, puzzled by the lieutenant's rudeness. They slowly stand and exit, but Tom stands in a slight daze, noticing the captain looks a little disappointed and shook up for some reason.

Tom takes two steps toward the captain when the lieutenant steps forward, so he fakes him out, veering off and out the door.

Captain Carrington grasps hold of the podium, frustrated, with fiery eyes that follows the lieutenant's movement toward the door and watch until he locks the door. He rushes up to the lieutenant, and when toe-to-toe, the lieutenant jerks then snatches the captain up by the collar "You listen here, you old od fart!" he harshly whispers in his ear, drooling with warm spit splattering in the captain's ear when the lieutenant's funky breath grows stronger. "If you screw up this operation, I'll personally see to it that you and your men pay dearly! Do you understand?" he says, spraying more funk-ridden spit in the captain's ear and alongside his face.

The captain frowns from the lieutenant's bad breath, then tenses and bursts into tears. "Hell, what's so damn secretive about briefing the men right this damn minute?"

"Listen, damn you! There are orders to be followed here, so don't even think for one minute that you'll be running a damn thing on this mission! Hell..., you should have told them what I politely asked, but noooo..., you want to be a stubborn old fool!"

Captain Carrington walks toward the door with the lieutenant is hot on his trail when the captain swiftly turns and raises his index and middle finger to the lieutenant's face. "If . . .!"

"If? If what, mother...?" he says, harshly forcing the captain against the back of the door. "That's what I thought, punk! You'll do as I freakin' say or wish you had!" he says, staring deeply into his eyes. "Now..., are you ready to conduct yourself like a freakin' real man?" the lieutenant says harshly with his chest stuck out.

The captain stares eye to eye, almost trembling. "Get out of my damn face, ya stankin' breath, pathetic little piece of crap! Screw you, dude!" the captain says, hacking up a wad of spit and holding it while still staring at the back of the lieutenant's head when turning.

The lieutenant flips around and closes in on him, toe-to-toe and eye-to-eye again. "Do it..., I freakin' double, triple dare ya! Heck no! Forget that..., no, I'm begging you..., please!" the lieutenant says sarcastically with his chest stuck out further, and his fists clenched tightly. "Do it and I'll knock the mud oucha (out of you)!"

The captain frowns from the bad breath again, and slowly swallows when shoving the lieutenant with his shoulder when he passes.

CHAPTER TWO:
U.S. MISSILE STRIKE PLATFORM (USMSP) DEPARTURE

Tom walks across the dimly-lit hangar and runs into a woman who he thought was the ship's navigator. "Excuse me, ma'am?"

"Yes, Chief," she acknowledges, smiling.

"Do you have a few minutes?"

"Sure," she says, blushing.

"Maybe we can talk on the fantail (after part of the ship), if it's ok with you?"

"Well, ok," she says, turning and following him at a distance yet distancing herself while checking out his physique, tight butt, and what she thinks is the sexiest walk ever.

They turn down another passageway, and she takes the lead, sensually staring back at him a few times to make her interest known. They turn again and come up on a watertight exterior door at the end of the long, dimly-lit passageway, and she stops with Tom leaning into her.

"Here, let me get that! Tom says, reaching over her shoulder with his firm chest pressed hard against her soft, well-structured back.

"My, my, my...! I love a strong man."

"I bet a lady of your caliber has plenty flocking at your feet, huh?"

"What does that have to do with having one more?" she says, smirking, winking, and licking candy-colored, glossy lips.

"Are you hitting on me, Ensign?" Tom asks, smiling when the door swings open from a short, brisk wind.

"Maybe..., and what if I am?"

"Then you need to get a more advanced novel than this amateur love story," he says, cocking his head back to one side with his eyes scanning over the cover while she holds it tight. "Maybe you should get something more advanced, like Tainted Obsessions, but the uncut version or Liberty Call..., Port of Spain by the same author if you need something comical as this supposed to be romance," he says with a smirk when turning and closing the watertight door.

"Yeah, right, whateva (whatever), man! Look, enough of the games..., why did you ask me out here?"

"Because I need to know how well you know Lieutenant Smith?"

"Well, all I know is he's been onboard for days and boy is he a damn jerk..., a pure asshole, why?"

"Well, it's just that whenever I try to get close to my captain, he's always in the way…, you know, as if he's intentionally guarding him or something."

The ship's whistle sounds one prolonged blast when Ensign Jones looks over at the warehouse. The ship slightly bobs up and down and then slowly begins inching away from the pier.

"Shouldn't you be on the bridge when the ship gets underway?" he asks.

She laughs. "No, no, no…, I'm the security officer, not the navigator, but don't be embarrassed because everyone mistakes us at times because we look alike, but I'm just a little taller and thicker in the right places, if you know what I mean," she says, checking to make sure the aft lookout.

She cautiously looks around, and then slowly runs her hands along her curvy hips in a playful yet seductive gesture when winking.

Tom gets somewhat turned on by her naughty gesture but plays it down with a smile.

They continue quietly watching until a tug comes alongside and receives the ship's prodigious mooring lines, then backs the ship into the middle of the basin.

She turns her walkie-talkie up to find the tug master giving maneuvering orders to the OOD on the bridge. "Mark your head, Bridge!" the deep male voice says.

"How does that sound?" the ensign asks, bursting into her silly giggle, then laughter.

"What's that?" He looks as if lost.

"Marking that head," she answers, hee-hawing even harder.

"Heading is 020, sir!" she hears the helmsman on the bridge reply over the walkie-talkie.

Tom shakes his head in disbelief at her blatant naughtiness and then smiles.

They proceed over to the other side of the ship when no longer able to see the tug, then walk over to the opposite side, slightly leaning over the lifelines, when hearing another tug pulling alongside to guide the ship farther out into the huge basin.

The tug shifts sides again, and they see two women and three male Boatswain Mates gathering at the front of the tug, tending to the ship's mooring lines.

Suddenly, the ship shifts in another direction when the tug on the port side pushes against the ship, keeping it steady.

The ship stands still for minutes, and then slowly advances until picking up speed for about twenty minutes. Instantly, the two tugs break off and peel away from both sides of the ship, paralleling a buoy line for a while until coming to a bare steerageway.

A white and red light appears out of nowhere; the pilot's boat bounces up and down across the top of mild waves as it makes its final approach. It pulls alongside, and the pilot disembarks via the rickety, florescent pilot's ladder, which bangs quietly against the ship's side.

Tom and Nicole stare at the boat until it vectors away from the ship, picks up speed, and quickly vanishes into darkness. They soon hear the ship's turbine engines mildly, and then loudly whistle in a mild and high pitch.

Within seconds, the turbine's spinning ratio increases the ship's speed through the cold, dark, and choppy waters until the sound is slightly unbearable when covering their ears until the high squelch levels out to a gentle whisper. The ship levels to cruise speed, causing the turbines finally to quiet.

Before long, the ship skirts atop five-foot waves, allowing a few more glimpses of the Chesapeake Bay light, which dangles back and forth before fading into pure darkness.

"I guess we'd better call it a night; besides, I've got to get up early," Tom says, standing a few feet behind her and still admiring her sexy body in the tighter-than-regulation uniform.

She stares into his eyes, barely able to see him. "Have a good night, Chief," she says, looking back at him with a teasing smile when winking in the moonlight as it clears the thick clouds. She walks off, opens the watertight door, and enters the passageway easing the door shut.

Tom stares back at the door for minutes, and then stares off at the diminishing skyline for a few more minutes before entering the ship, adjusting his eyes to the low-level lighting. He picks up his pace, heading for the berthing, where he quietly stumbles inside the partially-lit room and makes his way over to his bunk. He unfolds the rolled sheets and pillowcase, neatly making his bunk by the dim rack (bed) light. Tom opens his stand-up locker and slips out of his uniform, placing it and his shoes inside.

He tucks his tee shirt inside the liner of his underwear, adjusting himself from the three to six o'clock position for comfort, and then climbs between cozy sheets.

The ship begins bobbing up and down for long spells within the hour as it continues maneuvering south and farther out to sea. It pitches up and down, rolling side to side, when twenty miles outside the line of demarcation, sometimes taking longer than others to recover from the steep listing.

Without warning, a top bunk curtain flaps wide open with Johns flying out, screaming when heading for the cold, dark, blue-tiled floor. "Shit!" he shouts, bracing the lower bunk tight, straining against the following heavy listing, and climbing back in his bunk. He flops down, bracing each side of the mattress, holding on tighter when the ship takes more sudden twists and turns.

Later, forty-degree rolls even have Tom oppugning if the ship will recover while USMSP R. L. Peterson is sailing fifty miles off the coast. An hour later, the ship begins pitching and rolling in fifteen-foot swells, with waves rising well above the bow and covering the main decks at intervals.

Now, the USMSP R. L. Peterson was built by the finest of leading engineers and shipyard builders in the world. She's a powerful vessel and could easily withstand seas far more significant than those pressed upon her.

The female navigator leans over the chart table at the end of her eight-hour shift, examining the ship's last position when the ship takes a sudden hard port and then starboard roll. She instantly tightly braces against the table, balancing and sneering when looking over to find the male First-Class Quartermaster and female Second-Class Boatswain puking their guts out in the same trash bags.

The bow continually rises and falls, slamming hard into the sea, and after the fifth slam, it lifts the stern atop massive swells, abruptly dropping it at almost timed intervals.

Towering roadside waves continually clash against the ship out of nowhere, sometimes causing a solid vibration throughout the ship.

The sea raises the ship unusually high a few times and slams it down hard, causing an even heavier vibration with several things thrown about in various compartments throughout the ship.

The ship feels as though it is close to breaking in half at times, with even higher lifts and sudden drops.

A continual thick mist comes from the ocean's surface blows, with winds growing even stronger until mini golf-ball-sized raindrops pour across the bridge's wings.

The loud, roaring sea builds to greater heights as the ship fights its way through the cold night with faint port and starboard running lights fading occasionally and then barely reappearing in darkness.

The sun remains well hidden behind thick, dark clouds come morning.

The sea is almost as smooth as glass until sometimes rippling with schools of flying fish, which seem to appear out of nowhere.

The wardroom door opens slowly, with Strike Force One's XO slipping inside unnoticed. He stands staring at the back of Oggie's head for minutes, then takes a few steps toward Oggie, swiftly coming up behind him. His mind goes haywire instantly while thinking of something to say to ensure no one comes near the captain or his stateroom.

"Good morning, sir..., is the captain coming up for breakfast?" Oggie asks with eyes still cut back over his shoulder when hearing him breathing.

The lieutenant takes a deep breath to slow his heavy breathing when caught off guard and still looking down in somewhat of a daze.

He hesitates and then looks up with a stern face. "No, he's under the weather..., but the way..., where is your chief and ensign?"

"Probably sleeping in, sir. They were up pretty late last night with last-minute preparations and security checks."

"Well..., you make sure everyone knows that Captain Carrington wants to be left alone until he's feeling better but come to think of it, I think he's coming down with a slight cold, flu, or something."

"Sure thing, sir," Oggie says sarcastically with an unconvincing expression.

Down in the berthing, Tom wraps up his shower and begins shaving. Afterward, he finds a note from Oggie pinned to his bunk's curtain about the daily routine.

Oggie includes a comment about the captain's illness, expressly written to an overture of sarcasm, then informs Tom that he had put his breakfast in the refrigerator, along with a napkin with his name on it.

Tom gets dressed and enters the wardroom an hour later, finding the food, as Oggie had said. He sits eating with his back to the door, and when finished, the Food Service Attendant (FSA) walks up, removing his plate. Seconds later, Tom hears the door open and looks over his shoulder, not seeing anyone, then looks over the other, finding the security officer with her arms crossed. His smile comes and grows bigger and brighter by the second until she shakes her head, with eyes glistening, and then smiles just a little harder. "Oh..., so you didn't care to invite me to breakfast, huh?" she mutters lightly, taking a seat across from him and slowly stirring the cup of coffee just placed before her by the FSA.

"You can sit on this table and be my breakfast," Tom seductively says, taking a sip of juice and holding his laugh for as long as he can until softly giggling.

Her eyes sparkle more in excitement when looking around until spotting the FSA folding napkins near the pantry. "Excuse me! Please let me have a fruit, bagel, butter, and cream cheese."

"Yes, ma'am. It will take a few minutes because I have to defrost the bagels."

"Ok dear..., no rush, please..., take your time, love."

Ensign Jones attentively listens for the door's lock, instantly slipping her foot from her sandal. She slowly runs her soft, smooth, warm foot up Tom's leg, with toes gently working back and forth. She stops, thinking she heard the door open, then looks, not seeing anyone when driving her foot upward and deep between his gapped thighs.

She applies a few more back-and-forth strokes when feeling him growing fast. She tries gripping him with her long toes, as accustomed to doing so many times with other men, but Tom's just too thick. She tries several times just to tease him and get more satisfaction from the foreplay. "Damn! Mmm..., you talk a good game, don't you? Don't think for one minute I don't have a little secret place to put your sex ass through a few flex tests," she says, smiling.

She thinks she hears a door open again and immediately lowers her foot to the plush carpet, easing her foot back into her sandal. "I love aggressive men," she says, stretching her V-shaped collar to expose more cleavage. "So where were we, Mister Billy Bad-Ass?" she mutters.

"You were about to sit on this table, and she was about to bring your breakfast," he responds, digging the tip of his boots into the carpet and sliding his chair back. He stands, tucking his shirt into his trousers.

The FSA sits the wide, decorative dish before Ensign Jones and walks away.

Tom's eyes follow the FSA until she vanishes into the kitchen, then checks to make sure she is gone when playfully grasping his inseam, adjusting himself to ease the stiffness at his upper thigh.

"You know, I can help you with that, right?" Ensign Jones says, gazing at the thick, pipe-like bulge along his inseam with eyes browsing over his zipper to find a dime-size wet spot just below the inseam.

"Oh, yeah? Help me do what..., choke you with it?" he responds, grinning, winking, and walking out.

Ensign Jones' eyes stay glued to the door with attentive ears for minutes in anticipation, hoping Tom would walk back inside any minute, but he continues to the weight room.

Tom walks up to the weight room and stands, listening to his men before entering and listening to his men jokingly sparring back and forth, unknowingly.

Oggie is the first to spot him and stands with the others, quickly assembling around him, one at a time.

"As you know, I have not spoken with Captain Carrington yet."

"So what?" Johns responds.

"So what? Damn, son, what..., the lights are on in that head, but nobody's home or what? Look it..., here it is noon, and the captain is supposedly sick? Yeah, right..., go picture that bullshit! I tell you, this lieutenant character is up to no damn good."

"What do you have in mind, Chief?" Oggie asks, seeing Tom frozen in thought.

"Well, I was thinking..., there are vacant staterooms two doors from the lieutenant and captain's room. Tony..., Johns..., picks the lock and set up a special listening device. Oggie..., Bobby..., distract the captain and lieutenant by de-energizing lights in and near their room. Everyone, synchronize your watches to plus one-five," Tom says, adjusting his to fifteen minutes past the hour and relaying the correct time. "Whatever you do..., don't tell Ensign Terry anything about this because he'll go straight to the lieutenant or captain. Operations will run from 1900-2100, give or take, on the latter end. We'll use channel seven for reception and, oh..., no recording."

They immediately disperse and go about their daily routine.

Tom goes to the office and calls Kelley, awakening her from a long, peaceful nap. "Hi doll . . ." he says, expertly disguising his voice, remembering the pet name Jeff gave her, just to get a tease. "Were you thinking about me?" he asks, more playful but hoping she would fall for his plot in confirming his gut feelings about her still having deep feelings for Jeff.

"Jeff?" she drowsily answers, sounding somewhat excited yet confused, then in a more sluggish tone.

"Yes, doll," he answers, surprised yet anxious to continue just to see how far she'll go before recognizing his voice. "I need to see you."

"What..., for what? Huh..., you need to be seeing and taking care of your damn kids and not even be thinking about or talking about seeing me. Did you forget I'm engaged?" she replies with a childish giggle.

"Yeah..., but I miss you and can't help but think about you. I've been an ass, but let's put that behind us because I know you miss me and the way I used to put this down in those sheets," he says, forgetting to respond to the comment about the kids or her engagement.

She blushingly chuckles. "Don't even go there!" she responds when giggling harder and sounding somewhat cheerful for a quick second.

"Do you miss me?"

"Of course, silly..., you're my kids' father," she says unconvincingly when her mind quickly and deceitfully plots to attempt to lure him into her child support scheme so she can have him arrested for missing several payments.

"I heard your boy toy had to leave," he says, lying back, staring at the ceiling and continually blinking to absorb the tears that suddenly rush in from out of nowhere. "Are you expecting him back soon?"

"Oh him..., oh..., yeah, he had to leave unexpectedly, but I'm not sure for how long," she answers in a semi-trance. "Wait..., who told you..., how do you know?"

"I have my sources, babes..., I have my sources..., but hey, I'm at moms, so I hope we can get together for dinner, maybe a movie, just the four of us."

"Are you serious?" she answers, kind of in a rage when her voice slightly clears as she sits up after hearing him call her "babes," knowing Tom was the only one to call her by that pet name.

"Sure..., how about Tiffany's restaurant..., tonight? What time works for you, doll?" he says, realizing he used the wrong pet name.

"Hmm..., where are you calling from?" Kelley asks, recalling Jeff's mother was visiting relatives out of the state when lifting the caller ID and seeing the words 'U.S. GOVERNMENT' boldly flash across the window. Her eyebrows rise, with her eyes slightly bulging, becoming speechless.

"You know, Kelley!" Tom shouts in rage. "You're no damn different from the rest of these damn women out here, huh..., in love? In, love my ass! You are no better, claiming to be so in love!"

"Babe, I can ex—," she begins to say.

"Screw it! Don't! Hell..., just leave me the hell alone! Do you hear me?" he shouts out with more rage. "Just stay the hell away from me!" he says. He slams the phone down and drops back in agonizing pain.

She immediately tries redialing but gets redirected by the proxy switchboard and receives a recorded message that incoming calls are not allowed.

Tom continually wipes his teary eyes and looks off into space for some time until resting his head upon folded elbows and slightly nods off.

Minutes later, he's awakened by his ensign when the door slams. "Are you ready to discuss maintenance plans and weapons reports?" Ensign Terry asks.

"Do you have the invoices?" Tom asks, shuffling through his desk for eye drops.

"Yeah..., hey..., are you all right?" the ensign asks, hearing Tom sniff a few times while pretending to be clearing his sinuses and airway.

"What about the Command Center setup documents and master deployment plans?"

"Well," Terry responds in a daze, "the lieutenant said an ashore agent would handle the heavy stuff, but hey..., are you sure you are ok?" he asks again, but this time, staring into Tom's bloodshot eyes and then over Tom's desk.

"Yes sir..., probably allergies," Tom says. "Sir, normally we have the invoices by now, so don't you think that's kind of strange?"

"Sort of, ok..., maybe. Ok, look, maybe you're right. I'll go down and ask the captain for them," he says, taking a few steps toward the door.

"What? Didn't you get the word about the captain not wanting to be bothered?"

There is an abrupt knock.

"Come in!" the ensign says.

The door slightly cracks open. "Sorry to bother you," the navigator says, sticking her head inside before fully extending the door. "Hey..., I'm looking for Ensign Jones. Have you seen her?"

"Well..., what makes you think she would be here?" Tom rudely answers.

"Chief..., look..., I'll handle this! Come on in, Ensign," Ensign Terry says, easing a hand into each pocket. He nervously fiddles around with pocket change, pacing and quickly thinking of what to say next.

"Thanks for the invitation, but I really must be going," she slyly expresses.

"Excuse me, sir," Tom says, grabbing a few facial tissues and walking toward the door.

"What's the rush, Ensign? How about a quick tour of our impressive little setup," Ensign Terry says, sizing up her petite waistline and wide but lovely hips. He looks over her shoulder and watches Tom as he pulls the door shut. "Please don't think I'm too forward, but you have a great physique. Do you work out often?" he asks.

"Daily..., that's why I'm trying to find Ensign Jones: She's my workout partner."

"Then I have to go back to the chief's question. Why would Ensign Jones be here?"

"Well, can you keep a secret?" she asks, mischievously giggling.

"Sure, I'm good at secrets, trust me," he responds, smiling and leaning back against the wall, acting cool.

"Well, she's had a serious crush on your chief between you and me since she laid eyes on him. Heck! He's all she ever talks about, nonstop, and you have not even been onboard what..., not even two days."

"Well, hell..., she can just get her mind off Tom because he's madly in love with his fiancée, Kelley, and when I say madly, boy, do I mean madly."

"Oh, really now? Hmmm..., well, I guess you don't care to put up a wager, huh? I mean..., you do claim to know him so well, right?"

Ensign Terry thinks long and hard, with eyes intentionally drifting over her sexy body to ensure she knows he likes what he sees. "Deal..., but for the wager..., I want you," he responds, causing her to look away and blush.

"My! I see you have no problem speaking your mind, huh?" She shyly twirls a string of hair to look sexy, knowing that she's gotten so many compliments in the past from lovers and others trying to get next to her when doing so. "Well..., Ok..., well..., that's fine, as long as you can deal with the fact that I already have a married male friend."

"Well, let's see..., hmmm..., oh, yeah, I can handle that, as long as you can deal with the fact I, too, am married," he says, proudly flashing his wedding band.

"No problem," she says, marveling at what she was getting herself into on this deal.

"So then, it's a deal?" he says with a hand extended forward.

"A deal..., but you can never mention it to anyone..., and I do mean anyone or all bets are off..., that means not even your team," she says with a firm handshake. She winks and pulls her hand away when feeling him trying to pull her closer. "Not so fast..., you have not won yet," she chuckles. "Really..., I must be going, but I'll see you at dinner or movie call," she says, resisting his strong advances.

After dinner, the men meet in the armory and gear up. Minutes later, they exit, spread out along the long, dim, blue-lit passageway.

Bobby is quick at setting a timer and tripping the main breaker when de-energizing lights near the captain's stateroom.

Tom eases into his chair, pulling his headset from around his neck and covering his ears. He kicks back, riding on the chair on its hind legs when thumbing through a fitness magazine.

The four quickly maneuver through several dark passageways, remaining undetected by dipping into little cubbyholes or wall hatches along the way. They huddle behind machinery when hearing a watertight door open and proceed when the person's shadow passes.

Around 1900, the first radio signal transmits, and the lights re-energize.

"Testing, testing..., this is Alpha One Alpha, going live," Oggie whispers.

Oggie and Bobby adjust the equipment's knobs until they finally hear moderate voices from two different televisions. They accurately adjust the equipment's sensitivity with a few more turns and tweaks and manage to drown the strong television signals and make out the lieutenant's frail voice.

"..., tonight! How was dinner?" the lieutenant asks, watching the captain nod while gagged and handcuffed. "It won't be long now before the mission goes into full effect," the lieutenant says, looking mischievous. His face transforms into pure evil when sitting and staring at the captain's eyes, which are full of tears.

"Oggie, did you notice there was no response?" Bobby whispers.

"I noticed," Oggie says in excitement.

Without warning, mild springs from a door knob yawn from the equipment's sensitivity, and then a door slams, causing everyone to jerk their headsets slightly from their ears.

Instantly, the television's volume blares, totally drowning out the reception, and they hear heavy giggling, and seconds later, two women ensigns talking until they finally realize they're talking about how hot Tom and Ensign Terry are to them.

"Alpha One Alpha, sounding off," Oggie says, laughing during his transmission.

Oggie and Bobby wrap up their gear and turn off the lights, unsealing the door when the lights go out aft and reenergize minutes later.

Ensign Terry enters the office finding Tom putting away the expensive headset. He takes a seat, with curious eyes opening his mouth to enquire about the headset but doesn't, so he reaches for documents, and they commence the work on the personal evaluations.

Hours later, Tom stands, stretching before sitting back down.

"Looks like we've got them narrowed down now," Tom says.

The ensign glances over Johns' evaluation and notices that there happens to be a four-five-point mark. "Hey..., are you sure there aren't any last-minute changes?" the ensign asks, looking over Tom's shoulder.

"Why? Are there any doubts, sir? I mean, come on, man," Tom says, looking at him doubtfully.

"Well..., go ahead, just take another look."

There is total silence for minutes while Tom individually lifts and gazes over each evaluation except Johns'. "Well?"

"Well, what? Johns can't be as bad in leadership as you've marked him, can he?"

"Look, sir..., the regulations specifically state, in Block 55, 'tolerates hazards and unsafe practices and lacks the ability and integrity to cope with or tolerate above moderate stress,'" Tom replies, pointing at the thick evaluation manual's bold print.

"I see..., I see..., Ok, well, maybe you're right. I mean..., he does have a serious problem there..., but do you have to mark him so low?"

"Look, sir, I just call it as I see it, no more and no less. A spade is a spade!"

The PA system keys up. "Movie Call!"

Terry's mind scrambles. "Ok, now that it's final, what do you say we swing by and catch a movie with the girls? Besides, you owe me from Korea when I accompanied you on a blind date. I'll admit that was before you met Kelley, but you did promise to make it up to me for that ugly bat dressed in all black..., you know..., that chick from the dark side you hooked me up with."

"Wait..., what chick?"

"Don't play..., you sly devil..., I heard about you."

Tom smiles. "Hmm..., oh, I see..., well, consider the debt payable, but don't expect any miracles. We can meet there in a few, but I promised the guys I would swing by before it gets too late."

"That's fine, we'll be waiting," he says, smiling when reaching for the door and pulling it open.

"I'll put the evaluations in the top drawer so the captain can sign them whenever the lieutenant schedules our appointment."

"Appointment? Who needs a damn appointment? Hell, I'll walk right in anytime I feel like it and get them signed," Ensign Terry says, pulling the door open further.

"Damn, sir! You really are lost, huh? Where have you been the last day or so, sir?" Tom screams, throwing up his hands in frustration.

"What do you mean?" he asks, closing the door with a confused gaze.

"What do you know about this lieutenant..., this so-called XO?"

"Well, I know he's from the Washington Command Center and our XO."

"Is that it?"

"Well, nothing other than his bio, which I read; why..., is there more?"

"Just as I figured, with all due respect, sir..., you don't know, jack shit! You're walking around with your head so far up Ensign Haun's tail that you can't even see sunlight or smell the coffee."

"Now, you just wait a minute, Chief! What the hell does that mean?" he shouts angrily.

"Have you noticed anything strange with the captain?"

"Well..., no..., not really. You mean other than being under the weather?" Ensign Terry says.

"Under the weather, my a...," Tom responds, curving the curse word. "Then just let me say..., welcome aboard! You're a day late and a dollar short because we've already started the mission."

"What? Mission? What mission?" he asks with a chaotic stare.

"Listen..., and listen to me well. I had the guys set up reception in Captain Carrington's room tonight, but the team could only get a little information before Ensigns Jones and Haun cranked up their television, drowning the signal."

"What? Now, look here, Chief! That's an invasion of privacy, but anyway..., what kind of information were they able to retrieve?"

"I'm not sure, but it sounded as if the lieutenant was talking to himself because I never heard the captain respond..., ever."

"Are you sure?"

"Wait a minute," he answers, picking up the phone and dialing the berthing. Oggie answers. "Hello, Strike Force berthing...,"

"Yeah, yeah, yeah..., hey, Oggie, can you confirm there was only one voice tonight?"

"Yeah, Chief, there was definitely only one voice."

"Thanks, and by the way, cancel that little get-together that I mentioned earlier; something's come up."

"All right, Chief, I'll relay the message."

"Well!"

"As I said, sir, there was only one voice," Tom says, hanging up with concerned eyes.

The ensign concentrates for seconds, gazing at the floor, and then walks toward the door.

Tom turns out all the lights except one. "Let's get out of here," Tom says. He opens the door and walks out behind the ensign.

Tom and Terry enter the wardroom, finding Captain Carrington and the lieutenant near the pantry waiting on popcorn upon entering the wardroom.

Captain Carrington continually keeps his eye peeled over at the female ensign.

Tom steps off fast, leading the way with Ensign Terry hot on his trail.

"Afternoon, Captain," Tom says, swiftly approaching from behind.

"Afternoon, Chi—" the captain responds, looking over his shoulder before turning when interrupted.

"Afternoon, Chief..., Ensign," the lieutenant rudely says. "We were just leaving, so have a nice evening, gentlemen," he says, lightly shoving the captain in the back but trying not to make it too noticeable.

"But, sir," the ensign responds.

"Listen, Ensign, damn it, the last freakin' response from my freakin' lips was for you to have a nice evening; now, that's exactly what I meant! Are you deaf, dumb, or just plain stupid?" the lieutenant angrily whispers, with flaring nostrils and a thick vein protruding at his forehead. He shoves the captain again but harder, walking closely behind him as he leads the way.

The ensign looks over at Tom in shock.

"As I said, welcome aboard, sir," Tom says, also in shock from seeing the captain shoved a third time at the door before exiting.

"Did you hear what that prick said? Ooh..., I should have busted his damn wide open!"

"Look..., just put on your thinking cap tonight, sir. As far as I'm concerned, the captain is safe as long as he's on board," Tom says.

The ensign's short train of thought quickly refocuses when finding the two women sitting in the lounge with eyes constantly peering back.

"Look, who I see," Ensign Terry says, cautiously looking around before secretly pointing.

"Shush..., this is the best part!" Ensign Haun whispers, looking over at Ensign Terry and winking as they approach.

After the movie, everyone eventually wanders off, but Ensign Terry and Haun share a cup of coffee and mild conversation, leaving about thirty minutes later.

Ensign Terry walks her to her stateroom and then heads for his stateroom, which is dark when fumbling around for the wall's light switch, as accustomed and finally flipping it up, but nothing.

The lieutenant stands in Terry's stateroom with his back still pinned to the wall, holding his nose pinched tight and slowly breathing through his mouth. His watery eyes continually follow the ensign's hands and body movement, taking slow, deep breaths and holding his nose tighter with the awful feet funk continually rising.

The ensign's hands fumble around a little more, running up and down the lamppost until the switch flips up, but again, nothing.

Deadweight slumps over the ensign's back without delay with Hercules's strength when a cool, freshly-soaped hand covers his mouth.

A sharp, cold object presses hard against his throat and almost breaks the skin.

Perspiration rushes in like a whirlwind as Terry tenses, with both hands slowly raising high in fear.

"Slowly!" a low, deep voice whispers. "One wrong move and it's a wrap," the deep voice growls, then silences, with the lieutenant holding his breath longer and frowning harder. The lieutenant repositions his arm tighter around the ensign's neck, applying more pressure until it slightly breaks the skin, with sweat instantly burning the cut.

"Who are you? What do you want?" the ensign whispers, trembling with both arms even higher. His eyes widen and then slowly shift left, then right.

"You know damn well who I am, punk! Who else would be knee-deep in that ass! Stop with the fifty-damn-question bullshit! Listen..., and you listen well! This operation is serious shit! The Command Center specifically sent me to make sure there are no fuckups or failures," he says, still blinking his watery eyes when quickly closing his mouth and frowning until holding his breath again.

"I understand fully, sir," Ensign Terry anxiously responds, tensing and sniffing harder.

"Good! Look..., you and only you will report to me at 1200 hours daily," he whispers, slightly releasing the blade. His face frowns more from the unpleasant scent until he can no longer handle the overwhelming smell.

"Damn, man! What is that unearthly scent?" he asks, forcefully shoving the ensign to the carpeted floor. He sprints for the door and doesn't hang around for a response, with blue, dim lights suddenly flashing inside the room from the passageway as the door opens and abruptly shuts.

Ensign Terry remains in a fetal position for a while, and he stays on the floor crying for so long that he drifts into a deep sleep.

Come morning; the ensign is awakened abruptly by voices in the passageway when a watertight door slams. He sits up in a daze and wipes tear crust from his eyes.

Tom knocks on the ensign's door, listening until finally hearing a frail voice answer.

The ensign dashingly climbs from the floor, easing onto the edge of the bed. "Come..., come in," He says in a weak voice.

Tom slings the door open and falls back into the hallway, holding his nose. "Woowee!"

"Oh, hell..., like you never aired out your gym shoes. Man, get in here and close my damn door!" He says, seeing an enlisted female veer from the wall holding her nose when bouncing off the bulkhead (wall)."

"Woowee!" Tom whispers, walking inside and continually fanning and frowning until pinching his nose tight. "Damn, sir! What's with that awful-ass smell? Is everything all right? I mean, you didn't kill anybody in here..., did you? Well..., did you?"

"Yeah, whatever! I suppose all is well, but I've seen better days," he responds, looking down, astonished to find his toes wiggling back and forth in his frayed socks. He looks at Tom as if he wants to disclose what happened but then tries clearing his sad posture.

Tom grows curious when the ensign doesn't respond with his usual smile, seeing how Tom always cracks him up when being a comedian.

"Tamara and I argued after everyone left the movie call," he says with his lying eyes glued to the floor, unable to look in Tom's face because he's never lied to him.

Tom knows something is wrong but can't yet put his finger on it. "About what, sir, if you don't mind my asking?" Tom inquires, finally noticing the crusty little droplets of blood on his shirt.

"Nothing worth talking about, and I can promise that," he says, looking down and then away.

"I guess that scar under your throat isn't worth a discussion either, huh?"

"Well..., no, not really, but for sure, Tamara's a little fighter," Ensign Terry responds, looking down, somewhat embarrassed, when thinking of a quick lie to counter Tom's observations and comments.

"With all due respect, sir, I hope nothing happened to jeopardize your career or bring discredit to my men and me!"

"Oh, no..., I can promise it wasn't anything like that, Chief. Hey, look..., I want to rest more, so I'll get with you later. Oh yeah..., and by the way..., the rest of the time we're out here, please run everything going up to the captain by me."

"Sure thing..., no problem, sir. Hey..., I'll meet you in the office, say noon?" Tom responds, highly pissed and displaying it in his heavy breathing and demeanor.

"No..., let's say 1300," the ensign suggests, remembering the XO's new marching orders.

Tom stands and holds the door open in deep thought and then opens it further, exiting.

Ensign Haun slowly wanders through the passageway, with hands caressing both walls, concentrating on counting blue floor tiles, and unknowingly on a collision course with Tom.

"Good morning, ma'am!" he says, startling her.

"Morning, Chief!" she responds, a bit astonished to find his eyes roaming over her body.

"May I have a few minutes? I mean, if you don't mind and have time to spare."

Sure thing Chief," she says, slowly twirling a few times like a cheerful ballerina when following him. "Mmm..., Wow..., Nicole was right; you have a cute, tight, round tush (butt)," she says, giggling until she looks somewhat serious when Tom looks back.

"Thanks for the thorough assessment, and I can see that you two hold no punches. So..., how's your girl doing today, anyway?" he asks, briefly looking over his shoulder and into her lovely eyes, which she dims to look even sexier.

"She's probably in some corner crying her eyes out, seeing how you have been avoiding her like the plague today."

"I don't mean to..., it's just that . . ."

"Yeah, yeah..., I know, Kelley, right?"

"Wow! Ensign Terry didn't waste any time giving the 911, 411, 311, 211, and thorough background info, huh?" he says, laughing while opening his office door.

"You have to admit he's a pretty thorough little fellow. So, anyways, tell me, what do I owe for this invite?" she asks, standing to one side so he can close the door.

"I have a question, if you don't mind sharing," he says, turning again and locking the door.

"No, not at all," she responds, intentionally undressing him with her eyes from head to toe while seductively licking her pretty, full lips with heat waves instantly swarming over her body like a flood when she feels hot under the collar.

"I just left Ensign Terry's room, and he looks a mess, so what I'm saying is..., I just need to know things are all right with you two."

"Oh yeah..., sure they are! I mean..., after you guys left, we had a lovely evening of coffee and mild conversation, nothing more."

"Really? Then trivial, and you only get one correct answer, so..., tell me how he got scars under his neck?" he asks, puzzled.

"Scars? Necks? Around his neck? What scars? I'm puzzled," she says with lowered, confused eyebrows.

Tainted Obsessions

"You mean there was no altercation or anything physical?"

"Chief, look..., you'll see me laugh and joke a lot, but when it comes to work and this vessel, I don't screw around. I'm always in control, so I can wait to do my damn dirt on land."

Tom goes into a slight mediation. "Ok, ok..., maybe it's from him shaving or something but thanks, ma'am."

"You're welcome, and hey, by the way, Nicole wanted me to tell you that she heard a commotion coming from your captain's stateroom late last night.

"Oh yeah? It's probably just those guys lollygagging, but please let me know if you guys hear anything else out of the ordinary from those two clowns."

"Ok, that's a promise, Tom. You don't mind if I call you Tom, do you?" She smiles. "Hey..., I have been meaning to ask you this..., ok..., here it comes. Man, what have you done to my girl? She's mad crazy over you!"

"Really?" He blushes. "Yeah, maybe, but I like being the aggressor," he says, checking to ensure the door is locked when walking up to her, winking and smiling.

"What's that supposed to mean?" she asks, pretending to be clueless but gazing deep into his eyes and smiling.

"Hmmm..., I think you know exactly what it means, Tamara," he says, pressing his hard body gently against hers. "You don't mind if I call you Tamara, do you?" he asks, gently backing her into the bulkhead with rich fragranced aftershave suddenly rising deep in her nostrils.

She takes a deeper breath of him, closing her eyes in pure pleasure.

"Tamara, right?" he mutters, gently nibbling an earlobe until piercing the tip of his tongue deep in her ear and blowing soft, warm air creating the sound of a soft ocean breeze.

"Oh, Tom," she whispers, warming the shaft of his well-structured neck with her hot breath. "Why are you playing these damn games? You know I want you first!" she says, lightly frowning in confusion and then smirking.

"Games? What games?"

"You knew I had my eyes on you since the first time I saw you," she says, gently tugging at his collar until pulling him closer and giving him a peck on his lips.

"No, really..., I did not know, and I thought you were just being friendly but shy."

He leans deeper into her, slowly moving from side to side until gently pressing against her soft thighs and causing chills to run down her spine. He kisses the nape of her lightly perfumed neck.

She softly whines.

They begin to French kiss until she's working her hips in a circular motion, with a raised pelvis riding hard on his thigh. Their bodies grow even closer when she grasps his inseam and moves her hand around to find his zipper.

Heat swarms over her body like an inferno leaving no doubt that she wants him right then and there.

Tom's firm hand grasps hers moving it back when drawing closer with a long tongue slithering deep into her hot mouth, this time until their lips form a perfect seal.

She straightaway tries reaching for the zipper again.

Still, he playfully resists, and she grows frustrated after yet another attempt at his zipper when her hand scroll over what feels like steel when grabbing a hand full with eyes closed tight in imagination. She pushes him away, feeling dizzy and overheated. "Damn you! How could you have let things go so far with Nicole?"

"Well..., come on, now! Your intentions were never clear, and then again, I guess you can say for the same reason you let Ensign Terry get next to you," he responds. He draws her closer and palms her thin waistline in both hands. His warm breath flies up against her collarbone, with his tongue running across it a few times, sucking on it until it slightly stings.

"You just don't know how much I want you! It hurts to hear Nicole mention your name," she pouts, pushing away and then instantly pulling him closer by his collar. She stares deep into his eyes and breathes even heavier in the heat of passion.

"I know you're not getting sentimental on me, are you?" he asks, delicately licking his lips and moistening them when kissing her once more.

They continue in conversation a little longer and then comes more hugs and kisses until she pulls away, intensely heated. She feels woozy again, with heat sweeping over her body like a towering inferno until mild-to-heavy perspiration rushes in. Unnoticeable tiny beads of sweat build up on her forehead and nose.

"I'll see you later, darling," she says, shaking off the entertaining thoughts of stripping down to nothing and doing him right there when turning and gesturing a kiss before hesitantly walking out and closing the door.

Tamara returns to her stateroom to find Ensign Jones face down in her bunk. She gazes over Ensign Jones' perfectly curved figure and thick bottom, slightly uncovered and laced in the black silk G-string with spaghetti noodle strings.

"What's wrong, Nicole?" she asks, seeing her head rise and her hand wipe her teary eyes.

"It's Tom..., he hasn't even stopped by to see how I'm doing," she says, raising her head from the lightly dampened pillow, revealing pink, watery eyes. "He's avoiding me..., I just know it!" She pouts.

"Oh, girl, chill the hell out with that craziness! Men! Just forget about him! Don't you know that so many men would die to be with you?"

"Yeah..., maybe," Nicole answers, wiping her tears and staring at the floor in deep meditation. "Hey, thanks, Tam..., I knew you would put things in perspective. Hmm...; oh yeah, I'll play along with his little, silly-ass games," she says, easing out and leaning against her bunk. She grabs her khakis, hopping to get into them when slipping one leg inside, then hopping until she almost loses her balance when trying to get her other leg inside.

"So, what do you plan to do?" Tamara asks curiously.

"What else? Seduce him," she answers, donning her bra and cramming medium-sized breasts inside. Both hands reach back and firmly pull the straps. "Believe me! It has to happen before he leaves the ship because I have to show him he's not even all that. He has not gotten the best of me yet, huh? It may sound desperate and all, but after seeing that thick bulge in those damn khakis..., damn! Let me tell you..., it has been hard to get that off my mind. Damn, I've got to have him," she says. She shakes her head like a crazy woman.

"I won't let you do it! Damn that, I just can't, and I won't!" Tamara shouts. She drops onto her bunk, tense with her body somewhat numb because she knows Nicole is capable of swiftly executing her deceitful plans.

"What? What do you mean? What do you mean you won't let me? Girl, please! You don't have a damn thing to do with this, baby girl!"

"Damn you..., I'll tell Tom if I have to!"

"What, whore?" Nicole replies, staring slightly downward at Tamara with her face frowning and her fist drawn into a tight ball.

Tamara swiftly stands in a combative stance, forcing Nicole to the door. First and foremost, there won't be too many more whores around here!" Tamara says, forcing Nicole back a few more feet when Nicole loosens her fist out of fear of more aggression.

"Girl, you have no clue who you're messing with!" Nicole says, leveraging the playing field, though terribly frightened by Tamara's sudden hostile approach, a side never seen before.

"Then why don't you show me, Miss..., I have to screw every nice-looking man that comes along," Tamara says, degrading her yet instilling more fear as she fearfully backs Nicole against the door.

"Stop it, Tamara! Stop it," she cries. "I thought you were my friend. How can you say these horrible things about me?"

Tamara steps forward and presses her index finger into Nicole's forehead. Her well-manicured nail slightly creates a light impression. "Friend my ass! Oh, I'm your friend all of a damn sudden, huh? Hell, I am about fed up with all your pitiful-ass bullshit," Tamara says, pushing her finger forward and mushing her with the palm of her hand.

"I'm sorry, Tamara..., please forgive me..., please!" Nicole continually cries in a light whisper, sliding down against the gray metal door. "I don't know what's gotten into me, but please forgive me!" she cries, continuously wiping her tears.

"Then stop these childish-ass games! If Tom doesn't want you, so be it..., damn!" Tamara says easily and confidently, feeling she's gotten her point across.

Ensign Jones still cries until it tapers off to a light sniffle.

Several doors down the passageway, Ensign Terry eases to the edge of the bunk in deep thought again, still in a trance when climbing back into his bunk in his clothes. He yawns, not realizing how tired he is when falling fast asleep to be awakened later by a faint buzzing sound, which causes him to jump to his knees and look around. Terry continually looks around until finally realizing the noise is from the ship's service telephone. Without hesitation, he feverishly scrambles across the floor. "Ensign Terry, may I help you, sir or ma'am?" he asks, half-sluggish.

"You sure as hell can! Either you think this is a freakin' game of some sort, think I'm a damn toy, or you just don't give two flying shits!"

"Who is this?" the ensign asks, pretending to be clueless for seconds with hands nervously running through his greasy, messy hair when his fingers begin to replicate the movement.

"Listen, shit for brains! I don't have time for your lack of proper brain functioning. Damn it! Get your stupid, sweet little ass over to the captain's stateroom now! Do you hear me, chump? Now!" the lieutenant screams, slamming the phone down and jumping to his feet as if in a football huddle.

Ensign Terry slings the door open and breaks out of the room nervously, running straight into the bulkhead. He enters another passageway, swerves, barely missing the wall structure and angle iron, and then takes off at a slow and fast jog. Terry rushes down another passageway and slides to the door, overcompensating, when stopping and then sharply coming to attention outside the captain's door. He lightly knocks three times and then steps inside, promptly snapping to attention with eyes gazing over the dark, grim-looking room. "Ensign Terry, reporting as ordered, sir!" he says in a weak and somewhat reassuring voice.

"Bullshit! You were ordered here well over an hour ago," the lieutenant responds, staring at him for seconds without blinking.

"At ease," the captain says, trying to exert some authority before looking down, embarrassed.

The lieutenant stands next to the captain, sitting at his desk. His hand firmly grips the captain's shoulder tight from time to time, and he often cuts his eyes down and slightly leans forward to ensure the cuffs are not visible.

"Ensign, I would like an operational update," the captain says to ease the tension.

"One hundred percent ready and per Strike Force One's Command Guidance and Doctrine! By the way, sir..., my apologies, but I'll get the evaluations to you when done here."

"Just put them in my in-box, outside the door," the lieutenant responds to cancel the possibility of any further contact with the captain.

The captain blinks in Morse code, but the ensign never makes contact because he's too nervous to look in the lieutenant or captain's face.

"Sir, the men . . ."

"That's enough, Ensign!" the lieutenant yells. "From now on, I demand that you be at your place of duty and on time!" The lieutenant's eyes roam over Ensign Terry's wrinkled uniform. "That means not a second later, and..., my goodness man..., square away that wrinkled-ass uniform! Do you understand, recruit?" he shouts, leaning lightly over the captain's shoulder.

The captain and ensign somewhat frown from the smell of the lieutenant's bad breath.

"Aye-aye, sir," the ensign says, snapping to attention again. "Permission to carry on, sir."

"Permission granted," the captain says when lowering his head in disappointment.

Ensign Terry steps into the passageway, hearing a thug when pulling the door shut from the captain's head falling forward, from the lieutenant's fist being driven deep into the back of it, dead center.

"Ouch!" the captain murmurs.

"I can't believe you would try that damn Morse code bull!" he says with eyes still pierced into the captain's face through the mirror on the wall, which the captain had not noticed. "Look, I don't have time to play your freakin' little reindeer games..., do you hear me?"

"What the hell are you talking about?" the captain responds, rubbing the back of his head with the handcuffs pressed deep against his cheek.

"Let me refresh your damn memory?" the lieutenant says, drawing back hard and punching him harder in the same spot, causing the special forces academy class ring to stick slightly to the scalp and break the skin. "I'll help straighten up your damn act real quick," the lieutenant says, picking up the secure satellite phone, entering four digits, a secure access code, and then a long string of numbers.

Both their eyes watch the phone cycle to secure mode and then ring several times before someone answers. "Bear?" the lieutenant mutters. "This is Range Rover..., Captain Carrington is not complying with Command Center executive orders and policies."

"Hell, man..., put him on!"

"Roger that...," the lieutenant says, pushing the telephone into the captain's slow opening hand, instantly turning into a tight, balled grip when snatching the phone and making evil eye contact.

"Strike Force One Commanding Officer..., who is this? Oww!" the captain shouts, forced forward from yet another stiff and devastating blow to the head, but this time, the sting is even deeper in the same bloody wound.

The captain touches the sore spot, drawing his hand back to find blood smears at the tip of his fingers. The phone drops, and the captain pummels the lieutenant between his legs, fingers intertwined and hands clenched tightly.

A massive vein protrudes from the lieutenant's forehead as he drops to the floor in agonizing pain.

The captain swiftly turns and grasps the phone again. "Damn it, I asked who the hell this is!" he shouts angrily.

"The big, bad, damn bear who knows where 92435 Misty Cove is and how long Mrs. Carrington and Little Goldilocks have to live if you don't strictly comply with my orders," he says in a deep, hostile voice. The man's eyes cast over the computer monitor display of files containing the team's addresses until moving the mouse more with the cursor on Captain Carrington's home address again, clicking to expose his family history and phone number.

"Damn it, if you lay even a hand on a string of my family's hair, I promise personally to hunt you down to no end. I'll kill anyone in your damn bloodline, from the smallest to the greatest!"

"Captain, please spare me the bullshit! You're in no position to communicate or carry out any of these petty-ass threats. Listen to me..., just for the record..., your family is under twenty-four-hour sniper surveillance. These guys are ruthless as hell and don't give a damn about killing women or children. They know your family's daily routine and even know when your wife takes a dump or changes her stinking tampons. Damn it, if there's one more damn..., I don't give a damn if it's accidental; I'll have them shatter all your family's dreams in an instant. Stop screwing around and follow these damn orders!" the Bear screams. "Hell..., put the lieutenant back on, damn you!"

"Don't hurt my family," the captain sobs, passing the phone back.

The lieutenant grabs the phone, holding it while still kneeling. Minutes later, he manages to climb into the chair with what little strength he can muster when dropping down in unbearable pain and slightly releasing a sigh. "Yes, sir," he whispers with a slight but quiet moan.

"These are straightforward damn orders, so don't mess around and screw this up, or I'll have your ass as well! For the life of me..., I don't know why the hell I sent a boy to do a damn man's job," the Bear says, disappointed.

On the ship's bridge, the OOD receives a report from the radar room concerning a significant radar signal. The OOD rushes over to the starboard bridge window and looks through binoculars, vigilantly scanning the ocean's surface. He looks dead ahead, over the horizon, and sees two towering rain squalls and thick, dark clouds forming fast. He swiftly moves onto the weather deck when it starts to sprinkle.

"Boatswains! Pass the word for rain," the OOD yells over the heavy, sudden downpour.

Minutes after the word is relayed over the PA system, the rain stops, but it continually drizzles until becoming intermittent.

The bridge door swiftly swings open.

"Captain's on the bridge!" the helmsman shouts, being the first to notice the captain's presence. The captain paces the decks and stops near the starboard side radar. "What are your intentions, Derek?" he asks, lightly puffing on his pipe and looking around the quiet bridge at everyone working diligently.

"I intend to maneuver down the middle and clear both, sir; other squalls are closing from behind as well, sir."

"That's a splendid plan, Derek," Captain Pierite says, quickly checking the OOD's solution to satisfy any doubts. "It looks like you have it all under control, but remember..., if ever in doubt, call," Captain Pierite says, gently patting him on the back when walking off.

"Aye, Captain," the OOD says, walking away and not realizing the captain has gone back inside the bridge.

"Captain's off the bridge," the First Class Boatswain loudly announces, looking around and then back at the door after he hears it close securely.

The squalls vigorously close in and pass further away than the OOD's initial predictions when suddenly, light winds begin to gust.

Hours later, winds blow heavily and increase to fifty knots from the east-southeast.

The sea begins raging over the bow and harshly washing against the bridge wings and windows.

Per the OOD's directions, the JOOD notifies Captain Pierite of the abrupt climate change. The OOD has the First Class Boatswain announce the setting of the low-visibility detail seeing how the dense fog has set in earlier than anticipated.

Thick fog immediately clings to the ocean's surface, causing the visibility to diminish to less than half a mile.

Extra lookouts post as the primary navigation detail switches from the bridge to the Combat Information Center.

Loud, low visibility fog and horn signals sound as the ship journeys south in the turbulent sea.

The ship bounces and bobs over choppy waters, with the bow continually slamming into the sea from time to time before leveling out for a moderate ride.

"Officer of the Deck! Combat reports a new contact bearing two-two-zero..., ten thousand yards!" the status board operator reports, standing in front of the dimly-lit status board and plotting the contact's last known location.

"Very well!" the OOD shouts over mild whispers.

The OOD and JOOD stare at the radar for minutes.

The OOD reaches for the phone, cranking it down fast when calling Captain Pierite. His eyes wander around, scanning the surface until hearing the phone bumbling until hearing the captain's voice. "Sir, combat reports a surface contact bearing two-two-zero, ten thousand yards, but we don't hold anything visual or on radar, sir!"

The captain hangs up, and within minutes, the watertight door swings open, with the captain rushing inside.

"Captain's on the bridge!" the JOOD shouts.

"Where is the contact, Derek?" the captain asks, looking through several bridge windows.

"I still don't have a visual or radar, sir, but combat still has it on radar," the OOD says, pointing out where the contact should appear.

"Very well," Captain Pierite acknowledges, looking through the side bridge windows until glancing over his shoulder at the status board updates.

Water continues harshly washing against the windows at constant, timed intervals.

"OOD, combat reports the contact has faded..., the last known bearing and range are five thousand yards, bearing two-two-zero. The contact's last known direction is zero-seven-zero..., speed ten knots. The closest point of approach is one hundred yards dead off the bow," the status board operator nervously shouts, plotting the updates a little less legibly out of fear.

"Very well!" the OOD shouts. "Sir, based on the contacts last position, course, and speed, they're stand-on, and we're the give-way vessel!"

The JOOD plots the contact's information on a maneuvering board and begins working up a solution for an avoidance course recommendation. Immediately, the squawk box keys up with the Combat Information Center making an avoidance course recommendation, and when the JOOD hears it, he quickly checks his solution against it. "Sir, I concur with combat!"

The captain goes into mild meditation, calculating the recommendations based on vector logic. "I concur with combat and the rules of the road, Derek, but where the hell is it?" the captain shouts, breaking his train of thoughts when looking as far as the naked eye can see through the dense rain.

"Sir, I still don't see anything," the JOOD yells, hurriedly staring back down at the radar and then over at the status board.

"Very well!" the captain responds, still scanning the surface as far as he can see, but now with binoculars held tight in hand.

Suddenly, out of the dense shower, a little white-and-red light appears, the medium-sized vessel bouncing against vicious waves.

"There! There!" the captain screams, anxiously pointing through the forward bridge window with a firm finger dead set on the target.

"Right, full rudder, steady on a new course two-seven-zero!" the OOD screams.

"Course two-seven-zero, aye!" the helmsman screams, quickly acknowledging the rudder order and steering hard with all the strength he can muster.

The ship's rudder whips the ship around. "Sir, my rudder is right full, coming to a new course of two-seven-zero!"

"Very well!" the OOD and captain respond almost simultaneously.

Tensions rapidly grow on the bridge and in the Combat Information Center.

Several arms continually stretched forward, with the OOD and captain bracing the flimsy, metal tabletop near the bridge window.

The ship steadily continues altering course until, in a heavy lean with everyone throughout the ship, grabbing anything solid that they can get a hold of when holding on tightly while thrown about in every direction.

"Mark your head!" the OOD shouts, straining to keep from being slammed into the captain.

"Passing two-two-five!" the helmsman shouts, slightly shifting his stance, then digging boots deeper into the rubber matting when gripping the steering unit even tighter in his tightly-balled fist.

The other seagoing vessel continues on its course, bouncing across the sea until passing five hundred yards or closer down the port side.

The helmsman stops the steering unit, holding it with a death-defying grip as the ship steadies, then slowly levels out with a few slower leans to the left and right until slightly bobbing up and down and then left and right more.

"Sir, I'm steadied on a new course of two-seven-zero!"

"Very well," the OOD responds.

The OOD and captain release their grips and stare at each other with wide, nervous eyes.

"Great job, Derek..., close but great!" the captain says, wiping his sweat-covered face with his shirtsleeve.

Hours later, the winds diminish, and the sea calms with the ship traveling farther south throughout the night.

Within hours, a calmer sea and moonlit sky allow the ship to stand down from its low-visibility details.

Tom stands, leaning over the desk in the office to place the phone in the charger. He pauses, hearing footsteps in the passageway but pretends to be busy when the squeaky door slowly opens.

Ensign Jones steps inside, leaning with her back against the door while easing it shut tight, and then secretly locks it. She slowly strolls toward Tom, dressed in athletic spandex shorts and a tight halter-style top. Ensign Jones playfully flexes, showing off her firm, six-pack abs, sweating profusely. "Hi, mister!" she says when within arm's reach, seductively draping her warm, moist hands around the back of his neck with her soft touch raising the fine hairs on the back of his neck and sending chills down his spine.

Tom looks back to ensure the door is locked and then looks around for her, finding her climbing onto the desk next to him.

She looks deep into his eyes and smiles. She shyly awaits some type of confirmation that her behavior is welcome and receives it when he returns the smile.

Tom's eyes browse over her fit body, and she maneuvers, ensuring she has his full attention when leaning back on both hands and slowly spreading her luscious thighs wide.

"Nice thighs..., you must work out often, huh?" Tom smiles with eyes running deep between her thighs until he's gazing over her shiny skin.

"Not as much as I'd like to suga," she responds, slightly leaning forward until upright. She runs a hand up each smooth thigh and slowly pulls the material back as far as it will go.

Tom's eyes alternate between her hands, shiny thighs, and high-raised pelvis, which protrudes through the thin material. "Mmm, Nicole..., damn, that sure does look good."

"Then have at it, babe," she says, sliding over and onto his desk, spreading her legs until resting her back against the bulkhead. One foot eases onto one chair arm, then the other with her hand continually running across the curvature of her wide, raised pelvis until her fingers fade deep between her thighs and vanish, reappearing when she slides them out.

Tom grows totally aroused, continually watching her repeat the process a few times until he is in a deep trance, not realizing it when he licks his lips until drool drips from his chin.

She flexes her legs a few times and then stops when they're as wide as they can open, continually toying with him until gently stroking the back of his head and pulling him deeper between luscious thighs. "Go ahead, babe, it's all yours, sweetie..., have at it." She gently releases the back of his head, pulling his head midway her thighs, which slowly dry from the chilly air blowing directly from the air conditioner. "Is Egyptian Musk your flavor?" she whispers. "I know you want to take them off..., mmm . . ., maybe pull them to one side for a quickie?" she sensually says when grabbing a fistful of his hair and pulling his head deep again. She playfully closes her legs tightly against the sides of his light, stubbly face and then releases him.

Tom inches closer and instantly smells fresh Egyptian Musk when both cheeks slightly brush against silky thighs.

She closes and opens her thighs slowly and more seductively, then grinds slower, then faster, in a circular motion. She moans in a whisper when Tom's lips apply soft kisses deep into her soft thighs. She reaches forward, grabs him by the collar, and pulls him into her while leaning forward in the heat of passion.

Their mouths open wide, and her eyes close in sheer ecstasy when he feels heat from her hot breath as she pants in excitement.

She gets fully aroused when his hand caresses her face, with his thumb slipping slightly in her eardrums, when she flexes a little, then relaxes. Their lips collide with their tongues moving forward, breathing heavily.

A sudden, sharp knock come upon the door, causing them to jump up yet keep quiet.

Tom eases to his feet and almost loses his balance but leans and accidentally slides his chair back a few inches with a loud scrape against the floor, creating an even louder shrieking sound.

"Come in!" Tom says, hastily remembering that the door is locked.

In excitement, he gains his footing while Nicole nervously and quietly eases into his chair. Tom tiptoes over and opens the door, and without delay, he bends as if tying his shoe when giving himself time to settle back down.

"What's up, Tom?" Tamara asks, quickly looking around his muscular arm to find the back of Nicole's head.

"Oh, nothing." He pauses. "Oh, Nicole came by to say her last goodbye," he says, slowly standing after the stiffness subsides.

"What's up, Nicole?" Tamara asks with a frown, pointing an index finger at Tom's face to display disappointment.

The doorknob jiggles a few times, and Ensign Terry walks in.

"What's up, Chief?" the ensign asks, looking at the three surprised and as if he had walked in on something.

Nicole finally gets up, walks over to the copier, and bends over it.

Tamara notices a wet spot on the seat of her shorts. "Girl..., you know you need to go change those funky-tail shorts," Tamara says, secretly giving Tom the evil eye yet immediately straightening her face when Ensign Terry turns to look back at her.

Tom walks to his desk and eases into his chair.

Nicole frowns, embarrassed, still staring at the wall in disbelief until eventually turning and making eye contact with Tamara. "I'd better be going because this is getting too damn sentimental," Nicole says, rolling her eyes at Tamara. "You know I gotta get my beauty rest, babe..., but hey, here's my number," Nicole says, walking over and rubbing soft breasts firmly against Tom's face in a slow grind while mischievously looking back at Tamara until winking when scribbling more. She looks back again, running fingers through Tom's hair in a sexy moan when pulling away.

"Later, Michael," Nicole says. "Later, girl," she says, rolling her eyes at Tamara again.

"Whateva! Hoochi!" Tamara says, extending her middle finger up in Nicole's face as she passes.

"Yeah, trick..., you can apologize later!" Nicole says, slamming the door and standing and listening for seconds before walking off.

There is silence with Ensign Terry looking around with his back to Tamara and trying to hide his smile.

"Is everything ok, Tamara?" Ensign Terry asks, turning to her while straightening his face. He manages to hold back his giggle.

"Yeah, I get a slight headache when dealing with that crazy-ass chick, but anyway, all I need is something to drink and an aspirin, and I'll be all right," she says, taking a deep breath when a tear unnoticeably and uncontrollably rolls down her cheek.

"Have a seat, and I'll run down to my stateroom and get some change and aspirin."

She eases in the chair, crossing her legs and then her arms, slightly kicking her foot back and forth anxiously. "You know you have to go to the machine forward because the one aft is empty," she says, in her soft, sexy voice, with thoughts of the machine furthest from the office.

"Ok," Terry says, fiddling with the door and accidentally locking it when walking out.

Tamara stares eye-to-eye with Tom until he looks away. She sits anxiously, listening to Terry's footsteps fading. "You son of a bitch!" Tamara whispers, stealthily charging at Tom with full force, with him turning in time to find her little fist in full stride, and inbound, like a cruise missile. Her fist slams into his open palm, sounding like a muffled firecracker.

Tom jumps, coming to his feet fast and able to block the second tightly, balled inbound fist. He instantly locks her arms by her side, picking her up while she's wigging and kicking.

"Damn it..., how could you?"

"Calm down," he whispers, gripping her tighter while easing her onto the desk and spreading her legs wide when swiftly moving between them. "Sweetie, I promise nothing happened..., you can ask Nicole!"

She continually wiggles and kicks, finally realizing he's not going to loosen his grip when changing her demeanor and becoming somewhat calmer.

He leans deeper into her and slowly moves his hands up her thick, soft thighs, gently massaging them.

She runs her hand over him in an overheated fashion, with a firm grip on his manhood through his tight khaki pants. "We have to figure out a way to do this tonight, babe, please!" she whines.

"You don't mess around on the ship, remember?" he playfully says, reminding her of her favorite quote when she uncontrollably snickers.

"Uh huh..., mmm..., well damn that . . ., what about my office, later?"

Jingling keys brings them to silence, with Tom quickly releasing her and creeping over behind the door.

Tamara slips back in the seat and crosses her legs, with eyes on the door, anticipating the door opening when reaching for a blue notepad and scribbling.

"You must have locked it by accident, sir," Tom says, seeing the door retract when standing and reaching for the door as if reaching for the knob.

"Yeah, I must have...," Terry says, briefly standing in place and curiously looking back and forth between them.

Tamara looks up then away fast, not able to look at Terry until looking back up again.

Ensign Terry stares at Tom. "Hey, Chief..., do you think you can finish up tomorrow? I want to spend a little time with Tamara?" Terry whispers, passing Tom and handing her the soda and aspirin.

"Sure thing..., well, I'll see you when we get back, Ensign," Tom says, taking a few things from his desk drawer and reaching over, shaking her hand.

"Sure thing, Chief; you be careful out there," she says, secretly slipping him the sticky note while Ensign Terry walks back over to the door with his back to them.

"Have a good night, Chief," Ensign Terry mischievously says, gazing at Tom, winking.

Tom walks out and stops near a lit bulletin board, reading the sticky, telling him to call her stateroom, at extension 135, around midnight.

Ensign Terry double-checks the lock, and then pulls his chair up next to Tamara, gently pulling her closer by both hands when leaning forward with eyes closed when his lips pucker.

Tamara sloppily licks her index fingers, gently touching his lips. "Look, Michael, I don't mess around on the ship, so can you at least respect me for that?" She takes a sip of the strawberry soda and takes the aspirins, then stares at him with a devilish smile when taking another light sip before setting the cool can on the desk.

Ensign Terry concentrates on her curves with eyes slowly glazing over her for seconds in hopes of persuading her. "Damn..., why can't you be more aggressive like Nicole?"

"Nicole!" she screams, frowning. "How dare you compare me with that crazy-ass winch? I thought you had respect for me and liked me for me, but now I can see it's all about one thing; getting a piece of tail!"

Ensign Terry gazes in her eyes with suddenly drooped shoulders. "Well, I did not mean it like that, and you know it, Tamara!"

She springs to her feet. "Damn you!" she says expressly, dashing soda in Terry's face and quickly soaking him again. She tilts the can fast, turning it upside down over his inseam, draining it until it's empty, and then slams the can on the desk.

"What was that for?" he asks, stealthily wiping his face and looking dumbfounded.

"What for? Hell..., to cool your hot ass down! Look at me and hear me well! As long as you live, don't ever speak to me again!" she says, quickly faking her anger. She rushes for the door, walks out, and rushes down the passageway. A way down the passageway, she turns the corner, leaning back into the bulkhead and bursting into soft laughter. She quickly straightens up when a watertight hatch opens, hearing heavy footsteps approaching.

An enlisted woman appears smiling and nodding when quickly passing, and Tamara smiles and then giggles again.

Tamara goes about her business, entering her stateroom several hours later, and finds Nicole sleeping. She plops down on her bunk and turns on the television, lowering the volume when watching the end of a love story while anxiously waiting for Nicole to get up so she can validate Tom's story.

Nicole's alarm sounds around 2315, but she lies there for minutes, yawning and stretching before tossing and turning more until finally resting on her back. She raises the covers and pulls them to the backside of her rack, moaning in a somewhat seductive tone with hands gliding across washboard abs and slows at the rim of her panties' waistband. Her index finger lifts the rim of her panties; the tip slides inside and covers only the nail. She finally breaks her seductive concentration, looking over to find Tamara on her bunk, with her legs crossed, staring back at her when pulling her finger out. She sighs, and then pats the curvature of her hilly-shaped pelvis, tightly stretched in burgundy silk thong.

"Pretty tired, huh?" Tamara asks, still staring with a slight frown.

"Yeah, girl," she intentionally hesitates to keep her in suspense. "Tom beat this tight little thang up pretty bad," Nicole responds, slightly patting then rubbing the curvature of her pelvis again and patting it a few times. She rubs some more, but only because she knows she has Tamara's undivided attention and wants to piss her off.

"What! You mean you actually did him?" Tamara asks, sitting up, somewhat in a state of panic and frustration.

"Girl, please, just calm your ass right down because I'm just kidding, ok..., but it's a good thing you came in when you did because I was about to break him off a little somethin'-somethin' and show him what he's in for when we get off this ship," she says, cackling aloud at her senseless comment.

Nicole dresses for watch (work) and leaves minutes later.

Tamara changes into dark blue, cotton, crotch-less shorts and a top she typically wears to bed. She climbs back onto her bunk, turns on a video, and tightly snuggles into her pillow for seconds until comfortable. Within the hour, she grows restless, and her mind fades in and out but continually drifts to how Tom's hard body felt when he pinned her against the wall. Her mind soon drifts, with anxious hands sliding along the backside of the mattress, with deep concentration, until pulling out her nine-inch chromed toy she calls 'Azreay'l' with the small, attached top massager. She flips the miniature switch to the first notch, placing the lightly vibrating shaft at her neck and moving it slowly until it tingles. Her mind instantly drifts back to how great Tom smelled, finding herself in deep desire and wanting him and not the toy when flipping it off and placing it beside her. She drifts into deeper thoughts of doing him in so many ways until yawning a few times and then fading off and into a deep sleep.

CHAPTER THREE: THE PASSIONATE UNDERWAY

Tamara is awakened by the loud phone ringing well after midnight and manages to answer on the second ring. "Ensign Haun! May I help you, sir or ma'am?"

"Maybe" Tom says in a seductive voice. "So..., tell me..., what do you have on right now, sexy?"

"Umm..., a sexy little pajama set..., it's crotch-less." She giggles.

"Great, babe..., so..., here's what I want you to do..., take it off."

She hesitates and shyly giggles a few times and then senselessly chuckles before her laugh tapers off to a soft, silly giggle. "uh huh..., but how about this..., I need to see you. Please..., why can't I see you?" she asks, easing her hand under the covers for minutes and caressing her firm twins until her fingers slide slowly south. Her eyes slowly close in sheer pleasure, with soft, plump lips forming in a small circle and parting with warm air gently blowing through them. She grows heated when she begins to suck warm air in and out lightly, easing the phone from her lips, and seductively moans.

She breathes harder. " Please..., I need to see you, baby. Please..., tell me why can't I see you? Where are you? " she asks, easing her hand out.

"In the office, and I'm going to call your bluff so you can come up, but make sure no one sees you."

"Really? Ok..., sure thing," she says, blowing a kiss before hanging up. She grows full of excitement, quickly dressing and making a mad dash for the door. She reaches the step on the ladder well, hearing a watertight door open when expressly ducking into a dark corner. She waits until another door closes, then stays silent for minutes, peeping and running to the office door.

Her gentle taps come upon the door when it opens, and she darts inside, closing the door with her back against it. "I made it, not witnesses," she whispers, childishly giggling with hands still behind her back when locking the door. She stretches her arms out to him, engulfed in a firm embrace.

"Are you sure no one saw you?" he asks nervously, frozen in place, thinking he hears the doorknob jiggle and vigilantly listens for the release of the knob. Without haste, he resumes Tamara's warm body's deep embrace until his hands caress the lower part of her spine as her warm, soft flesh melts in his hands. He anxiously slips both hands down and around her round apple bottom. His hands spread even wider as he palms each cheek, continually massaging them together and then apart as if they are professional size basketballs.

She slips into a trance yet still thinks about his question. "Mmm..., yeah, babe,

I'm sure no one saw me," she says, slightly hanging from his neck, with feet barely touching the deck.

"Well..., we had better go inside the maintenance room in case Ensign Terry shows up."

"Ok, sweetie, but why would he be up here this time of night?"

"Who knows, but he's just weird like that," Tom says, unlocking the other door and taking a step inside.

Tamara steps in behind him and stands to one side while he locks the door and pulls out the key.

They indulge in a deep, long French kiss that lasts for minutes.

He slides both fingers into her waistband, easing her shorts down, and then kneels, kissing each warm thigh until kissing them alternatingly.

She slips her fingers in the waist of her panties and childishly giggles like a little elementary school girl.

Tom stands, and she grabs a fistful of him and falls into deep thoughts of taking him on like a true rider, but then thinks longer and with some reality when whispering out loud. "Damn, who am I fooling? I'm not sure if I can handle all of this, babe," she says, looking down, surprised to find his hardware pressing hard against his pants like something that's about to explode or bust at the seam.

"Oh, yea..., sure you can, sweetie," he responds, assuring her that she would be fine yet thinking about over-pleasing her and making himself unforgettable. He removes her hands from his raging bulge and steps out of his pants, now down to just briefs.

They fully undress and waste no time going at it; the heat of passion feels like an eternity for her, but she takes the continual pain, warming up to him when comforted. They try a series of positions, including some obtained from porn videos or others in their past.

Halfway through their heated encounter, they grow exhausted and take a break, which works particularly well for Tom when needing a quick reload or time to catch their breath from trying to set an example that will be hard for others to follow.

An hour later, their bodies are dripping with sweat.

Out of nowhere, a sudden thump brings them to a standstill, and they freeze with wide, excited eyes with hearts pounding in fear.

Their bodies soon tremble from the heavy blowing air-conditioning unit that activates directly overhead.

Tom motions for her to stay quiet when listening harder, then slowly move, pointing to their clothes.

Tamara looks up as he stands and hungrily gazes at him as if in another world. "Damn, where did you learn how to satisfy a woman like that?" she asks, slightly reclining on the desk for a few minutes before slowly reaching for his clothes, only to look back and find him staring at her beautiful naked body in a daze.

"I had my skills at birth," he says with a smirk while speedily dressing.

She's dressed first and looks back once more to find him admiring her hot body as her clothes conform to the curves of her body again.

"Here, hang onto this," he says, handing her his old work cell phone. "Hey, look..., there are many uncertainties about this mission, but I'm not at liberty to explain it right now, but I need you to contact me if you can get through to my captain after we depart the ship. My new satellite cellular number is on the back should you need to contact me in an urgent nature only. You have to promise you will not involve yourself in this craziness, please, because it's just too dangerous," he says, kissing her again when taking her to the bulkhead in a deep sensual kiss that has her reaching for his zipper again when he backs away quickly smiling.

"I'll be fine, baby..., you just take care of yourself and come back to me safely," she says.

"If it's meant to be, I will, sweetness," he says, pulling her back in his arms, cuddling with her soft, apple-fragranced hair shampoo rising in his nostrils.

They grow quiet, attentive to the sounds in the front room when drawing close to the door until their ears are against it.

Tom eases his hand to the knob, turning it slowly until he peeks out with fast wandering eyes, finding the room empty.

They tiptoe inside, making it over to the door where they feel more at ease when cuddling and kissing more and so long that they are both heated again.

She becomes the aggressor, pushing Tom into the bulkhead, and before he gets his mind around what just happened, she has his trousers unfastened again and begins begging for more.

He grasps her hand easing it away but continues kissing her some more while zipping his trousers. He kisses her again until her frustration rises, and she pushes away, but he quickly pulls her back in his arms to comfort her and calms her when kissing their last goodbyes.

The following morning reveals light-blue skies and scattered clouds. Temperatures rise to the mid-eighties with the ship skirting across the calm sea off the coast of Florida.

The forces are now four hours from their final operational destination and eighteen hours from the Special Forces' final departure.

Ensign Terry stands outside the captain's door, tucking his creased shirt into his somewhat neatly pressed trousers. He looks down at his freshly polished shoes, sticking his chest out with pride when knocking twice, but he gets no answer. Ensign Terry hesitantly then swiftly makes his way to the wardroom, easing inside and finding the captain and lieutenant. "Good morning, Captain, Lieutenant!" he says, easing into a seat across from them.

"Good morning, Ensign," the captain responds, looking half dazed when staring at a few patrons over the ensign's shoulder and then back down at the table before cutting his eyes over at the lieutenant.

The lieutenant slyly gazes into the ensign's eyes until frowning. "Have you forgotten your damn table manners?" He pauses. "If I'm not mistaken, you're to request to be seated by the most senior-ranking officer."

Ensign Terry swiftly snaps to attention when the strong smell of bacon and pancakes rises in his nostrils as another patron passes with a fresh plate of food. His head and eyes go straightforward.

"Ensign, please sit," the captain says, staring at the lieutenant with a war-torn, mean face.

"Surprisingly, you're early," the lieutenant says quickly, checking his watch. "There are no special orders this morning, so what can we do for you?" He slices his grapefruit with the gold butter knife.

The ensign's eyes nervously rove over to the captain. "Captain, I was wondering when the briefing will take place. Your policy is for us to brief as soon as we're onboard."

"Yes, but this mission is per the Command Center's guidelines, not mine, Ensign," the captain responds, conjuring up a quick lie.

The FSA places a plate before the captain, and he leans forward, pouring warm maple syrup over his golden-brown, fluffy, buttermilk pancakes before taking a bite of hickory-smoked bacon.

The captain breaks his concentration to see if the lieutenant is looking and then plays it off by looking down at his watch when realizing that the lieutenant is more observant. "How about we brief after dinner?" the captain says, staring at the lieutenant and quickly looking away after eye contact.

The ensign looks over at the lieutenant with a smirk when the lieutenant slams his utensils down and stares deep into the ensign's face until his face turns bright red. "Listen up, dipshit!" he says, leaning across the table and whispering while his eyes drift about the room. "You're freakin' in charge of these guys, so take charge, damn you! Stop with this clueless-ass bullshit!" he says, leaning forward more until his index finger is inches from the ensign's face. "Listen, Ensign, and hear me well! If you plan to keep your position as the Officer in Charge (OIC), I suggest you pull your head out of your four-corner contact! Make some freakin' decisions around here, like real quick, or I'll have your dumb ass terminated from this mission and sent stateside on the first damn thing smokin'." the lieutenant says, slowly easing into his seat and embarrassingly looking around.

"Roger, sir, request permission to be excused..., Captain."

"Permission granted, and oh, by the way, I still need those evaluations," the captain says.

The ensign instantly snaps to attention. "Yes, sir, I'll get them right down."

Ensign Terry exits the wardroom in a flash and stops by Ensign Haun's stateroom. He walks slower and deeply thinks of what to say, hoping to apologize for his behavior, but he doesn't get an answer after several knocks. He hesitates, knocks again, and then steps away, staring at the floor as if in a daze.

"Good morning!" Ensign Jones says, unknowingly coming up behind him and finally noticing him. "Man..., you must have torn my girl up last night. Did you try and set a new record, or what?" she says, giggling a little louder, and then looks around until quieting down.

"What? What do you mean?" He pauses. "Oh, no, it was not even like that, honestly!"

"Yeah, right, Michael. I guess that's why her shorts were so stained, huh?"

"Shorts, stained? What shorts? What are you talking about?" he asks, even more confused yet curious. "No, really, what do you mean? Honestly..., nothing happened..., for Pete's sake, Tamara will tell you the same thing!"

"Yeah, right. Well, I'll find out when Tamara wakes up from her total exhaustion," she says, winking.

"You just tell her I want to see her as soon as she's on her feet!" he curiously says, taking a few steps behind her and toward their room.

Ensign Jones gives him a smirk. "Sure..., that's when and if she wakes up," she says. "Besides, Tamara has never slept in this late; she's always up no later than 5 a.m., watching the news or cartoons," she says, still advancing toward their stateroom when looking down at her watch. "Oh crap! She hasn't even done her..., oh, man!" she thinks aloud, surprisedly, placing her hand over her mouth.

Surprisingly, she turns the doorknob and opens the door, rushing up to Tamara's bunk. "Tamara, Tamara!" she calls out, pulling Tamara's arm from under the sheet and jerking her forward. "Girl, you've got to get up and do your Navigation Report!"

Tamara lies totally limp until jerked again. "Nicole, stop it..., I'm getting up, Ok?" Tamara shouts, turning and finally sitting to find Ensign Terry in a semi-trance, adoring the sight of perfectly cupped, nude breasts with the prettiest nipples.

Ensign Terry's head drifts down beside the bed, quickly spotting her slightly stained shorts.

Tamara grasps the sheets, tucking them securely under her arms. "What the hell are you looking at, pervert?" she screams. "Get the hell out of here, you jerk!"

"Sorry, Tamara, I didn't mean to leave the door open," Nicole says, backing him out with firm hands to his chest when backing and slamming the door shut. She briskly walks back over to Tamara's bunk, apologizing.

Ensign Terry stands frozen, trying to figure out why Tamara's shorts are so messy when going into a daze, until he slowly turns and walks away.

When he enters his room seconds later and turns on the television, then eases onto the side of his bunk, fully dressed, as if traumatized. His mind focuses on

Tamara's hot body for minutes before drifting to her heavily stained shorts again. He continues in deep thought until breaking his thoughts and picking up the phone, dialing his men's berthing.

"Strike Force berthing, Specialist First-Class Ogwin, may I help you, sir or ma'am?"

"This is Ensign Terry..., put the chief on."

Minutes pass then the phone bumbles around. "Yes, sir," Tom responds.

"Can you come up to my stateroom?"

"Aye, sir, give me a few minutes," Tom says, hanging up. He walks back over to his bunk, straightens his rack, and leaves about ten minutes later, quickly lunging up from the ladder well. He swiftly passes Nicole and Tamara's stateroom, with eyes upon it, when noticing their door cracked open a little. He backs up, reaching to knock, but accidentally pushes the door slightly open.

Ensign Haun's eyes rove from her boot over to the door when she hears it yawning on the hinges and finds him smiling. "Morning, babe," Ensign Haun whispers, smiling, winking, and blowing a few kisses while she still sits on the edge of her bunk, still lacing her boots. "You wouldn't believe how bad Bianca is throbbing right now," she mutters with an even heavier giggle that takes off fast.

"Throbbing enough for some of this?" he says, twirling his tongue around in a slow, circular motion. "Or more of this," he says, squeezing a fistful of himself.

"Stop it, babe!" she says, looking at the tube-shaped bulge in his trousers.

"I hate to rush you, but I'm running late, but hey, maybe I'll see you later."

He blows her a kiss, closes the door, and continues down to Ensign Terry's room, where he knocks but does not get a response, so he waits for a few seconds and then turns the knob about the same time he hears the ensign finally responding.

"Come in," the ensign says a second time, but clearer.

The pungent aroma of the ensign's funky feet rises in Tom's nostrils as he eases into the unpleasantly scented room. "Woowee..., what in the hell is that awful-tail smell you still have imprisoned in here?" Tom pinches his nose and holds it for minutes, sometimes squeezing it harder and taking slower breaths.

Ensign Terry frowns and then smiles when taking a deep inhale. "Oh, hell, man..., it can't be that bad," the ensign says, twiddling toes and long, sharp toenails through his raggedy, hole-riddled socks.

Tom frowns, exhaling and inhaling even slower. "Bad isn't the word! Those feet smell like Limburger cheese mixed with sour greens!" Tom says, looking around fast until with eyes dead set on the air freshener on the nightstand. He snatches, then vigorously shakes the can and holds his breath, spraying for seconds. "Heck! Maybe you should consider patenting your funky-feet? You know..., maybe sell it to the Navy as a nerve agent cause (because) it damn sure as hell has me gasping for air. I'm sure a submarine would surface quickly with this funk poisoning the waters; not too sure about the number of fish that would surface first, so that could be catastrophic altogether," he says, letting off another thick blast when the funk overpowers the initial spray. "Hooootttt (Hot) damn!" Tom yells, smelling the feet getting stronger.

"Come on, Chief, enough is enough! Are you trying to use up the whole can or kill us?" the ensign asks, coughing a few times and then fanning fast.

"Death would be easier," Tom says, finally coughing but still holding his breath and spraying another quick blast until staring at each other, fading into the thick fog and then visible again.

"So, what's up, sir?" Tom asks, reclining and placing the can next to the chair.

"I want you to know I was around the captain twice, and he could have given a sign if he was in trouble, but he did not do anything along those lines. Anyway, he plans on briefing us after dinner."

"Sir, I hear you..., but I still don't trust this lieutenant; he's just bad news..., I can feel it. I mean, just think about it: the captain has never had an XO since assuming command, not to mention one who has not trained up with any of us. Also, he treats the captain like a crock of shit!"

The ensign sits, meditating, and never looks Tom in his eyes but keeps his eyes peeled to the floor, but on his third attempt, he finally makes firm eye contact. "Damn that..., let's talk, Tamara. Hey, I need a big favor."

Tom is stunned with his mind scrambling, trying to figure out what just had happened in the conversation, when refocusing on the ensign's comment about Tamara. "What? What have you done, sir? Have you shown her your little friend, and I mean your tiny friend?" Tom asks, guffawing when reclining.

"Ha, ha, ha..., very funny, you smart-ass, unpaid comedian!" the ensign says with a grin that quickly vanishes. "Anyway, I saw Nicole earlier, and she commented about Tamara's shorts, insinuating that Tamara and I had sex or something. I mean..., I did see her shorts, and they were somewhat stained..., you know..., smeared with something white?"

"What!" Tom says, laughing so hard that he falls to the floor on his knees in even deeper laughter. He pretends to guffaw even harder but instantly jumps up when the feet funk from the carpet rushes deep into his nostrils.

"What's so funny?" the ensign asks with a frown.

"Give me a few minutes," Tom says, throwing up his index finger and laughing while half bent over until he jumps upright when the feet funk rises deep in his nostrils again. "Damn!" he says with a frown, shaking his head and gasping for air.

"What..., what?" the ensign shouts in rage and total confusion.

"Oh!" Tom says, trying to get the funk off his mind and get his train of thought together. "You mean you think she had sex because of her shorts?"

"Well, do you have some other explanations, Mr. Sherlock Hopeless?"

"Why, yes!" Tom responds, flopping down in the chair and putting on a semi-serious face. "Well, some women use powder to keep their kitty fresh and dry, a yeast infection, or maybe even self-oral pleasures from sexual frustration you pissing her off."

"I should've known better than ask the damn resident love expert."

"Hey, sir, the way I see it, you asked a stupid-ass question, and I gave you a couple of logical answers," Tom says, standing and tucking his shirt neatly in his trousers.

"So, will you talk with her? You know, put in a few good words for me?"

"Sure, sir, I'll put in a few good words, sir."

The ensign goes on to tell him all that had transpired in the conversation with her and then what he had seen in the room until Tom has gotten enough information to understand what was going on and where he was going. Tom walks to the door, still pretending to be laughing when exiting.

Tom enters the berthing twenty minutes later to find his men cleaning their bunks and locker.

Upon noticing Tom's presence, his men form a semicircle around him. Tony and Bobby sit on the floor while Oggie and Johns lean against the dark blue and black striped bulkhead.

Tom looks off and then back at them. Oggie, Tony, and Bobby check with the Chief Boatswains on our unclassified gear, and Johns, continue cleaning."

The phone rings minutes after Johns leaves to go after cleaning gear.

Tom answers. "Strike berthing, Chief Powells..., may I help you, sir or ma'am?"

"You sure as hell can..., you double-crossing bastard! What's all this white crap on the floor and desk in the maintenance office? You damn dirty son of a bitch!" Ensign Terry shouts, slamming the phone down and racing for the door.

Tom hangs up; stands distracted for minutes, then take a slow step and stops again in deep meditation, vividly replaying the sexual encounter. He steps off again, heading for his bunk, and before reaching it, hears a loud bang from the door slamming heavily against the metal trash can, slinging it up against the bulkhead.

"I've got your two-timing ass now!" Ensign Terry screams, expressly turning the corner. He freezes with bloodshot eyes, sprints, lunging, and then diving into Tom's chest at full force.

"Motherfu—" Tom yells, absorbing an abdominal tackle and having almost all the wind knocked out of him.

They fall into the laundry bin and then to the deck but recover like precision robots.

"I ought to kill your two-timing punk ass!" the ensign shouts, swinging with all his might and his fist slightly missing Tom's face by centimeters.

"What's your problem, you little young-ass punk?" Tom shouts, raising Ensign Terry by his hair, and expressly punches him in the nose a few good whacks. "Your mama never taught you respect, punk?" Tom screams, elbowing him in the ribs a few times.

"Why, Chief..., why?" the ensign screams with tears falling as he swings again with all his strength but misses Tom by inches this time.

"What the hell are you talking about, chump?" Tom shouts, grabbing Ensign Terry's hand, folding it behind his back, and pushing him face-first into the lockers, heavily denting them.

Oggie approaches the top of the ladder hears a loud commotion and rushes down the ladder and inside the berthing. "What the!" exclaims Oggie in disbelief, trying quickly to assess the situation when lunging forward, breaking them apart, but Tom's able to ram the ensign's face into the lockers one last time.

"What in the hell's going on?" Oggie shouts.

"Ask this two-timing, backstabbing cocksucker!" Ensign Terry shouts, bent over, breathing harder to catch his breath while staring intensely into Tom's face.

"Hell..., I don't know why you're down here wigging the hell out," Tom says, breathing slower to catch a second wind.

Without warning, the ensign charges toward Tom when Oggie tackles him and secures his arms by his side.

"Let him go, Oggie! I'm going to finish his young punk-ass up!"

The ensign's head falls backward and doesn't retract, but blood is heavily spewing from his bottom lip.

Oggies eye light up. "Damn, Chief! You knocked his ass out!" Oggie mutters in shock, quickly stretching Ensign Terry's limp body over the cool tile floor.

They stand nervously watching him for minutes until Ensign Terry's leg jerks, and he begins coming around within seconds. He braces against Oggie's shoulder, half-dazed, and tries standing but staggers a few times from his blurry vision.

"You still ain't shit!" the ensign shouts with a fast-wavering finger, finally able to stand. He wipes his bloody nose with his hand. "You hear me? You ain't shit!" he screams again, pointing an index finger at Tom with one hand while holding his abdomen with the other, still hunching over.

Tom and the ensign continually exchange offensive words for minutes while maintaining eye contact and being ready to strike without notice.

"What's this all about?" Oggie asks again.

"From what I can make of it, something about me getting a tail in the office last night," Tom says, shaking his head and pretending to be clueless, when winking at Oggie, finding the ensign looking down.

"What? Well, that can't be," Oggie says in a peal of zealous laughter, winking back and smiling. "Bobby had the keys to the maintenance office last night."

"What? So what are you saying..., it was Bobby!" Ensign Terry shouts, balling his fist tightly and gazing over at Oggie.

"No, no, no..., not with whoever you're talking about; he ran into a girl from the Deck department that he already knew," Oggie replies, scheming hard to get the chief and ensign back on favorable terms.

The ensign stares at Tom, under-eyed, quickly lowering his head in humiliation but continually looking away until taking one last look. "I owe you an apology for flipping out over a chick I hardly know," Ensign Terry says, heading for the door.

Tom looks over at Oggie when the door closes. "Hey, thanks, Oggie..., I owe you one," Tom whispers, rubbing his bruised side. "Just make sure Bobby knows, should Terry follow up," Tom says, patting Oggie on the shoulder as he passes.

After Oggie leaves, Tom calls Tamara and gives her a play-by-play synopsis of the incident.

The two are on the phone for a spell and deep in tears until Tamara pauses and waits for Tom to quiet. "Well..., have you heard? The first wave into the beach will be at first light; well, that is how it stands right now. Hey, I have to go, ciao!"

With a few sexual innuendos, he blows a kiss and hangs, turning to watch a television commercial while waiting for one of his men to return from dinner.

The berthing door springs open before the word 'dinner for the crew' is passed, and Tony walks in, chomping down on a hot chicken drumstick partially wrapped in aluminum foil.

Tom looks over his shoulder. "Hey..., a reliable source informed me that we're rolling out at first light, so let everyone know," Tom says, tightening his military uniform's appearance, and then walks out. He comes up on the wardroom's deck minutes later, spotting Nicole and another officer ahead of him while slowing to give them space to avoid her. He stops at the next corridor, waits for her to enter the wardroom, and then stops outside the pantry door getting the FSA's attention. "Hey, can you get me three wings, some potato salad, and collard greens, please? I must get back to work, so I'm trying to avoid the long line."

"Sure thing, Chief," she says, smiling and turning away.

She returns minutes later. "Here you are; I put five wings on there because I bet you can tear up some fried chicken," she says, handing him the Styrofoam plate when reaching back, handing him a cup of lemonade.

Tom thanks her, makes his way to the office, performs a few maneuvers at the door, and balances the cup against the plate. He sits at his desk and flips the lid off the plate with hearty flavors flowing forward, mingled in streams of steam, which continually rise deep in his nostrils. His feet unknowingly and continually tap lightly against the floor as he grows anxious to plunge into the meal when the fork shovels up a heaping load of well-seasoned greens, with chicken in the other hand.

Tom finishes the meal in record time, disposes of the plate and utensils in the trash can near the door, then heads back to his desk when suddenly a light knock sounds, followed by a few soft giggles.

"Come in," he says, easing into his seat and slightly looking over his shoulder for seconds with the door slowly easing open.

"Hi, Chief, I'm Specialist Third Class Early, and this is Specialist Second Class

Blount. We're here to do PMS on your air conditioning unit. You know..., preventive maintenance..., PMS."

"Oh..., ok, well, don't let me stop you, go ahead and have at it," he says, turning around and pretending to be busy, but watches while they place their tool belts on the table.

Specialist Blount grabs a flat-head screwdriver and climbs onto the desk, immediately unbolting the first screw and looking professional while removing the screw.

Specialist Early bends over the desk next to Tom, pretending to supervise when looking up slyly and then back down at him. "So, how's the food?" Specialist Early asks as the light aroma of the devoured food heavily lingers.

"Quite tasty! Boy, do they know how to make it mouthwatering, for sure," he says, standing and slightly turning his chair at a different angle when noticing Specialist Early's perfect, hourglass shape. His eyes scroll down her backside, over her bold-stenciled name tag, above her back pocket.

"If you think it's good, my food will make you gnaw your fingers and beg for more."

"Are you serious? Do you mean to tell me you can cook? What's your favorite dish..., these?" he asks, pulling out a pack of jerk noodles from his drawer and bursting into deep laughter.

"Please!" she acknowledges with a semi-serious face when looking deeply and sensuously into his eyes. "I can cook anything under the sun and make it damn good," she says, looking up and then staring at Specialist Blount's sexy shape.

"No offense! You just look so young," he says, staring at her thick, round bottom in her skintight dungarees, which appear painted over her sexy body. He continually admires her sexiness as if half-mesmerized.

"You like what you see, huh?" Specialist Early asks, looking back to find him in a daze with a grin when bursting into laughter, realizing he has not heard a word. "Chief!"

"Yeah," he finally acknowledges, still somewhat in a trance when looking off to the side of her hips and into her baby face, which barely sticks out past her hips.

"I asked if you like what you see when you look at this pretty face and sexy-ass bod (body)," she says, running soft hands and freshly-manicured nails over the curvature of her hips. She pats the roundness of her thick apple bottom.

Specialist Blount bursts into laughter upon hearing Specialist Early's comment and accidentally drops the screwdriver, and Specialist Early picks it up and hands it back to her.

Tom continues glancing between her broad hips and pretty face with a stare to let her know she has his undivided attention.

Specialist Early leans forward and further over the desk to tune the ship's entertainment system to a jazz station, and then adjusts the volume to just above normal speaking level.

"Oh, girl..., that's my damn song!" Specialist Early screams, looking up at Specialist Blount, who stops and meditates on the song, then seductively rolls her hips in a Jamaican-style dance.

"It sure is," Specialist Blount says, removing one vent and then playfully and over seductively twirling her hips again.

Tom leans his chair back on hind legs, staring at Specialist Early's wide hips, moving even slower in a grind, yet in a sexual rhythm. "You know you need to stop, right?" he whispers, rubbing his upper thigh and adjusting himself when his trousers tighten at the upper thigh.

Specialist Early continues in mischief, pretending not to see Tom's hand at his thigh but continually watches between the wide gap in her upper thighs. She looks over her shoulder, moistening her full, thick lips. "What's wrong? This non-cooking girl is turning you on, huh?" she says, reaching for his inseam, gripping and squeezing him tight. She grows in excitement with an even tighter grip, eyes closed tight, shaking her head. "Uh, uh, uh," she moans.

Tom keeps his eyes peered up, ensuring her friend is not watching when leaning and squeezing a handful of her soft, plump bottom. He palms one cheek firmly until his hand slips off from her jeans fitting so tightly.

She pulls away when turned on by his touch and releases him. "Do you still think I'm a little girl?" she whispers, sliding into the seat next to him, gazing deep into his sexy eyes and winking while licking her full, glossy lips.

"Oh yeah, of course, you are..., you're just a little baby; besides, you have not proven any different, now, have you?"

"Ok..., then do you think you can handle these, Daddy?" she whispers, leaning forward and poking out her chest until the buttons tighten and look as if they are about to pop.

"The question is, do you think you can handle this?" he whispers, grasping hold of what looks like a steel pipe bulging at his upper thigh.

She licks her lips and wink. "Mmm..., wee..., it's like I already have," she says, winking and pointing at the big, silver-dollar diameter wet spot, holding back her laughter as long as she can. She turns red when finally dropping forward in great laughter, which grows silly and louder.

"You got me on that one, but that's only because I am backed up from being out here on this damn water," he whispers, senselessly giggling.

"Poor baby," she says, finally able to taper off her laughter.

He grabs a document from the desk and hurriedly covers himself.

"You're lucky your girl's in here or those jeans would be off, so we can really see if you're about it," he mutters.

She leans over the desk, grabs a pen and paper, and scribbles. "Here, man, call me when you're back in Virginia, and we can see what's up," Early says, scribbling a little more.

"Sure will..., so, tell me..., who do you live with?"

"It's just me, my girl, and my baby. We have an apartment off Cypress Crest."

"As sexy as you are, I know you have a lot of guys or someone stalking your pretty ass."

"Yeah, ole girl," she says, pointing at Specialist Blount.

"You mean...?"

"Duuuh! Yes!" she says. "How would you like to do us both? Do you think you can handle us, Daddy?"

"Oh, no problem..., the two of you and then some," he says, looking up at her girlfriend's thick round bottom and bow legs, which Tom has failed to acknowledge up until that point.

"Let's go, girl! We're going to miss this meal!" Specialist Early says, heading for the door when her sidekick steps off the table into a chair and lays the tools down.

Tom stands with the document in front of him and closely follows Specialist Early.

Specialist Early reaches for the door handle and turns, grasping him by the collar and pulling him closer. She slips her tongue deep into his hot mouth.

Specialist Blount walks up from behind, reaching around his body, fumbling, and then clutching his zipper. She moans in his ear, nibbling on it, and then sticks her tongue deep inside. "Ummm..., I can't wait to taste your sexy ass."

Tom drops the document and reaches forward, palming Early's perfectly round bottom while reaching behind, stroking Blount's fat camel-toe-shaped pelvis, stretched tightly in the dungaree material.

Specialist Early stops tongue-kissing him and begins breathing on his neck while working her way up and around his ear. She blows and sucks on his earlobe until piercing the tip of her tongue deep inside his ear hole.

Her wrist comes forward, and she stares at her watch. "Shit! Girl, let's go before they close the galley!" Specialist Early says again.

Tom's eyes go over his shoulder and back to the desk. "The air conditioning?" Tom asks, looking back at the parts scattered over the desk.

"Hell, we don't know a damn thing about air conditioners," Early responds, giggling and causing Tom to grin. "Call the engineering log room and get the air conditioning team up here," Early says, slipping through the door behind Blount.

Tom leaves the office after some time and heads for the flight deck, where he steps through the watertight door, looking at the moderate waves rolling away from the ship. He eases over to the lifeline's metal bar, leaning when seeing bright, and fluorescent blue water glowing while trailing graciously away from the ship.

"What's up, Chief?" Tony asks, walking up from behind.

"Sup, playa?" Tom responds. "I mean playa hater."

"Naw (No), Chief..., come on, man, why would you say some lame-mess like that?"

"Easily, hmm..., I've been meaning to ask if you remember the tall woman we met at Club Vogue in Virginia Beach..., you know, the woman you left the club with that night?"

"Yeah, I remember well, but it was only because she begged me to take her home."

"Bullshit!" Tom says, leaning forward, playfully and intentionally forcing the word boldly underneath his breath. "She had intentions of leaving with me, but you told her I was a womanizer."

"Naw (No), Chief! Come on, man..., I would never hate on anybody for a piece of tail, man, never!"

"Bullshit!" Tom says again, playfully and intentionally forcing his word boldly underneath his breath again.

"Naw (No), man..., she could not have told you any mess like that. You're just making shit up, right?"

"Ok, then check this: For one, she had her own car, so your first comment is already a lie because you did not drive her anywhere. So..., two..., she lives at 13941 Oak Leaf Cove, drives a burgundy 300Z, thirty-five, with two beautiful little girls and a handsome little boy. Should I say more?"

"Hey, ok, maybe you did run into her!"

"Then check this: You guys arrived at her house, say, around 4 a.m.? The two of you were in her bedroom, and she cut off the lights. There was a little freakiness going on, but nothing serious. You went to the bathroom, and coming back, you got sidetracked and stumbled around in the dark," Tom says, looking out at the sun setting, smiling with tears filling his eyes.

"Ok..., well it seems like she told you everything," Tony says, deeply meditating on that unforgettable night and not trying to smile and confirm that Tom is on the right track.

"Yeah, she did that, for sure," Tom replies, smiling even harder.

"What?" Tony asks, looking at Tom's blushed face in the dim sunset yet fighting to keep from bursting out in laughter.

"What's with her grandmother?" Tom finally asks, laughing so hard that he causes a few nosy people to cackle.

Without warning, Tony glows, slings his hand out, snapping his fingers loudly in a 'gotcha' notion. "Man, I can't believe she told you that bull!"

"Well?" Tom says, inquiring for more details before bending over, chuckling, expecting Tony to tell him the part the woman refused to tell.

"Hell, I screwed up..., so sue me!" Tony says, bursting into a burst of more resistant laughter.

"Naw (No), man, I want to hear your side," Tom says, slightly hanging onto the lifeline bar and then leaning back when seeing a male Safety Petty Officer approaching and motioning him to get off the lifeline.

"Well, it's like this..., I left the bathroom and walked into the first room I came upon, whispering ole' girl's name, but there was no response, so I undressed and climbed under the sheets, cuddling. I mean..., I heard her light snore but thought she was plotting because she didn't want to give up the goodies. Well, I slipped to the foot and started kissing and sucking those toes, and at first, she whisked her foot away, but that made me immensely persistent.

"Minutes later, she started moaning, 'Oh, Henry!' in a deep, slurred voice. Well, I thought her voice sounded like that because she was trying to clear her throat, but then again, I was mad as hell for her calling me freakin' Henry. Anyway, I moved my hand up her thighs until touching something hairy and coarse, instantly recalling ole' girl being totally bald. Man, let me tell you..., sweat set in fast when jumping up, hearing ole' girl's voice whispering my name from the hallway. Hell, it was useless trying to get away from Granny's leg-lock when she started hollering 'Oh Henry' a few more times."

"So then, what happened?" Tom asks, crying in laughter.

"Hell, I kept trying to get free, but Granny kept pulling my hand between her legs. Man..., we were wrestling under those covers for minutes until she fanned that heavy-ass quilt, straining when that funk rose up and grew stronger!"

"Funk? What funk?"

"Man..., Granny messed around and busted one of those old silent-but-deadly-ass farts. Damn! I mean one of the stinking reindeer farts, if not worse."

Out of nowhere come a few low outbursts from nosy bystanders.

Tony briefly looks back, finding a few folks quieting while still trying to get an earful.

"Dude!" Tom screams, bent over to his knees, giggling even harder, until gaining his composure seconds later and long enough to listen to more. "Then what?"

"Well, ole' girl cut the lights on, screaming when she saw me lying there in a defeated struggle," Tony whispers, somewhat embarrassed that others had overheard. "Man..., I can't believe she told you that mess," Tony says, looking into Tom's frown and teary eyes when Tom lets off an unexpected burst of laughter.

"You have to promise not to tell the guys, Chief!" Tony says with a serious face.

"I've got something on you now..., so don't ever screw with me!" Tom says, smirking.

Their and the bystanders' laughter finally tapers off when Tom and Tony step off and enter the ship's interior. They stand in the dimly-lit passageway, adjusting their sight to the low-level blue lights, and then make their way down to the second deck.

Tom goes to the wardroom, and Tony heads to the berthing.

Strike Force One is finally closing in on its final destination.

The USMSP R. L. Peterson is steaming two hundred nautical miles off the Coast of Grand Bazumi Island and closing fast.

The operational plans and orders are to close within seventy nautical miles and remain well outside of the island's surface-radar detection so they can launch the six-man assault wave undetected.

"Standby!" Someone shouts out in the wardroom, with everyone coming to parade rest in total silence, waiting for Captain Carrington and the USMSP R. L. Peterson's Commanding Officer to enter.

Lieutenant Smith walks in. "Standby!" he shouts, holding the door against his back.

"Atten-tion!" Ensign Terry shouts, seeing the commanding officers enter and move to the head of the table.

Captain Pierite looks around at several smiling faces and then nods to the chaplain, who begins blessing the food and ends the prayer with the room still semi-quiet until mild conversations level out again.

Tom glances around, getting a feel for his men's mood, which seems distant.

An hour later, and after most of the tables are clean, Captain Carrington stands and looks around. "May I have your attention?" he says, tapping his gold dinner fork against the crystal glass as the room quiets. "Ladies and gentlemen, the information I'm about to divulge is privileged. During Strike Force One's last mission, we had casualties and lost the entire sister team. Well, at least we thought we did, until this mission."

Tom's men stare at each other surprised, and a few mouths surprisingly drop open.

"Strike Force One is grateful to have only lost one, but losing one is too many. Now I said that to say this..., as we march into the unknowns of this mission, we must realize the seriousness of our jobs in our day-to-day supportive roles."

Captain Carrington goes on to finish his speech, then nods to Ensign Terry when Tom and his men stand and look at one another, confused.

"Strike Force One, draw your weapons at 0100!" Ensign Terry shouts.

Tom and his men huddle in a semicircle, mumbling to one another.

The team draws their Special Forces weapons as if in a rehearsal and assembles in the conference room.

The lieutenant enters the conference room unnoticed while Captain Carrington's restrained in the stateroom. He breathes heavily from rushing up the steep ladder wells. "May I have your attention, please," he says, waiting for the mild chatter to cease while slowing his breathing more.

"Gentlemen..., this may be the last time you see me until the end of your challenging mission. This disk is classified," he says, holding the clear disc well above his head. "Though it's not of the best quality, it is of great value," he says, loading it into the DVD player. "Please hold any comments until after the briefing."

The disc plays for some time, and bright lights illuminate the room at the end of the presentation.

Everyone sits, trying to refocus their sights.

The lieutenant scans the room and notices two men wiping their watery eyes with their long-sleeved, dark swimwear. "Strike Force One's mission is to go in and rescue Strike Force Two!"

"What?" Tom shouts, slamming both hands down on the table when standing swiftly. "Hell, I thought they were all dead!"

"Well, Chief..., that is what the enemy wanted us to believe, and why Ronnie's body was the only one delivered back to the United States. The images are of a heavily-sedated team who seems to have been injected with a sedation drug of some sort."

"What! You mean to tell me that we've carried this heavy burden, and the government knew the team was alive all this time?"

"No..., the government immediately activated you guys when they got word. Intelligence determined they're located in an installation called the Underground, or Compound. You and your men are hereby tasked to locate the Underground and Command Post, which is being run by a traitor, a major with whom you have had the pleasure to serve in the past, Chief. You'll perform a rescue extraction, kill the major, destroy his post and communications links, and kill all militants."

Tom takes a deep breath and swallows when recalling the major who practically saved his life during an ambush in Afghanistan. Tom feels a few of his men staring at him, so he calms down yet keeps the distasteful thoughts of killing a dear friend weighted deep down, not wanting to discourage his men.

"Furthermore, you're to destroy the disk and original command satellite chip, so they have no satellite uplink capability."

"How long do you think this will take?" Johns asks, thinking of his unborn child.

"We anticipate a month, tops, though the captain mentioned it taking longer. We're on borrowed time, gentlemen!" the lieutenant says. "Is there anything else I can answer?" he asks with both hands sunk deep in each pocket, fiddling around with loose coins in one pocket and keys in the other.

"What if we can't locate the Underground or Compound in time, sir?" Tom asks.

"Then God bless us all, son because this will shatter our ties with the UN and other countries," the lieutenant says, pretending to be in deep sorrow when slipping his hand out and shaking his head. He reaches for the desk, passing the confidential communications and frequency plans to Ensign Terry with fast-gazing eyes swarming over the room. "I wish you all the greatest luck on this mission, gentlemen! Now, put your blue-tooth headsets on and conduct communications checks. These are the new Sky-Tel cellular phones, fresh off the assembly line," the lieutenant says, pulling one from the box.

He hands the phones out and then spreads a large-scale map over the table, motioning Tom and the ensign over.

The three stand strategically, looking over the rough terrain for minutes, scanning the island's contours for the best undetectable approach.

"Meet me in the hangar in twenty minutes," the lieutenant says, turning and rushing off.

"Here!" Tom points. "Looks like a four-hundred-foot drop, but we've climbed five times higher or more."

"Ok..., everyone, synchronize your watches," the ensign yells with attentive eyes. "On my mark..., the time will be zero one fifteen, fifteen-second standby, five, four, three, two, one..., mark!"

Everyone activates synchronization, and chimes loudly echo throughout the room, adjusting the volumes until the chimes are very low.

"Switch to secure, silent mode," Tom says, pushing a button on the side of his watch. He places the map in its watertight case and seals it tight.

Everyone picks up an antenna and extra charger from the table near the door as they single-file out and head down the ladder well.

They stand relaxed in the middle of the hangar bay and talk amongst one another about their sister strike team.

"Attention on deck!" Johns shouts, being the first to notice both captains and the lieutenant approaching from a narrow passageway.

"Gather around, gentlemen," the lieutenant says.

"I'm Captain Pierite, the ship's commanding officer! It is a proud feeling knowing the United States Government has sent only the very best to handle this extraction. My crew is proud to be a part of this covert operation. Best of luck, men, and know my prayers are with you. Ensign..., the ship's disbursing officer, has the team's cash ready for pickup. The rest of their money is in the Islander's Bank and Trust. Your credit cards are readily accessible, and the secure Sky-Tel cellular phones are active, but please, keep your calls to a reasonable limit. "Are there any questions?" Captain Pierite asks, proudly smiling.

No one verbally acknowledges, but everyone shakes their head in a negative response.

"That's all, men!" Captain Pierite says, turning with Captain Carrington.

"Attention on deck!" Ensign Terry shouts, keeping the men at attention while waiting for the three to exit the hangar.

The lieutenant briefly stops to pick up a pen that fell from his shirt pocket. He looks up and quickly finds himself at a distance, picking up his steps, and is hot on Captain Carrington's trail until snatching him back when finding his arm extended forward for the ship captain's shoulder.

Captain Carrington and the lieutenant reach the next corridor, with Captain Pierite now a ways ahead when the lieutenant snatches Captain Carrington by the collar. He pulls him into a side passageway and looks around for witnesses.

Captain Carrington struggles to gain footing when falling into the bulkhead and bouncing back. "Oohhh!"

The lieutenant quickly grabs him in the back of the collar and forces him headfirst into the steel bulkhead, almost knocking him out.

Captain Pierite looks back then looks again when calling out to them, before backtracking.

The lieutenant shoves Captain Carrington through an open door and drapes his hands over his mouth.

The ship captain calls out to them again until stopping, then picks up his pace with his next call out fading.

Ensign Terry talks to the men a little longer and puts them at ease. He then veers off to discussing the initial approach to the island in detail, and afterward, he leads them to the disbursing office, where they sign for cash and credit cards.

They finally reach the fantail an hour later, with eyes glistening over the glassy water, when finding two boats bobbing up and down while standing off at a safe distance.

Tom catches a glimpse of the quarter moon's reflection, which shines just enough to support the covert landing.

The boat coxswains keep an eye on the red landing approach lights, and as soon as it turns green, the two ship's coxswains increase the speed of their engines, slowly making their final approach alongside the ship. They tie up alongside quickly with eyes dead set on the OOD, awaiting his following command.

The OOD stands talking to another officer, then looks down at the boats and motions to the team again when the coxswain motion Ensign Terry and his men forward to board.

Strike Force One's men are all loaded with 100 pounds of gear when single-filing down the poorly lit, flimsy Jacob's ladder, which quietly bangs against the side of the ship.

The first boat, then the second, is quickly loaded with five men in each when the coxswains ease from the ship with the new trawler motors active.

The coxswains soon secure the trawlers, decreasing the sound of the muffled engines when the first boat's engine blasts and they commence a full-power run into the beach.

The second boat replicates the movement within seconds and follows close in the trail, as if in a precision rehearsal.

The men sit uniformly dressed in black turtlenecks, black canvas pants, and black steel-toed boots covered with waterproof frogman suits and fins. Each carries a backpack loaded with deceptive civilian dry-pack clothing, which is shrink-wrapped.

The coxswain even wears all-black gear to prevent detection. They continue to cruise at a high rate of speed, with boats continually rising and falling over moderate to high waves. They instantly slow getting a radio message from Combat Information Center (CIC) advising them when they've reached a distance where those ashore could hear the engines. The boat coxswains shut down the main engines, activating the silent trawlers, and securing them seconds later.

The choppy waters begin mildly, then heavily rocking the boats back and forth when the team grasps the paddles, rowing inland in unison to prevent disclosure.

The team lunges into chest and chin-deep water when the first boat touches down on the sandy beach, and the second group does the same. The team grabs personal items from the boat and mounts items on their backs before joining in and pushing the boats offshore.

The coxswains restart the quiet underwater trawlers and slowly propel the boats further from the beach until several miles away and top, raising their binoculars. They zoom in on the team with a sense of pride, being a part of their first covert operation.

Chief Powells takes the lead and continues advancing with the team, scaling the mountainside until becoming almost transparent to the coxswains.

Strike Force One constantly scans its perimeter and grasps the cliffs' dark, rugged edges to support their steep climb. They clear a large boulder twenty minutes or so later that stands out from the mountainside when a solid and continual gust of winds picks up.

The team makes it through three-fourths of their climb when the boat coxswains crank up and rev the massive main engines in a slow turn, in unison when sprinting, side by side, into pure darkness.

The team freezes several yards from the top of the cliff when hearing a fast-revving engine closing in fast, with weak radio transmissions quickly blaring in the background.

The jeep's tires come to a screeching halt, and dust rises several feet high, with a huge dust cloud extending several feet over the cliff's edge and fading into darkness.

Instantly, a floodlight flashes over the team's heads, shining out to sea and slightly piercing through dust and darkness with foreign radio transmissions blaring in the background.

The coxswains look back, finding a dim, tilting beam of light shining in the water in a zig-zag pattern, dancing around a few hundred yards away from both boat's sterns before fading away with distancing.

The island guards keep shining the light to where they hear fading engines fading faster with foreign radio transmissions blaring in the background.

The floodlight stands still and slowly shifts to the left and right before piercing straight off the cliff and then sharply shifting downward, shining on a portion of the cliff sticking out close to the water.

Johns' head tilts back, nosily peeping up until drawing close to the mountainside.

The short guard tilts the light down further, thinking he saw something black move, and keeps the light steady with eyes steadily combing the exact spot where Johns' head popped out for minutes.

Chief Powells holds his fist tightly to signal his men to hold their positions until the light finally goes out.

The island guards pull cigars from their pockets, easing the radio volume down a few notches.

The tall patrolman eases out, slipping a pint-sized flask from his back pocket, and takes a swig. He eases to the mountain's edge and unzips his pants with a cool hand slipping deep inside. He rocks back and forth for seconds, drunk and straining until finally, pissing as hard as he can when a long, gruesome burp comes, with a loud, long, obnoxious fart following.

A soft but sudden, forceful wind turns against the tall guard's solid stream of piss, spraying back and against his pants leg and boots, when the man groans a few more times, pissing for what seems like every bit of five minutes.

Tom and his men frown, soon smelling whiskey mingled with what smelled like rotten eggs.

The team strains, continually holding their breath and positions.

Tony and Bobby jerk a few times in a soft, silent giggle, though fearfully, a few fights hard not to burst into laughter.

There is total silence for minutes until the two men finally climb back in the jeep, crank up and sit idle until finally pulling away, with engines fading within seconds.

Tom motions the team to climb swiftly and advance on the windy cliff, where they kneel and survey the hillside, which looks like a deserted lover's lane.

The team remains kneeled but forms a semicircle, closely watching the jeep until its floodlights come back on again as they patrol quickly further down the far end of the cliff.

"All secure," Tom whispers through his mouthpiece, adjusting his headset.

The team stays focused on the jeep and the silhouette of the two guards beneath a street light, one with a machine gun propped up in his hand, when the jeep turns swiftly and rolls down a steep hill.

Ensign Terry tweaks a few knobs on his communicator. "I'll take the lead! Everyone, switch to channel six," he whispers. He pulls out a map and navigation instrument, checks the coordinates, and then leads the way through the thick brush.

They continue their journey and soon see dim city lights fading through a light haze when close to their destination, where their contact is to pick them up at 0400

Tainted Obsessions

hours, but due to their aggressive approach, they arrive with thirty minutes to spare.

A ten-passenger transport van pulls up out of nowhere as if rehearsed with headlights going out, followed by three, two, and then one short flash which reflects off a reflective kg speed limit sign.

Ensign Terry approaches from the rear, signaling to the team, who quickly run over and dive in through the side door, rolling to the floor without delay and expressly shifting to the rear to make more room.

"Let's go!" Ensign Terry says in a moderate tone when hearing the door slam shut.

The driver steps on the gas pedal with wheels heavily squealing, leaving a huge plume of dust and black smoke.

"Are you all ok?" a feminine, removing her black knitted cap and briefly looking back into a few of their excited faces.

Responses come delayed and lowly spoken as everyone sits in shock, finding not just a woman but a gorgeous woman informant.

Ensign Terry instantly falls into lust mode with one look.

"Hello, everyone..., my name is Nadine," she says, looking back again and swaying back into the lane when hearing a car's steady horn and seeing bright, flashing headlights.

The ensign climbs in the passenger's seat, staring at the beautiful blonde. "I'm Ensign Michael Terry!" He begins pointing to the rear. "This is Tom, Tony, Bobby, Jeff, and Robert."

Periodically, Tom catches Ensign Terry's eyes browsing over her curvy hips, which fit snuggly in her too-tight fatigues, especially under the bright streetlights that light up the cab.

She cuts her eyes back with a glance at each of them. "Hey..., we will go over to my place for now," she says with the sexiest foreign accent. "Later, we'll meet with my boss," she says with an even friendly, beautiful, sexy, and foreign accent. She drives a good twenty-five minutes or so along beautiful moonlit beaches and shorelines.

Finally, she slows and turns down a road with houses that look like mansions spread several hundred feet apart. She makes one more turn and drives farther without seeing another house, then turns again and pulls up to an immaculate mansion. She comes up on the gate, stops, and leans onto Ensign Terry's knee, balancing.

The men ease up, amazed at the beautiful architecture of the miniature mansion.

Nadine balances again, reaching into the glove compartment, and activates a button, causing the gate and garage door to open simultaneously. She sensually runs her hand on Ensign Terry's knee, then deep inside his inner thigh, making eye contact when winking. Nadine slowly pulls into the well-landscaped yard with her feet easing off the brake a few times as she coasts inside the garage.

The men vigilantly monitor their surroundings.

"This is home for a few hours, but please excuse the mess," Nadine says, smiling but continuing to give only Ensign Terry special attention. She exits the opposite side with well-manicured nails slipping inside the rim of her fatigues, wiggles her hips to get them free, and then drops them.

Tom and Oggie watch Nadine's head through the driver's side mirror.

Tom grips his gun, still cautious, until she stands.

Nadine bends over again and stands, tossing her fatigues into the laundry basket.

Tom's mind furiously searches as he tries to remember where he had seen her.

Nadine walks onto the porch, and all their eyes rove over her lovely body and large breasts filling her size thirty-eight bra. Eyes rove over her long, slender body in the too-short and sexy miniskirt that fits just so while she reaches into her purse, feeling around for her keys. "I know they're in here, somewhere! Oh well," she says, slowly bending over and reaching under the doormat yet intentionally remaining bent over for seconds while pretending to be feeling around for the key.

Bobby, who is in the rear, sees everyone's head snaking around the person in front of them as they fight to get a sneak peep at Nadine's perfectly tanned, pretty, round bottom swallowing her dark-blue G-string, down to her swollen pelvis, which forms as a softball stretched in the thin material.

Nadine looks back and smiles while still bent over. "Naughty, naughty, naughty," she says, catching them turning heads swiftly to pretend they are not looking. She stands with her key high overhead and then slides it into the lock while they continue admiring her sexy body while quietly straggling and following her inside.

Nadine throws the keys on the counter, and the men are startled by some unfamiliar, high-pitched screams, which cause them to jump and draw their weapons.

They all instantly zoom in on her pet miniature monkey, which frightfully rattles the cage and furiously continues to scream even louder.

Nadine rushes to the cage, extending her hand to comfort the monkey with baby talk when he calms down with her opening the door and stroking his small head a few times.

Ensign Terry raises his hand and motions the men to withdraw their weapons.

The monkey grows quiet, and she closes the door, reaches into the cupboard, pulls out a fifth-sized bottle of liquor with shot glasses, and pours a quick round as if she's a skilled bartender.

Each of them grabs a glass, holds it, and waits for Tom's approval.

"Could you please give us a few minutes, Nadine?" the ensign asks, smiling

"Sure suga..., I'll be in the last room on the left if you need me, honey," she says, very observant that they had not devoured their first courtesy round. She winks and gazes at Ensign Terry, then gently brushes up against him and squeezes between him and the counter. "Just make yourselves at home," she whispers, looking over her shoulder, winking at Ensign Terry again. She runs her fingers through her long blonde hair and unravels it with curvy hips, seductively swaying until she squeezes her round, firm cheeks, one cheek in each hand, and releases both so they jiggle.

"Listen!" Ensign Terry whispers with eyes still lustfully glued on her hot body.

None of them heard a word because they also stare until she vanishes around the corner.

Tom snaps his fingers, getting their attention, then motions them to pour the drinks out, but Ensign Terry is hardheaded and holds on to his. Tom dumps his and sits the glass next to the cage, accidentally knocking the glass over and spilling a large amount on the counter.

Tom does some type of fancy handwork, motioning them off, and they begin cautiously securing the perimeter around 0430.

Everyone breaks off, dispersing into little cubbyholes.

Tom pulls out his .45 and snuggles next to the four-way, glass-encased, lit fireplace to see the kitchen door.

The men settle in and look around, finding Ensign Terry walking around, assessing their positions.

Ensign Terry takes one last look and then walks toward the dim, red light shining into the long hallway. He stands at the door and looks inside for seconds before turning up his shot glass and smiling. "Is it ok if I join you?" he almost shyly asks, finding her in a sexy, sheer, black, see-through gown with a black G-string. She leans back on giant pillows with legs spread wide, continually opening and closing luscious thighs while gently stroking them and moving them sensually until resembling giant butterfly wings.

There's no response, but she nods yes, and he enters and immediately shuts the door.

Nadine's hands slip under the pillow and grow tense when gripping and holding a long surgical needle.

Tom tosses and turns, unable to stop his thoughts of Kelley, the mission, Nadine, the lieutenant, and the captain. His mind stays full of sporadic thoughts, soon realizing that trying to sleep is useless, so he sits up.

Ensign Terry undresses quickly and playfully climbs on the bed, somewhat pouncing like a lion on its prey. He begins kissing her soft thighs, working his way to her pretty belly button until stopping at tender breasts.

Nadine's hand cups the back of his head, and she pulls him deep into her sweetly fragranced bosom.

Nadine and Ensign Terry's low giggles grow like a whisper in Tom's ear.

The two get louder when Tom hears her light out of nowhere and then loud laughter for minutes when distracting Ensign Terry.

Nadine strokes his head a few times, and then runs fingers over his eyes, motioning him to close them. She kisses his eyelids until they close again, and then eases the surgical needle out, plunging it into his neck, filling him quickly, and not leaving a teardrop of the milky-looking tranquilizing medicine.

Tom hears a squeaky bed, moans, jerks, and then a few kicking motions from the bedsprings and chuckles at the thought of how quickly the ensign lost it prematurely to such a knockout chick. He grows in need of a good guffaw, when he leans forward with a hesitant smile and continues listening.

The ensign's stale and slow drooping eyes stare up at the ceiling, paralyzed by the drug and unable to see her, while she moves stealthily about the room without a sound.

Nadine creeps around, pulling out her surgical bag and other tools, which she places on his chest. She attaches a long rubber hose to a funnel-like hollow chrome tube with a v-type tip, easing it into his heart.

The tube's bitter end falls to his side when she releases the pinched clip, and blood gushes out, slowly outlining his body.

She eases up and stands on the mattress, dancing over him, then quickly removes her top, lightly giggling as if stoned. Her perfectly-cupped breasts flash before his weak eyes for minutes until she quickly covers herself and then gives strip teases. She smiles harder until a frown replaces her devilish smile when she spits on him and then reaches under the pillow for a thin wire, which Nadine wraps around his neck until she sees him losing consciousness. She attaches a T-bar piece of metal to the two bitter ends of the wire and slowly twists it until the wire begins cutting deep into his flesh and vanishing underneath his skin. She quickly strips down to nothing, using the lingerie to wipe her hands.

Tom sits longer, waiting for Nadine to either burst out in laughter or start venting, but neither ever happens.

Minutes later, Tom notices how toasty the room has gotten when easing up, flipping off the fireplace's switch. He quietly moves about the room and passes a window, uneasily drawing his weapon quickly when gazing into what looks like a man's face when aiming and quickly realizing it's a shadow from a tree. He tries slowing his heart rate, and then makes his way to the kitchen, sitting at the table.

Thirty minutes pass, and Tom hears a door lightly squeak, but in short intervals.

Nadine peeps down the hall toward the living room, then tiptoes out, slightly pulling the door shut until the lock quietly clicks.

Tom squints and soon confirms it's her before realizing she's nude.

Nadine doesn't notice his presence when advancing, but he keeps his eyes on her as she quietly tiptoes and sneakily peeps around.

"Good morning," Tom says, startling her as she fades into the living room, fearfully and nervously jumping. "Ooh..., shiiii...! You almost scared the bejeebeez out of me, suga," she mutters, hurriedly wrapping her beautiful, naked chest and pelvis with hands and arms while moving over to the couch. She grabs a knitted throw covering her lovely body. "Would you like some coffee, tea, or breakfast?" she asks, still covering herself, yet leaving more of herself exposed to entice him.

"No, thanks," Tom says, shaking his head yet admiring her gorgeous body. Nadine looks away and leaves more of her breasts open, and then all of it when tightening the throw around her curvaceous hips.

The monkey jiggles the cage instantly and then kicks while fighting to regain his vision and strength from the residue in Tom's overturned glass.

Nadine freezes, staring at the empty shot glass on the counter, then more turned over in the sink, the one on the counter with a trail of droplets. She slowly looks back to see if Tom notices the monkey's strange behavior, then nervously licks her lips and slightly clenches her bottom lip between her teeth in thought. She fades behind Tom, but he speedily gains sight of her through various sparkling, stainless steel countertop appliances until she moves further out of his view.

Tom nervously looks about the room until he sees her again as she walks up to him. He looks down the hallway with his mind going haywire, anticipating the ensign fading in, and out of the darkness, like a raging, jealous beast. Tom grows a little tense, knowing the ensign is no longer unarmed, so he's not up for taking him on as he did on the ship.

Nadine continually runs her fingers through Tom's hair, making his heart race faster. She grows nervous and gets so fidgety that her body feels warm and tingly when easing into him, pressing her bare chest against his face, teasing until aligning her nipple with his ear and playfully sinking it deep inside. Her index finger gently slips into his other ear.

Tom's hearing briefly goes numb as she gently presses harder and rubs her breasts in circles to get him aroused.

Her finger eases deeper into his other ear and moves back and forth gently.

Tom's heart races faster with eyes continually glued on the hallway until his eyes water as he blinks fast to clear them.

Nadine backs away slowly and then leans forward, slipping her tongue deep into his ear. Her lips suck the shaft of his neck until she pulls her head away after she caresses his face.

Tom's eyes swarm over her beautiful twins, then her pretty belly button, noticing a smear of what looks like a dried, reddish-brown mark on her hand. He thinks about it, assuming firsthand that she might be on her monthly, and secondly, he is imagining things. He leans into the table, unsure, yet unnoticed, and slowly draws his ten-inch double-blade dagger, 'Big Bertha,' from his thigh holster. He nervously shields the knife and then slowly rocks back and forth. "I'll have that coffee, after all, Ms. Nadine," he says, nervously looking up and into her stale, black eyes, which transform into pure darkness when quickly looking away.

She stares at him in deep thought. "Sure thing, honey," she seductively whispers, though nervous when drifting out of deep thoughts when thinking of what to do or say next. "That ensign sure is something, huh? How can he totally satisfy a woman with an appetite like mine?" she asks with a fake and nervous snicker.

Nadine finally notices the faint, bloody streaks when making her way to the sink. She turns on the faucet and hurriedly washes when her mind swiftly oppugns. "Maybe I should have taken a big, strong stud like yourself in the Queen's Quarters. I'm willing to bet top dollar that you would still be in there handling your business right now, right, huh, suga? I bet you would have been so deep it would have been as if you were drilling for oil. One thing for sure: I doubt we would be talking food or beverages right now," she says, distracting him as she cuts off the water and dries her hands with her back still to him. She folds the bloody, soapy cloth, quickly covering it with a few dirty dishes with slippery detergent at her fingers.

Tom feels sensual, merely from her sexy accent and the thoughts of having hardcore sex with a woman so gorgeous and firm yet so sexy in her seduction. He quickly thinks about the many positions he would have loved to have her in as vivid images flash through his mind until he refocuses and finds it hard to keep his eyes off her. Still, his sensual visions are fleetingly overcome when drifting and refocusing again.

He hears a tap, then a nervous tap, when he turns to find her manicured nails nervously tapping on the edge of the counter. He grows unattached quickly and knows something's wrong with the whole ordeal. He quickly thinks back on the insecure ensign again and how he had not popped up on the scene with eyes wandering back over to the hallway.

A light bang comes from the cage when the monkey grips the bars, yawning and then observing Nadine's movements as trained.

Nadine opens a cabinet, fumbling around a few glasses, and nervously bangs them together until reaching deeper, slowly easing out a loaded gun when jumping in a stance and snapping the weapon into view.

"Raid!" Tom screams at the top of his lungs, shooting straight up with all the strength he can marshal when everything seems to go into slow motion.

The monkey screams, confused and heavily rattling the cage with his little monkey fists tightly gripping the aluminum bars while whisking the cage back and forth in rage as if a wild, diseased animal.

"Raid!" he cries again with bucked eyes staring at her, trying to cock the weapon while in a backward fall and unbalanced yet still in slow motion. . Her throw falls, revealing her nude body as he's leaning forward.

Tom comes back with brute force with his elbow again, missing her, and becomes unbalanced as he falls in the opposite direction. He quickly braces against the counter and pushes off from her to regain his footing but overcompensates.

Nadine braces against the counter, half slumped over, tugging at the weapon, and tries to cock it with her body well off balance and out of alignment.

Tom manages to throw Big Bertha while still unbalanced, hearing a quick, slight grazing sound when slowly spiraling in slow motion a few feet from the floor, the sharp blade sticking out of her chest cavity, dead center.

Nadine grabs her chest with slippery fingers, which slowly inch toward the knife's sharp blade, still training the uncocks the weapon at Tom's face, and presses hard on the trigger. She clenches the blade tightly with slippery, bloody fingers and jerks it hard with the knife, slightly budging when splattering more blood that trails to her stomach.

With a few mild clicks, the knife's backside rib notches lock, preventing her from pulling the knife out, but she screams louder and strains through severe pain. With each pull, she tugs even harder until her fingers are unintentionally sliced in large chunks.

The monkey shrieks louder and jerks so hard that the cage rocks back and forth until it almost tilts.

Nadine takes one last tug, and finally, she chambers a round with a sad yet painful smile growing on her stale face when her eyes transform to black again, like shark eyes.

The weapon's chambering makes Tom cringe, and his heart drops when he tightens his hands over his head and curls into a fetal position.

"Ahh!" she screams. Her face abruptly frowns and then grows into a pained smile when aligning the weapon with Tom's chest.

A blaze of gunfire erupts abruptly, echoing throughout the house.

The wooden kitchen cabinets begin and continue crumbling.

Nadine's hand instantly drops down by her side, with several more rounds hitting her hand and causing her to release the gun. Her body trembles from each automatic round's deep penetration until she slowly slides against the cabinets and down in a puddle of blood, gasping for air until her body halts and her eyes remain open.

The monkey momentarily deciphers the events when he releases his death-defying grip and drops down in the cage, whining for minutes. He keeps his head down and slowly looks at Tom with pity and sadness.

Tom lowers his hand and looks over his shoulder through a smoke-filled room, finding Oggie and Johns in a standing, prone position.

The room remains filled with the spinning sound, with Oggie's barrel still spinning with a high whistling sound until winding down to a whisper.

The smoke lightly clears with all weapons still trained on Nadine's body until slowly precision scanning the room.

Tony and Bobby stand at bedroom doors with their weapons drawn. They peep toward the semi-smoke-filled room and quickly advance and come up behind Oggie and Johns.

Tom swiftly climbs to his feet, signaling Tony and Bobby to check on the ensign when the three come up behind them, following closely down the hallway.

The five slow when coming up on the room the ensign is in, with Oggie slowly turning the knob and pushing the door open with the muzzle of his weapon.

The door squeaks until pushed harder and flings open, finding Ensign Terry facedown, handcuffed, gagged, and spread eagle. His partially-nude body lay outlined in an inch-thick puddle of blood.

Tom and Oggie move closer, barely able to make out the thin, somewhat transparent wire wrapped around his neck until moving closer. Their eyes wander over the rubber tube and metal that extends from the side of his chest.

Tom moves forward and then steps back when his foot rises from stepping on the metal T-bar.

"What are we going to do now?" Johns screams, standing at the door, trembling while staring toward the kitchen where Nadine's foot is slightly visible past the cabinet.

Tom walks into the living room and flops down on the plush leather couch with everyone single-filing in and stands around in suspense.

"Damn, she killed damn Tee!" Johns screams, nervously stomping in total confusion when Oggie turns, grabbing him by the collar on his third turn and taking him to the wall, slapping his face a few good whacks. "Damn it, Johns! Snap the hell out of it before you get us killed!"

Tony and Bobby walk through different rooms, looking through windows, and then scanning the front and back perimeter of the house until surveying along the hillside for anything suspicious.

Tom eases to the edge of the seat with eyes wandering over to Johns. "Johns! Get my knife out of that trick's chest," Tom says, drifting into deep thought.

"What? Shiiiiii..., no way man, I'm not even touching that crazy-ass chick!" Johns' mumbles unclearly.

"Damn..., I knew I should have left your punk ass behind! Listen, you had better get your head out of your tail this damn minute!" Tom screams, walking up to Johns and grabbing his weapon after noticing the safety's still on, and the cold barrel runs a chill up and down Tom's spine, causing hairs to spike on the back of his neck. His eyes drop at once, inspecting the weapon while turning from Johns. "How many shots did you fire?" Tom asks, briefly looking at Johns over his shoulder.

"Nu-nu-nu-nu-none, Chief," he chatters tensely.

"None? Damnait, Johns! That could have been me over there dead instead of

Tainted Obsessions

that crazy-ass bitch!" Tom screams, turning with a tightly-balled fist when rushing up to him. "Here! Take this damn weapon!" Tom says, throwing, grasping, and forcing the weapon into Johns' chest. Tom presses Johns' back hard against the marbled mantle. "The damn time you forget to use it, I'll be sure to use it on your monkey ass!" Tom says, shoving the weapon deeper into Johns and then backing away.

Gee tilts and then presses his boot into the side of Nadine's chest, straining and slowly pulling out the knife.

Everyone turns upon hearing the blade scrape the bone when everyone turns simultaneously, finding Gee whisking the bloody knife out. "Here you go!" Oggie says, passing Tom the knife with the thick blood smear on the blade and handle.

Tom goes into a deep meditation and then stares with eyes wandering over the blood-smeared knife. He wipes it with a different throw from the couch and then places it in its leather sleeve. Tom eases up, dumping Ensign Terry's valuables from his backpack, still thinking about what to do next.

Ensign Terry's pictures of his wife, a pocketknife, two weapons, the secure Sky-Tel cellular, and sixty thousand dollars freely fall and bounce on the tightly-stretched leather cushion.

"So, what's next?" Oggie asks, walking up to Tom.

"We should let the ship know Ensign Terry's dead," Johns says, swiftly lifting his headset.

"Damn it! Drop it, Johns! You stupid idiot!" Oggie shouts, rushing up to him and drawing back but holding his spring-loaded backhand inches from Johns' face.

Johns tenses staring at Oggie, and then looks over to find Tom's frowning.

Tears swell in John's eyes as Tom's face clears when he drifts into deep thought again.

A loud bang causes the men to train their weapons in the kitchen and even faster at the monkey's cage, finding the monkey with a liquor bottle nozzle to his lips; the bottle angled through the back of the bars.

They closely watch him take a few heaping swallows, which sets their minds at ease when bursting into a mild, then great laughter to ease the tension when they lean into one another, uncontrollably laughing harder.

After more laughter, even Johns eventually cracks a smile after becoming teary-eyed while trying to be hard and hold his laughter inside.

One at a time, they turn and retrain their thoughts when something louder slams into the counter, distracting them again when they promptly turn, frowning and eagerly watching the monkey try to lift a small six-shooter from a silver box behind the cage. Everyone instantly brings their weapons to eye level with steady aim.

Tom signals them to hold their fire while bringing the monkey into his crosshairs. A red beam of light floats over the monkey's body until the sound of an old, weak camera flash charging grows to a loud and steady tone. A red dot sits dead center in the monkey's little peanut-shaped head until he staggers to the left and right, dropping the gun after a few more funny-looking staggers with a few steps. He freezes in place, drops, and kicks a few times, and then stops moving.

Tom withdraws his weapon and swiftly, yet cautiously walks up, inches from the cage.

The monkey jerks inaccurately, snatching the gun and aiming, then fires off a shot, causing Tom to duck, barely missing when everyone hits the floor and takes cover.

Tom brings up his weapon and takes steady aim when the monkey falls back, and the gun falls freely. Tom mounts his weapon, opens the cage, and slowly reaches inside, breathing hard while removing the gun and checking the monkey's pulse. "Hmm, dead as a doorknob," Tom says, lifting the glass and then the bottle and smelling both. "I guess this was her way of doing us all at once. You guys owe ole' chief for not allowing you to drink to your deaths," Tom says, winking and smirking.

"So, where were we...? Oh, Strike Force Two! Hell, I don't know what's going on with that bull, but could anyone make out the high-ranking official?" No one acknowledges as they stand in a daze. "Well, given the circumstances, I think it's best that we head for the nearest city for concealment and split up to buy ourselves more time to figure out this mess."

Oggie takes a seat and leans back with his legs crossed. "Great idea, Chief!" Oggie responds. "I'm sure when this trick fails to call in or show up, they will come in full force," Oggie says, half-dazed until looking over to find Johns looking down in a daze.

CHAPTER FOUR: THE COVERT LANDING

Tom drops onto the couch and begins dividing the money evenly, but he keeps the ensign's share. He lifts his handset and dials the ship's emergency monitoring frequency. "Nestor, this is Eagle, over," Tom says, looking at a few of his men's concerned faces and then at the floor.

"Nestor, send your traffic..., over!" the ship's radio operator responds.

"The eagle has landed. We are two hours late due to car problems, over," Tom says, lying to confuse their location so the ship can't pinpoint them. Now at this point..., they trust no one outside the team or anyone inside for that fact because paranoia has set in deeply, and it is in full force.

"Nestor, roger, report when at third base, over..., Eagle, this is Nestor..., did you copy..., over?" The ship makes several efforts to reach them, but Tom and the men sit listening until Tom closes the communications circuit and directs them not to respond.

Gee and Tom walk back into the bedroom, cautiously looking around until something lightly flaps intermittently and catches their attention.

Tom's eyes quickly go to the finding a thin, braided strap extending from the windowpane and mildly blowing back and forth in the wind.

Oggie carefully examines the camouflaged bag to ensure it is not an attached trap, and then eases it inside. He slowly unzips the bag and soon realizes it is full of C4 explosives. "Damn, there's enough C4 to level this whole damn community!" Oggie says in disbelief.

Tom comes close to Oggie. "It's a good thing she couldn't fit through this port-sized window, or she would have bailed out. Hell, had she been able to, we would all be dead. As a matter of fact, had she been able to make it through the kitchen, her plan would have probably been to detonate the C4 with this remote," Tom says, flipping open the clear plastics pouch.

Their eyes closely gaze over the detonator and charger.

"Man, the newest model at that," Oggie says, flipping the charger over to find the manufacturer's production stamp on the bottom. His fingers roam over the shiny seal, and his eyes grow wide, finding the date to be weeks ago.

The rest of the men stagger into the room and everyone stares at the ensign's blue face for minutes in total silence.

"What do you want to do with his body, Chief?" Oggie asks.

"I was just thinking of what we can do to preserve him. Put him in the deep freezer in the garage. A proper seal on the door should preserve him long enough for the recovery team to arrive. Yeah, that should work, at least until the American

Embassy team arrives," Tom says.

"Do you think he even got a piece, Chief?" Oggie asks, shaking his head in disbelief.

"Hell no, I know he didn't because there's the unopened condom," Tom says, pointing at the silver and gold condom packet, slightly extending from under the pillow. He flips the pillow back to find the empty syringe and bent needle.

"Damn..., killed for nothing. That chick should have at least had a little decency to give Terry a shot at it before taking his life," Oggie says, slinging his sniper rifle over his shoulder.

"Shit! Let's not be too judgmental because that could have been either of us lying there," Tom says, leaning into the wall, cleaning dirt from under his fingernails with the tip of his knife's blade. "My guardian angel was definitely watching over me," Tom says, reaching down, grabbing the blue comforter, and spreading it over the bed. He motions to Oggie, and they begin rolling the ensign's body onto the comforter but leave his face exposed.

They carry Terry to the garage, where they empty half of the stocked freezer, place him on the cold meat, and then repack as much as possible. They leave the food that will not fit on the floor; then everyone gathers around and looks into the ensign's face and can't help but stare at the deep laceration around his bloody, bruised neck.

Tom leads off in a lengthy, devotional prayer, and afterward, each places their hands over their hearts, taking turns bidding him a farewell.

They spend the day taking turns catching up on rest and alternate the security rotations to provide three-hundred-and-sixty degrees of surveillance.

After sunset, Oggie brings the thawed T-bones, shrimp, and lobster tails inside, from the garage floor.

Oggie and Bobby cover Nadine's nude, bloody body, and then Oggie drapes a white apron over his body and prepares the team dinner in the blood-covered, bullet-hollowed kitchen.

At midnight, Tom directs them to bury the freezer alongside the garage. They finish around 0130, then clean up and change into civilian attire for the remainder of their covert operations. They break down their miniature backpacks and leather cases and then repack their weapons and personal items.

"What about the Operational Control Center, chief?" Johns asks.

"Damn, Johns, do I look like a freakin' grand wizard? Shit, the OCC may have never existed, and if so, we have no contacts to lead us to it..., now, do we?"

Tom signals them to grab their gear.

They destroy the things they leave behind beyond recognition and start loading the van.

Tony and Bobby set time-delayed C4 packets in electrical wiring and high-impact areas.

A head pops up and peeps through binoculars at a distance and the top of the hill with eyes roaming over the yard and windows of the mansion.

Another body soon low-crawls alongside the first body within minutes and then another.

The three watches closely as the garage and the gate open in unison when the shielded bodies slowly back down from the hill and run to the limousine, speeding off.

The Strike Force One team rides along the island's east end minutes later when the C4 detonation levels the mansion, sending debris over a radius of at least half a mile or more, vibration the van with mild light flashing, lighting up the mountaintop, in the background.

All eyes scan the area as the van picks up speed.

Minutes pass in total silence.

Johns happens to look over his shoulder and two headlights when unnoticeably jumping and doing a double take, finding it gone, but he keeps it to himself, looking back several times.

The van shoots past a cab parked in an indentation in the road, with its headlight turned off when Tom's head goes back with keen eyes. "Here..., here!" Tom yells, pointing to Oggie. "Get your gear!"

The unidentified vehicle stops and stays hugged against the road, giving the van time to advance down the long stretch of road to stay undetected.

The van makes a sharp turn with the signal light coming on when Tom points toward the gravel and forward into the path with trees on both sides.

The unidentified vehicle's taillights flicker a few times, then eases from the side of the road, picking up speed, then stops again just before the curve, inching out with all eyes peeking ahead, finding the road empty when pulling off fast.

"There..., there!" the person in the unidentified car yells, pointing over the headrest and off to the left when the car veers off the road, taking a narrow path.

The van slows when they shoot out on the other side in a clear field when the ocean comes into view.

The brake lights flicker a few times, and then stay steady with the van rolling a few more feet until close to the cliff's edge.

The driver's door flies open, and everyone exits from the closet door, with all doors almost closing simultaneously.

Tom is the first to drop his things, followed by the others when he motions them to the rear, then walks to the driver's side, easing a hand inside and throwing the gear shift to neutral. He rushes to the back with hands on the bumper, and they all join in, lightly rocking then lunging the van forward, ditching the van, and backing off, watching it burst into flames when hitting the thick boulder at the bottom near the water.

The aft lookout on the ship instantly reports the bright ball of fire on the shoreline.

From a distance, two heads pop up until the third pop up, taking turns looking through binoculars, scanning over and around Tom and his men, looking for the van while the team stands near the cliff's edge.

Tom cautiously looks around and then motions his men back when picking up their things and beginning the mile or so hike south to a cabstand they just had passed minutes ago. Tom takes off in a slow jog, leaving his men when rushing up and knocking on the window, startling the driver out of his sleep, with hands rubbing across slobbering lips and then dim eyes.

From a distance, three heads pop out from the edge of the woods, tiptoeing closer to the road, observing Tom and his men climbing inside the taxicab.

Tom slides in last, pointing the driver to the dim and hazy lights in the distant background.

They ride for twenty minutes or so until bright city lights pierce through thick, patchy fog.

The driver turns onto the main street and stops when Tom points to the side of the road. He exits quickly with sleepy eyes and frequent yawns, rushing to the back, popping the trunk while Tom stands, counting off seventy-five dollars for the fare until adding a few more dollars for the tip.

A black, silver, and chrome stretched S.U.V. limousine pulls up at the far end of the street, next to the curb. The driver dials a number and presses the phone tightly to his ear, avoiding the background noise of the women in the back, making several murderous and slanderous remarks.

A slender, feminine, curvy body slumps over the chauffeur's seat, crossing her arms with her chin settled on the seat's backing to get a better view.

Tom passes the money to the cabbie and then turns to his men with eyes on the cabbie's back as he jumps back inside. "Remember, cash only so that the electronic transactions can't trace back to this area," Tom says, looking for agreement through precision head nods.

The team stands in mild discussion for minutes when the limousine driver pulls out a handheld device and smiles.

Tom and his men turn and advance up the long strip of well-architected buildings to include eateries, shops, banks, and hotels.

The limousine cranks up and follows them at a distance until immediately speeding up, with windows rolling down fast and automatic to semi-automatic weapons trained on them but well hidden behind tinted windows.

The team veers off in another direction and breaks off in different directions.

The limousine stops for pedestrians crossing the congested crosswalk with anxious eyes gazing down at the device's crystals, watching each team member separate yet continue tracking individually.

The traffic and pedestrians clear, and the limousine driver floors the gas pedal, finding Tom and his men vanishing quickly into the busy crowd of early workers.

The limousine doors abruptly open when three men and two women hide their weapons and jump out, canvassing the area. They spot Tom and his men at a distance and split up individually, each person one-on-one.

Tom acquires a room at the Oman Resort, checking in. He sets his watch for 11 a.m.; before taking a long, hot bath and sleeping. He's awakened by the loud beeping of his watch when deactivating it and lying there longer until finally getting up and getting himself together. He keeps a keen eye on the time, establishing a secure conference call with Oggie as agreed, and plans to meet at Oggie's hotel later.

Afterward, Tom sits around trying to piece the mission together up to this point, though it is difficult without accurate intelligence information to analyze.

Tom thinks about Kelley and the kids, realizing they could be in danger, so he drops his pride, calls the house, and Martha answers.

Martha puts Tom on hold immediately, leading the kids downstairs so she can talk privately.

Minutes pass until he hears her pick the phone back up.

"Are you still there?" she asks, easing into the chair and taking a deep breath before easing back.

"Yes, I'm here..., is there something wrong, Martha..., are you ok?" he asks, easing his back against the headboard when hearing her lightly sniffing a second time.

"Why yes..., yes, something is wrong..., it's very wrong! Now just listen to me and hear me out," she says, meditating on how to break the bad news.

"Ok..., you have my undivided attention, Martha." Tom sits forward, listening closely to her low whining and more sniffling.

"Ok..., whooo..., where do I start." She lets out a light burst of air, getting her train of thought together. "Ok..., well, Kelley told me what transpired between you two on the phone call. Well, after that call..., Kelley followed through with her plans to meet with Jeff so she could have him arrested for delinquent child support." She takes an even deeper breath this time. "Well, the arrest worked out just fine, but her plan backfired when Jeff posted bond and came to the house that night and beat Kelley badly.

A tear runs down Tom's cheek. "Oh really? Well..., are you sure something else didn't happen to set him off?"

She stays quiet for a second or so in deep thought. "Well, Tom, I can't swear because it's not right to do so, but Jeff's known to be out of his mind throughout these events, and every encounter I've had with him or heard of..., he's just a pathetic, stoned alcoholic."

Tom stares at the floor until he slowly shakes his head in frustration. "Ugh..., I'm going to kill that son of a...," Tom declares when refraining from using profanity.

"Tom..., Tom..., just please calm down! Look..., Kelley will be fine, but you need to hurry home. We love and miss you!"

" Same here," he responds, wiping teary eyes. "Wait..., wait, Martha, the reason I called is that I want Kelley to take leave and stay in Richmond with you until she hears from me."

"Oh, Tom..., there's no need for that because he's no longer a threat; he's back in jail."

"Really? Ok, but look..., I'm not referring to Jeff but more so to this tricky mission. It's just not safe for Kelley and the kids to be in the house so get out now and don't even bother packing a thing. Tell Kelley I'll be transferring ten thousand dollars to our checking account later today..., now go!"

She sits nervously, rocking her leg with her mind scrambling. "Alright..., alright, Tom, but know that God is with you," she says, wiping her watery eyes. "

"Go, Martha..., go now!" Tom hangs up and sits back, reminiscing about Kelley and what she must have gone through.

An hour later, Martha sits still, stuffing bags and luggage, when receiving a call from Kelley, who had confided in Martha, telling her all the different trivial reasons why Jeff had jumped on her.

Kelley hangs up and sits smiling, then giggles as if stoned off cheap drugs.

Tom sits still, puzzled, until beginning to feel sorry for not being there for her. In even deeper thought, he breaks his meditation, grabbing his bag. Tom counts off sixteen thousand in large bills, stuffing the money in various pockets. He straps on his .22 and leaves the hotel, remaining vigilant when heading for the bank and, afterward, growing more cautious. Tom proceeds to the tailor's shop, leaving an hour later with both arms filled with bags of new threads. He returns to his room, unpacking, and when exhausted, he sits around for hours, then takes a short nap until 1615, and when awake, dresses, strapping one .22 around his ankle; the other in his holster, under his sweat suit.

Tom leaves the hotel, cautiously walking the streets until entering Oggie's hotel. He looks back and stares into the face of a beautiful, old, gray-haired woman who has her arms filled with bags, seeing the double doors about to close. He reaches back and grasps her cart's handle, which she leans forward to grab.

The two front wheels of the connected, heavy trunks roll over the door's ledge, lightly rocking, and with one last tug, Tom rolls the back wheels over the raised ledge.

"Thank you, son," she says, taking a deep breath.

Tom helps the lady to the elevator, loading her things inside, and with one final wave, he bids her farewell and walks over, taking a seat. He sits longer, growing restless, and takes a seat, finding Tony passing the large window. His eyes followed Tony through revolving doors.

Azreay'l

"Chief," Tony says, walking up to him and nodding, and when they are within arm's length, they turn and walk up to the gold-plated elevator doors. They stand back, patiently watching the elevator lights descend until the bell rings and the door fully extends.

A tall, beautiful island woman stands to one side in the elevator with her handheld mirror, touching up lipstick until closing the mirror, finally noticing them standing there and looking surprised when smiling and walking toward them. "Hi, handsome!" She winks.

Tom holds the elevator door open, looking back at her long, firm legs and well-proportioned body until she fades behind a few people in the lobby.

She reappears at the door's turnstile, walking out and climbing into the backseat of a smoke-gray limousine.

They reach Oggie's room and spend hours going over different scenarios with minds at full throttle, trying to figure out the mission when coming up clueless, repeatedly.

They grow bored hours later, heading for the lobby and inquiring about the area's nightlife.

The clerk stands thinking for minutes while looking down, and then looks up surprised when recommending Club Annabelle's.

Tom walks outside, pulls out his cell phone, dialing, and Tamara answers minutes later.

"Hi, babe..., I need a favor. Can you pretend you received an emergent injury transmission over the bridge-to-bridge circuit? I need you to tell your captain the coordinates are where a mansion once stood on the west side of the island," he says, rattling off coordinates pulled from a map earlier.

Tamara urgently scribbles the coordinates on a pad and rips it off. She folds the paper, slipping it into her pants pocket.

"I'm sure the local officials can easily direct the American Embassy to the location. Hey, listen..., I have some bad news. Look..., Ensign Terry's dead; he's the one we want to be recovered as soon as possible. He's in a freezer buried next to where the mansion's garage once stood."

"No..., Tom," she cries in a low voice when the phone bangs quietly against the plush carpeted floor when she runs for the bathroom, vomiting when bursting through the door. She returns minutes later. "All right, Tom, but please, sweetie, please be careful," she says, rubbing her stomach and wiping her mouth with a damp paper towel.

"All right, babe," he says, ending the call and walking up behind his men, who are standing and waiting for the attendant to wave down a taxi.

Later, and hours into clubbing, Tom still sits, not mingling with any of the local or foreign women passing or giving a smile or wink. He continues meditating on Kelley and the kids until breaking his concentration when feeling like someone is walking up on him.

"Do you come here often," a soft, sexy, feminine voice speaks over the loud, jazzy, island upbeat that had just started playing.

Tom looks over his shoulder, finding the tall, beautiful blonde from the elevator earlier.

The bright lights reflecting off the shiny disco ball reflect upon her beautiful face when she stares deep into his eyes with a long, smooth arm forward.

"Hi..., my name is Nichelle," she says, with a firm handshake, gently squeezing. Her soft touch melts in his hand until feeling bony fingers but in a firm grip.

"Excuse my manners..., please come around," he says, patting the leather seat in excitement.

Nichelle comes to the front and steps up and inside the booth with her body turned slightly to one side when slipping between the decorative metal bars at the opening of the circled couch.

Tom stares and can't help but notice what an amazing body she has when she wiggles her curvaceous hips past the table's edge.

"I see you like staying fit."

"Yes, I have to because I travel so much," she says, taking a seat.

Nichelle and Tom continue in conversation when she notices Tom staring at the dance floor from time to time.

He looks off and then back at the dance floor, and before he can ask her to dance, she informs him that her feet are killing her from standing so long to get inside.

She gains his full attention when putting on a sexy smile and winking. She smiles again, extending one foot at a time onto the couch next to him. "Do you mind?" She asks.

He smiles back and then puts on a semi-angry face. "You've got to be kidding me..., right? I mean..., first, you blow me off on a chance to shake a leg, and second and third, I don't even know you or your ole" crusty feet!" he responds lowly and jokingly.

Nichelle looks away briefly, offended when lowering one foot, and Tom smiles, grabbing her other soft, warm foot before she can retract it.

Tom gently strokes her foot as it grows warmer to the touch when she leans back, licking her full lips and closing her eyes while he gently continues kneading her foot and toes.

"Wow..., please..., please don't stop", she moans, arching her back to soothe her tingly spine.

Tom's crafty hand massage, which he's mastered over the years in turning women on, drives her crazy with touches and strokes, making them very horny.

Tony walks up from behind Tom and Nichelle. "The girls want to take us to the boardwalk."

Tom looks at Nichelle, who immediately stares back.

"Not no, but hellz (hell) naw (no)..., I'm not doing any more standing on these dogs tonight," she says, smiling when tilting her drink and taking a sip.

"Come on..., the water will be therapeutic," Tom says, winking to get a blush.

She thinks for a quick second and then turns up the last sip of her mixed drink. "Ok..., what the heck; besides, I'm leaving tomorrow, so I may as well, right?"

Tom finally notices her wedding ring and band. "So, where's the mister?"

"Oh..., he's around," she responds, smiling and then winking her beautiful eyes.

The group exits, catching three separate rides. They arrive at their destination twenty minutes later, and Tom detaches from the group, paying the three drivers but only generously tips his driver.

Tom turns and almost bumps into Nichelle but plays it off by lifting her into his arms, and it works when she falls into him, wrapping her arms around his neck.

She holds on tightly with her head at his neck, her soft lips slightly brushing against the shaft of his neck. Her curly hair dangles about his ears and face as she kisses his ear a few times until sucking his earlobe. She playfully blows long, warm breaths of air in his ear, arousing him as he closes the boardwalk.

Tom crossed over to the ocean side of the boardwalk, accidentally bumping against her thigh when putting her down.

She looks down with excited eyes when feeling his stiffness but looks away, shadowing her smile.

Tom also looks away, somewhat embarrassed when staying quiet for a spell, looking out at the roaming waves with the wind blowing his hair.

The embarrassment diminishes when she touches his hand and smiles, assuring him that it is appropriate.

Later, Tom and Nichelle find themselves separated from the group but continue walking along the beach's edge, holding hands.

The cool ocean water rushes across their lovely feet, and the sea roars from the medium waves in the distance.

Before long, they found themselves near a boulder that waves heavily clash against, causing them to talk a little louder as they walk a few yards under the flimsy pier and into a poorly-lit area, cuddling.

They walk off and eventually reach an even darker point, where roots stick out of the sand, so they turn around.

Nichelle strikes up another conversation, leading to her telling him about her husband when fabricating her cruise to the island when heading under the pier again.

Tom and Nichelle walk, looking at the sand go from dark to pristine, and they are distracted, finding four shadows extending swiftly across the sand, and closing fast.

Four gang members carrying knives, sticks, and chains draw closer while spreading apart. "Give me wallet, jewelry, money," the tallest islander with short dreads shouts in a broad island accent.

"What? Man..., please..., give me a freakin" break," Tom replies, laughing at the man's broken language.

Tom gently back Nichelle toward the water's edge, assuming his favorite karate stance.

Nichelle screams when seeing the tallest, well-built man approach Tom swiftly and within arm's length when Tom kicks the man in the throat twice, forcing him face-first into the sand.

The second man throws a jab at Tom's face with a pocketknife in his tightly balled fist, and Nichelle screams even louder, with the loud waves drowning her cry for help when jumping up and down, waving in the direction of Tom's men.

She looks back for Tom, seeing him dropkick the second guy in the chest and grab the knife.

Tom rushes over to the third man, swiftly breaking his nose when Nichelle screams again, but even louder, while still waving for Tom's men.

The third man backs up with his bloody nose in his hand.

The fourth man helps one of his friends up, and the two begin cursing and swearing in their native tongue.

The taller man pulls the arms of two of his friends, and they stagger toward the dark end of the beach, instantly fading into pure darkness minutes later.

Nichelle runs up from behind Tom, draping her arms around his waist and pressing the side of her face into his back, crying. "Honey, are you ok? Honey!"

"Me?" Tom laughs, then bend, laughing harder while catching his breath. "Yeah, I'm fine..., heck..., that was fun," he says, hee-hawing as if just getting off a thrill ride at a theme park. Tom looks back a few times, making sure the men are gone, and then stops, catching his breath when hitting the light on his watch. "Hey, it's getting pretty late; I'd better get you back to your ship," he says, facing her and drawing closer until he runs a hand down her delicately structured, curved spine, and a chill runs through her hot body.

"I don't have a curfew, dear; besides, I'm a big girl."

They walked a ways further into the more lit area, looking toward the dark sea, spotting huge waves fading in from the darkness.

She cuddles tighter and looks down, somewhat shy, playing with a seashell with her toes until turning it over with the side of her great toe. She turns, looking deep into his eyes, batting them to look bashful when playfully whining. "Hmmm..., maybe we can go back to your room and have a nightcap. You can show me how American men treat foreign women, but nothing intimate. I wouldn't want you to get the wrong impression," she said, batting her long eyelashes again to look even more seductive.

"Mmm..., my kinda (kind of) girl," he responds with a smirk when walking further with his arms around her shoulder until gripping her firm waist tighter, from time to time, enticing her closer.

She runs her hand over his muscular back, massaging him, and then softly leaning into him, gently kissing his neck and sucking on it until it stings a little.

"Aww..., a hickey," he says, smiling then laughing when backing off a little. "I haven't had one of those since what..., seventh grade, but it's still as effective as ever. You know..., you really should be careful about how romantic you're being because one might just take advantage of such a fine woman as yourself," he says, staring into her pretty, baby-blue eyes.

"Really? Umm..., well, maybe I'm giving you an open invitation, sweetie. I'm no little girl, and I think I've told you that before."

They walk down the beach to where her shoes are, and then head up the steps and onto the boardwalk.

Tom faced her so that her back is to the hand railing, slipping his hands to the middle of her firm bottom, palming a handful as she ride back into the railing, pressing her abnormally raised pelvis at his thigh.

Nichelle instantly feels her sheer panties tighten as he draws closer, feeling him grow hard when pressing harder into her upper thigh in a slow grind.

"We'll link up in the morning, Chief!" Oggie yells over the swells when appearing from out of nowhere.

"Cool"! Tom properly responds, backing away from her when bending over and picking up her shoes when the men and women break off in different directions.

Nichelle and Tom arrive at his hotel a little later than the cabbie predicts due to the heavier-than-normal traffic. They pass the front desk when the elevator attendant presses the elevator button.

"Evening, ma'am, sir."

"Evening," Tom responds, watching Nichelle nod and smile, hearing the bell and seeing the door retract with soft music gently rising like a gentle whisper when walking inside.

The young, handsome attendant stands with his hands neatly tucked behind his back, staring at Nichelle and winking when Tom looks away. Tom feels the guy's advances but pretends he's focused on the polished panel when the bell rings.

Nichelle eventually cut her eyes at the young man, blushing until the door shuts.

Tom reaches for her hand instantly, swinging it back and forth when leaning into her ear. "You know..., I would never have guessed you to be such a flirt, Chelle."

"What?" she says, pretending to be clueless.

"You heard me," he says, grinning.

"What..., that young boy? Man, please! I'm old enough to be his damn mother."

"Yeah..., well, that's my point."

"What? That's absurd..., I'm offended by such a ridiculous-ass statement as that." She snatches her hand away.

The elevator bell rings, and the door quietly opens with a gorgeous brunette standing off to the side, waiting for them to exit.

"Alright..., I apologize," he says, holding the elevator door open as she exits, intentionally brushing against him and walking off in the wrong direction.

Tom continues holding the door for the brunette, then walks off, heavily and jokingly clearing his throat. "The room's this way, sweetness," Tom says, waiting for her to turn around.

Nichelle rolls her eyes as she approaches him, trying to look pitiful, when making eye contact with the brunette when she peeks out and jumps back before Tom looks back. "I see you can be such an ass!" She smiles before slightly trying to frown.

"Really..., I'm sorry, babe." He grabs her hand again, pulling her into him and kissing her cheek as she passes. He spanks her gently on her firm bottom, playfully palming it yet releasing her when the brunette walks back off and heads in another direction.

She glows with seductive eye contact. "Where's the room," she asks, giggling.

"Right after this one." He points to the double door with gold-plated handles, passing her and opening it. He switches on the lights, and she floats gracefully inside past him.

"My! So, this is how the royal suite looks? My friends mentioned how nice they were..., umm..., not bad..., not bad at all," she says in deep thought while vigilantly peeping around and barely hearing the elevator bell ring again when the brunette enters.

"Definitely the best I've ever seen and a lot better than most four-stars by a long shot," he says, walking up behind her as she eases off, peeping into the bedroom. "So, what's your preference?" he asks, turning and escorting her over to the bar.

Her eyes continually scroll over the well-stocked selection until pointing to the gin, giggling.

"They say if you're ginning, you're sinning..., so are you planning on a little sinning, because for sin, this gin will make you sin." He chuckles at the senseless comment and then stares at her pretty smile.

"Well, to be honest, it's my favorite, so we have something in common already."

Tom pours their fill, then grabs both glasses and walks through the bedroom door, placing the glasses on the foldout table near the dresser.

"Not to be forward, but do you mind if I slip on one of your shirts and get comfortable?"

Tom smiles and removes a shirt from the closet, draping it on the edge of the bed.

She lifted the shirt with eyes roving over the tags. "You're a big spender, honey," she says, looking at the high price tag dangling from the cuff with eyes going back over her shoulder to him while easing the shirt down.

She does some playful dance and spins out in a stance with her back to him. "Could you unzip me, please," she asks, backing deeper into him until pushing firmly against him in a slow, seductive grind, feeling him press into her fast. "You're such a tease." He slides the zipper down, with sun-tanned skin, slowly exposing it and revealing smooth skin.

"There you are," he says, slightly backing away while growing fast and out of control.

"Thanks, darling," she says, pulling the dress off her shoulders and giggling while looking over her shoulder.

"You sure you don't need any help getting that off?" he asks in a daze, with eyes on curvaceous hips with fingers slipping into her waistband while she tugs at the dress.

"No, I always have a hard time getting this butt in and out of certain things." She stretches the dress over her firm curves until dropping the dress and giggling when looking back and catching him gazing in a semi-trance.

"Nice G-string." He licks and then moistens his lips.

"Honestly? Well, my husband says this butt is too big for a G-string," she says, palming a firm yet delicate cheek in each hand and releasing both simultaneously before tensing each cheek and rotating each up and down as if on a runway at a strip club.

"Damn, babe..., that's a perfect apple bottom if I've ever seen one and boy, do you know how to work it..., damn! Hell..., many women claim to have an apple, but you, my dear, have the perfect apple, and no one would ever question that!"

"Do you really like it, darling?" she asks, grabbing a cheek in each hand, again lifting it and then allowing it to fall, but this time allowing it to jiggle firmly back in place quickly.

"Like it..., is an understatement..., I love it!" he said, bending over, kissing her right cheek, and gently patting it.

"Babe, you've got to stop being so romantic because I'm so damn horny right now. Look..., let me be totally honest with you. I've never had a man so romantic outside or in the bedroom, ever." She pouts.

She motions him to unbutton her bra, and his hands rub her warm flesh, gently massaging her skin while working toward the snaps.

Tom holds one strap out, allowing her to pull one arm out, then the other. He reaches for his silk shirt, opening it wide, gazing at her smooth, soft-looking thighs with deep concentration until snapping out of it. He stares at her nicely curved hips, her slim, tanned waist, and then back up to her firm breast while she takes her time buttoning from bottom to top.

"Umm..., aren't you going to comment on my small knobs?" she snickers in a silly tone.

"Small? Hell, anything more than a handful could sometimes be considered a waste." He kisses her left breast before she can fasten the third-to-last button. "Besides, I'm a pretty pearl, camel-toe, gap, nice, thick-round-bottom type guy," he says, causing her to blush.

"A what?" she responds, senselessly giggling.

"Oh, nothing..., I was just being silly." He uncontrollably laughs.

Nichelle slowly guides her hands between her warm thighs, running her hand over her raised, silk-panty-covered pelvis, which looks like a softball pushed through sheer, black fabric.

Tom reaches for her, slowly unbuttoning the shirt. He fully exposes one breast, staring at the areola expanded into the circumference of the rim of a shot glass.

"You've got me, babe," Nichelle says, slipping into a deep-rooted, sexy language he'd never heard. She grabs him at the inseam with hands, squeezing tight when closing her eyes and slightly nibbling her bottom lip. "No, no, no, I can't do this," she moans in frustration. Her face slightly frowns when childishly stomping. "I just can't..., I mean..., I want to..., no, no..., I need to, but honestly, babe, I need more than just a one-night fantasy screw. You see, right now..., well, you're telling me anything I want to hear so you can get up inside this good loving; and oh yeah, I can promise you, this will not be some of the best, but the very best you've ever had in your life, sweetie. To be honest, honey, this shit is so good, it'll make you wanna (want to) fly home and slap not just your mama, but your grandma, and not just once, but every time you think about how good this was to you," she says, uncontrollably giggling yet being real silly. She takes another sip.

"Naw, really? I mean really?" he excitedly asks. "Then just let me put the tip in," he says jokingly. "Naw..., I'm just kidding, but Nichelle, I do want to be with you."

"Then it's possible for you to wait until I go home and come back, right?" She blushes. "Honey, I'll be back, I promise, and when I do, I'll let you do anything you want, darling..., and I do mean anything," she whispers, leaning deeper into him and gently kissing his lips. She looks deep into his eyes, sliding her tongue deep into his mouth when indulging in yet another deep-throat French kiss.

His tongue quickly warms to her cool, liquor-tasting tongue. "I feel you, babe, and I have to respect your wishes, he says, pretending not to be pissed when mustering up a friendly smile. He walks over and tunes the radio to a jazz station.

Nichelle keeps a curious eye on him, with eyes swarming over his masculine backside. "Thanks," she lowly responds, sliding onto the large, fluffy pillow with her drink. She buttons the shirt, except for the top button, with Tom watching, slowly dropping his tension, knowing there would be no sex, so he tries downplaying his frustration.

Tom turns in deep thought and exits, returning with a bucket of ice and an unopened bottle of gin.

They rested on the covers, indulging in more drinks until Nichelle was tipsy and had nodded off when hearing snoring.

He eases from the bed, leaning back, covering her, and wakes her to have her snuggle on his chest.

Four hours later, Tom eases out, sliding into his pajama pants. He walks over to the big picture window, slightly pulling the curtains back, observing sunrise, then closes them, quickly ordering room service.

Forty minutes later, a sharp knock comes at the door, and Tom jumps, springing from the mattress, waking her. He clutches his robe and .22, slipping it into his pocket unnoticed.

"Room service!" a male voice lightly sounds off.

Tom peeps through the peephole, finding the elevator attendant when relieved and opening the door wide enough to get the decorative cart inside. Tom digs deep in his pocket for a couple of dollars from the money roll, looking back up and back with eyes goggling into the room where the attendant is staring. He freezes, staring at the attendant with stale, then fiery eyes. "Damn..., you sure are nosey!" Tom says, acknowledging that he locked onto Nichelle's beautiful feet and long legs, which slightly hang from the bed. "You..., you..., Get the hell out of here before I get you fired, you little punk!" Tom murmurs under his breath, balling and pushing the healthy tip deep into his pocket.

The attendant backs up further and then rushes toward Tom, executing a last-second fake move at lightning speed, dashing past him with eyes still over his shoulder, inches from the door when slamming into the metal doorframe. Dazed, he scrambled through, lightheaded.

Tom stops in his tracks, uncontrollably bending over in quiet laughter and watching him struggle to gain footing. He grows weak, easing into the chair, still quietly laughing until walking over, and slamming the door shut. He grasps the cart, pushing it toward the room, chuckling and unable to clear his mind until entering the bedroom. "Breakfast time, sweetie!" he says, lifting the tray's cover and watching as she eases onto the large pillows, fluffing them and happily leaning back into them.

The strong aroma of bacon, eggs, and toast fills the room.

After breakfast, she dresses while they continue talking.

"Here's my number," she says, passing him a gold-plated card while quickly looking at her diamond-framed expensive watch.

Nichelle gathers her purse and makeup, sitting it on the dresser and looking into the mirror again before turning to him.

He smiles, leaning into her. "Alright, one more kiss before you go, babe," he

Tainted Obsessions

says, intentionally French-kissing longer until she playfully pulls away and smiles.

Tom begins to slip into something more appropriate when she motions him to stop with her hands, declining his offer to walk her out, so he stays at the door, half-nude and chatting while she waits for the elevator.

The woman in the room across the hall eases from the bed, looking back over her shoulder at her heavily snoring lover, continually listening to the voices in the hallway. She peeks through the peephole with a smile noticing Tom's half-naked when her eyes bulge. She cracks the door open without him noticing, gazing between his legs until lightly drooling with her mouth slowly dropping.

The elevator bell rings, and the door slowly retracts with the room service and the elevator attendant standing nervously and with a smirk, peeping around in anticipation of Tom appearing. His eyes continually browse over her hot body until she looks up and into his eyes, and then back at Tom, waving. She blows Tom a kiss with her hand and walks out of sight.

Tom eases back with eyes finally dead set on the woman when jumping back and barely seeing her fast-motioning hands for her to come to his room when the door clicks.

Tom proceeds over to the big picture window.

Nichelle and the attendant stay pressed against the wall with eyes locked for seconds until breathing hard like raging bulls. Her eyes swarm over the control panel, pulling the emergency stop and forcing the young guy back into the wall. Her tongue sinks deep inside his hot mouth, fondling to feel his arousal, but due to her aggressiveness, there's nothing.

The emergency buzzer sounds off.

The guy somewhat withdraws, too nervous to respond and intimidated by this knockout blonde.

She attempts to guide him into sheer pleasure, but he immediately turns her off, so she backs away, frustrated, and stares into his face, registering the irritating buzzing.

"Sorry," he murmurs with eyes peeled to the floor as if in a daze, embarrassed and looking as if he'd lost his best friend.

"Shit! Sorry is right!" she shouts, rolling her eyes until she stares at the elevator lights and pulls the red stopper to silence the buzzer. She patiently waits for the ride to be over, anxiously tapping her foot a few times.

Tom stays in the window until growing impatient. His eyes meandered over the parking lot longer until dialing Oggie on the Sky-Tel phone.

The elevator's bell rings, and Nichelle walks up to him, toe-to-toe, staring deep into his eyes, not blinking.

The young guy slowly raises his head, finally making contact, gazing into pretty blue eyes until they turn black and empty when he falls abruptly to his knees from a sudden, hard thrust of her knee to his groin. A vein rises in the middle of his forehead as he tries standing but immediately drops, looking up in anger. "What! What in the hell did you go and do that for?" he asks in a pained voice.

Tom comes up on his tiptoes, now looking over the front of the hotel.

Nichelle stares down at him with the meanest look. "What for? Hell..., you're not using it, so I brought the business!" she acknowledges, holding the door open with the buzzer now humming. She stares longer with eyes swarming out the elevator door, not seeing anyone when hacking up a wad and looking again, finding an old couple sitting and staring in disgust. She grows embarrassed, holding it when walking out and briskly strutting across the large lobby, with eyes dead set on the old couple whose eyes stay on her until easing from the seat, with eyes on the young guy's legs as the door closes.

She flies through the door, spitting with a few patrons looking at her in disgust. He picks up her pace with a hand high over her head, waving for her limousine while strutting across the walkway.

"Hey..., hold on, Oggie," Tom says after he finally answers when finally gaining sight of her as she climbs into the backseat of a black limousine. He walks from the window, satisfied, and starts in on a conversation, which leads to him arranging a time to meet the team over at Oggie's room later.

Within seconds, an old, gray-haired woman walks out of the hotel's double doors and climbs in the limousine with Nichelle, throwing the brunette wig to the floor.

Tom ends the call and hangs up with several clicks on the phone, missing them.

In a dungeon-looking room, a Cuban woman sits at the Cuban Headquarters, listening longer until terminating the eavesdropping.

Around 1630, Tony and Bobby show up at Oggie's hotel with Johns already there.

Tom walks in ten minutes later, and they cease their conversations, focusing on Tom. "Hey..., I thought up a little plan to put us in a safe haven until we can get a grip on things and decide what's what!" Tom fiddles around in his pocket, pacing the floor. "One thing for sure, we have to establish a fake Operations Control Center (O.C.C.), so we can reestablish communications with the ship. If they think the mission is a failure, the Command Center will not hesitate to get the approval of assigning another strike team on station and easily from out of Europe."

"You're right, Chief, but where would we set something like that up?" Bobby asks.

"Well, for one..., in that old hotel." Tom pulls the curtains back, pointing across the street. "It's under construction, so there probably aren't many occupants there. We'll need a remote monitoring suite we can monitor from inside this hotel but from above Oggie's room..., Johns, Oggie, here's twenty thousand dollars." Tom pulls the large bundled rolls of large bills from his backpack, passing them to Oggie. "I stopped by the bank earlier and took money out of the equipment overhead. Bobby..., you and Tony reserve a room here above Oggie's, room and across the street, but on a lower level over there so we can have a good downward view into the room."

The four cheerfully exit, and as soon as the door clicks, Tom pulls out his Sky-Tel phone, punching in numbers while walking onto the balcony.

Tamara answers on the third ring.

"Hi, babe," Tom says with eyes gazing down below. "Hey..., did you relay the urgent message to your captain?"

"No..., not yet..., couldn't because all communications circuits were down during radio silencing, but they're reestablishing communications as we speak. Hey..., Nicole has the CONN; so now's even better."

"Alright, I just want to get Terry out of there and get him a proper burial. Hey, look, I'll call you around 1900." He looks down at his wristwatch with eyes still rambling over the streets until finding his men crossing at an intersection.

"P.S, miss you..., bye for now, sweetie," she says, folding the phone shut.

Hours pass with Tom now deep in tears of laughter, watching the new dual comedy, part of LIBERTY CALL..., Port of Spain and now, STITCHES: both written by Azreay'l. He pauses in the middle of laughing, hearing the door's electronic key insertion, and instantly startled when easing up on the back of the chair, removing his gun from his holster. He leans, taking a steady aim with his finger tight on the trigger when one eye closes tight, realigning the shot.

The door cracks open slowly and then flings forcefully back, banging against a floor statue with a glass of liquor, slowly rocking off-balanced until falling the statue's flat surface to the floor as the door retracts halfway.

The stairwell door slightly cracks open with two sets of eyes meandering out; one woman standing and the other kneeling, watching the guys playfully lined up against the hallway and acting silly.

The door closes to a hairline crack, but it's still held in a tightly-gripped fist.

The women begin whispering and smiling, quietly plotting their ambush with Tom's men still quiet and bowing forward in deep, silent laughs.

Bobby laughs the hardest; holding in the burst until it bursts forward, causing the rest of them to burst out in laughter when staggering inside, single-file, in tears, and closing the door.

Tom stares at each of them in disgust as they come into view. "Dumb shit like that'll get you messed up," Tom says, pissed.

The stairwell door flings open abruptly, and the two women spring forward, taking aim and bringing their weapons to shoulder level. Their trigger fingers ride hard against the triggers when advancing down the hall, swiftly looking around and taking cover through another stairwell door, stopping on the stairwell's porch.

They continued giggling for minutes, trying to get most of the laughter out, and when somewhat calmer, they join in, setting up the equipment. They work diligently for hours, ensuring the equipment works together, and then dismantle it, restacking things in a hard side case or leather transport carry cases.

Hours pass until finally, they establish communications and live-circuit camera coverage.

Tom stands in the background, noticing Tony and Bobby excessively playing with the camera's monitors. "Alright..., enough! Let's put it on auto and record."

Minutes later, Oggie and Johns entered.

"Man, this suite is awesome," Johns excitedly says, pulling a seat up to the table and staring deep into the twenty-seven-inch monitor. "What's next, Chief?" Oggie asks with inquisitive eyes.

"Well, first, we need to flood the ship with fake coordinates so they can't pinpoint us, but at the same time, we can get valuable information passed along. Also, we need to set up a satellite tracker near the window for early warning," Tom says, walking up to the window and looking up at the sky. "We must ensure the ship is not targeting our movement as well."

"I thought the same but didn't mention anything around the ensign," Oggie says, staring at the screen and refocusing on the camera, slowly scanning in a three-hundred-sixty-degree radius, in the other hotel.

Ensign Haun jogs through the passageway at a slow pace, reaching the bridge and spotting Ensign Jones scanning the surface for other seagoing vessels, then the air for low-flying crafts, reported earlier. She walks up next to her quietly for seconds until Nicole notices that she's there.

"Nicole..., Terry's dead,"

"What! What do you mean dead? What happened?" she anxiously asks, dropping the mini binoculars to her chest and allowing them to dangle on the nylon strap. She felt nauseated.

Tamara scans the ocean in deep thought, thinking of what to say next, yet keep Nicole from asking about Tom or why Tom would leave her his phone. Her eyes light up when a clever thought comes. "Hey, look, Tom somehow got through to Radio Central but didn't give details. He said we have to get Terry's body out of there ASAP! So look..., I'll let Captain Pierite know one of our guys took a hit and then provide the coordinates that Tom passed along," Tamara says, hugging Nicole to comfort her when a tear rolls down her cheek. Tamara stands around a little longer and then peels off.

Tamara shows up outside her captain's cabin, straightening her sharply-creased uniform when coming to attention, but before she can knock, the door swings open swiftly.

The captain's wide eyes dim when backing back inside and motioning her forward, with Tamara expressly spilling the information as if well-rehearsed, then handing him the coordinates on a sticky note.

The captain down jots a few notes and leans forward for the phone, calling the bridge to have an announcement made for Strike Force One's Commanding Officer and Executive Officer to report to his at-sea cabin.

The PA system key up seconds later with medium squelch when the Officer of the Deck makes the announcement.

Captain Carrington and the lieutenant are in the stateroom eating ice cream and cake in silence when the announcement comes, curiously looking at each other until looking confused.

"Shall we?" Captain Carrington anxiously asks, hesitantly springing up, hoping to get the cuffs off, maybe a chance to escape or just notify someone of the coercion.

"Yeah, but look, none of that fancy crap!" The lieutenant digs deep in his pocket, then deeper, nervously un-cuffing him.

They exit swiftly, making their way through the back passageways, rushing up on the ship captain's door; both almost out of breath from the swift ladder climbing.

The lieutenant knocks three times and enters when told to enter.

Evening, Captain Carrington, Lieutenant," the commanding officer says, nodding and greeting them with firm handshakes before sitting with surprised eyes. "Gentlemen, two of my officers overheard a faint Mayday over V.H.F. The emergency sounded as if it might have been one of our boys, and they mentioned a man is dead," Captain Pierite anxiously says, passing Captain Carrington the coordinates when walking them over the operational area map.

"Did they say who?" Captain Carrington asks with sad eyes.

"No..., no..., it was a brief transmission; besides, they would know better than to divulge that classified information over a secure circuit, huh?"

Captain Carrington stares into space, trying to remember if he'd seen the coordinates on the map earlier or if it was coded by one of his men when drawing a blank. He breaks his concentration instantly, noticing that the lieutenant is in deep thought when attempting Morse code, but stops when the lieutenant becomes more observant.

Captain Pierite keeps alternating eyes on both of them, awaiting some kind of response. "Well, Captain, will there be problems extracting the men from the operations area immediately?" Captain Pierite looks over at Captain Carrington, who has just taken a deep swallow.

The lieutenant keeps his eyes glued on the floor with his mind spinning until a frown comes. "Things have just started, so no extraction is required. We have to carry out this mission, or we're doomed. Captain, we must call headquarters!" the lieutenant mumbles, standing over Captain Carrington while the captain's slithering into a chair. "Now, captain!" he shouts, somewhat nervously.

Captain Carrington cuts his eyes over at Captain Pierite, finding him in shock from the insubordination yet tensed and waiting for Captain Carrington to tear the lieutenant a new one. "Thanks, Captain Pierite." Captain Carrington shoots up, wobbling a little from the ship's abrupt change of course before leveling back out. He steps toward the door, and the lieutenant slightly shoves him in the back as the door shuts, leaving Captain Pierite unsure of what he saw, so he ignores the sign.

"Damnait, I want to make this damn call now..., not later," the lieutenant snarls.

"You'll get to make your call, you pathetic little cockroach! I won't delay anything, now, will I?" The captain stumbles into the room onto the floor, forcefully shoved and then clipped by the lieutenant's fancy footwork.

"Hmmm..., do you think this is a damn game? One more call concerning your resistance, and BLAM!" the lieutenant yells lowly, removing his trigger finger from the captain's protruding temple.

The lieutenant reaches for his hidden gun with a silencer from his pillow, unnoticed, sticking the gun in his jacket pocket and grabbing the handcuffs from the desk drawer. He continually swirls the cuffs around on his index finger. "Get your sweet little ass over here and turn around!" The lieutenant briefly stops the cuffs in the palm of his hand. "I said get your sweet ass over here now! Damn you! Don't screw with me, Captain!"

Captain Carrington stays eye-to-eye until the lieutenant goes out of view. He accurately judges the lieutenant's distance through the mirror, tightening his tightly sprung arm and swinging his right elbow back with brute force. His devastating blow connects with the lieutenant's temple, causing him to stumble backward when coming up high, swiftly executing a roundhouse kick, knocking the lieutenant's head into the steel doorframe, and rendering him somewhat unconscious.

The captain's eyes float down to the secure phone, slamming it to the deck several times until destroying the phone's cryptographic components beyond recognition. He angrily stomps the phone one last time and picks up the diamond chip, looking back when hearing the lieutenant moaning. He immediately pivots, finding the lieutenant struggling to get something shiny out of his pocket, quickly realizing it's a gun when calculating the distance and knowing he's unable to counter the attack in time when running to the door.

Two metal rattling, silenced rounds sound off almost simultaneously; the second round grazes the captain's right arm when darting into the hallway, indecisive of his direction. He slams the door shut.

A heavy rattling comes at the door's knob, then a click when the lieutenant's head barely pops out at the door handle, quickly looking to the left and right when he slams the door shut. He eases into the desk's edge, plotting out his unplanned backup plan.

Captain Carrington's momentum slows with eyes clued behind him, scanning his surroundings when dashing up the steep ladder well. His feet hit the next deck, and he comes up to top speed, making his way to Captain Pierite's at-sea cabin door, bursting through with brute force, and almost out of breath.

"What the hell, man!" Captain Pierite nervously screams, springing up and slamming his back into the bulkhead with eyes wide and rolling over Captain Carrington's bloody shirt. "

Captain Carrington slams his back into the door with fearful eyes. "Sir, you have to set a security alert immediately! The lieutenant is armed and dangerous!" he screams.

Captain Pierite props a metal chair against the door, locking it and dialing the bridge in hands-free mode.

Seconds later, the public announcement (P.A.) system sounds loud and clear throughout the ship. "Security alerts! Security alerts! Security alert on stateroom four! All hands not involved with the security alert stand fast! The security reason is an armed person: Strike Force Executive Officer Lieutenant Smith! This is not a drill! I say again..., Security alert! Security alert! Security alert on stateroom four! All hands not involved with the security alert stand fast! Security reason is an armed person: Strike Force Executive Officer Lieutenant Smith!" the Second Class Boatswain's Mate nervously screams.

The lieutenant burst through the door, hearing the full transmission, heading for the closest armory, realizing that if he's to survive, he has to overtake the security team before they draw their weapons.

Now, the lieutenant is totally dedicated to this mission because it is the biggest payday ever..., permanent retirement kids of pay. Also, he's determined not to fail his tasks given by shady officials; all officials deemed most honorable.

Captain Pierite removes his .45 from his security safe, strapping it on, Western style, and then donning his shorter-than-regulation bulletproof vest. His eyes drift over his shoulder, glued on the knife when pulling it out and handing it to Captain Carrington, both fearfully discussing a quick contingency plan.

The lieutenant anxiously waits in the dark corridor, watching four men approach, halfway out of their clothes and still dressing, fighting zippers and lacing boots. He backs deeper into a corner, anxiously waiting for all of them to enter, then rushes up, slinging the vault door back, spraying un-aimed, silenced rounds from the automatic weapon.

Their loud, dreadful screams echo loudly through distant passageways, the stray rounds penetrating bodies when continually ricocheting off steel bulkheads in a continual whirlwind until exhausted.

The Security Forces team leader finally shows up, stopping at the top of the ladder after hearing more muffled gunfire and death-defying screams. He turns back, signaling other security members who are swiftly approaching to go back when the remainder of the security team regroups, heading for the mess decks, where the team leader calls the bridge, making an urgent report and requesting permission to use the aft armory to reassemble the team and draw weapons.

Azreay'l

Captain Carrington heads for the radio room for the next-to-last secure phone, and Captain Pierite stuffs his cabin's phone in a security safe, leaving the door open while bending, picking up a few rounds that fell to the floor before turning to the safe.

A loud, thunder-like sound comes when the door's locking mechanism shatter, scattering across the room from the lieutenant's abrupt dropkick. Captain Pierite reaches for his gun and sloppily falls into the lockers with a single round striking him at the waist.

Captain Carrington hears ricocheting from the metal locker when freezing in his tracks with eyes nervously scanning the passageway ahead. He presses his back against the door, pulling the knife out and slipping the blade between his teeth.

Captain Pierite slides upward against metal lockers until he's almost on his feet when standing limp against the locker for as long as he can and sliding down, tensed. He clenches his teeth tight, with a finger still on the trigger when trying to stand again, and accidentally squeezes off a delayed round with the gun still in the holster.

The bullet penetrates the metal locker, and the gun freely falls outside an arm's reach.

The lieutenant looks for Captain Carrington with eyes quickly over his shoulder several times when taking tense steps toward the captain. His foot slid hesitantly forward, looking back again when kicking the gun further away, then snatches it fast, emptying it. He looks around quick, jerking his hand when throwing it behind the strong, seaworthy, and secured desk fastened to the wall.

Captain Carrington hesitantly creeps up near the captain's cabin with fast-scanning eyes. He veers off quickly, easing up to a power distribution panel and gazing over it until opening it. He tries figuring out which switch controls the passageway lights. He studies it a second longer, unable to make out the faded diagram. He leans in, quickly flipping four switches and de-energizing the lights in adjacent passageways, making it pitch-black with eyes slightly adjusting from the light shining upward through a scuttle, from the lower decks.

Captain Carrington slides around the corner, quickly closing in on the ship C.O.'s door as fast as possible, and when turning the last corner, he spots a small beam of light through the captain's smashed door. He tiptoes closer and finally sees the lieutenant bent over and concentrating on the secure phone's junction box.

Within seconds, there's a soft click from the phone's jack securing in the junction box when the secure phone's lights begin rapidly recycling to activation mode.

Captain Carrington draws closer and finally hears Captain Pierite moaning in a painful whisper, but he can't see him.

The lieutenant anxiously pushes numbers, and then hangs up, redialing. "What the hell is wrong with this damn phone…, is it password protected?" the lieutenant screams, aiming the gun at Captain Pierite's stomach and slowly coming up to his chest.

Captain Pierite slowly maneuvers and reclines on his back and flat against the floor when moving more until slowly propping his head up against the locker. "I don't know," Captain Pierite acknowledged, frowning in more pain yet pretending to cough so hard a few times that he couldn't talk.

"Damn it!" the lieutenant screams, nervously aiming at the captain's head now with a trembling hand. He tightens his grip on the gun with his index finger slightly pressing on the trigger.

Captain Pierite's eyes slightly roll backward intentionally and then go stale, in fear of dying, so he keeps his eyes closed and breaths slower, sometimes holding his breath in long intervals.

Captain Carrington reaches up high on tiptoes, feeling around in the overhead cabling when sticking the knife between his teeth again. He gets a good grip on the cables, swinging lightly until viciously swinging back and forth and latching his feet around the cabling. The captain maneuvers, clinging to the wire harness, and maneuvers more until his back is parallel with the floor when slowly advancing. He holds on tight when coming upon brackets, bracing his feet in the well-structured angle iron, mildly straining when pushing up, and securely locking himself in the wiring harness.

"Damn this..., I'll just use the one in radio central!" the lieutenant shouts when looking back at the captain, whose eyes stay barely cracked open and stale. The lieutenant waves the gun over the captain's body until, aiming for a direct headshot. A mean frown unfolds until his face clears when he squeezes off a loosely precision round, hitting the captain in the left side of his chest.

The captain moans and then cringes, with eyes stale and piercing upward.

The lieutenant cut the lights off and peeped out, slowly creeping into the passageway, listening while taking a few small steps. He stops, hearing something pop lightly, and looks around, listening again.

Captain Carrington strains with all that is in him, feeling himself slipping when straining more when the cables yawn as if about to snap when Captain Carrington breaks wind, and the scent does not hesitate to give off its pungent scent.

The lieutenant frowns, bringing an elbow to his nose when frowning more with the cable louder this time when eyes go up, and the dark manly silhouette instantly drops in an express turn.

Captain Carrington clobbers him, dropping him limp to the floor and causing the gun to fall freely and slide a few feet across the dark deck.

A thin beam of light instantly pierces through Captain Pierite's cracked door, partially lighting the passageway with him struggling to balance against his desk.

The two wrestled back and forth with the knife in the narrow passageway. The lieutenant initially gets the best of the captain, and then vice versa, as they struggle for what seems like an eternity.

Now, with victory in both their minds, they grow exhausted fast from the fierce blows they are administering to one another.

Suddenly, the captain manages to get a few more good whacks in until the lieutenant strikes Captain Carrington in the temple with a fierce blow, almost knocking him out.

Captain Carrington quickly regains strength while the lieutenant continually struggles to free the knife from his hand.

The lieutenant climbs on top of Captain Carrington with one more last roll, pinning him, then slowly rocking the sharp, shiny blade back and forth, trying to penetrate his heart. He continually rocks more, and the knife barely touches the captain's uniform, and then presses hard upon his flesh until it slightly breaks the skin.

The ship captain's legs kick, lying face down, stretching to get the gun and bullet when sitting fast, loading the gun, and then jumping up and throwing the door wide open.

Bright lights instantly light most of the passageway when hearing heavier moans, grows, and cursing.

Sweat continually rolls into Captain Carrington's eyes when the pinpoint of the blade slightly penetrates his flesh a second time, but deeper. The point drives deeper until it slightly scrapes the bone.

The lieutenant grows greedy and strains harder from resistance, thinking the blade is deeper when turning it to the left and right.

A loud, single shot rings out, and the lieutenant's body grows weak and fast.

Captain Carrington punches the lieutenant in the face with three good whacks, easily gaining control of the knife. He snatches the lieutenant up in the collar and pushes him onto his back, jumping to his feet with eyes roaming over the floor for the gun.

Captain Carrington looks toward the light with blurred vision, finding the ship captain's shadow extended with his gun still drawn as his vision slowly clears with a smile. He leans back, leaping over the lieutenant's body toward Captain Pierite when the lieutenant musters up all the strength in his body when lunging out with one last death-defying swipe for the captain's ankles but misses by inches.

Captain Carrington tilts forward, riding high on one foot when turning the tip of his raised foot, thrusting it deep into the lieutenant's stomach and causing him to ball up in the fetal position and cough up blood.

The lieutenant's body retracts, stretching back out, with his body jerking and rolling when Captain Carrington's shuffling feet continually hit the deck, maneuvered to retrieve the lieutenant's gun.

"Are you ok, Skipper?" Captain Carrington asks Captain Pierite while pushing the gun inside the back of his trouser.

"I'll be fine, but next time, I'll take the Supply Officer and Doc's advice on wearing a much longer vest. Hell..., I only chose this one because it is comfortable for sitting, but damn that!" He grins and then frowns in pain.

Perspiration quickly grows over the ship captain's face while Captain Carrington guides him to his chair.

Captain Carrington drops down in the other chair and looks after his bloody knife and a pained gunshot wound.

Captain Pierite reaches for the phone, calling the bridge. He secures the ship from the security incident and dispatches the medical team to care for the wounded. He eases to his feet, heavily breathing when opening the first-aid kit above his desk and then dropping back into the seat.

Captain Pierite's eyes go stale in deep concern when asking Captain Carrington about distracting the men again when Ensign Haun walks up.

Captain Carrington sees her first. "Excuse me, Ensign..., was there something you wanted to say," Captain Carrington asks, slyly cutting his eyes at the ship's captain when Captain Pierite looks away to tend to his wound.

"Sir..., I have the chief's cellular phone," she says, reaching for her belt loop. "He asked me to give it to you," she says, handing it to him when he secretly strokes her soft hand until she nervously withdraws when her captain looks up.

"This is great!" Captain Carrington says, making sure Captain Pierite isn't looking when winking and gesturing a silent kiss that leaves her looking away and over blushing.

The PA system keys up, asking Tamara to report to the bridge, and when heard, she walks away, forgetting to mention Tom's number is attached to the back of the phone.

The lieutenant continually tries slowing his breathing while not moving, though in excruciating pain and growing weaker by the second. He lies attentively, listening to the two captains go back and forth for minutes. He quietly leans to one side with a hand sliding into his waistband, pulling out a small gun, and the other hand covers his wound as he sits up quietly. He struggles to stand, a little dizzy but quietly leans against the bulkhead, moving closer to the captain's door. His vision worsens when raising the gun, and he can barely bring Captain Pierite in his aim when limping once more, taking a more direct aim, when abrupt gunfire rings out. Automatic rounds continually penetrated his back, frantically shaking while falling into the bulkhead.

Both captains jerk with hands tight over their faces with knees rose high, screaming.

The lieutenant instantly drops forward and to the floor.

The Chief Master-at-Arms stands frozen in a standing prone stance.

At the hotel across from Oggie's hotel, outside the fake control room, two Cuban men dressed in maintenance attire walk around with small handheld voice monitors and two types of electronic handheld devices. The tall Cuban tampers with the door while the short Cuban slides a mirror-type device under the door. The tall Cuban rechecks the handheld electronic tracking equipment's coordinates until pushing another button on the device and verifying the navigational inputs from the transmissions made when Tom's men tested the control room equipment earlier. For seconds, he looks down at an electronic device, which looks like a palm-sized calculator. He stares at the five joined crystals, pressing the uplink button to update the location of Tom and his men's Sky-Tel phones. "This is it!" the tall Cuban whispers while the other Cuban looks through a bore scope. "No one's inside!" he declares.

Oggie accidentally adjusts the volume, thinking he heard voices in the background. "It's a monitoring room of some sort. Hell, we'll make them come to us!" the tall Cuban says.

Oggie rushes to readjust the volume to a point where the receiver almost pegs out to a loud squelch when pressing the headset closer to see if he can replicate the voices again.

The tall Cuban watches the camera while the other Cuban runs a few doors down, placing his hand over the fire alarm. He makes frequent eye contact, patiently waiting for the camera to sweep away when motioning his partner with a stern thumbs up when pulling the alarm.

"Damn!" Oggie screams, throwing the headset to the floor and grabbing his heavily ringing ears.

Several patrons pour into the hall with their ears covered when rushing for the stairwell.

A few intrusive patrons rush by and stare at the two men, who suspiciously look back.

The Cubans wait until the hall clears when jamming a device in the door's lock. They patiently wait for the camera to scan away again and then swiftly enter, quickly spraying the camera's lens with a thick, slow-dissolving, sensitive film.

"Damn..., what now!" Tom screams, thinking that maybe his eyes are playing tricks when seeing the two shadows ducking and vanishing with shadowy projections against the wall.

Tom and his men patiently wait for the camera to scan over by the balcony when quick glare flashes across the wall and the monitor before the screen grows dark in a slow, downward motion, clearly displaying the room again.

The short man reaches quickly for the wall, energizing bright lights.

The loud fire alarm continues blaring from Oggie's headset until disconnected with the volume rest.

Oggie notices light at the bottom of the screen before it disappears and reaches over in a flash, switching the equipment's knob to infrared. "Damn..., what next!" Oggie shouts, looking into the dark screen.

The team gathered around instantly and closely, watching the dark screen.

"Hmm..., the fire alarm must have blacked out the power. I'll go over and reset it after the police and firefighters leave." Johns looks over the rest of the gear's monitoring displays, which have normal readings.

Twenty minutes after the firefighters arrived, the alarm ceases.

CHAPTER FIVE: ISLAND OF ECSTACY

Johns waits well over thirty minutes and then tucks his gun under his windbreaker, darting out of the room.

Oggie continually manipulates the controls to see if he can resolve the camera's problem before Johns reaches the other hotel room.

The tall Cuban exits the room, running across the hall and hiding in the maintenance room.

The short Cuban picks the lock to the vacant room next door and slips inside with his back against the room's door, with his heart pounding as he looks down at the tracking device, noticing that one of the dots has broken off from the others. He pushed away from the door with great force, rushing to the window, looking over the busy intersection, and finding Johns at the red-light controlled intersection. He spots a police cruiser quickly pulling up and skidding wheels with blue lights flashing.

After some time has passed, Oggie notices the picture clearing faster from the top down, but not really giving it much thought. "Hot damn..., Johns knows his stuff! The camera's fine now!" Oggie said, not considering the fact that the lights were on now, either.

Outside the ship captain's cabin, on the ship, the Chief Corpsman and a few enlisted men from the security team maneuver around in preparation for removing the lieutenant's body.

"Hmm..., I wonder where the hell my X.O. and Operations Officer are..., they should've been up here by now. Hell..., I need to put this first-aid kit down and work on this incident's initial voice and message traffic!" Captain Pierite says, shoving the kit to Captain Carrington when seeing him looking inside his open, stained shirt and rolling his sleeve up.

"Sure, sir, but I highly recommend delaying and keeping the initial report generic because this mission is tainted! We don't want to give away information that the lieutenant's accomplices can act upon because, for sure, he's not working alone!" Captain Carrington says, deeply thinking while his eyes scroll over various sizes of bandages in the first-aid kit.

"Yes, of course, and for the safety of your men," he said, slouching in the chair.

"Are you ok?" he asks, seeing Captain Carrington rip open a few bandages and shove them down his shirt when nodding 'yes.' "We'll both go down and see Doc Wellington when they've had time to care for the others. "

"That would be great; besides, mine is not that serious, just a deep cut, but it's not bleeding bad anymore." Captain Carrington strains when applying more pressure.

Tom stands looking at his watch, pulling the phone out, and dialing back in Oggie's hotel with it ringing a time or two.

"Hello..., Tom!"

"Captain..., Captain Carrington!" Tom says in joy.

"'Why, yes..., yes..., tell me..., what's going on out there, Chief?"

"No, sir, the question is, what's going on with you?" Tom responds sarcastically.

"Ensign Terry's dead, as you must know by now!"

"Yes, yes, I know that someone was dead, but I didn't know who. The transmission came in garbled, or so the ship's captain told me,' he says, curiously cutting his eyes over at the captain and then looking down. "But wait..., I can explain everything..., I was under duress! Several times, I tried signaling the ensign, but it was a lost cause. Eventually, I realized I had to play along with the lieutenant's games to prevent harm from coming to our families!"

"Aye-aye, Captain, but now what, and what's with the lieutenant?" Tom asks.

"Dead. Dead as hell! Captain Pierite and his security team put that poor bastard out of his misery!"

"Well, sir, our primary communication is on the back of my phone!"

"Ok!" He flips the phone over, quickly bringing it back to his ear. "Hey, I have a friend there, Major Fields, whom you served with some time ago."

"Yes sir, I remember him..., I practically owe the man my life." Tom instantly thinks about the Major and reminisces on his encounter with death and the major saving his life. "The only problem is he's one of them!" Tom mumbles, thinking out loud.

Captain Carrington doesn't recognize Tom means his friend, the major, was of the opposing forces. "Well, he owes me a big favor. The last time we spoke, he tried to get me down here to help run some special operations," he says trying to recall the name of it. "Ah, ah, ah..., the Underground, I believe."

"What? Wait! Did you say Underground? That's where Strike Force Two personnel are being held, hostage. That's the outfit we're to eliminate, along with Major Fields, per the tasking order!"

"What? Wait..., no, no, no! Wait, Tom. There must be a misunderstanding. The intelligence information the lieutenant provided me was of another organization, War Fighters, or something of that nature. Anyway, I'll get back to you; I promise you can trust me on this, Chief!"

" Well, sir, he must have double-briefed to cover something up. For sure, he mentioned the major and my having dealt with him. For sure..., it was gut-wrenching to hear him mention the Major, but anyway, I'll be waiting for your call, sir..., Chief Powells, out!" Tom says, terminating the call.

Johns covers his ears, riding the elevator up anxiously when walking out whistling a jazz tune until taking off in a sprint.

The tall Cuban man presses an uplink button on the handheld monitoring device, noticing one crystal moving quickly to the middle of the screen. He cracks the door, peeking out again, and hears Johns' boots slamming into the carpet when slowing and then coming to an abrupt stop outside the door.

Johns' nervous eyes swarm over the door's frame with caution.

The tall Cuban closes the door until there's just a needle-sized crack in the seam, and he's barely able to see Johns. He eases the door closer, pulling a thin wire from his pocket and quickly unraveling it, then wraps it tightly around both gloved hands. With brute strength, he tightly snaps the wire apart a few times, and then slowly opens the door with Johns gone.

Johns presses his back against the monitoring room's door until it lightly clicks, and instantly, he freezes in his tracks, finding green, thick slime dripping to the floor from the base of the camera's lens. He immediately recalls not having to turn on the overhead lights when the thought flashes in his head. "Compromise!" Johns screams, instantly drawing his weapon. The muzzle of his weapon slowly sweeps around in a three-hundred-sixty-degree radius.

"Johns, get the hell out of there! Get out of there, now!" Oggie nervously screams.

The short Cuban overhears Oggie's loud scream, and without delay, he dashes through the balcony's door, swiftly maneuvering over the low-cut partition. His hand digs through his small leather handbag, quietly gluing two gray C4 packets alongside the door's frame.

Johns begins slowly moving about the room, with his shadow extending through the sheer curtains. He works his way over, backing up to the balcony and looking over his shoulder at the curtains.

The short Cuban's eyes widened, seeing the shadow extending slowly and outward across the half-sun-exposed porch.

The tall Cuban exits the maintenance room after receiving chirps on his phone. He ran down the long hallway at top speed, almost colliding with a sleepy-eyed young lady who had just stepped out from around the corner with her little child.

The tall Cuban and the woman's ears stay slightly covered when he drifts quickly to one side in an attempt to miss the two, maybe a three-year-old little girl. He dances back and forth expressly until going forward fast and unintentionally knocking the child down but keeps running while continually looking over his shoulder. He dodged into an adjacent hallway.

The child abruptly rolls from side to side, screaming until her mother lifts her and brushes her dress down; finally covering the child's ears when her face turns bright red.

The mother's mind fills with all sorts of curse words, but she refrains from screaming. For seconds, the mother stares back at the upper corner of the door, trying to make out what is protruding into the hallway against the door's frame, and thinking the worst, she quickly distances herself, fearing it's a gun.

"Is she ok?" an old, concerned couple asks, expressly intercepting the woman and child outside the monitoring room with their ears slightly covered.

"Oh, yes..., she'll be fine," the mother responds, kissing her daughter's flushed cheeks.

Tony immediately notices movement on the balcony behind Johns when the camera scans past. He turns swiftly with eyes piercing through sheer curtains until he rushes up, pulls the curtains back, and lifts his binoculars.

"Someone's on the balcony!" Tony shouts, thoroughly scanning the balcony. "What the..., it's C4!" he screams, gazing over the too-familiar packets when staring back at Oggie.

The short Cuban hears their loud voices over even louder monitoring speakers, scrambling back across the low partition and easing back into the room.

Johns trains his weapon on the balcony, slowly backing away.

Bobby's hands rapidly and nervously pat against his pants pockets and then his upper body. He reaches for his weapon, tucking it inside his jacket, doing some hand sign to Tom when storming out.

"Johns..., C4! Someone's on the balcony. Get the hell out of there right now! Now! Johns, damn it! Hurry!" Oggie screams.

Oggie flips a switch and begins manually controlling the camera, keeping it trained on Johns' movement.

Tony tucks his gun inside his jacket, motioning hand signals to Tom when sprinting out.

Minutes later, Tony's finally able to catch up with Bobby near the busy street where the police are directing the congested traffic.

They quickly cross the street, looking up to see the man peeping through the balcony door.

Johns backed up against the door with hands drifting down the side of the door until grabbing the doorknob and cracking the door open with abrupt, near-silenced rounds spraying the doorframe, some rounds hitting the wall, splintering wood and metal.

The three adults drop to the floor, screaming a dreadful, loud cry for help.

The little girl stands looking in fear and fluttering and then screams when the next barrage comes.

Another long burst of firepower comes, shattering more of the door's frame when the child's mother finally sees her standing and nervously reaches, snatching her down.

The child fearfully burst into a deep scream, trembling.

Johns lowers against the wall when several more rounds whistle past in a sporadic spray, barely missing the door. "People are screaming out there!" Johns nervously acknowledges, somewhat in a daze. His heart beats faster, and his mind drifts to his wife and unborn child.

"Johns..., just stay down! Tony and Bobby are on the way!" Oggie yells.

Tom's cell phone rings, and he backs away, gazing into the big screen to find Johns anxiously rocking back and forth with his head tucked between his knees.

Oggie keeps the camera's lens zooming in and out on John's for seconds, and then begins zooming again.

Tom finally answers, bringing the phone up and quietly holding it for seconds.

"Tom, are you there? Tom..., this is Captain Carrington..., look, Major Fields and his men are positioning now to take out the Cubans soon. I don't have the details, but the Cubans are behind this whole plot!"

When Johns finally registers the type of weapon it is, a barrage of fire hits the door, and his mind goes haywire, expressly recalculating the rounds expended. He thinks longer until assuming there are only ten left before the reload. He swiftly stands, anticipating the next burst, in hopes of escaping.

"Tom!"

"Yes, sir," Tom responds, pulling the phone to his ear when hearing the captain's faint voice.

Oggie grows impatient, with fingers nervously tapping on the table's edge to calm his nerves until a loud blast comes over the speaker. His fingers go in slow motion until frozen and lightly trembling, then vibrating microseconds later, causing him to yank his headset off about the same time the screen blanks out. His fingers grip the vibrating table again until it heavily shakes when jumping and trying to support the moving equipment.

The elevator door opens and jams.

Lights flicker, and plaster sprays deep inside the elevator's doorway and shaft. The doors slowly retracted about halfway.

Oggie stares deep into the big vibrating window, settling back in disbelief, and covering his ears from the loud, increasing ringing.

Tom focuses on a full glass of water on the table, which, after rippling, has started to stabilize.

Tony and Bobby slowly stand in disbelief.

The elevator bounces a little, with cable yawning as if about to snap. Tony and Bobby low-crawled to the edge of the door, looking to the right to find a tall man running toward the far exit of the hallway.

Tony jumps up, grabs Bobby by his jacket, and pulls him to his feet when they lunge forward, heavily covered in white plaster. Their faces and clothes stay covered with thick globs of plaster that continually drops from them as they run down the long hallway, at top speed.

Tom and Oggie close in on the large picture window, shocked by the heavy debris still falling on the pedestrians scattered below to quickly clear the building.

"Tom, what is it?" the captain screams, finally registering the speaker's sounds and static.

Tom stands confused and soon hears the phone's amplified keys continually pressed when backing up and slowly pulling the phone to his ear. Tears roll down his cheeks. "Somebody's going to pay dearly, Captain!" he declares in an angered voice. "Damn..., it's Johns! He was in the hotel setup with our command and control gear, just blown away with C4!"

Tony and Bobby stand at the stairwell with their ears pressed to the door until Tony slowly opens it. They scanned the ladder well until fast-paced footsteps and the mild chanting of foreign voices in their ears.

Suddenly, a door below them slams.

Bobby pushes the door open, and they run down the first flight of stairs at top speed.

They slow down at each corner, picking up their pace until reaching the next to last set of steps, where they slow down again.

Tom stands with the phone to his ear, in a daze.

"Did you hear what I said about Major Fields' team being in the position to take out the Cuban forces?" the captain asks. "The Cubans are behind this whole plot!"

"Aye-aye, sir," Tom says in a daze and with a heavy heart when a tear drops. He stares at the phone, unconcerned when pressing the red button and ending the call.

Tony and Bobby peep through the exit and then rush into the parking lot after hearing a car's wheels squealing.

The black limousine continually skids across the lightly graveled lot until fishtailing, steadying, and straightening when increasing speed.

With precision-trained weapons at shoulder level, Tony and Bobby hurriedly aim, and then quickly disengage when pedestrians run in the crosshairs, clearing the car's path.

Frustrated, they turn, looking back at the building, and hearing distant sirens closing fast when taking off in a sprint toward the loud, fire-alarmed building.

From the back of the hotel, they see a thin trail of thick, black smoke rising over the room and coming from the front of the hotel.

At stealth speed, they make their way up the back fire escape, rushing past a few firefighters further down the hallway who screams for them to exit and then veer off.

They enter the floor of the O.C.C. and close in on the monitoring room when Bobby is stopped by Tony.

"Clear these people out of here while I get Johns' things!" Bobby yells above the loud alarm while staring into the concerned faces of non-compliant guests, finally exiting and nervously gathering around the four covered bodies.

"Excuse me, everyone! You have to clear the building. We think there's another bomb set to go off any moment!" Tony shouts, barely heard over the loud alarm when the people scream and, like ghosts, disperse as if never there.

Bobby peeps through the busted door into the smoke and dust-filled room. He heavily pushes his shoulder against the splintered, jammed door a few times and then leans into it with brute force. With one last push, he forces the damaged equipment and some of Johns' body between the mangled door and crushed wall.

He fans thick, plaster dust and smoke from his face in the war-torn, smoke-filled room, slowly advancing and fearfully when inching up on Johns.

"Hey, Bobby!" Johns says, coughing with dust-filled lungs, lying on his back, and breathing hard to remain conscious. He grits his teeth and holds the makeshift waist tourniquet in both hands, from time to time, twisting the tourniquet with weak strength, causing blood to gush out of his main artery while growing weaker slowly.

"I need you to hang in there, man," Bobby calmly says, removing Johns' tag from his upper body, which is intact but dislocated at the waist. Bobby looks around for his other body part and finds his identification tag standing upright but tilted in another corner.

"Hang in there, huh?" Johns said, slowly blinking and sweating profusely, when finally seeing a boot with part of a leg extending from it, becoming delusional when his mind expressly drifts, and he calls into question whether his eyes are playing tricks when looking drunk and smiling. "I know I'll never see my little girl, Bobby," he says with tears filling his eyes until even his dislocated leg becomes blurry.

"Sure you will! A cheerful ten-pound bouncing little girl," Bobby says at once, remembering Johns' baby's last reported weight and adding the cheerful word to make it more welcoming.

"Come on, Bobby..., you're kidding me, right?" He coughs up thick chunks of blood, then dry-coughs non-stop until smiling until his face becomes stale with eyes frozen open.

Tony continually looks up and down both sides of the hallway, training his weapon at the slightest sounds until tense with a finger barely pressing on the trigger.

"Bobby, hurry before island authorities come!" Tony mutters, vigilantly looking around and then down at the covered bodies with legs extending from under the covers. He freezes, fixated on the little girl's shoe, up against the wall with the leg detached at the kneecap, when instantly thinking of his daughter.

Bobby's mind draws a blank, looking over the blood-covered room with nervous eyes wandering around for anything he might have missed.

"No, man, you have a big, ten-pound, bouncing baby girl," Bobby says with an unusual, un-assuring laugh, teary-eyed, and with his back to Johns when picking up Johns' mangled phone.

He slowly turns to look at Johns' face with eyes filling with tears when a few fall on his cheeks when kneeling and placing his hands over Johns' eyes, closing them with his other hand at Johns' neck when he jerks his I.D., breaking the chain.

"Bobby..., let's go..., now..., now!" Tony yells, seeing Bobby slowly move past the door when he reaches inside, grabbing Bobby by the shoulder. He snatched him up, pulling him into the hall, with his body tensed to brace himself. He braces against Bobby to help him balance when Bobby almost stumbles over the dead bodies.

With brute force, Tony leans into him again and manages to stabilize him when pulling Bobby by the collar and guiding him to the nearest stairwell. They hear loud, authoritative voices giving commands in the hollowed stairwell when Tony stands with the door slightly against his shoulder, so they creep out onto the platform, softly sprinting upstairs. They reach the next level, crack the door open, enter the quiet hallway, and make their way over to the maintenance room, where they pop the door's lock and enter. They scanned the room, finding a huge air conditioning unit against the far wall, quickly unbolting butterfly nuts, climbing inside, and leaving the panel leaning against the mainframe.

Within minutes, S.W.A.T. team and Explosive Ordnance walkie-talkie communications and verbal commands grow louder as a team of officers advance in the hallway.

Gloved fists pound upon doors as the officers wait for the assistant manager to unlock each door.

Tony's leg slips out of the unit, and he leans over for the panel, speedily turning it and pulling it back against the unit when keys jiggle at the maintenance room door. Tony backs one leg inside, straining to steady the heavy plate with the riveted panel tightly held when looking through the crack, which slowly narrows, finding shadows cast upon the far rear wall.

Heads bob around one another, and shadows enlarge as the team slowly advances toward the air conditioning unit.

Tony times the loud communications and pulls the panel against the mainframe when the walkie-talkie sounds off again. He eased the panel shut tight with Bobby in a standing prone stance, flipping his weapon to automatic and aiming over Tony's shoulder.

The S.W.A.T and E.O.D team's point man eases up on the corner of the air conditioner until he can look against one of the back walls.

The point man checks the next wall, which is too close to the unit for a body to fit, feeling comforted when backing out, and due to oversight, he misses one of the unit's screws tucked alongside the crease of the back wall.

Tony and Bobby hear distant voices and then more soft poundings upon doors as S.W.A.T and E.O.D work their way down the hallway. Tony begins sweating and straining to keep the panel from slamming onto the concrete floor.

Minutes later, they hear the last transmission from the walkie-talkie, then a heavy stairway door slam when there's total silence.

Tony holds the heavy plate for seconds longer and then lowers it to the floor until it slips from his numb grip and loudly bangs against the wall.

Bobby tenses, slinging his weapon in its holster and maneuvering quickly in tight quarters when grabbing the plate and quickly backing into the unit. He holds the panel shut for five minutes until he is sure that the coast is clear.

Over an hour later, they exit the maintenance room and occupy a vacant room across the hallway. They get settled in and comfortable, then establish communications with Oggie and Tom, providing a situation update and informing Tom of their delay due to the additional security posted in and around the hotel.

When the last security team leaves their post later that night, Bobby and Tony wait an hour longer and then exit through the back of the hotel.

They emerge onto the street from an alleyway, heading to Oggie's hotel, not noticing a black limousine tucked away neatly on another side street.

Tony steps out from the curb with his head in the crosshairs immediately.

The blonde's steady aim follows him for seconds until the other blonde reaches forward, easing the AK-47's barrel down when spotting two island patrols coming up the main road on motorcycles.

The driver and five other women in the back patiently watch Tony and Bobby until they enter Oggie's hotel.

The limousine remains parked for half an hour longer and then cranks up, slowly pulling away from the curve with all eyes glued on the hotel's front door.

Oggie's door flies open, with Tom and Oggie training weapons back fast, lowering them, and slowly shaking their heads.

Bobby sadly walks over to the desk, passing Johns' things to Tom.

The four sit around, mourning in silence a little longer until, starting with Tom and one-by-one peeling off to their hotels, but Oggie stays.

Now, per Tom's orders, at 0600, Oggie puts the equipment on voice recording and then leaves for his room.

A gray limousine pulls up outside Oggie's hotel.

The male driver slumps down, adjusting the rearview mirror to get a better view of the two women kissing in the back. He looks away at his surroundings, and then gets another glance, eyes locking onto one girl's hand, which slips into the other girl's slacks. He leans heavily to one side, easing out a tracking device, noticing the crystals separating when grabbing a pillow from beside him, and cramming it in the corner of the door. His eyes stay on the hotel entrance for minutes until he drifts off to sleep.

Hours later, the driver begins tossing and turning from the sweltering, hot sun's rays beaming through the side window and windshield; at high noon. He finally awakes, profusely sweating with fast stretching hands going forward, blocking the bold rays until quickly adjusting the sun visor and massaging his stubbly face. He straightens up with fast eyes roving over and into the rearview and then back over his shoulder at the two beautiful women cuddling, nude and asleep. He pulls the tracking device to his face, yawning and quickly growing excited when finding the crystals converging at the center.

Now, as previously decided, Tom and his men assemble in Oggie's room.

Tom walks around with his hands in his pockets until taking a seat and meditating on what to say to get them in good spirits. "Hey, listen..., we've all suffered a great loss over the last few days, but I promise you, we'll get our revenge. Right now..., well..., right now, we have to focus on our surroundings, and later, who's to pay."

"Chief, they plan to kill us off, one by one. I mean..., damn, we're like sitting ducks out here!" Bobby nervously says, shaking his head in disbelief.

"Well, anyway, I confirmed last night that the captain has indeed been under duress. I didn't get the details, but I can assure you the lieutenant's out of the game because he's dead."

"Dead? Really? So when were you planning on telling us?" Bobby asks, standing.

"That was need-to-know information at the time, and I didn't think you needed to know," Tom says, breaking out into a smile when cackling.

"So what now?" Oggie asks, standing.

"The captain's old friend Major Fields is here on the island, and it appears he's an ally and in charge of the Underground."

"What! The Underground? Isn't that where they're holding Strike Force Two, and aren't those the clowns we're supposed to eliminate?" Tony asks, anxiously sitting up on the edge of the bed, confused.

"No, no..., obviously, the lieutenant and his accomplice wanted us to kill the major and his men for them or commit suicide attempting to do so. Anyway, the captain has arranged for us to meet with the Underground, who can hopefully make sense of all this mess. He also mentioned the Cubans being behind this as well."

Now, somehow, the conversation continues, and then ends in a joke, and then joke after joke until everyone is somewhat in good spirits.

Two hours or so later, Tom and Tony leave first, but Oggie and Bobby remain in mild conversation and more jokes.

After some time, Oggie thinks they've clowned around long enough when looking at his watch. "Hey! You'd better get up there and monitor those radio circuits. You know Chief..., he's probably calling there right now, checking," Oggie says, still pointing at the door.

"Yeah, he would do that, huh?" Bobby eases the door open, sticking his head out, cautiously looking down both sides of the quiet corridor before exiting. He takes the stairwell and ounces out on the next level, approaching the monitoring room, paranoid when slowing and drawing his weapon, then slowly opening the door.

He slips inside with eyes over his shoulder, hearing a door open and easing it shut with his back heavily pressed against it. He stays glued to the door, attentively listening to soft giggly voices with fast, swarming eyes covering the room.

Two females rush by the door whispering with hands inside deep purses, clutching Locks when picking up their pace and vanishing into the same stairwell Bobby had taken.

Bobby stands, heavily breathing when peeling off fast and slowing when inching up to the balcony. He slips a hand alongside the curtain, slowly pulling it back with dim eyes scrolling over the balcony, then double checking and at ease when finding the structure enclosed.

On the next level up, a maid receives a call to go to a room for cleanup and arrives within minutes, knocking and announcing herself for seconds until easing in the key in the lock and opening the door slowly.

A Dominican-looking woman expressly comes from around the wall, meeting and happily inviting the maid in and easing the door shut with eyes on a woman walking by, nodding to her with a welcoming smile. She quickly turns with eyes swarming over the huge suite when rushing past the maid, showing her to the other side of the room, near the bed where she claims to have spilled something that messed up the carpet. She points with the maid's eyes still looking into her face, then quickly at the thick white substance that appears to be baby powder until guessing its cocaine when finding the thick white cocaine-type bag wrapping beside the bed.

The maid eases a whisk broom from her pocket, easing to her knees like a true addict, quickly bringing a nail full of cocaine to her nose smelling, and then taking heavy sniffs until cleaning the nail, then easing her finger in her mouth, massaging her gums. She excitedly cuts her eyes back at the woman finding her smiling when reaching for a steno-type decorative notepad from the nightstand, whisking up the cocaine for minutes. She stops when most of the substance is on the pad and dips her finger in the white substance, looking back and up fast, and surprised to find it's uncut when feeling numb. She goes down again and stays longer, this time making sure there is nothing left when finally turning to look back, with something fast and fierce coming yet seeming to be in slow mode when the steel-plated butt of the AR-15 knocks her out.

Bobby walks about the room, feeling it too quiet when tuning in to a jazz station, walking over to the balcony, and looking at the pretty bright city lights. He begins rocking his head in unison with the mellow tune when the transceiver's needle pegs out a few times.

The indicator light begins steady, lighting the room with little flashes of what look like searchlights.

Bobby finally comes off the window, noticing a distinctive light reflection in the glass. He looks over his shoulder, seeing flashes when rushing over, turning the music off, and turning the transceiver up a few notches while sliding in the seat, tensed.

"..., Fireball, over!" the broken transmission comes then ends with a short delay. "This is Fireball, over!

Bobby nervously scrambles for the mic. "This is Eagle-five, over!"

"This is Fireball..., is Eagle Two there, over!" the deep, authoritative voice speaks a third time.

"This is Eagle-five, negative, sir, over."

"This is Fireball, roger; relay to Eagle Two that the American Embassy military liaison has picked up both KIAs and will transport them back to Mother (the United States) tomorrow, over!"

"Roger, copy all, sir, over!" Bobby responds, quickly underlining the last comment but holding the pen, ready to copy more.

"That's all..., this is Fireball, out!"

Bobby hangs up and, without hesitation, calls Tom's hotel to find him unavailable. He relays a shorter version of the long message on Tom's voicemail encoded and then sits rewriting the message more legibly.

A sharp but soft knock comes upon the fake control room's door, startling Bobby, who stands slowly, then drop the pen, grabbing his 9MM. He takes soft, calculated steps toward the door until standing off to the side. He turns slowly and hesitantly until bending and looking through the peephole and into the face of a beautiful Puerto Rican-looking woman dressed in a maid's outfit.

"Room service!" she finally whispers in a light, sexy voice.

"What? Oh..., uh..., uh..., wrong room! I didn't order any service," he says, slipping the 9MM into the back of his trousers and covering it with his shirttail.

"Well, sir, it says Room 345," she says, pointing at the pink slip of paper held tightly in her hand. She smiles, hearing the lock click, and smiles harder seeing the slight crack in the seam.

Bobby extends the door open until holding it open fully with one hand, the other hand tightly gripping the gun, with a finger easing into the trigger well. He stares at her beautiful face and slanted eyes with eyes slowly wandering over the ticket with the room number neatly scribbled at the top. He admires her hot body from head to toe in a quick, sweeping fashion, and with a long gaze, he pierces his eyes on her cleavage, down to her thin waistline and curvy, broad hips bursting out of her illegally tight outfit. He looks deep into her beautiful eyes again, and his heart instantly fills with lust.

The chick slips her hair back over her shoulder and starts running fingers through her long, coal-black, semi-curly hair. She twirls one long, sexy curl that slightly covers her face, smacking hard yet sexily on bubblegum until blowing a huge bubble.

Bobby smiles at her, quickly extending an index finger, pretending like he's going to burst it when causing her to back fast, chuckling. "Give me a minute," he says with a smirk, easing the door shut and rushing over to close the door housing the communications and satellite gear. He removes his 9MM, placing it on the dresser and under his backpack against the far side of the room.

Within seconds, he fully extends the door so she can easily get the decorative cloth-draped housekeeping cart through.

"Well, it took you long enough..., I was about to leave," she whispers with a naughty but playful stare until winking.

"Wouldn't I have to sign a form declining your services first?"

"No, I would just pass it along to the next shift because my shift is almost over."

Bobby eagerly listens to her speak so confidently about her job and recalls the room number on the ticket when letting down his guard and putting himself at ease.

Bobby eases a hand to the cart, helping her push the cart beside the bed, where she's very persistent in guiding it. He pauses, thinking of something interesting to say. "Hey..., can I get you a drink?"

"Maybe after work, if you're still up to it?" she responds, sitting on the edge of the bed, crossing her firm, pretty legs until easing them open and slowly spreading them wide.

"So, are you originally from the islands?" he asks, lightly turning the music up a few notches to set the tone when looking between her thick, silky, smooth thighs several times before finally noticing a black patch.

Now, he perceives her to have on a black G-string, but he is not sure, so he looks again, and then looks away fast, feeling her staring.

The chick continually rocks back and forth to the low, soft music, as she's practiced plenty of times to make her miniskirt roll up around her curvy hips. She touches his lips with her index finger, gently running other fingers up and down his thigh until she raises her feet onto the bed and spreads her thighs until her eyes close. "Damn, man, I'm so freakin horny," she seductively whispers, opening her eyes and looking deep into his eyes. "Mmm..., so can I get a taste..., please..., please?" she pouts, licking glossy, candy-colored lips to make them even shinier.

Bobby thinks long and hard with eyes swarming over his shoulder back at the room with the equipment. He slowly looks back at her and into deep black transitioning eyes, missing the transformation and forgetting all about the previous deaths and the mission. "Well, only if you don't mind dimming the lights because I'm a little shy," he says, excitedly giggling and walking over to light a candle, then moving to the lamppost, anxiously running upward, turning off the lights.

She eases up, quickly repositioning the cart even closer to the bed, when standing at the foot with her hands slipping to her back, unzipping her miniskirt.

She slightly tugs to get the skirt over her broad hips and then drops it, removing her headband, spreading her legs wide, and unsnapping her bodysuit. She slowly removes the maid's top in a playful seduction, with her hands grasping the bottom of the bodysuit. She pulls the body suit over her head, shaking out long hair, which unravels all over her head until he runs his fingers through it, slightly combing it back down.

Bobby eases closer and into her, gently sucking on her collarbone and kissing her soft, perfumed neck until she moans, running fingers through his hair.

She slips a finger in his ear, rotating it in a slow circular motion until lightly blowing into it when moaning. She backs up, lowering onto the king-sized bed, and then eases back, resting on her back with her feet slightly hanging off near the cart.

Bobby climbs next to her like a lion on its prey until leveling off to one side, resting next to her but on his side. He strokes her soft thighs until she guides his hand deeper between her thighs, moaning and breathing hard upon his neck when curling into him, slightly perspiring.

Bobby does everything he knows to get her exceptionally hot for over twenty minutes until he finally succeeds when her soft cheeks press hard into the mattress, alternating in a grinding motion until she is about to explode.

She grasps him, swiftly maneuvering to her knees, straddling him with warm, thick thighs clenching each side of his rib cage, warming his body with little perspiration. She grips him tightly in a closed fist, squeezing harder as Bobby flexes and expands. "Ooh..., I like it like that, Daddy..., Mommy loves it," she whispers when having him feel things he's never felt before when he's turned on to the max and about to lose his mind, knowing no woman has ever been so sexual and playful, yet so gentle at the same time.

She looks down and guides him deep between her thighs, teasing him until he feels her getting hotter each time she lowers her body onto him. She gets tease at times, gripping him tighter until tensing more, and looks down, finding his face slightly frowning.

His eyes close tightly, trying to hold on as long as he can. "Whooaa!" he softly breathes, over and over, trying his best not to lose his manly composure. His train of thought shifts from this chick's tight, warm grip to things like; car tires, bells, whistles, desk work, or anything else he could think of, far from sex.

She leans back, but further than the first few times, and with one last lean, she brushes up against the cart. She jerks in a forward heavy lean and into him, with his eyes wide when shushing him in a light whisper with something cool and sharp pressed hard at his throat.

Bobby freezes with nervous hands coming up slowly.

"Don't move, or your ass is as dead as your two friends!" she growls, transitioning from grey to black eyes when staring deeply into his eyes with one slightly raised eyebrow rising higher and her pretty face mildly transforming into something out of a horror flick.

Bobby breathes deep, taking lighter breaths to ease the pressure on his neck. He swallows and then slowly lets out a breath of warm air when her face grows fiercer.

"I said for you not to move!" she softly growls with warm breath heavily pressing upon his face and slightly warming it fast. "I should kill you right now for not letting me get mine! Damn you! You should always wait until a woman gets hers first, you inconsiderate-ass bastard!" she shouts, tightening the sharp blade until it slightly burns underneath his Adam's apple.

A few drops of blood soon trickle down the side of his neck, with some trailing along the thick blade's edge until dropping off the back of his neck.

Bobby rolls his eyes slightly until he brings his raised backpack into view, sees the tip of his 9MM barrel exposed slightly in a deep desire, and unknowingly extends a hand toward it with uncontrollable tears rolling from his eyes.

She snatches his face, turning it to her, and stares deep into his watery eyes as if staring through him.

The door jiggles with keys heavily, distracting her when she suddenly jumps, swiftly turning at an angle and, looking back and applying more pressure to his main artery now, until sweat runs over the wound, slightly burning it when more jagged-edge teeth dig deeper into his flesh. Sweat continually dripped from her body onto his.

A teardrop of sweat forms at her chin, slowly filling until dripping on his neck and face when she snaps back, looking at the door, then him.

She becomes tenser, breathing faster and as if in an adrenaline rush, excited to kill. Her eyes begin alternating between him and the door until she swallows hard a few times. Her adrenalin rises instantly to an even higher level from nervousness. "Not a word or I'll go ballistic and rip your freakin' main artery to shreds. Don't even flinch, chump!" she softly growls deeper into his ear when turning again, staring over her shoulder.

The door swiftly opens, shining a bright ray of light inside when her hips rise and begin slowly grinding.

Oggie takes a few nervous steps inside the dim room, closing the door, not noticing them lying there while focusing his eyes in the candle-lit room. He steps off and finally spots them, pretending he doesn't see them with nosey eyes roving over her pretty naked flesh and curvy hips. He slowly backs up with his eyes still glued on her pretty round bottom, still raised even higher.

She slightly twirls, sometimes lowering and then raising higher with eyes dead set on Oggie when playfully giggling, winking, and twirling her hips a little more to make Oggie think things were fine, but keeping the blade covered. At times, she presses the blade harder to Bobby's throat, with the blade's teeth gripping so tight that he barely could move his neck.

"Hey! I'm sorry!" Oggie finally says, feeling stupid from standing there so long yet still staring at her perfectly curved hips and pretty face when he clumsily backs into the door, quickly opening it and backing out. He pulls the door tight; hearing the lock click when checking to make sure it wouldn't open, and heads for the elevator.

She stays pressed even tighter into him, attentively listening until the elevator bell ring, when comforted. She eases from him and tries lifting him with the knife still to his throat. Her other hand slides to the back of his head, and she drops back from Bobby forcefully head-butting and falls flat on her back, rolling almost as if transparent. She paws and claws like a cougar, throwing the cart's cloth back and diving for the partially-covered shiny object.

Bobby balances on one leg half off the bed, attempting to leap in the direction of his weapon, completely startled, when realizing she has a handgun. He falls back in a sharp turn, sprinting for the door when one silenced round whistles centimeters from his head, the other hitting him in the leg as he dashes through the fast, swung-open door. He quickly advances with eyes over his shoulder until midway through the hall, when coming up to full speed and quickly slowing and exiting through the stairwell door. He eases onto the platform and freezes after hearing foreign women's accents on the lower decks. He looks upward, pushing off the wall, moving fast, forward, and up the stairwell.

The Puerto Rican-looking chick continues frantically running around the room, looking for her top. When partially dressed, she snatches her bodysuit and her other semiautomatic weapon, throwing the maid's top to the floor. She steps into the hall topless, her eyes drifting back and forth until finding a few drops of his blood soaked into the carpet. She leaps forward, coming up to speed and in stealth mode, viciously slinging her bodysuit in her hand when moving even faster. She slows near the stairwell door, spotting more blood trails but bigger droplets.

She slightly pushes on the door, barely cracking it open with hands hurriedly training the weapon in a sweeping motion, inching onto the quiet platform. She stays quiet, listening until hearing a door below slam shut; when she eases the door shut and slips into her top, allowing the snaps to dangle. Her eyes meander around until regaining another spot of the faint blood trail. She gets a tight grip on the gun with a silencer, slipping it into her skirt and slinging the semiautomatic's strap over her shoulder. She dashes up the stairs almost in stealth mode and as if transparent.

She slows again when approaching the roof's entrance, slowly cracking the door open with the muzzle trained around the dark roof, covered with gravel and pipes, some standing as high as twenty feet and eight feet wide. "Come on out, punk boy! You scared to deal with a real woman like a man should, huh?" she shouts, bending and leaning forward sharply when training the weapon around more pipes and metal bins. "Let's see how bad you want this good-good now. Come on out and take it like a real man!" she shouts, grabbing her crotch and laughing as if stoned on cheap drugs.

She backs into a dark corner easing out a vile from an ankle band; opening it, and taking a deep hit of cocaine, snorting loud until senselessly giggling. "What's wrong? Cat got your tongue, sucker?" she screams over the sound of the distant waterfall and low-humming hotel power transformers, which grow louder as she approaches the other side of the roof. "You know, you American men always let your little head do all your thinking!" she screams, reaching down and finally turning on the infrared laser beam, which sounded like the activation of an old camera's flash.

She looks down, finding a few more small droplets of blood where the dim spotlight shines outward from around a pipe. Her eyes fleetingly scan over the roof, training the weapon in the direction of the second and third droplets, leading to a spot where Bobby had confusingly stumbled around looking for a hiding place. She steps off, walking another zigzag blood pattern, finding another confused-looking circle of blood droplets that Bobby intentionally made, attempting to confuse her.

Bobby tiptoes with one last step backward when his foot rests on a medium-sized piece of broken brick.

"I know you're up here, punk! Listen! There's no time to play hide and go seek, wimp! Get your dumb ass out here so I can earn my pay! No! No! On second thought, how about coming out and eating a little trim before you die? And oh yeah..., you better be damn good too because you'll be doing it with a freakin' barrel to your freakin' head!" she senselessly giggles, stoned, and half bent over when leaning forward and peeping around a few more pipes.

She disappears from his sight, but Bobby soon catches sight of her through two pipes several yards away when she has her back turned to him.

Bobby strains through the pain, reaching undetected, grabbing the brick, gripping it tightly, and losing his grip when jerking forward and catching it. "Whew," he sighs.

"Look! You're starting to piss me off now! Your resistance only makes me want to kill you slower, so come on out and die fast and with pride like your two punk-ass friends!"

Bobby leans back in pain, and with all his might, he lunges the rock high over her head, hitting a metal transformer and causing her to immediately turn and fire on automatic. His mind goes haywire, realizing it is his only chance to take her, when tensing and in stealth mode, silently charging with full force while she still had her back to him. He screams several feet away to scare her when executing his famous dropkick with a foot connecting at the side of her face.

The brute force spins her out of control with her screaming while firing on automatic; with four of the ten rounds penetrating Bobby's upper and lower body and knocking him back onto the coarse, rock-covered roof.

Her silenced weapon falls from her skirt with ten rounds prematurely expended as she forcefully twirls over the ledge with a long, high-pitched, fading cry.

Two women stand outside the limousine, trying to figure out where the long, endless screaming is coming from, and fearfully jump, hearing a loud splash and thick slap. Both their eyebrows rise, with eyes over their shoulders, finding the woman's body slumped over the concrete, quad deck water fountain. They sprint, quickly drawing near with firm observation revealing the woman is one of their own.

Bobby strains to stand, then reaches for his leg and waist, straining to limp over to the ledge where he leans, looking down and alongside the building. He begins to squint until he finds her body stretched over a water fountain with the male statue's sword pierced through her back and protruding from her chest.

The pink water in the top basin suddenly turns red, trickling to the second and third basins and into the main well.

Bobby continues surveying the grounds until scanning the lot, finding two women walking away from the fountain and then turning and standing outside a limousine, staring back over at the fountain until the short woman points to the roof and Bobby ducks quickly.

The tall woman stares until he peeps again, pulls a black veil over her face, and climbs back inside the limousine.

The car sits idle until the driver activates the flashers.

A transit bus rolls through the crowded parking lot, making its way alongside the hotel, until coming to a slow roll when stopping.

Tony jumps off wearing his headset, bobbing his head to a dope beat. His eyes wander alongside the hotel finding a car's flashers when doing a double take, finding the sexy-looking, medium-built woman waving until climbing into the limousine. He stops with curious eyes, waiting for the limousine to come closer, when suddenly it stops a ways from him and then veers left and speeds up.

Bobby grows weaker, turning and heading for Oggie's floor. He passes a decorative table in the hallway, snatching the cloth off and wrapping his nude body. He steps off and stumbles, light-headed, almost losing his balance when falling against the wall, taking deep breaths until he can push off in a slow stagger, but falls into the wall again. He staggers more, finally coming up on Oggie's door with little strength. "Oggie!" he lowly shouts, half out of breath and with a faint knock. "Oggie!" he shouts again, but in a weaker voice.

The door rattles and swings open, with Bobby falling into Oggie's arms, almost out of breath, then breathing heavily and fast.

Oggie drags him inside and then kicks the door shut, with arms wrapped around Bobby's waist as he helps him over to the couch.

Several seconds later, a few heavy poundings come upon the door. "Hey, Oggie, open up..., it's Tony! Is everything ok?" Tony shouts, staring at the heavily-saturated, bloody carpet when instantly chambering a round while nervously listening and looking down both sides of the hallway with caution as he turns and presses his back to the door.

Cynthia, the girl Oggie had met at the club and spent time with at the boardwalk, stares into Tony's eyes when he looks away and over his shoulder, staring back into her watery eyes. He quickly leans, staring over her shoulder to find Oggie kneeling over Bobby when rushing in, un-chambering his weapon and slipping it back in his holster. He drops to his knees and slides a few feet next to Bobby, who is breathing heavier and clenching his teeth to absorb the excruciating pain. "Call an ambulance! Who did this, Bobby?" Tony screams, crying and holding Bobby's hand tighter. "Who did this?"

Bobby coughs up a little blood, and then coughs up more with eyes dimming after every blink until sweat beads on his face. "That...!" he begins to say in pain when slobbering and clenching his teeth tighter.

"Hang in there, bro! Please let him live, please God..., please!"

Bobby takes a deep breath with a death grip on Tony's hand when his eyes grow wide open and stale.

"Cynthia, grab your things! Tony, we've got to get out of here, man!" Oggie screams.

Oggie grabs Cynthia when passing, taking her into the connected double bedroom, where he eases her onto the edge of the bed, kneeling while wiping his tears and then hers. "I can explain later, precious, but right now, I need you to get dressed and help get this stuff out of here." Oggie pulls bags and clothes from the closet, tying them in a bundle with the bed sheet, when his mind goes into overdrive until he remembers the room across the hall, closed for repairs. He extracts his intrusion kit from the table, checks the hall, and then runs over and opens the other room's door. Oggie gives the front room a quick look over and then checks the back rooms and eases to the door, checking the hall once more when rushing back across, swiftly closing the door.

Tony remains next to Bobby, unclearly mumbling. "I should never have left you, man!" he mumbles clearly, continually crying and unclearly mumbling more.

"You've got to strip his tags, Tony!" Oggie shouts, racing toward the back room again, then to the door, cracking it open and peeking out, checking the halls, when dragging the bundle across. He thrusts the bundle inside and closes the door. Oggie floods back on once more and look at Tony as he passes at a swift pace. Tony, strip him down, now, now, now!" Oggie shouts in a low tone.

Tony continues leaning over Bobby, crying and religiously chanting, when Oggie rushes up, reaching over Tony's shoulder and grabbing Bobby's dog tags, but before he can pull them, Tony forcefully shoves Oggie's hand back. "No, Oggie, damn it! I'll do it!" Tony says, clutching and yanking the tags with all his might. He begins patting Bobby down for valuables and other identifiable items.

Oggie checks the hall again and quickly guides Cynthia into the other room.

Tony stands, slowly backing away but keeping his eyes on Bobby, still wiping tears when backing into the door, accidentally shutting it, when grasping the knob from behind, and opening it. His vision blurs when wiping his eyes once more when exiting and entering the other room, abruptly closing the door and looking over at Oggie, who is easing onto the couch.

Oggie grabs the phone from the bundle of gear and dials star (*) one and reports the incident to Tom, quickly informing him of the new room they are occupying.

Thirty minutes later, Tom knocks, identifying himself with one of their memorable knocks, then enters with bloodshot eyes rolling sadly over to Tony and Oggie before noticing the girl standing off in his peripheral vision.

"Are you going to be all right?"

Tony acknowledged, 'yes,' nodding a few times.

"Come on, Oggie..., we don't have much time," Tom says with curious eyes on the girl.

Tom and Oggie check the hallway and step out with eyes instantly drifting to the carpet, soaked in blood. Tom steps forward toward the door when Oggie grabs him by the shoulder. "No, Chief!" Oggie guides him off in another direction.

They step up to the control room, and Tom freezes in his tracks, noticing more droplets of blood trailing down the long hallway. They slip inside the room and turn on bright overhead lights finding thicker droplets of blood trickling from the door with the blood thicker near the bed, and on the floor, with a large circle of blood on the bed.

Oggie's mind goes haywire, feeling faint when recalling being in the room with Bobby's killer when sweat instantly beads on his forehead and his body heavily perspires.

Tom inches up on the equipment room, finding a notepad that he holds up and reads, recalling the voice mail light flashing when rushing from the room.

Tom walks around in a thorough inspection of the room. He quickly spots Bobby's weapon under his backpack when cutting unbelievable eyes over to Oggie and finds him looking away. He slips the gun into his waistband in a stare while shaking his head in disbelief. "How in the hell do they know where and when to strike? It's as if they're zooming in on us one at a time," Tom says, half-dazed when pulling the transport dolly out of the closet and freezing. "What about your woman companion? Do you think she'll talk?" Tom goes into deep meditation for minutes. "How do we know she's not shadowing us and feeding information back to these crazy people?"

"Naw, Chief..., she's good. She just happens to be totally disoriented from Bobby's death."

"We have to make sure she won't talk, Oggie..., we can't afford to be identified!"

"I'll handle her, Chief..., you have to trust me..., she'll be fine."

"What if she goes to the police and tries to clear her name?"

"What? What are you saying?" Oggie asks, staring deep into Tom's eyes; his fists balled tightly at his sides. "Are you insinuating we kill her?"

"Do you have a better idea? I mean, think about it, Oggie..., really. How do we know she's not one of them? They could be targeting our position as we speak!" Tom frantically screams, cutting it short.

"Hell no! We're not going to do anything to her..., she's not one of them, and I can almost promise she's innocent!"

"We'll discuss this later, but right now, we need to get this equipment out of here. When blood is reported outside your door, the hotel clerk is sure to call the authorities."

They freeze; hearing a man and woman's voice whispering in the hallway, but continue packing quietly. They soon check the hall and make their way back and forth, and with everything loaded, they rescan the room and become cautious when cracking the door open. They manage to pull the large box in the hallway and roll it back to the room quickly, and with things unloaded, they make several trips until arriving with the last box.

Tom takes a seat and then jumps up, searching for the phone after the first ring. He tears through the sealed bottom box, rummaging through the equipment and clothes until finding the phone on the third ring and answering on the fourth when greeted by Captain Carrington.

Tom greets him professionally and provides details surrounding Bobby's death though short, refraining from mentioning foul play or Bobby's improper protocol when flipping out a pocket device up-linking and providing the hotel's coordinates for having Bobby picked up.

"What about the Underground, sir? We sure could use some support and intelligence information, so anything would be better than nothing," Tom says, looking through the large picture window at the quiet downtown.

"Yes, I've arranged for them to move you guys to a safe haven in a few hours."

"Not to question you, sir, but how do we know we can trust them?"

"At this point, Chief, we don't have much of a choice..., now do we?"

The captain gives Tom a secret number and password for the Compound. "Look..., just call and arrange for transportation, but hurry because it won't be long before Cuban forces show up in full force," the captain says, taking a sip of his hearty vegetable soup.

"Alright, sir, Chief Powells, out!" Tom hurriedly ends the call and activates a secure call mode when the warning, 'INITIAL CALL FAILED, flashes in the LED. He terminates the call and tries again in non-secure mode, and it rings.

"Compound..., request you verify your password!" the feminine voice says.

"Trigger," Tom responds, gazing over the notes and password he'd written on the paper.

"Wait one moment, please! All right..., we'll be there in about thirty minutes, so keep the door locked. I'll knock three-two-one, ok?" the woman says, waiting for a response.

"Got it, but I didn't catch your name," Tom responds.

"Tee!"

"All right, Tee..., I'm Tom. We're at the Westside Hotel, third floor, across from Room 345, the room across the hall from the blood-stained carpet," he whispers, looking over at Tony, who sits with his eyes closed, nervously tapping his feet. "We'll be waiting."

Tom strolls to the bedroom door and stops in his tracks, motioning for Oggie to come over, and they indulge in another conversation concerning the girl. Tom keeps staring from time to time at the back of the girl's head.

The girl continually looks down into the parking lot at a few suspicious characters, deceptively moving about outside of a limousine until distracted, finally hearing Tom mention her and becoming more intrigued when eavesdropping.

The conversation grows out of control and gets louder.

"I see..., so I don't have any say regarding my life? What kind of people are you?" she screams, staring at Tom and then slowly and questionably looking over at Oggie.

Oggie walks over, reaching for her hand, which she briskly pulls away, when he pulls her into his arms, hugging her tightly until both cut their eyes back at Tom almost simultaneously.

Tom's eyes float to the floor quickly, in embarrassment. "Ok, here's the deal..., the Underground or Compound personnel are en route to transfer us out. If they ask, Cynthia is a team member," Tom cleverly says, but in doubt.

Oggie smiles, releasing her yet guiding her to the other room, where they neatly pack a few things.

Tom eases into a chair, uncertain as to whether he's making the right decision by allowing her into a secure environment. He goes into deeper thought, wondering if she's wired and how much of a breach he would be injecting into the Compound or Underground. He stays in deep meditation until thinking about the standard security protocols for any secure environment, which puts him at ease.

"What about Bobby and his stuff?" Tony asks with his eyes still closed.

"Arrangements are in place to have him picked up by the American Embassy. We'll worry about Bobby's hotel and his things tomorrow," Tom says, thinking more about the whole ordeal up until this point.

Oggie pulls Cynthia in his arms, removing his weapon from his holster, unloading it, and showing her how to use it.

Tom wanders over and takes a seat across from the room where Cynthia is standing, and Oggie sits on the edge of the bed. He looks up, hearing a chuckle, when finding Cynthia playfully jumping, turning, and pointing the gun into the living room at Tom, unknowingly. He launches off to one side, screaming while diving to the floor and reaching for his weapon while the curved sofa slides to one side.

Oggie jump from Tom's movement with wide eyes, grabbing the gun from her hands, swiftly throwing his hand up, and motioning to Tom that it is alright.

Tony falls forward in a burst of deep, uncontrollable laughter, staring down at Tom, pointing.

Tom eases his gun down and crawls to his feet, sitting with a frown until drifting off in thought, though still embarrassed. He soon sits reminiscing on his fallen men until looking back into the room and over at Cynthia and Oggie, cuddling.

Oggie continues showing her the gun's features while she sits between his legs with her back to him.

Tom attentively watches until thinking back on Kelley and how they used to cuddle when he was teaching her about weapons, though for some reason, she always seemed to be a fast learner. His mind drifts again, and he marvels at how Kelley was so proficient with weapons in such a short time. To him, she seemed to be better than him when it came to quick draws and breaking down weapons. He meditates more and thinks harder when it puzzles him until breaking his concentration.

Several heads in the limousine slump down when they find three high, head-beam vehicle lights approaching in the parking lot.

A camper rolls through the lot and heads over near the side of the hotel.

Two escort SUVs break off in different directions, covering both hotel entrances as the camper parks with heads inside bobbing around, staring at the dead body on the fountain.

The camper's side door flings open when the rear electronic door opens and four soldiers in fatigues exit. The driver comes around to the back of the camper and assists with pulling several large transport cases out.

The soldiers stand off to the side, stacking boxes neatly on the sidewalk until grabbing two apiece and head for the hotel's side door.

A young Cuban man exits the back door of the limousine parked in the dark part of the hotel's parking garage undetected. He walks to his car and jumps inside, revving the engine for seconds, and then pulls away and parks in front of the camper. He jumps out of the low-rider, waving his hand as if waving off smoke from the engine until raising the hood and pretends to have car problems. He stays well hidden from the SUVs but slips between his and the camper's bumper, attaching a tracking device under the camper's bumper. He jumps up and rushes around to the front of the car, slamming the hood down, then climbs back in the car, revving the engine for a few seconds before barreling out of the parking lot, burning rubber.

Like clockwork, three soft, quick knocks come upon the door, followed by two, then one.

Tom peeps through the security lens, finding two women and two men.

"It's Tee," she joyfully acknowledges.

Tom opens the door and straight away stares into welcoming faces and then over at the long transport cases stacked behind them, quickly motioning them inside.

Everyone stands and forms a semicircle when Tom and Tee take turns introducing their team.

"Cops will soon be swarming this place like crazy," Tee says, tucking her long hair back under her toboggan.

"You're right..., let's get a move on!" Tom says, lifting one end of the case sitting next to the door and loading it with things from the bundled sheet.

Everyone helps load and restack the cases; afterward, they break down the other boxes and stuff them in the last case.

Tony opens the door and stares over at the other room door, walking out empty-handed and stepping over the large, blood-stained carpet. He kisses his hand, placing it on the door, when Oggie and Tony's hands come to his shoulder with their hands on the door as well. Tom whispers a few heart-felt final words.

The three drop their heads wiping tears and then break off, helping to lift cases when Oggie walks over to help Cynthia lift a case.

They single-file outside with cases between them and are a few feet from the camper when Tee makes mention of the messy fountain, but none of Tom's folks catch on until she points.

Tony and Cynthia lay the last box in the camper and slide it to one side.

Tony comes up on the side of the camper beside Tee, staring over at the fountain until his face transforms into a frown when stepping off at a fast pace and slowing when crossing the plush lawn. He pulls his knife out, rushing up, seeing her chest still lightly rising with her taking short agonizing breaths when lifting the woman's head by her long, black hair, staring deep into her face when driving the blade through her heart.

Her eyes open wide in a weak scream, taking a deep breath and heavily jerking.

Tony's tightly-balled fist twists the knife back and forth a few times, with her finally giving up being tough when letting out a death cry with eyes weak then stale. He slowly pulled out the blade and wiped it against her top.

"Hardcore!" Tee whispers, staring deep into Tony's eyes when he passes.

The driver and Tee climb in the front, and Tom sits behind her while others scatter about the van.

The driver revs the engine and then raises his fist out the window.

The two SUVs' bright headlights pierce from darkness, falling in close behind the camper when one takes the lead and the other follows closely.

The limousine's engine starts, but the lights stay off when pulling away after the last SUV turns the corner with one of the girls in the back screaming in pain with eyes still dead set on the fountain as they pass.

The limousine's passenger reaches for her phone and calls the Cuban Headquarters, providing a tactical update and obtaining authorization for shadowing the convoy. Upon receiving permission, the limousine driver drops back and tails them from a greater distance.

The limousine driver nods to the front-seat passenger, and she pulls out the tracking device, motioning for the driver to drop back even further.

After a thirty-minute or so into the drive, Tee directs her driver down a wooded trail, but the SUVs continue straight until their taillights vanish at the top of the hill.

The camper slows fast, and the tracking device's light fluctuates from light to dark green.

The passenger's hand comes up quickly, motioning the limousine driver to stop.

The camper stops outside a secret passage and waits for the wall to extend fully open.

The limousine driver goes slower after the tracking device's lights turn light green, and then green, and back to bright yellow.

The limousine passenger stares at the device with a quick fanning hand, motioning the driver to drive faster when the limousine driver's eyes widen as he steps into the gas pedal.

The camper continues its three-mile drive along the dusty, wooded trail until taking a sharp curve into a heavier wooded area, where it stops at a small brick guard shack.

Two armed guards swiftly approach.

The tall man walks up with his weapon drawn; the other has his weapon slung over his shoulder.

The short man holds a rod in his hand with a mirror attached at the end, walking around the front while motioning the vehicle safely into position. The camper inches up more until well within the red lines, when the guard activates the infrared beams, allowing time for synchronization.

The short guard keeps shyly cutting his eyes over at Tee, blushing when making his way around the camper's right-side undercarriage and catching Tee smiling when passing the side door and heading for the front bumper. When distracted by Tee's pretty smile, he rushes past the bumper, missing the microchip tracker painted the same color as the bumper.

The tall guard looks into each of their eyes. "Please stand clear of the red line, and whatever you do, don't break the infrared beams," the tall guard said, motioning them out. He waves to his partner and heads to a porta-potty (portable bathroom).

After minutes of positioning and adjusting for the camper's height, the electronically-guided laser beam begins scanning the camper. At the same time, they stand in the encased glass, observing the highly technical computerized system.

The short guard enters the waiting area, scanning personnel items, starting with Cynthia. Obsessed with Tee, he stands at the rear, cutting his eyes over to Tee's hot body.

Tony accidentally closes the door marked 'never to be closed.'

The system scans the camper's front again when the guided laser's beam beeps, but the short man is too distracted again while running the wand over Cynthia's body and watching Tee's great curves, stretched in black, glittery spandex.

The tall guard flinches, cutting his whirlwind of piss short when his head nervously crooks to one side, and he stares at the ceiling, recognizing the distinct beep. He slowly looks over his shoulder in disbelief, still frozen and holding his urination, when the beep comes again as the system scans past the tracking device's transmitter a second time while the short guard gives directions while being nosey in conversations.

The limousine's front-seat passenger looks out the window and then down at the tracking device again when it flashes and changes from green to yellow and then red, and instantly causes eyes to widen. "Whoa, whoa, whoa, back up!" she says, excited when the driver slams on the brakes, backing up a few yards and then over a hundred feet or so, staring at the edge of the road until finally finding tire impressions in the tall grass. He turns the wheel snappily with feet still on the brake and then gas.

The high beams come on, instantly shining against a rock-like wall, which he closes in on at a slow pace.

Two Cuban men jump out from the rear and walk around, examining the path and the wall. They look in the grass to see if they can find a tire actuator along the tire's tracks but find nothing when guiding the limousine driver directly in the beaten-down tire path. They grow confused after a short time and jump back inside, and a few converge around the tracking device, staring at the lights, which flicker between red and yellow.

The limousine driver eases his head out the window going from drive to reverse until he rocks several times unsuccessfully until well aligned. He slowly inched up until the bumper slightly touched the wall.

With one last forward lunge, the front wheel presses upon the well-hidden actuator and electronically opens the wall.

Inside the trap door, a few Cubans nervously stare back at the gate as it closes. Others stare at the tracking device until about a mile from the gate when the driver pats the brakes, stopping and putting the limousine in park gear when turning off the headlights when the tracker fluctuates between red and yellow.

The short guard finally enters the camper and is inside for minutes when rushing to the door. "Come inside!" he excitedly says, pointing to Tom and turning.

Tom comes up beside him when he scans the boxes again, and the LED lights up as if malfunctioning.

Tom slams his fist against the wall without warning, denting it. "Man..., no wonder they always knew we were separated..., by the damn Sky-Tel phones. Thank you!" Tom said, walking off and away from the camper, pissed.

"What's wrong?" Tee asks, seeing his frown.

"Our Sky-Tel phones were bugged with satellite tracking crystals, no doubt. It's obvious now why the lieutenant was so anxious to have us communicate on these damn bogus phones!" Tom looks over at Tony, who turns away, continually wiping teary eyes.

The tall guard finishes funkin' (scenting) up the bathroom and his zipper finally comes up about the same time his phone rings, and he answers instantly, distracted by an emergency call from home.

The short guard removes everything that didn't scan properly and debugs it, and with a clean bill of sanitization, he allows them to re-board.

The camper's engine revs a few times when the driver looks through the side mirror as the short man guides him out of the pit. The camper backs all the way out, about to make a U-turn, when Tom touches Tee on the shoulder and points to the tall guard running toward them, frantically waving.

"Stop!" Tee touches the driver's arm.

The limousine driver's eyes shoot to the passenger's hand, seeing the device's lights flicker in reverse order, with eyes growing wide quickly. "Shit..., get your weapons! Take cover," the driver says as he and the passengers jump out, leaving the doors open.

The tall guard runs up to the short guard, snatching him by the collar. "What the hell are you doing? You need to pull your head out of your ass! Hell, you act as if you have never seen a damn woman before. Didn't you hear the two beeps? Hell, I was in the shitter, and I heard it..., heard it twice, you freakin' idiot!" the tall guard yells, motioning the camper forward again and ordering a rescan, which detected the tracking device while they sit in the camper.

After the third clean sweep, they back out again.

The camper driver turns around and heads back down the same wooded trail, and half a mile before the camper rounds the curve where the limousine is parked with the Cubans well hidden in the tall grass, Tee directs her driver to veer left. They head down a hill, almost parallel to the path they'd entered. He drives about two hundred more yards and pulls up to another security shack with a secret wall.

Tee and the driver flash identifications to the first guard and pass through to the other side.

The camper proceeds with the dirt road, quickly turning into an unevenly paved road, which soon turns into the new pavement with fresh markings.

The limousine driver looks at the tracking device's steady lights when pulling out the Sky-Tel phone's tracking device and notices crystals still dead ahead and down the path taken initially. The limousine driver immediately motions them to load up when climbing inside. He slowly pulls away and then stops at intervals with eyes bucked and scanning the perimeter. The limousine moves faster, with everyone's eyes excitedly gazing forward and looking to the left and right and deep into the tall weeds when suddenly slowing.

Their hearts race fast as the driver slowly creeps but stops several times while the men and women continue training their weapons out of the windows.

Five minutes later, the camper arrives at another security gate, where the guards open the electronic gates and stop the camper about twenty feet within the yellow-striped lines.

An alarm moderately sounds when red lights begin flashing, causing the road to rise like a draw bridge.

The driver waits until the hydraulic lift extends fully, and then drives inside the steep, dark tunnel.

Completely inside, the lights flash red, yellow, and then green as the tunnel lights up along the long wall ahead as the camper advances with single, bright, white lights a few feet ahead, energizing one at a time.

The camper advances at a moderate pace and then increases speed, as they begin moving so fast that lights become a steady beam ahead as far as the naked eye can see.

The limousine's passengers grow tense, seeing the tracker malfunction when the driver slows, and everyone's eyes focus on crystals fading, one at a time.

The first two checkpoint guards stand off to the side of the shack, smashing crystals against a concrete wall with a sledgehammer.

The Cubans grow excited with eyes bucked when the limousine's front-seat passenger pulls the tracking device to her face, and everyone quickly gathers around. A smile grows and then quickly vanishes when the tracking device turns red when the tall guard slams the sledgehammer into the last crystal.

The limousine driver and his crew grow very nervous fast, sweating profusely when the driver steps into the gas, causing the limousine to swerve along the narrow trail with dust rising high. The limousine goes even faster and slows, coming into a steep curve with the corner of the small brick guard shack unexpectedly coming into view.

The two guards finally hear the mild engine and turn swiftly approaching with drawn weapons.

The short guard rushes to the wall, retracting his weapon when nervously reaching for the mirrored rod when the limousine slows.

Surprised, the limousine driver stops, nervously sitting and looking at the enclosure, yet driving straight toward the shack when seeing the tall guard waving more frantically. He slows more so they don't alert other guards or checkpoints and blow the element of surprise.

Everyone in the limousine lowers their weapons and hides them as directed by a backseat passenger.

The limousine slows a little more before almost coming to a complete stop and moves forward again when directed.

The tall guard motions the limousine forward a few more feet and into position when the limousine comes well within the red lines.

The tall guard walks over to the glass enclosure.

The short guard begins scanning the undercarriage, starting at the rear, taking his time, this time, and slowly making his way around to the other side.

The Dominican-looking woman keeps her back to the short guard but raises her weapon under her sweater, aiming at the tall guard heading for the driver's door in somewhat of a rush.

The short guard looks up while inspecting the vehicle and, from time to time, finds a few heads moving around. He continues, and when almost finished, the tall guard activates the synchronized electronic infrared beams. The short guard stands at the rear side view window, finally noticing the Cuban men through the back window that's cracked open slightly. He grows curious, noticing the driver is Cuban as well when he accidentally removes his glasses through the slightly cracked open, tinted window. He quickly gazes over the passengers and grows tense. "Cubans!" the short guard screams, dropping the rod and drawing his weapon.

The limousine's windows shatter from those in the back seat firing on automatic.

The guards lunge backward as if in slow motion when falling toward the low-cut partition, breaking infrared beams.

The taller guard hits his leg, and the short guard grazes his rib cage, trying to clear the concrete wall.

Both guards slam into thick hay and mulch, covering their ears.

Mild then fast-growing high-pitched whistling sound roar with cannon-like guns popping out of metal trap doors mounted in the ground.

Several large shells from all angles launches, continually riveting the limousine into shreds with large hot, smoking casings falling on the guard's backs as they scream low-crawling away from the limousine, which is heavily shaking from side to side, for seconds.

The guards lay tense with hands tight over their heads until hearing the loud buzzer alarm and jumping up and running, diving into a high pile of straw and leaving behind another concrete barrier with steel reinforcements.

The concrete floor opens, and a small compartment filled with lethal dynamite charges explodes, bringing the car several feet off the ground and creating a huge, mushroom-shaped dust cloud.

The guards pierce their heads from behind a barrier, standing slowly. They limp, covering their wounds while making their way past the burning limousine and rushing inside the shack, calling the Compound to report the security breach.

Further up the road, guards wave Tee's driver through from a distance at the last checkpoint.

"Whatever you do, don't walk around in the wooded area from which we just came because it's filled with land mines, motion detectors, beam-guided remote-controls, and automatic weapons," the driver says, looking through the side mirror and smiling.

Tom and his men's eyes brighten, watching and admiring the awesome superstructure of the beautiful bridge and towering buildings.

The driver stops when he sees a couple of small formations of troops approaching with weapons drawn.

The team leader immediately identifies the vehicle and spots Tee, motioning his group to lower their weapons and return to their post.

"This is our stop. Here, tag your things with these labels," Tee says, passing Tom the green-and-gold labels. "They'll bring your things to your rooms later, so no need to worry. We don't normally go through all the security stuff, but it's a precautionary measure for first-timers. There's a quicker way back in, but security is tighter than a gnat's ass in the dead of summer."

Tom's men open all the containers, sticking labels on as much as possible, when Tom intervenes, telling Tee to send anything not tagged to his quarters.

"Here, let's get your security badges and room keys." Tee points them to the main entrance.

"This place is awesome, huh, Chief?" Oggie says, full of excitement.

The whole group goes through several scanners, and Tom's team goes through fingerprints and photo sessions before being indoctrinated on procedures for entry and exit of the facility.

Next, Tom and his men attend a ten-minute film on security and safety, which is mandatory.

Tee waits for them after I.Ds and badging, and then escorts them down a long corridor to their living quarters. "Here you are," she says, stopping outside Tom's quarters. "For your convenience, the rooms are fully equipped with wave-less king-sized waterbeds, spare bedrooms, living rooms with an S-curved sofa, bars, stereos, saunas, Jacuzzis, and sixty-inch state-of-the-art televisions. You will also find your suites equipped with completely stocked, stainless-steel kitchens for your pleasure, and room service is available twenty-four/seven."

Tom and his men quietly retreat to their quarters.

Tom showers and relaxes in the sauna with a chilled glass of wine.

Tony showers and thinks of his brother until he is fast asleep.

Oggie and Cynthia put on some easy-listening, island-style music, play around, and then make wild passionate love in the Jacuzzi.

After some time, Oggie goes into the heat of passion, turning her away from him.

Cynthia leans into the side of the Jacuzzi, grasping both thick, firm cheeks, one in each hand, when Oggie kisses the nape of her neck, mounting from behind.

Oggie gently eases into her and then slowly moves back and forth before playfully thumping her hard a few times.

Instantly, she releases her cheeks, and he grabs them, spreading them even wider when power driving until hearing thighs spanking against her firm but jiggly bottom until growing to a whisper. "Damn, baby, damn..., harder! Damn you! Harder!" she screams over the mellow music. She keeps her head down, constantly looking between her wide, gapped thighs finding his thighs moving fast, sometimes faster than others. Her eyes go almost stale when focusing on the water, noticing a lightly-dimmed texture of the water swaying with the trail of something pink. Her eyes widen, and she lifts high, falling back into him. "Damn, mon! You done made me come on my damn period, mon," she says in her deeply-rooted accent, forcing him back even further when grabbing a towel.

"Oh, man..., sorry about that, sweetie," he says, still looking down surprised while stroking her firm back to support her stand. Oggie stares at the reddish-pink swirls until they slowly vanish, dips down in the water, runs his hand over his body until clean, and then grabs a towel to dry off.

She wraps up even tighter and then exits, staring back over his physique and manhood while shaking her head and smiling before winking.

Oggie stares into her pretty, slanted eyes, winking until blowing a kiss.

Cynthia wanders off, taking care of her personal hygiene, showers, and then wanders out, finding Oggie fast asleep, though pretending to be. She eases onto the side of the bed and pulls the covers back, standing and admiring his muscular body for minutes before partially covering him and leaving his head to upper thigh exposed.

She eases back onto the side of the bed, gently stroking his thigh with manicure nails, barely touching his skin until feeling as if something is crawling over the fine hairs.

Oggie tries holding back until a slowly growing face comes when bursting into a crazy, heavy laugh. He opens his eyes, pretending to have been rubbing them before looking over at her and making eye contact.

She winks, easing her head down to his navel, softly kissing him before making her way further south, but at a snail's pace.

Before long, Oggie is tense with well-manicured and firm hands grasping the sheets, balling them in his tightly-balled fists as he fights to keep from losing it too fast.

Tom wakes around noon, lying there, staring at the ceiling in deep thought of everything that has happened until breaking his train of thought and reaching for the phone.

Later, he calls his hotel, checking messages, and the desk clerk relays several calls: Bobby's, Nichelle's, and Kelley's, which was in detail when drifting into deep thoughts. He hangs up, remembering he had left his phone directory at the hotel, so he gets dressed and calls for a driver, who shows up outside his door ten minutes later.

The driver escorts Tom through the various checkpoints that lead to the car garage, which is filled with over twenty polished, high-profile SUVs, limousines, and luxury cars.

They climb into the silver sports car and buckle up, with windows automatically rolling down on both sides, when the driver revs the engine and speeds off.

Within seconds, the driver comes to a quick halt near two steel doors, leaning toward the glove compartment, opening it, and pressing a gold button to activate the electronic doors.

The driver keeps steady eyes on the traffic light on the lamppost until it turns green when the car moves into another tunnel.

They slowly approach a joined road, where the driver advances out of thick Weeping Willow tree limbs and onto the cliff's edge, flashing his I.D. to two weapons-carrying security guards.

"I didn't catch your name, sir..., I'm Tom."

"J. Taft, but just call me Joe..., it's a pleasure." Joe shakes Tom's hand, slows down at the second set of doors, and moves forward until the bumper slightly crosses an infrared beam.

A small mountainside opening slowly rises out of nowhere.

The wall lowers after the car's tires cross the actuator when they come to a slow roll, then take off and, minutes later, reach the highway.

Joe pops in a CD and cranks up the tunes, with both heads soon rocking from side to side.

Tom is dropped off at his hotel an hour later, with the driver passing Tom a business card with instructions on the back for reaching him on short notice.

CHAPTER SIX:
THE ISLAND OF TERROR

Tom reaches his room twenty minutes later, opening the door and checking for signs of forced entry when the phone rings, startling him and then ringing twice before he can get to it.

"Hi, darling," Nichelle seductively whispers

"Perfect timing! How are you, sweets?"

"Just fine, Honey! So tell me..., where have you been..., out there giving my stuff away?"

"Now, why would you say something silly like that? I told you I was saving it for you, babe, but hey..., what's with the noise in the background?" Tom asks, hearing the chambering of several weapons until the phone goes muffled, and he's unable to make out the sound when it ceases from her fast-waving hands.

"I'm at the airport, Honey..., with all the messages I left, I thought you'd be here by now with open arms."

"Well, I would've been had I known you were here or got your messages; I'm dying to see you."

"Well then, don't make me wait, Sweetie," she says in her sexy accent, making a seductively, long kissing sound and ending the call.

Tom straps on a weapon and heads out front, waving down a taxi.

Half a block away, a Cuban limousine driver fumbles around with the SATCOM phone, with eyes over the hotel entrance, and can't get a signal. He toys with the device for a few more seconds until briefly looking up and then doing a double-take, surprised to find Tom when he passes a stone pillar with his phone to his ear. The driver's face looks confused when pressing more buttons and trying to re-link the SATCOM phones.

The limousine driver fumbles with the device more, but the display stays blank, so he calls and informs the Cuban Headquarters that the phones are no longer traceable. He keeps his eyes on Tom with his head slowly tilted back into the headrest while adjusting himself and then leans back into the plush seat with a smirk.

Tom climbs into the taxi, and the Cuban driver patiently waits, and then looks in the side mirror, pulling away and quieting the five women and three male passengers as he closes in on the taxi.

Tom arrives thirty minutes later, pays his driver, then slips into a street shop, purchasing six long-stemmed red roses.

Nichelle's phone beeps several times, but she continues in conversation.

Tom walks around, finally spotting Nichelle on her cell phone with her back to him. He begins tiptoeing with one hand behind his back, clenching the roses tightly and attempting to sneak up on her.

Nichelle's eyes wander until she's distracted, finding a woman signaling her to Tom's presence; looking off and staring into the big hobby shop display window, she notices Tom. She immediately terminates the call but pretends she's still talking, then turns as if surprised, greeted with beautiful roses and sensual kisses when motioning him to wait while saying her goodbyes.

They indulge in a third-long kiss that lasts for what feels like minutes when he forgets he's in public with a hand grasping her waist and sliding down her backside.

His eyes slowly drift over her shoulder, somewhat embarrassed, looking up to find an older couple watching with their noses turned up when hastily reaching for her luggage and leading her to the lower-level baggage claim area.

Over half an hour later, they walk through the ticket area after finally claiming her luggage.

A British-looking woman steps out from behind a beam, secretly taking still-shots of them until satisfied, then quickly uplinks the pictures to the Cuban Headquarters and walks out, strutting across the street. She stops and looks around before climbing into the backseat of a limousine and easing the door shut.

"What shall we do today?" Tom asks, successfully flagging down a taxi.

"I don't care, sweetness, as long as it's with you."

They are deep in conversation and have not noticed that most streets are roped off with yellow police tape near the hotel.

The driver slows and pulls up to the red light when Nichelle stares over and into the face of a beautiful blonde sitting in the limousine next to them. "Sir, why are the roads blocked?" Nichelle asks, winking at the woman and quickly making eye contact with the cabby through the rearview mirror.

"The annual parade," the driver says, staring into her lovely eyes after noticing Tom sightseeing out the side window when looking back into her pretty face and smiling.

The woman in the back of the limousine sits behind the dark, tinted windows with her head leaning against her open hand. She continually stares at Tom until her eyes wander to the floor, and a tear falls from under dark shades, rolling down her cheek. The other eye fills until there is a steady stream of tears when she adjusts her arms and rests her head against her knuckles. Her keepsake bracelet falls to the thick part of her arms, dangling back and forth while she keeps her blurry eyes on Tom, not blinking until he becomes clear.

Tom's head slightly eases back as the cab thrust forward when traffic begins to move again.

Nichelle sits in deep thought with eyes scanning over every street they pass.

Tom sits in silence longer until in a delayed thought. "You know..., a parade does sound nice," Tom says, turning and looking into her eyes when she gently strokes his hand.

The cabbie drops them blocks from the hotel, and they enter the back of the lobby minutes later.

They make it to the room, and when inside, Tom helps her unpack, and they jump onto the bed, kissing until loud cheers are heard outside the window as the big bands draw near. Within minutes, they rush into the streets, holding hands, forcing their way through the thick crowd, and soon stand near the corner where the parade is to pass. They finally find a vacant spot where Nichelle stops and stands in front of him, pulling his arms around her waist, cuddling and swaying in good spirits. She begins toying with him, and when thinking no one is watching, she slowly and seductively grinds on him.

Tom presses forward, settling deep into her and slightly stretching the thin nylon skirt. "Any harder, and I'd penetrate this little thin-ass skirt at the seam and be deep inside you," he playfully whispers.

"Please do..., babe, please," she sighs, slightly turning to look up and kiss him.

Two hours later, the last banner pass, and people begin dispersing, but the street traffic grows thick with vehicles, and the sidewalks instantly are crowded again.

Tom and Nichelle stop at a corner bar for drinks and stay there for an extended spell, but after sunset, they head for the fancy restaurant connected to his hotel.

Nichelle finds the scenery very soothing and relaxing. "This place is somewhat romantic and cozy, babe. I want to eat in..., hey..., how about over there?" she says, pointing to the cozy little corner away from everyone.

A waitress comes over to seat them. "Good evening! Will it be dinner for two?" the tall, skinny Asian waitress asks, slightly bowing and smiling.

"Yes, we'll take that booth." Nichelle points to the cozy little corner again.

Tom pulls out a chair across from where he's going to sit, and she eases into it, reaching for menus just placed in front of them.

Their eyes gaze up and down the menu and then over a few colorful pictures.

The waitress turns to talk to another worker when Nichelle reaches across the table and strokes his hand, then retracts her hand when the waitress turns to them again. The waitress walks away briefly and then comes back, easing down cloth napkin-wrapped utensils when smiling and staring deeply into Tom's eyes when noticing Nichelle's not looking.

"I'll take your drink orders if you're ready," she says, winking and then smiling to let him know she really is feeling him.

"I need a few more minutes," Nichelle says, turning the menu over and scrolling down the wine list just for the hell of it.

"No problem, I'll come back to you in a sec," she says, slightly sucking in her bottom lip, then winking again before turning and walking off.

Nichelle looks over to find Tom with a childish look, and he blushes uncontrollably. Her eyes wander to the waitress, who is now standing at the computer punching in numbers, but gazing back over to their table from time to time until noticing Nichelle sits staring back, without breaking her stare.

She reaches for his hand to regain his attention and then stares at him with a concerned look to let him know she's attentive to what is happening with the waitress; then abruptly releases his hand, letting him know she disapproves of his actions. She stares longer and then looks away, slightly shaking her head and smiling when he smiles at her. "Mmm..., what do you think? Chicken and broccoli, maybe?" Nichelle says, pointing at the dish on the menu when reaching for his hand again.

"I think I'll have Mongolian house with shrimp, beef, and chicken or hot pepper chicken with hot and sour soup," he responds, laying the menu down when gazing deep into her beautiful eyes, and running his index finger across the back of her soft hand.

The waitress walks back up, and Nichelle lifts the menu quickly, scrolling through it, and takes even more time to piss off the waitress. "Umm..., Merlot and a side glass of ice," she finally says, looking over at Tom to let him know she's being rude intentionally.

Tom's eyes ease from her and go to the waitress, who seems to be in a daze, smiling like a kid with a first crush. "The same," Tom whispers, smiling and then quickly looking back at the menu when seeing Nichelle with a firm stare.

The waitress scribbles down their drink order and walks away with her eyes wandering back over to Tom a few times.

"Hey, you..., don't you think you're a little too far from me?" he asks, smiling and then winking to regain her attention and break the chill.

Nichelle stares with a firm look. "I don't know..., maybe..., what do you think?" she responds, somewhat rudely, while looking over Tom's shoulder at the well-dressed suspicious-looking Cuban gentleman standing with the curtains pulled slightly back.

She looks around the room cautiously and finds the waitress standing off to the side, talking to another waitress and nodding over at Tom when slipping one sandal off and placing her warm foot against Tom's inner thighs, continually moving it back and forth, playfully.

She slumps slightly under the table, feeling him instantly swelling, and continues in foreplay until the tip of her toe becomes lightly moist.

"Naughty girl, now look what you've done," he says, totally aroused by her foreplay when reaching down and readjusting himself.

Nichelle eyes wander again, looking for the man again, noticing he has vanished, so she scans the through the crowd.

They continue in foreplay and become lost in mischief, failing to notice the waitress' presence because her voice is slightly lower than the mellow jazz playing in the background.

Nichelle notices her first, pretending not to have seen her, with eyes slowly drifting upward to find the waitress's eyes locked on Tom's inseam.

The waitress sighs, seeing him reposition himself a second time.

Nichelle grows fierce until turning red when loudly clearing her throat and still staring at the waitress, who finally looks down at her and then away, somewhat embarrassed. "Damn! Yes, Mongolian house with shrimp, beef, and chicken," she says rudely.

Tom sits in deep thought. "Ok..., well, I'll have the hot pepper chicken with hot and sour soup," he says, laying the menu down and staring back over at Nichelle and then the waitress finally registering that Nichelle's tone has changed.

Minutes later, the waitress appears with a co-worker, placing their plates and drinks on the table.

The waitress stares at Tom when Nichelle pretends to look away and then winks before turning.

Nichelle instantly catches the gesture but not the wink when frowning, throwing up a middle finger behind the waitress' back, causing Tom to spray a mouth full of wine into the seat next to him when trying not to laugh.

The lovely evening continues with them humoring each other the entire meal and becomes more playful until it's time to leave.

Another waitress walks up, placing the bill before him, and he digs deep into his pocket, counting off enough extra for a healthy tip which Nichelle snatches right before the waitress while Tom turns his head.

They exit and enter the lobby, and Tom grows very cautious, seeing several curious-looking eyes staring and then quickly looking off. They ride the elevator up a few flights until Tom pulls the emergency button, gently forcing her against the mirrored wall, kissing her exposed cleavage a few times, and then the nape of her neck up to her ear lobes. He slips his tongue deep into her mouth when the elevator's loud buzzer causes them to jump.

Tom stops her at the room door, showering her with more kisses until opening the door and slipping the electronic key into his pocket. He lifts Nichelle in his arms, stepping across the threshold; he leans back, shutting the door against his back.

She kisses him around his ear, sucking his neck as he carries her to the bed, where he eases her onto the edge of the bed, kneeling and removing her sandals.

The softness of the carpet soothes her feet when she begins sliding her feet back and forth across the plush carpet until reclining back on both elbows.

Tom excuses himself, heading to the bathroom, where he fills a porcelain basin with hot, soapy water and places it on the floor at her feet. He slightly raises her feet, dipping them, but at her pace and comfort, and when her feet are soft to the touch, he massages them with strong hands, relaxing her.

Nichelle fully reclines back, and before long, she's softly snoring.

Tom eases up and sits in the chair, admiring her beauty for minutes before removing her feet and drying them and, afterward, rubs them in lotion and baby oil until no longer slippery but soft to the touch. In an obsession, he slowly raises her foot, kissing the top of one foot and then the other alternatingly. He kisses her toes, one at a time, until taking her big toe deep in his warm mouth when she is slightly awakened and softly moaning in sheer pleasure.

Somewhat coherent, Nichelle finally registers the full sensation when trembling, quickly snatching her feet back and letting off a loud, silly scream of laughter until, like greased lightning, she jumps up. "No, no, no, I can't take it, babe!" she moans, uncontrollably giggling until it tapers off, and she stands slowly, turning from him, unwrapping her wraparound skirt and dropping it. Nichelle looks over her shoulder, seductively winking and motioning for him to unbutton her.

She stands tense, feeling the last button loosen the top, slowly lifting it from her body, smiling in a playful spirit until she is down to her matching bra and G-string. She climbs on the bed, swaying her hips, and then gently rolls over onto her back with smooth-shaved, long legs apart, slowly enticing him. She begins continually stroking her silky, smooth thighs from her knees upward, slowly and seductively, then slightly eases her G-string to one side with one finger, teasing as she pretends to show him his treat.

Tom rests on his side with his head propped against one hand, watching her continually toy with him for over ten minutes until he's overheated. She finally reaches for him, pulling him into her arms, softly kissing him with her tongue deep in his mouth when her hand slides down his thigh, grabbing a fistful of him. Nichelle squeezes harder, totally turned on when then harder, temporarily cutting off his circulation, and within minutes, he's numb but refuses to complain.

Tom grows overheated when standing, loosening his trousers and dropping them, and opening his shirt as she gazes over his masculine body.

She swiftly, then slowly, mounts on the edge of the bed on her knees with her feet hanging off the side until turning her round, smooth, apple-bottom in the air, burying the side of her pretty face in the silky pillows. Now with plans to tease Tom right off, she giggles childishly.

After an hour of nonstop rough sex, they cuddle, drenching in sweat, still breathless while French-kissing.

Before sunrise, Nichelle awakes, having to use the bathroom and sits tingly with her feet easing to the cool carpet. She sits nude and summarily stands, weak, instantly losing her balance, and dropping yet manages to break her fall when grasping the edge of the bed. She sits longer until she feels stable, with her knees still slightly bent, her strength comes back quickly, and she tries to stand again.

She stays in the bathroom longer, and when she finishes, she doesn't flush, so she doesn't wake him.

The door cracks at the seam and slowly spreads wide open when she eases out, heading to the living room with mildly rubbery legs.

Nichelle flops on the couch, still tingling, and quietly listens to see if she has woken Tom. She reaches for a pen, comforted, and begins scribbling a note, then orders him room service.

Tom's mild snore grows louder as she quietly walks around, gathering her things and rushing while dressing.

A gentle knock comes at the door as she zips her last piece of luggage, rushing to the door so as not to wake him, and opens it wide.

An old man pushes the food cart forward, stopping it a few feet inside, gazing into her lovely face, with eyes slowly browsing over her hot, sexy body. He smiles, bows with his eyes closed, and then opens them, greeted with a healthy tip, bows again, and walks out.

Nichelle carefully listens while growing anxious and nervous when easing onto the edge of the sofa, removing a small, shiny, silver bottle. She pours half its contents into the cranberry juice and slips her index finger into the cup, slowly stirring. Nichelle wipes the residue from her fingers with a napkin from the tissue box, gathering the rest of her things and placing them on top of the largest piece of luggage. She opens the door, leaving it cracked when pulling her belongings into the hallway, walking inside, and rolling the cart over near the bed.

Tom snores even louder, but he abruptly opens his eyes when hearing the door slam and the lock click. Still exhausted, he sits up against the headboard with a hint of bacon and sausage rushing into his nostrils, but with a full bladder, he jumps to his feet and runs to the bathroom.

He returns to find a pink, folded, lipstick-stained note and climbs under the sheets, unfolding the note with eyes running over her lovely handwriting, then the perfectly stained lips, until registering the first word.

Good morning Honey,

I had a ball, babe! Now I can honestly communicate with my girlfriends in lovemaking conversations. I'll know what they're talking about exactly when they discuss sex in detail; thanks, sweetness. I couldn't handle telling you I was only in town for a day, so I left this cute little note, which I hope you will enjoy. I hope you enjoy your breakfast, darling. After all your hard work, you make sure you drink plenty of juice to get your strength back up, especially my favorite, cranberry juice. There's one thing for sure: how you handled your business last night and this morning will forever be painted in this girl's mind. Just know this, and I say it honestly: No man has ever handled me like you, babe. Actually, there's little doubt as to if one ever will. Mmm..., you're the greatest. P.S. I love the way you broke me in. Damn! Mmm..., and I loved it when you called my name like a little bitch! Xoxoxoxo (kisses)!

Tom instantly grows excited, and a big smile comes, reading and pretending she's standing, telling him those things in her beautiful, foreign accent. He rolls over and sits, eating, and afterward drinks the milk and orange juice, which are his favorite. Tom wraps up the dish and lifts the cranberry juice to drink it when the phone rings. He lowers the juice onto the cart and dives across the bed with one hand extended when grasping the phone on the third ring. "Hello."

The person on the other end abruptly hangs up.

A sharp, hard knock comes at the door almost instantaneously, causing him to jump and grab his robe with the gun. "Room service, sir, we forgot your fruit."

Tom buries his hand deep in his robe and aims the gun at the door when he opens it, looking an old woman over, from head to toe. "Thanks, but I'm full..., but wait..., you can take the cart, please."

The woman rambles inside, placing the beautiful, decorative fruit bowl on the cart. She rolls the cart to the door with Tom close on her trail and with wandering eyes all over her lovely shape, which she switches a little more than usual from having a younger man behind her.

Tom stops her at the door and slips her a healthy tip, then extends the door wider so she can get the cart through.

The phone rings several times when the door locks, and he answers to find the caller hanging up, but after the fourth call, he leaves the phone off the hook. He reclines and relaxes, with his mind filled with thoughts of Nichelle, before falling fast asleep.

Nichelle sits continually calling several more times, then eases back into the plush limousine seats smiling when reaching for her favorite top-shelf drink and toasting with five others.

Several hours later, the phone rings in the limousine, and Nichelle answers with eyes instantly filling with tears when receiving word that her sister, Nadine's body, has been identified in the coroner's office. She breaks down, crying hard until, in a light whine, there's total silence amongst the others. Her hand comes forward, tapping the driver's shoulder when instructing him to drive in the opposite direction than usual when going to Nadine's mansion.

Within half an hour, they pull up to where the immaculate mansion once stood, spotting the massive rolls of crime scene tape blowing in the wind.

Nichelle goes into a deep depression when breaking down even harder for a long spell until finally reminiscing on her sister's bold speeches about strength when she pulls out a black, sheer scarf from her purse, covering her head and face.

Oggie and Cynthia lounge around, waiting to hear from Tom, who finally calls while they're napping.

Tom obtains an operational update from Oggie, and then lounges around longer before calling for a rental car.

Hours later, Tom's phone rings.

"Good day, sir; there's a rental agent here for you. You will have to come down and sign for your rental," the desk attendant says, gazing back at the agent's name tag.

Tom approaches the counter shortly after that, scanning the lobby thoroughly for any suspicious activity. He waves to the agent greeting him, then follows him outside, looking over the shiny, metallic-gray, high-profile, super sports car.

The agent shows off the car's features and then turns, passing the agreement, which Tom glances over and signs before settling the bill. Tom gives a firm handshake and then waves goodbye, unlocking the secured first T-top and then the other top. He arrives at Tony's hotel within the hour, picking the key lock and retrieving his personal belongings, and then heads to Bobby's hotel, where he enters through the back door near the pool.

He makes an illegal entry into Bobby's room, pulling his belongings out and stuffing them in suitcases. He quickly shuffles through drawers and closet, then makes another quick round, zipping the last bag, when hearing a loud thump on the balcony. He instantly drops down, drawing his 9MM when low-crawling near the window, and slowly standing with his back pressed against the wall. Shortly after that, he hears another bump, taking a couple of deep breaths with beads of sweat dripping down the side of his face.

With a deep breath, Tom throws the curtains back abruptly, training his weapon around when rapidly dropping his aim below his waist at the sudden movement.

"No, no..., not my baby!" the child's mother screams, staring into Tom's eyes, shocked, while continually waving Tom off until he slightly lowers the weapon when she reaches over the low partition for her little boy.

Tom swiftly fades behind the thick swinging curtains with his back still pressed against the wall, taking intense breaths to slow his rapid heart rate. He gets his thoughts together and quickly walks off, making another quick sweep of the room until satisfied, yet still somewhat dazed from the near-death incident with the kid. Tom bundles other items together and grabs the suitcases, and rushes out. He expressly comes up on the passenger side door, dropping suitcases in the front seat, and rushes to the other side.

A faint scream rises, and he looks up, finding the woman standing next to a hotel worker, pointing down at the rental when Tom jumps over the driver's door and revs the engine, burning rubber and skidding wheels out of the parking lot. He comes up on the stop sign slowing, then gunning the engine when shooting out in front of a car, skidding wheels to miss him when he guns it, then slows quickly, coming up fast on an unmarked police car.

Tom makes a few stops and arrives at his hotel, unloading the suitcases on a dolly and then placing the T-tops back on. He cautiously makes his way to the room with attentive eyes, even more, cautious when entering his room. Tom begins stowing the suitcases in the closet and then reaches into his bags, removing his .22 and strapping it to his ankle. He places the ammo cartridges in his pocket, slips the 9MM into his backpack, and closes the closet door.

Tom grows bored later, so he goes sightseeing, and along the way, he spots a few cars that seem to have been tailing him, so with swift maneuvers, he shakes off any suspicious vehicle before entering the city. He soon arrives at his hotel and parks on the upper level, where he sits cautiously, looking around until exiting and entering the lobby and closing the desk with fast, swarming eyes. "Excuse me, sir, room 3579, can you tell me if I had any calls or visitors?" he asks the desk clerk as he turns to the desk.

The clerk turns away with a fast-scrolling index finger until pointing at Tom's in-box. "Why yes, sir..., a Ms. Kelley, thirty minutes ago; she would like for you to return her call," the clerk says, passing Tom the several messages previously relayed to him over the phone.

Tom surveys his surroundings while waiting on the elevator, and then quietly rides up with an old grey-headed lady with dark shades on until exiting and bidding her a good day with no response when waving him off with an unconcerned hand when he's out of view. Tom eases inside the room, unstrapping his .22, and placing his .357 under his bed pillow, then showers and sits around in a semi-trance until falling fast asleep on top of the covers, half-nude but draped in a towel.

Six hours pass when Tom jump, awakened by keys dropping outside his door when glimpsing over at the digital clock, which read 2:05 a.m. He finally notices the message light intermittently flashing when sitting, then easing to the edge of the bed, somewhat nervous. His heart races while sliding his hand under his pillow, grasping his 357 Magnum while tightening his towel at his waist and reaching for his trousers. Instead, he quietly rolls to the floor, assuming a prone position when hearing the lightly jiggling doorknob.

He spots two shadows frantically moving back and forth underneath the door when reaching for his trousers again, realizing there's no time to dress when leaving them. He moves forward until hearing women whispering, though the conversation is unclear, so he makes his way closer to the door, hearing the woman's voices mutter again when keys softly jiggle in the lock. He backs away softly until against the wall and moves behind the couch to procure a better aim when taking a deeper cover. His hand slides to his waist, tightening his towel again when patiently waiting and profusely perspiring.

The door slowly opens though mildly squeaking, until fully extended with an array of light shining in from the hallway and lighting half the room.

Tom watches the hotel worker's hand fold as she collects her large pay for the illegal entry, with lights slowly fading when the door eases shut and the room dims.

A five-foot-eleven, beautiful, firm, native woman with a medium build and long black hair draped just below her breasts quietly stand in the dimly-lit room, looking around until her eyes adjust.

Now, she's wearing a short, sleek, black sundress with black high-heel pumps; a total knockout. Well, she stands listening, takes a few quiet steps, and floats about the room.

"Freeze!" Tom whispers in an authoritative voice upon seeing her hand slip inside her purse.

She slowly removes her hand, dropping the purse and freezing, then eases a hand on her hips and sticks her hip out one hip in a sexual gesture.

Tom keeps trained eyes on her. "You..., you..., over to the light!" he nervously stutters when she steps off, swaying her hips when stopping over by the night light and across from the couch. He slowly trains his gun directly at her face and then quickly moves to the door with eyes glued on her until she cuts on the bright-white overhead lights. "Well, well, well..., what or who do I owe for this late-night or should I say early-morning visit?"

"Nothing and no one," she replies. "Major Fields asked me to deliver a disc." The woman smiles in deep thought with eyes swarming over his body, then slowly walks up to him with a more sensual smile with her index finger over the barrel and guiding it down. Her lovely eyes slowly close with her warm breath heavily against the shaft of his neck and chest when her eyes slowly open, and she stares deep into his eyes.

He stares in disbelief. "Hell, I could have killed you," he says, looking deep into the woman's beautiful eyes but backing away, uneasy.

"Yeah, but you didn't. Besides, that was a chance I was willing to take," she replies.

"Yeah, and you could've just counted yourself dead! Just consider yourself lucky because I was seconds from popping a few slugs in your ass!" he says in a moderate tone.

"Ok, look..., enough of the bullshit, already! Do you want the disc or not?" she asks with an even sexier islander accent.

"Well..., of course I want it!" Tom hesitantly replies.

"Then start being a little fuckin' nicer or I'll leave your punk-ass without it!"

"Yeah? Well..., just know this..., I've got your punk-ass hanging!"

"Really? Then show me or shut the hell up!" she says, leveraging the playing field.

"Look..., just give me the damn disc!"

The woman walks over and picks up her purse.

Tom closely watches her, wondering if she's legitimate or if he is about to be had by some two-bit, beautiful skeezer but thinks to himself that she has to have the finest woman he'd seen.

She fumbles through her purse and then looks up at him a few times, and Tom grows impatiently tense and eases a finger in the trigger well.

Now he doesn't trust her and isn't about to let her gain the upper hand.

She fumbles around more and then slowly pulls out a small disc inscribed in the major's handwriting, and when the signature becomes legible, Tom instantly remembers it from previous missions.

"So, is this what you want, or is it me?" she asks, noticing he's lost in lust when seeing his eyes stale and mouth parted.

"Well, I don't mix business with pleasure," he nervously replies, slowly peeling his eyes from her beauty at a snail's pace when finally looking at the disc and slowly backing away, a little less tense.

The woman throws her purse on the couch and proceeds toward the bar but stops a few feet away, looking into the tilted mirror and then back over her shoulder. "Riiiggghhhttt (right)..., don't mix business with pleasure, huh? Yeah? Well, I can't tell from the way you're making me hot as hell from staring so damn hard at this firm, soft booty," she says playfully, patting a thick, round cheek in each hand and letting it jiggle just so.

"What! So you have eyes in the back of your damn head now?" he sarcastically responds, easing onto the chair's arm.

She looks at him, then at the tilted mirror, then back at him, but he doesn't get it. "No, but that wall mirror is big enough to see everything in this damn room," she says, staring at him through the tilted wall mirror again and then walking over to the couch and flopping down.

Tom slumps in the chair, feeling stupid after such a dumbass question and being handed his ass by some smart-ass, beautiful woman. He realizes she's no amateur but a real professional and seems always to be one step ahead, making him slightly uneasy.

"Do you mind if I have a drink?"

"No problem, but first, I'll have to search your purse, then you," he says, creating a lame excuse for putting hands all over her sexy body.

She mischievously stares at him, dimming her eyes to look even sexier.

Tom quickly searches her purse, and then anxiously throws it on the couch, motioning her to stand and turn around.

She smiles, turning and reaching for the back of the couch, spreading bowlegs a few inches apart, then poking her bottom out more.

Tom's eyes rove over her, and he can't help but notice the beautiful curves of her sexy body, the smell of her perfume, and her smooth, butter-pecan, sun-tanned complexion.

Now through her short, sleek, sheer sundress, Tom sees lightly sun-tanned cheeks protruding from the bottom of her faintly red-and-black ruffled, satin garter when growing overly impressed with her overall beauty and spirit. For sure, she's left nothing to the imagination as to how drop-dead gorgeous she looks without the clothes she'd literally poured into oh-so-well.

"Well, are you going to search me or stand there looking stupid?"

Now at this point, Tom is lost and doesn't even hear a word until it finally registers when placing the gun on the table. He positions both hands firmly on her shoulders when she expressly flips him onto the couch, senselessly giggling. She swiftly comes into her favorite karate stance, playfully rocking back and forth like a true professional but in a peal of even sillier laughter.

Tom lunges for the gun in deep fear, but she clips him to the floor, rolling him a few times when an even louder outburst of laughter comes as she playfully stands with her hand masked over her face. She jumps and swiftly grabs the weapon, pointing it at him while senselessly giggling again.

"Whoa, mama!" he says with one hand slightly covering his face and the other nervously trembling.

She giggles more, and then leans, putting the gun back. "Honey, your ass is seriously slipping," she says, holding a hand out when he declines, speedily jumping to his feet, embarrassed. She smiles again, reaching for the back of the couch, spreading her bow legs while uncontrollably giggling senselessly. Now, when she finally gets most of the laughter out, she looks back, batting her sexy eyelashes.

Tom eases up on her, straddling her legs more to ensure she can't pull another roll stunt, then runs fingers through her soft, long hair. He continues, working his way down to her perfectly structured neck, her firm shoulders, and bulging just-right breasts, taking one breast in each hand, gently squeezing and then releasing them with eyes slightly closed. Tom slowly moves a hand down, stroking her upper ribcage, then six-pack abs a few times. He freezes, listening when hearing someone pass the door, then proceeds to her firm, muscular thighs, kneading them thoroughly before pulling her dress up and around her hips to make her readily accessible for a more thorough search.

Now, from his angle, her high-raised pelvis looks like a balled fist pushed through a G-string.

Tom grows aroused madly with eyes swarming over her smooth, raised skin, protruding from each side of her G-sting, making him expand like a balloon on helium. He steps back and instantly feels the towel pulling and tightening at his waist and backside. 'Damn!' he thinks almost out loud, palming her warm, soft cheeks, one in each hand, as they melt like the softest of the highest quality cotton.

She lightly moans, turning him on, when slowly turning her head and batting long eyelashes. "If you like what you see, then why don't you just take it, honey? Now, just make sure you're brave enough to handle me like a real man or step off because I haven't had a man do this right in quite some time!"

Fully aroused, Tom feels the towel tightening again until thinking the tucked material would unravel. Although very tempted to go for it, something won't let him tighten it or trust her just yet, so he proceeds, running his hands between her inner firm and more relaxed creamy thighs.

"Ooh, babe, please don't stop!" she whispers, tensing from the slightest touch. She begins breathing harder and harder until she is completely turned on and twirling her hips in a slow, sensual dance.

Tom instantly feels the towel loosening more, and within seconds he feels that it is almost to a point where it no longer clings to his waist.

"I've got to have this," she pouts, looking back at the still-stretching towel while moaning in sheer pleasure. "Please don't make me beg," she moans louder, looking back with the right side of her bottom lip pulled between her teeth and dimming her eyes to look sexier.

"Ok..., you're clean!" He backs away, tightening the towel. "Let me get you that drink," he says, picking up the .357 and continually watching her through the mirror while proceeding to the bar.

The woman drops dropped down on the couch, seductively staring at him.

"Sekif's Treasures: cognac, brandy, or gin?" he asks, placing the gun on the bar but keeping his eyes glued on her hands or browsing over her hot body.

She looks through the mirror at him, winking, kissing, and then dimming her sexy eyes. "Whatever you prefer," she says, slowly straightening her clothes and then sitting up, ladylike when crossing her legs. She reserves a few more seconds to better straighten her clothes before fixing her hair and tidying up her makeup with just her fingers.

Tom pours the double shots of Sekif's Cognac on the rocks. He turns to hand her the drink, catching the towel at his lower thigh.

They make immediate eye contact, and her surprised look assures him that she'd gotten an eyeful when seeing her eyes still bulging. She stares longer with eyes coming upward fast with his quick hands when slowly lowering her head, realizing she won't get to see him totally nude.

She stares deep into his eyes, then seductively at the towel while licking her lips. "Get dressed, or drop the towel right now..., it's your call."

"Fair enough," Tom responds, handing her the drink. He reaches for his drink and takes a sip, walking back over and picking up the gun. "Excuse me while I slip into something more appropriate." He walks into the bathroom and then back to the door, peeping to find her touching up her hair again in the mirror.

Tom cautiously remains near his firearm while dressing and then finally walks back into the room, easing the gun down on the opposite side of her when starting a conversation about Major Fields, leading to more personal things about her life when getting around to formally introducing themselves.

The more they talk, the more at ease he becomes, especially knowing how familiar she is with the Major Fields.

"So tell me..., how well do you know your captain?"

"Quite well, I would say. I've been working with this captain for quite a while..., why do you ask?" he responds, feeling totally comfortable knowing she knows of his captain.

"Nothing, it's just that the major has always spoken very highly of him and more than his own blood brother." She eases up, grabs both glasses, and walks over to the bar.

Their eyes meet up in the mirror, and she winks. "Tom, right..., another?" she asks, rattling fast-melting ice cubes.

"Sure, a double," he says with eyes continually wandering over her hot body until staring at her backside from head to toe.

They sit longer, chatting before she suggests dinner later.

"It's getting late," she says, looking at her locket when lifting her purse.

"You mean early," he shyly responds, yawning at about the same time that she does.

They guffaw, looking eye-to-eye until their eyes drift off somewhat shyly.

She looks away longer, and then looks again, staring deep into her pretty eyes, when she gently kisses him on the cheek. "You know you could easily persuade me to stay, right?" she says, smirking.

"If I have it like that, then stay," he confidently responds while questioning if he's making a good decision or a grave mistake when she does some silly gesture, dropping her purse, thrilled when running into the bedroom, diving onto the bed. "Do you mind if I sleep in my panties and bra?" she asks, easing one foot to the floor and then standing, looking at him over her shoulder.

"That's totally up to you," he says in a smooth but unsure tone when going back for the gun and moving it to the bedroom.

She reaches for the back of her neck, unbuttoning her snaps, and then pulls at her waistband, wiggling her hips to stretch the material around her dangerous curves until the dress freely falls.

They climb onto the bed and talk longer, and before long, they snuggle and talk a little longer until they fall fast asleep.

Hours later, Tom is awakened from a nightmare, sitting up, still exhausted, but straining to look at his watch and then over at the clock on the wall, comparing times. His eyes drift to the gun, easing in under the edge of the mattress when looking at the time again. "Latisha, its 6:20!" he says, yawning and stroking her soft back.

"Wow, really!" she sluggishly responds, springing for the phone beside the bed.

Within seconds, Tom slightly hears the phone ringing and cuddles closer, putting his arms around her and caressing her soft, half-naked body until stroking her gently.

Latisha closes her eyes in a light moan swaying her hips a few times, laying sideways in a belly dance and stopping when a woman's voice answers. She immediately moves his hands back, giggling.

Now, after making arrangements with her sister concerning her daughter and then work, she hangs up and turns back to him, finding him smiling and rolling onto his back. Her hands massage his hairy chest, slowly working their way to his six-pack abs. "Ooh, what a lovely six-pack!" she says, continually rubbing soft hands over his washboard abs until he can barely feel her touch when she begins lighting her finger off him. She kisses his firm neck, slowly moving her hands past his navel when the rim of his boxers gently presses against her fingertips which work back and forth a few times. She makes several attempts at stretching the material so her hand can slide inside, but the boxers are too tight for the large, clustered diamond ring to pass through. "That's not even fair, honey! Why do you have on these tight-ass kiddy boxers? Man..., can you even breathe in these things?" she asks, giggling.

"Wait a minute! You agreed this was going to be strictly platonic." Tom rolls onto his side and slides closer to her, looking deep into her eyes with warm breaths against her skin. "Latisha, I've got to give it to you..., you're the finest woman I've seen in my life..., hmm..., then again, there was this one other here, but she is not in competition with you," he laughs, jerking back when she takes a quick, playful swipe at him. "Are you sure you're not married or involved?"

"No, really..., thanks for the compliment, but no, I'm not. I mean..., I do date, occasionally."

They are quiet for minutes caressing and playfully toying with each other until she looks at her watch and sits on the edge of the bed in deep thought.

Tom eases up as well, and they continue in conversation while dressing.

Latisha walks over, looks in the mirror, straightens her hair, and then starts making the bed. She turns back, straightening the covers, and then throws the comforter over the bed, not satisfied, and makes one last tug and is finally ok.

"Look at the time..., look at the time. So tell me..., are we on for a late dinner?"

"Dinner? I was thinking breakfast, like right now," he says, winking.

"Look now..., there's work to be done, honey, so let's say 8 p.m., at my place, so here's my address and number," she says, scribbling on the notepad next to the nightstand.

Tom eases the gun into the back of his pants, and they exit.

They approach the lobby, and a new female at the front desk stares back at Tom, smiling as he walks past with Latisha snuggling on his arm.

Toms stops her at the door and kisses her until she playfully pulls away, then waves to her when she looks back, waving when approaching a row of parked cars.

Now off in the opposite direction, a limousine sits parked out front, with heads either looking at Tom or Latisha.

Suddenly, a woman's body slumps forward through the window behind the driver's seat with hands resting on the headrest. Her eyes go back and forth between Latisha and Tom until teardrops make light trails through her lightly made-up, veil-covered face. She finally feels a tear near the side of her lip, licking it away and slouching while drifting into a trance. Her eyes browse down over her hand with a gun held tightly in her fist. Her eyes wander over the keepsake bracelet that the man she loves so much and her kids had given her a few years earlier for Valentine's Day.

Latisha's taillights finally come on, with the gearshift tight in hand, when she begins backing out. She motions her arm out the window, and two black, tinted-window SUVs close in swiftly on the tail of her car. She waves to Tom again and moves toward the intersection, where one SUV takes the lead and the other close in as they merge into heavy traffic.

With one last wave, Tom proceeds back to his room. "Excuse me, sir!" a male clerk says, reaching for the in-box. "Powells, right? You had a call earlier," he says, staring at the note. "Kelley said to call her at Martha's tomorrow," he says, passing the note. "And please tell Johns' he's the father of a new, nine-pound, bouncing baby girl, Robianna," he says, smirking when leaning under the counter, passing Tom several complimentary hotel cigars.

"Well..., thank you, sir." Tom grasps the cigars, immediately turning when his vision blurs from the quick thought of his fallen men, but clears when noticing the elevator door is still open. He turns in a slow jog and sticks his hand toward the retracting door with eyes on the woman when she comes into view.

"Sorry, I didn't see you," the old woman he had assisted days earlier says with a serious look and then a fake smile.

"No problem, ma'am..., I didn't know you were in here," he says with his back slightly turned to her while trying to dry his tears with his shirt sleeve, unnoticed.

They ride up quietly with her still behind him, looking him up and down with a frown that quickly transforms into an evil face when the flashes of Nadine's dead body flash across her mind.

"Well, you have a prosperous day," he says, hearing the elevator bell ring.

"You do the same," she responds, breaking her frown and smiling when Tom turns and smiles before walking off.

The woman watches his foot vanish, and the doors retract when adjusting her wig and straightening her shades, mumbling under her breath until outraged and crying, repeatedly smashing her cane against the mirrored walls like a crazy woman, shattering a few.

Mild to heavy growing bangs and shattering glass rise in Tom's ears when backing fast and pressing his ear against the elevator's door until the sound momentarily fades as the elevator car rises higher. He stands longer until he cannot hear the bangs when hasting to his room and packing everything. He removes his .22 from the pillow, straps it around his ankle, and then searches through drawers and cabinets, with his mind wandering over all the things that happened up to this point. He does another quick search and, feeling assured he has everything, grasps two of the four bags and exits.

The elevator soon opens, and he stands back, staring at the broken mirrors and the crumbled glass strewn over the carpeted floor.

Tom reenters the room, picks up the last two bags, and eases onto the side of the bed, accidentally knocking the .357 Magnum to the floor, stuffing it inside an outer pocket of the black leather bag. He exits and is soon standing outside the car, in deep thought, thinking he has forgotten something, and this time, he enters through the bar. He fades into the half-filled room, still holding the door's locking bar until the door is almost closed when from the parking lot, a set of eyes gaze between Tom's car and the hotel door for minutes.

The hotel's door lock clicks, and feet shuffle with doors slamming.

A manly, gloved hand extends under the bumper of Tom's car, attaching a small tracking device alongside the tailpipe. He quickly stands, cautiously looking around, then walks to the bar's door at a fast pace and steps inside. He quickly scans the room, looking for Tom before speedily heading for the stairwell.

The old, gray-haired Dutch-looking woman and a middle-aged Indian-looking woman stand patiently for the elevator. When the door opens, they wait patiently for an elderly gentleman to exit and grow impatient when the old woman's arms go forward, snatching the man's arm and slamming him into the wall, almost knocking him to the hallway floor.

"What the...!" the man shouts, bracing the wall while staring back as the door slowly closes when managing to flip a middle finger with the old woman's gun-toting hand coming up fast and vanishing behind closed doors.

Instantly, the women load two weapons each and conceal them again under thin Windbreaker-style trench coats.

The older woman anxiously taps her foot, looking at the three lit lights on the panel.

Tom makes one final sweep and sits, calling his driver before leaving the room, exiting through the stairwell where he freezes, hearing mumbled men's and women's voices that suddenly grow louder and fade.

Sandy-bottom shoes quickly shuffle up a few stairs and then slow down, and immediately, there comes the loud sound of metal slamming together while weapons are chambering.

Tom tiptoes down a few steps and slightly bends over the handrail, noticing two gun-toting shadows cautiously advancing upward against the wall. He backs away fast with his back drawn against the wall, removing the .22 until holding to the inner handrails when creeping upward to the same exit with his shadow scurrying up the wall.

The exit door slams open with Tom and the two shadows frozen in fear, surprised.

A tall Puerto Rican-looking woman clutches her handbag, making eye contact with Tom. "Freeze!" she screams, still training her bag upward, reaching for the heat (gun) and trying to bring it down when a blast echoed through the stairwell.

Tom's bullets penetrate her heart, and then there is another blast to her forehead, dead-center when the woman falls back and tumbles past him.

Silenced rounds ring out below as Tom climbs the staircase at top speed. His feet shuffle fast and then slow down at each turn.

The elevator door's bell rings, and the old and middle-aged women exit, creeping down the long hallway quickly. Their eyes gazed at every room number while advancing at an even faster pace, drawing weapons and cautiously looking around. They move slower when inches from Tom's door, abruptly stopping with the old woman knocking and then pounding on the door several times. She grows impatient, firing a silenced round at the door, with eyes swarming over the door, thinking she heard the door knob jingle. She backs up a few feet and dropkicks the door, dismantling it from top to bottom.

A man and woman rush up on their team leader on the stairwell. Peaches' ass is down!" the woman screams, looking over the tall Puerto Rican woman's body when quickly checking her pulse and not getting a response. She and the tall, built man in the wife beater rush off with their weapons training ahead.

"His ass is mine!" the male's voice echoes in the hollow-paved stairwell while Toms makes it to the eighth floor, where he cautiously enters the hallway but accidentally allows the tightly sprung door to slam shut.

Tom rapidly runs to the end of the hallway, pressing his face against the thick glass and looking down. He heads halfway back down the hallway, training his weapon at the exit door, patiently waiting.

The man and woman stop on the seventh floor, peeping then tucking their heads inside, looking and listening with sweat-covered faces, fast-scanning eyes, and nervous hands.

The man leans further into the hallways, finally notices two kids playing undisturbed, and figures that Tom hadn't come that way.

Tom positions himself behind a large steel support beam when noticing the staircase door slowly open when firing one silenced round, with the door slowly closing and then slowly opening again.

The manly body rocks back and forth until finally lunging across the hall, spraying automatic, silenced 9MM rounds toward Tom and landing in an adjacent hallway, breathing hard. The man's heart pounds heavily, with heavier sweat dripping from his face.

Tom tucks himself close against the pillar, repeatedly peeping to get a better angle on the door again, and finds the door still cracked open until hearing light whispers when the woman sticks her head out and cursorily pulls it back, spotting the muzzle of Tom's weapon.

Tom trains his gun to the middle of the hallway, where he anticipates she will drop and roll, and seconds later, he sees her shadow against the floor when she props the door open with something. He watches her slowly rock back and forth a few more times and then lunge forward when Tom expends four rounds into her lower body with a tight trigger finger, rendering her motionless with screams of great cry.

Instantly, the man's hand reaches forward for the woman's hand.

Their fingers barely touch when the man's sweaty hands lose grip.

Tom quickly repositions, taking a steady aim when expending two more rounds: one in her leg, the other in her foot, with the bone impact severing her main artery and causing her to kick and scream until her body drops with legs snatched out of view when the man takes one last deep reach and pulls her into the adjacent hallway.

Tom quietly loads another clip, listening to the deep sound of the man's whiny voice, which begins crying louder when closing his eyes and prejudging the distance of the drop until distracted by the man's loud crying again.

Seconds later, there is total silence as the man quietly reloads.

Tom meditates and then whispers a quiet but quick prayer when coming up, easing forward with eyes on the staircase door, spraying two piercing heads and dropping them back with the door slamming. He fires two more rounds, launching forward at full speed, with a quick look back over his shoulder, firing ahead on automatic, into the glass, until the clip empties. He takes one last hard leap with hands coming upward when diving toward the bullet-riddled thick glass window in midair. His gun goes forward, with elbows finally bent and arms still folding over his head when slamming into the glass. He flies through it, his body quickly vanishing downward with muffled distant and closer shots ringing out with legs finally clearing the window's frame.

The man screams, continually firing on automatic while running even faster with eyes still glued on the tip of Tom's shows which instantly vanishes.

Tom descends quickly, dropping faster until stretching both arms forward, then together and above his head, jackknifing into the hotel's twelve-foot deep-end section of the swimming pool and plunging straight to the bottom. Upon expressly touching the bottom, he pushes off toward the side closest to the hotel's wall, slightly sticking out like a bastion while still submerged with eyes going back quickly, spotting tracers from another bullet flying by with red-smeared streaks of blood from patrons, hit topside.

He swims for the surface, and before he makes it, a bloody body falls backward, with another falling sideways into the pool. He looks to his right, finding a woman in a full stride, swanning, kicking her hands and feet until she is shot in the head, rolling over, and floating upward. He draws closer to the side and finally surfaces, finding a lot of movement along the pool's edge until people vanish from the edge.

The screams seem to fade when his head breaks the water's surface, hearing muffled shots and noises and mild screams as patrons from afar scatter.

The shooter and his accomplices continue spraying more silenced and unsilenced rounds in and around the pool, pissed with no concern for innocent people when firing upon anyone moving.

A few times, Tom hears cannon-like booms from a larger, more powerful weapon, but sometimes in unison with other weapons while still protected by the building's structure until swiftly climbing out. He glances back, finding the young elevator attendant floating face up, with his bloody hotel uniform full of bullet holes.

Tom runs to the garage in full stride, jumping in the car, loudly revving the engine twice with tires immediately squealing and burning dark black rubber tracks across the lightly sanded pavement. He approaches the attendant's booth almost invisibly and slows, continually looking through the rearview mirror while extending his free-parking pass. He steadily blows until a head pops up, and he stares in the face of the attendant, who fearfully stares back at the hotel and then nervously takes his time collecting the pass and raising the guardrail.

The attendant's hand remains out while Tom pulls away with eyes glued on the hotel, where the shots grow louder when out of nowhere, the attendant's head snaps to the left, seeing something flash by, almost invisible. He jumps up, looking over his shoulder, finding someone with long hair running down the long drive toward the back of Tom's car.

Tom speeds to the intersection light with eyes stale in the rearview and side mirrors, watching the guardrail come down slowly. His foot begins nervously and lightly patting on the floor while impatiently waiting for traffic to pass.

Instantly, another vehicle's tires squeal in the garage until overpowered by stronger gunfire.

Suddenly, a few rounds ping off Tom's bumper when he ducks and then looks through the rearview, finding a long-haired individual closing from the rear on the driveway.

Tom's hand impatiently bangs against the steering wheel until the last car passes. He anxiously looks again, finding the long-haired individual's face transforming into that of a beautiful Chinese woman as she appears to slow down and stop taking precision aim. He drops, leaning to one side when flooring the gas pedal, running the red light, and merging into busy highway traffic. He immediately swerves, missing oncoming cars, and then steady on the straightway.

A car flies past Tom with its front window shattered; the driver slumps over the steering wheel and the car swerves until veering off the road and into a pole.

Tom looks over his left shoulder, finding the attendant diving through the booth's window just before a black sports car slams into the shack and rips it to shreds.

The black car swerved into oncoming traffic in a flash and swiftly closed in on Tom with several semiautomatic rounds hitting the rental car's trunk and bumper.

Two rounds pierce the back and front window, and Tom ducks, punching the accelerator, bringing the car up to top speed, leaving the black car a ways back and in a thin black smoke trail.

Tom dodges around a few cars and looks in the rearview mirror again to find the black, nitrogen-powered car tight on his tail and trailing even closer like a heat-seeking missile. He tries a few combat maneuvers, dodging through a few more cars, but the black car manages to counter each of Tom's evasive maneuvers in stealth mode.

The black car bumps Tom's bumper a few more times, rams the rear, slightly tearing off some of the bumper, and then tries hitting the side bumper to put Tom in a tailspin.

Both vehicles finally clear the congested traffic outside of town and come up on the open highway when Tom leans toward the passenger's seat, grabbing his .357 from the side of the leather case. He pulls away, making several more maneuvers, increasing speed. With one last ounce of hope, Tom punches the accelerator again; pulling away, then immediately spins the steering wheel hard to one side. He slams on the brakes, the car sliding sideways several feet through the intersection when unloading two rounds into the black car's windshield and a third into the engine block. The last round penetrates the front driver's tire, causing the black car to spin out of control and slam into a parked car at 80 plus when the hood folds with the car bursting into flames.

Tom thrusts forward toward the lack car and abruptly stops, slamming the transmission in reverse when backing up and then throwing the car in drive, punching the accelerator. He rolls slowly, pulling up next to the smoke-filled sports car, gazing at the long-haired Dominican woman who is unconscious; her body slightly slumped over the door.

Blood drips from the deep gash onto the door, then gushes out of her forehead onto the door until dripping onto the pavement. Her eyes flinch a few times until she quickly regains consciousness, slowly pulling herself back inside and trying to unbuckle when looking over the hood and seeing the high flames. "Help me, help!" she screams, staring at Tom while trying to detach from the jammed seatbelt.

Tom smiles, winks, and revs the engine then speeds off.

Bystanders from afar instantly close in on the wreck as first responders.

"Help me, you fuck! Help!" she screams, waving to nervous bystanders who stand back, looking at the high flames going higher. Her eyes wander over the floor until finally spotting her gun and stretching for it a couple of times, until looking over, yelling at the men again.

The men nervously approach when the fire seems to die down, and without a second thought, they sprint, leaning in and trying to detach the seatbelt when gas fumes grow strong.

A few drips of gas hit the pavement, and a slow and then steady trial comes from the gas tank of the super-charged sports car, slowly making its way through deep grooves and down toward the rear of the heavily damaged and blazing parked car. The gas soon forms a puddle in an indentation in the pavement under the parked car's rear bumper, and in a flash, a fireball swarm over the parked car.

The flames reach the back, and heat begins instantly melting the bumper until dripping black, wax-like fire to the ground.

The second drip of burning plastic hits the ground and rolls within centimeters of a deep fuel puddle, and one man runs up to the rising blaze, warning the others that there is more fire and gasoline at the rear of the car.

The pedestrians try to free the woman, and then back off quickly when the man rushes back up, yelling and tapping on their shoulders one last time.

"Help, help!" the Dominican-looking woman screams, finally managing to unbuckle when reaching for the door handle when the car explodes in flames, creating a huge fireball and mushroom cloud.

Tom is distracted by movement in the rearview mirror, catching a glimpse of the fireball, then a black cloud while staring into the rearview mirror, then the rear of the vehicle, finding the flame-covered, hair-singed woman staggering in circles before being pushed to the ground by two bystanders.

Within seconds, a second explosion comes, consuming the three, with others running off fanning flames.

The black limousine pulls up half a block from the burning car, with back windows rolling down and two heads sticking out from each side, looking at the inferno.

The other four heads begin bobbing around in the back, looking through the tinted windows for Tom's car.

One woman in the back points, finally spotting Tom's car at the top of the hill and motioning to the driver, who pulls away fast.

The front-seat passenger also points and then jumps around excitedly, reaching under her backpack and flipping the switch up on the tracking device. The receiver's light turns green and flashes before turning yellow and red as Tom punches the accelerator, bringing the car up to speeds well above ninety and then slowing when thinking he's far enough from the scene.

Tom accelerates again faster, spotting something at the top of the hill through the rearview but in the distance. A few miles down the road, he turns at the intersection and slows down long enough to call his driver to inform him of his delay, and within five minutes, he pulls into the upper part of a two-level car garage next to his driver's car. He jumped out and unloaded his luggage without delay.

"Great seeing you again, Tom," the driver says, walking over to assist with his bags. As he walks up, a smile grows on the driver's face, shaking Tom's hand. He shakes his head in a delayed response, with eyes roving over the rental's new bullet holes, cracked windshield, and busted rear bumper.

"It was close, but I survived on a little prayer," Tom sneers.

The limousine finally approaches the top of the second hill. The hotel's garage quickly comes into view, with the limousine driver slowing and pulling to the side of the road beside the four-story hotel. He whips the limousine beside a bus but parks so they can only see the top of Tom and the driver's heads, which moves quickly between both vehicles.

Tom and his driver make one last trip, and their heads vanish for seconds when the limousine maneuvering closer to the garage's exit, where it stops.

A sharpshooter jumps out, standing beside the wall with a miniature, silenced rocket launcher. He pulls a miniature tracking chip device from his shirt pocket, meshing it in clay-like, formed putty, and then loads it in the gun.

Tom's driver pulls out of the garage and stops, waiting for the gate to lift when the sharpshooter low-crawls in the high weeds.

Still well hidden, the limousine driver steadily leans into the horn.

Tom and the driver's heads bob around for the car's horn until looking ahead and along the highway.

The sharpshooter brings the scope into view with the car's hot tailpipe, firing a silenced shot and attaching a tracking device inside the tailpipe when the horn ceases.

With the lift fully extending open, Tom's driver brings the car up to top speed, and they fade over the hill, with the limousine replicating the car's speeds but keeping its distance and allowing the tracking device's light to fluctuate between yellow and red.

Tom's and the driver's heads are soon bobbing from the smooth jazz until forty-five minutes later, when the driver eases the music off and closes in on the Compound's secret entrance forty-five minutes later, with the driver pulling over to the shoulder.

The driver calls the security shed, requesting an area scan from the security tower, and receiving a positive acknowledgment of the coast being clear, he pulls back onto the road and drives another mile. After another fifty feet, he makes an immediate left turn into what looks like a deserted, dark cave, camouflaged well by long, hanging, Weeping Willow branches. He drives through thick, tilting branches and turns on bright headlights when slowing to five miles per hour, per the posted speed limit markings, cautiously looking around and watching the speedometer very closely while accelerating and decelerating.

The limousine passengers look through binoculars. Not seeing the car ahead or below on the winding road or along the hillside when the front-seat passenger motions for the limousine driver to pick up speed. The limousine driver swiftly takes a few sharp curves until he almost runs a few oncoming cars off the road.

"Why are we going so slow, sir?" Tom asks with curious eyes.

"This cave is booby-trapped for security reasons."

"Oh, I see..., a drop of some sort, huh?"

"Yeah, at least two thousand feet into inches of shallow water..., a shallow grave for sure," he says, looking nervous at Tom with sweat beading on his forehead before finally tittering when a green light begins spinning and extending the bridge when activating steel doors while lighting the tunnel.

The limousine zooms past the cave's entrance out of nowhere, on the straightway, when the tracking device's lights turn yellow, green, yellow, and red with the driver noticing the change. His curious eyes bulge when slamming on the brakes, burning rubber on asphalt, and creating a thick black smoke cloud. He stops, throwing the transmission in reverse with a foot immediately hard on the gas pedal, squealing tires, burning more rubber, and backing down until the light turns yellow, then green.

The limousine driver looks carefully at the mountain-like structure, noticing a few drops of oil extending from in front of the huge Weeping Willow's limbs that sway back and forth. He cuts the wheel hard, following the oil trail and inching up to the tree's hanging limbs when advancing through it.

Everyone in the limousine sits armed and ready as they roll down windows, some nervously staring through the long, encased side windows.

The loud sound of a waterfall grows out of nowhere as they slowly advance, looking around with caution with the tracking device's lights fading when the sports car's taillights fade under the closing steel door.

The limousine passenger flips the switch back and forth a few times and then turns it over fast, checking the batteries.

The men in the well-hidden guard tower stand frozen in disbelief, watching the breech of the maximum security boundary.

The senior Compound guard calls to inform the Compound and Underground of the incident, anxiously providing minute-by-minute updates as things occur.

The other guard continues looking with his hand held over the sandy-covered floor's manual drop button, which the limousine's wheels are feet from and steadily approaching.

The limousine's bright headlights activate as the limousine slows to five miles per hour per the speed limit postings until the car stops fully inside the wall when it closes with the limousine aligned, per the initial deceptive alignment instructions posted below the speed limit sign.

Within microseconds, infrared beams shine across the limousine's tail, reflecting off its shiny body. The beam's reflection activates the electronically-controlled locking device, which triggers and opens the bottom safety layer of the trapdoor.

Everyone quietly listens to metal clips flinging away and sounding like mild bombs released, dropping deadweight from a fighter aircraft, while everyone sits mumbling and reporting any movement while looking around in fear. They continue covering the perimeter with tightly held, trigger-ready weapons until they quiet with the sound of a loud waterfall growing louder again with the second drop security floor slowly unlatching until a thin metal bar is supporting the weight of the limousine when it lightly bounces.

The senior Compound guard reaches for a remote, activating the video recording that automatically sends video footage to both command centers when a loud buzzer sounds with the latch's spring trigger slowly opening.

The front end of the limousine drops, and screams blare out when the car expressly drops, with the driver and front passenger gripping the dashboard while others held on tightly to the back of the seats or anything they can grab for the long, deadly drop.

Within minutes, a loud splash mixed with a huge explosion and a big fireball comes, with screams abruptly ceasing when the peaceful waterfall grows loud again.

Out of nowhere, a loud hydraulic sound grows louder with steel doors rising from camouflaged bushes, boxing in the car's remains until crushing the car into an almost perfect cube shape.

The senior Compound guard slams the phone down and quickly maneuvers shift-like levers, engaging the large, round, metal magnet over the cube. With perfect alignment, he lowers the magnet, lifting the metal wreckage mingled with clothing and blood, and loads it onto the back of a flatbed truck that pulls up.

Tom's driver pulls around to the main entrance, finding Tee with both arms folded, dressed in a tight, leopard-skin bodysuit.

The driver eases from the car. "Man, I'd give anything to get up in some of that..., damn!" the driver says, standing and returning a salute to the guards and then her.

"I know what you mean," Tom says, standing and cutting his eyes over at the driver over the roof before smiling.

Tom slips his hands in his pockets when Tee's arms slide snuggly through his when they turn and walk through various checkpoints, flashing security badges.

"Would you like to have dinner? Man, I can throw down on some lasagna!"

"Lasagna? I don't do lasagna, but a tasty surf and turf would be great, if not a problem."

"My room is around this corner, 119." She points ahead, breaking off, and continuing down another corridor.

Tom stops and stares at her slim upper body and thick, round bottom until she fades around the corner. He steps inside his room, finding his bags stacked, so he heads for the shower and afterward rummages through his bags. Tom pulls out a pair of gym shorts, a tank top, and sandals. He stands at the door, looks around, takes a few steps over to the bar's cooler, reaches for a bottle of wine, and walks out.

Tee opens the door after the second knock, dressed in an orange see-through body scarf with an orange-and-yellow halter top, and a dark, matching thong. "My..., you're not as late as I thought you'd be," she says, looking at her wristwatch.

Tom smells a hint of steak before hearing a slight sizzling upon entering the kitchen. "Where should I put this?" he asks, extending the wine bottle to her.

"Here, let me take it," she says, reaching over the counter and placing the wine in the refrigerator before pulling out an identical, chilled bottle and placing it on the counter.

Tom walks around the island-type stove and climbs in the high chair with eyes wandering over her sexy body, checking out Tee's sexiness as she prances around preparing the hearty meal.

When she is almost done, Tom pulls two long-stemmed glasses from the wine rack and pours drinks while she fixes their plates.

They share dinner amid candlelight, soft music, and mild conversation, and after dessert, she places the dishes in the washer while Tom sits in deep meditation for seconds.

Tom sips his third glass of wine and cracks the other chilled bottle open. Deeply distracted, he soon becomes more distracted by bright orange colors in his peripheral vision when taking another sip and looking up to find Tee at the door with her hands on her curvy hips.

"A movie?" she asks, turning and heading back down the hall after his positive response. She twists her hips; enticingly leading him into the immaculate Egyptian-designed bedroom, then dims the lights, staring at the remote, confused, until pushing a few more buttons.

Tom slides his sandals off, climbing onto the black, padded Egyptian leather couch and resting on his back when she climbs next to him, resting her head on his chest.

Feeling playful, she rubbed her soft feet against his with their toes playfully and sensually, fighting back and forth.

Tom is slightly distracted by her sensual sense of foreplay and finds it hard to keep his eyes off her sexy, curved hips, which rise to a peak while she rests on her side.

They watch a short clip of a Western flick when she flips to porn and instantly becomes turned on when massaging his upper thigh a few times before grabbing him in a balled tight fist.

Tom continually looks away at the screen from time to time. "You mean you actually watch this stuff?" Tom frowns, somewhat disgusted.

"Sometimes it's exhilarating..., especially when I'm alone with my toys, which is almost always." She stares deeply into his eyes while rubbing Tom's upper thighs until he is somewhat aroused.

"Huh, a lady as fine as yourself alone, with all these men who worship you and the ground you walk on?"

"Worship, right..., they just like to look at my beautiful, luscious bottom, these curvaceous hips, robust thighs, and..., ooh, la, la..., these firm breasts, but these lowlifes know they can never have a queen," she says, ever so arrogantly.

"Hmm..., a queen, you say? Then whose queen?"

"The major's, of course," she proudly says, bursting into a silly little laugh.

"Are you telling me you're the major's wife?" he asks, jumping up with an even more disgusted look, keeping her at a distance with hands held out as she playfully jumps up and continually tries grabbing him.

"No, silly!" she says with a smirk. "His mistress! Besides, we have a daughter together. Now what I really need is for a man to put it to me right," she says, easing back down and lying back while stroking her thick, smooth upper thighs.

"I can't..., I can't do this, Tee, honestly!"

"What? What do you mean you can't do this? Do you not find me attractive?"

"Come on Tee! That's a loaded question, and you know it. Hell..., what man in his right mind wouldn't find you attractive?"

"Then take me and do with me as you please, darling..., I'm all yours."

"Well, out of respect for the major, I just can't! Damn! The man practically saved my life!"

She stares at him until her smile diminishes. "I understand, Tom..., trust me..., I'll never force you to do anything you feel is immoral, but I'm desperately in need of great sex but not desperate enough to beg for it."

"Can't we just be friends and watch television?"

"What? Hell naw! No way..., so you can get your crap and get to steppin'! I am about to handle my business," she says, even more, pissed when pulling out a thick, gold-plated vibrator from the nightstand.

"I'll just lock the door on my way out."

"Yeah..., you just do that," she says, wickedly hee-hawing while cranking up her vibrator to super-charge.

Tom enters his room and phones Latisha to postpone their date, but her phone goes to voice mail, so he leaves a sweet little message. He sits in thought, and with a desire to get down to business on piecing the mission together, he sits longer until restless. With eyes swarming over the room, finally noticing the half-opened computer cabinet, he opens it and removes what looks like a new disc of footage, which he slides into the player. Instantly, he recognized that this copy is more straightforward and more defined, and he drifts into deep meditation when watching it. He stands before the disc end, and before he can reach for the remote, it continues to a scene he'd never seen when freezing and slowly easing back into the seat, watching two women climb onto the stage. The cameraman slowly zooms around the room as if intentionally keeping the camera down to hide faces when the camera steadies on the two women again and then slowly sweeps past the lower part of a high-ranking official's waist.

Tom immediately switches the recorder to still play with eyes widened when noticing the Strike Force tattoo underneath the officer's uniform sleeve. He zooms in on the hand and identifies the distinctive Special Forces ring, which was distorted before, but is now clearer. Tom rises, banging hard on Oggie's wall twice.

Within minutes, Oggie knocks and then enters, looking down at Tom before rushing over and taking a seat when Tom's hand pats the couch.

Oggie's eyes grow wide-eyed, seeing the expanded Special Forces ring.

"Get Tony, now!"

Oggie immediately exits and walks in with Tony seconds later.

"Here's our lead," Tom says, pointing at the tattoo and then the ring.

"Hell naw! Hell naw! He's one of us..., I'm going to kill this mother..., with my damn bare hands!" Tony says, cutting the curse word short when seeing a female officer walking past the open door.

"This is great, chief! Where did you get it?" Oggie asks.

"Compliments of the major, I guess. I found it in the cabinet minutes ago," Tom says.

Captain Carrington stops by Captain Pierite's cabin. "Evening, Captain; I'm ready to go ashore once we have communications established with Knight Hawk Air Command," Captain Carrington says, adjusting his shirt collar and tie.

"What time do you need a ready deck for helicopter operations, Captain?" Captain Pierite asks, staring up at him and then quickly back into the computer.

"The Operations Officer will inform me when they have established communications with the helicopter, which has already launched from the base, as you very well know."

"Yes, I approved it earlier. Hey..., will you be all right ashore?"

"It's part of the job, you know, just part of the job," Captain Carrington repeats, deep in thought when thinking of his wife and daughter. "If you receive any calls for the lieutenant, please inform them we went ashore to identify bodies. The caller will more than likely call a few times before I return, so please stall him as long as you can for my family's sake."

"So, there's still no word on your family, huh?"

"Nothing yet, but here's my home number," he says, scribbling on a pad. "Please have someone contact my wife, and if they get a hold of her, just have her execute plan alpha, and she'll know what to do."

"Will do, Captain!" Captain Pierite says, standing and shaking Captain Carrington's hand before he turns and walks out.

Within the hour, the loudspeaker announcement sounds throughout the ship to immediately set flight operations.

Thirty minutes later, out of nowhere, a helicopter flies low over the ship's tail and then banks hard, heading away a few miles until circling while waiting for a ready deck.

Ensign Tamara Haun walks into the helicopter hangar and stands off to the side, looking at the well-organized flight crew who work diligently as a team.

Captain Carrington surprisingly comes up from behind Tamara with eyes locked on her pretty shape, stretched in tight dress slacks. He soon gains focus on the airborne helicopter, hovering several hundred feet off the back of the flight deck and slowly approaching.

The two of them make it over to the hangar bay's edge, where Captain Carrington stops next to her, watching the signalman performing the hand signals for landing the aircraft safely.

Tamara goes into a daze with eyes on the waves. "So, are you still planning to leave her?" Tamara asks, straightening her clothes and then looking around again before making eye contact.

"Yeah..., as planned," Captain Carrington acknowledges, staring back into her lovely eyes and trying to assure her that he would leave his wife by confirming it with a straight face and then smiling.

"Ok, so it's good to know nothing has changed because we need to be a family and raise our son as a unit. My son needs his father in his life daily, and not just when you feel like you want to play house," she says, looking around to ensure no one is close enough to hear the conversation.

Captain Carrington's eyes drifted from her back onto the flight deck to find two crew members running out to chock and chain the helicopter to the deck.

When everyone boards, the captain, two pilots, and two helicopter crewmembers sit patiently, waiting for flight deck personnel to detach the chocks and chains.

Soon, the order comes from the tower, granting them a green light for takeoff.

Well over an hour later, the helicopter lands in a deserted airfield inside the confines of the Compound's air radar coverage area. After landing, Captain Carrington transfers to another helicopter for further transfer into the Underground.

After takeoff, they make several security inbound and outbound runs over coastal waters.

"Excuse me!" the captain shouts to the young man in the back who is handling the M-70 machine gun and looking at the ground through the side window. "Is there any reason why we're flying in circles after all this time?"

"Yes, sir, in the exercise of an extended new approach pattern and direction procedures. We have to ensure unidentified aircraft can't just fly into the operations area undetected," he says, looking around for the backup machine gun.

Due to security procedures, the trip takes an hour longer than anticipated, but the helicopter finally heads for the landing pad on the roof of what looks like a newly-constructed oil refinery with numerous, huge satellite dishes.

The helicopter touches down and steadies, with Major Fields emerging from behind steel doors. He holds his hand over his head, rushing out to greet Captain

Carrington in a firm handshake followed by sharp salutes.

The copilot runs over, passing the captain's handbag to the Underground's soldier, and salutes the captain and major before heading back to the helicopter.

"It's a pleasure to see you, my friend!" the major yells over the loud blades, sneering as they embrace. "My, my, it's been a while," the major says, patting him on his back while escorting him away from the helicopter.

"Man, this is quite an impressive setup you have here. I know it had to have set your government back a couple of billion, huh?" the captain says, looking over the exterior of the huge facility in amazement.

"No..., no..., not really, the drug cartel alone paid for it and continues to pay for upgrades and the newest, state-of-the-art technology." The major turns, looking back at the helicopter, still hovering when it lifts fast, banks, and drops down off the side of the building as if crashing but comes back up fast, almost as if transparent.

"Man, I thought that chopper had gone down," Captain Carrington says with his hand still fearfully over his heart.

"No, no, no..., we will use it as part of a new takeoff procedure we've been testing in case the craft is ever under fire after landing or taking off," the major says, smiling. "It will save us billion in asset recovery." He escorts the captain to his quarters, which is three times the size of the Compound's typical living quarters.

CHAPTER SEVEN: THE JOINING FORCES

The captain freshens up, and half an hour later, the major gives him a guided tour of the laser-guided weapons system and then the command and control centers.

"You've got to meet my daughter later. I've told her so much about you and your chief, whose life I saved. I can barely remember his name but think it was...," the major says, trying to recall Tom's name.

Captain Carrington is very impressed with the facility and is in deep thought and has yet to hear all of the major's comments. "There's no way they could have penetrated this place," he thinks aloud.

"Penetrated? This place?" he chuckles. "Who?" the major finally asks, grinning and then chuckling again.

"Strike Force One has been deceived on this mission..., they were tasked to take down the Underground."

"The Underground?" He burst into a burst of great laughter. "You've got to be kidding me, right? Who would be stupid enough to send the team on such a suicide mission?"

"Not sure, but obviously, wiping the team out must have been their main objective."

"Well, whoever planned it deserves a medal or two because he would have easily succeeded. Hell, man, this place is as tight as a gnat's ass on the hottest day of summer!" the major says, laughing and pointing him to the next office on the facility tour.

"I should've figured foul play from the download of Strike Force Two's covert operation," the captain says, somewhat in a transition between thoughts.

"You mean that special operations footage? Shit..., yeah, right..., all fabricated. Our intelligence officers picked up on that footage the first time they viewed it in 3-D, zoom. Someone spliced the exclusive footage from an old movie shot here, on the island eons ago. The only part not fabricated is the ending and their executions," the major says, guiding the captain down another long corridor.

"Executions? What executions? I didn't see any executions!"

"That's it..., they sent you only what they wanted you to see so you could rush to judgment. The part you didn't see had to be digitally decoded, regardless," the major says, leading the captain into his plush study.

"So are you saying Strike Force Two's personnel really are dead?"

"Hell, yes! They are as dead as a damn doorknob, and from the looks of things, they were probably buried, some possibly alive. Here," the major says, picking up the remote and fast-forwarding.

The captain watches intensely as if seeing the disc for the first time, gritting his teeth and tightening his fists in anger. "And this disc..., the Cubans know we have the digitally decoded version?" Captain Carrington asks, deeper in thought.

"No, it was confiscated by one of my intelligence officers who secretly dated one of the women Cuban intelligence officers. He slipped her a pill, injected her with a truth serum, and worked his magic. By the way, I heard you lost three of your best men on this trip. You know you should have called well before things got this bad, right?"

"You know I would've had I known the operation was illegitimate, but then again, I was under duress at the beginning of the mission. From the looks of things, my guys were on a suicide mission from the word go."

"Did I mention the satellite phones they had were bugged with tracker devices? The crystals loaded in them were satellite traceable, and I guess that's how the Cubans knew when they were most vulnerable."

The captain stares into space longer. "I can't believe someone would do such a harsh thing to human lives for the love of money."

"Money? Is that what this is all about?"

"Hell, what else could it be?"

"What's your government up to now, Captain?"

"I wouldn't say government, but more so the greed of a few high-ranking individuals."

"So, do you have the situation under control?"

"No, not really; all we have to go on is this deceptive footage and fake intelligence. As of right now, the only thing real is some unknown entity has threatened to download this fake footage into our worldwide telecommunications systems if the U.S. does not comply with their demands for money."

"Well, I'm a hundred percent sure it's the work of the Cubans. Look, we have targeted these Cuban operations for some time now. They have made uncountable, unsuccessful attempts to gain access to the Compound and Underground. Weekly, they unsuccessfully try and penetrate this place. All of their management and most of their teams consist of very attractive, powerful, and persuasive women. I've somewhat countered their poison tactics by staffing my department head billets with straight women because some can be so gullible in such sex-driven instances."

"No doubt," the captain says. "It must be very hard to have to think with two heads all your life," he said, chuckling.

"Hell, you've got to give this Major Davis credit. Hell..., he's managed to kill hundreds here on the island with the help of these sexy-ass, beautiful women, not to mention three of your very own."

"True, he deserves a plus for innovation, but I doubt he'll live to enjoy the full victory."

"Let's not forget he also wiped out Strike Force Two with the help of one of your own, too, right?"

"Yeah, but that mission was like leading hogs to the slaughter!" the captain responds.

"Here, look...," the major says. "The man in the white uniform is a senior officer; a damn traitor!"

"No doubt..., and those men more than likely confided in him, so he must be the leader. If we zoom in or map the film's top, we can figure out more about this traitor."

"Yeah, we tried but could not due to the special effects used in splicing the film. They modified it, so there's no altering capability, just zoom. Whoever made it was very creative and clever, I must say."

"So what do we do now?"

"As we speak, my top leaders, battalion, and field commanders are discussing the final details of Operation ELI."

"ELI?" the captain asks, confused.

"Yes, short for Operation Elimination. I'm expecting to receive a tasker on destroying the Cuban Camp within twenty-four to forty-eight hours. I thought your team would want payback, so I put them up in the Compound so they could get acquainted with their comrades." The major leans forward, pressing a speaker button. "Control..., this is Major Fields..., please prepare a car for the Compound."

"Aye, Major, it'll be ready in three minutes, sir."

The two of them, along with the escorts, arrive at the Compound an hour later, greeted by Tee and her staff as they pull into the Compound's heavily-guarded gates with everyone already at attention.

"Evening, Major," Tee says, blushing while saluting them.

"Good evening Theresa..., this is Captain Carrington," the major says, standing and pointing to him.

"It's a pleasure to meet you, Captain," she responds, shaking his hand and then interlocking her finger with the major.

The troops on the ground and in the tower continue standing at attention, and it's so quiet that you can hear a pin drop.

"Attention on deck!" the security guard shouts when the three enter the main entrance.

"At ease!" the major says, waving for them to carry on.

"I missed you," he whispers with a kiss on her cheek when they're out of view of the guards. "Did you miss me?"

"You know it, honey. Hell, I even had to take care of myself again last night," she whispers.

"I know, babe, but the wife's been on me hard lately. I think there are some loose lips around here. You know what they say..., loose lips sink ships," the major says, smirking.

"You know what? I don't even care to hear that bull...! You know I need to be able to get mine just as much as your wife," Tee says, frowning and smiling after realizing Captain Carrington is being exceptionally nosey.

"I promise things will get better, babe. So tell me, how's our little angel?"

"Why ask? Especially after I've arranged for her to stay right down the street from you at my mother's; yet you never go over and spend time with her?"

The captain follows closely, pretending not to be listening as the three walk down the long, hollow, concrete corridor with escorts further behind.

They come up on two double steel doors, which Tee opens with her security badge on a lanyard held out to the wall's reader.

"Attention on deck!" she screams, holding the door open against her back.

They flow into the control room, and the major greet the senior watch officer and then the team.

Tee breaks off and exits and the major continue his tour with just Captain Carrington, showing him the high-tech electronics and intelligence monitoring displays.

Outside Major Fields' home, a black SUV cranks up and revs the engine. His wife waves from the window for the escort to take the lead while the other car falls behind her.

Minutes later, she arrives at her mother's, where she drives into the security gate past the well-hidden guard, attempting to park in the backyard when one of the escort drivers notices one of the Compound's cars parked out back but pays it no mind, thinking it could have been the major's escort vehicle.

The yard guard makes a strange sound, then does it again and walks off satisfied.

Without warning and not hearing the early warning, the mother finally hears the car door slam, dropping down hard on her lover a few more times and moaning in her deep cigarette voice, deep in pleasure. She jumps from the bed and rushes out of the room, dripping with sweat and standing near the door, thinking she's missing something, until she remembers leaving her panties in the bed.

The major's wife lifts the keys from her purse with her white ruffled gloved hand, opens the door, strolls across the lawn, and enters through the back door.

"Mom, are you here? Joe?"

Her mom steps back into the hallway, looking for her panties until her hands nervously go down, tightening her robe. Her eyes continually gaze over the hallway as she becomes more anxious. "Yes, I'm here..., I live here, don't I?" she responds with a nervous laugh, taking a last puff off the cigarette and nervously lighting another when out of nowhere comes a big cigarette ring, which floats toward her daughter's face as she enters the dim hallway.

Her daughter steps back, fanning the smoke away. "Damn! You know I hate the smell of smoke. Do you really have to do that crap? Really..., do you?" she asks, frowning and backing up a few more feet, fanning again.

"Girl..., you getting on my last damn nerve..., no you look here..., this is my damn house, so if you don't like what I do in own my damn house, then get your ass to steppin'!" she says, cackling and walking away. She looks down at the floor in her junky bedroom for her panties with fast wandering eyes.

Joe, Tom's driver, walks out of the shower and stands in front of the dresser, wrapping himself up in a towel, hearing the major's wife call to him a second time when combing his hair. He tightens the towel tighter around his waist and looks back quickly when the door flies open, and he turns, pretending to be surprised when Mrs. Fields rushes into his arms with a strong embrace, kissing and hugging him. "Hey, babe!" he says, slightly backing away when she bumps against him, and he acts sexy toward her, trying to get excited, but can't from her mother draining all his strength.

"You look drained..., poor babe! They must have worked you too hard last night," she says, looking into his strained, bloodshot eyes.

"Yeah, babe-doll, I pulled a double, then a late shift. I was parked out back for a while, but your mom was nice enough to let me get some rest and shower. I thought you would have been here hours ago so I could've gotten some of that good lovin'," he says, holding her tight yet slightly backing away when feeling the friction when rubbing against her thigh again.

"I know, honey, but my husband didn't leave as early as expected," she says, running her lips over soft, damp chest hairs. "It's not too late for some of this good lovin'," she says, slowly unbuttoning her top button and then the next one. She leans into him lightly sniffing. "Hey..., you been smoking?"

"Hellz naw! You know I don't smoke," he says nodding to her mother. "This house always smells like a chimney." He happens to look back in the mirror, and something red catches his attention out of his peripheral vision when concentrating on what it might have been when his mind goes haywire. He thinks harder, instantly realizing it's her mother's red satin thong, slightly exposed from under the pillow.

"Do you know if he's still messing with that bitch?" she asks, waiting for him to turn his head to her when holding onto the third button with anticipation for an answer.

He looks into her eyes fast. "Oh, yeah, yeah, yeah, he was there most of yesterday. Something is going on because yesterday, Tee switched shifts twice. Rumor has it that they have a second baby on the way," he says, lying to keep the major's wife committed to their little secret, sexually motivated affair.

"Hey, sweetie, can you get me a beer? I have to get back to work in a couple of hours, and I have other business errands to run as well," he says, buttoning her top and turning her in the opposite direction of the mirror and bed. He closely follows her toward the door, and when she exits, he scrambles for the thong, slipping it under the mattress, and then rushes, dressing. He eases into the hallway, and her mother motions and then whisper about her panties when he gives her the signal that he'd found them.

The mother lets off a sigh of relief, winking, and spanks him on the butt as he passes, causing him to nervously pick up his pace when following him toward the kitchen.

The daughter walks up to Joe as he rushes into the kitchen, still looking back at her mother with a slight frown. She passed him the ice-cold beer with her mother easing into the chair with her daughter sitting next to her.

"What did you cook this morning, Momma?" she asks, looking at her mother put out another cigarette and lights another.

"Girl, it ain't nobody here but me. Now, why in the hell would I cook when I can have someone run out and pick up my breakfast?" she says, rolling her eyes over at Joe. "Joe..., why in the hell are you dealing with this spoiled-ass brat? She thinks Mama gone (is going to) get on the damn stove every time she comes busting up over here unannounced. Look, what you need to do is start calling before you come popping up at people's houses like you own it. And learn to knock some damn time! Damn, I could've had my lover up in here, getting my groove on, on top of the stove or table, for all you know," she says, chuckling.

"For what, Mama? Mr. Jeff probably can't even get it up with all those damn jelly doughnuts and jelly beans he is always eating," she giggles.

"Ms. Smith, you're something else," Joe says, bursting into laughter.

Major Fields' wife sits staring at the corner of her mother's mouth. "You must have had someone here because you got crust running down your chin and droplets of something white on the top of your robe," her daughter says with curious eyes.

Her mother looks down with hands running across her chin. "Damn! You and Joe can get your asses out of my house. I'm a grown-ass woman! Hell..., I can't even eat breakfast and spill something on my clothes..., without insinuations."

Joe eases into a seat next to the major's wife, and her hands go straight to his thigh, stroking him with his face turning red from the intense friction burning when frowning with each stroke and looking away, trying to play it down.

Her daughter looks at her and then at Joe, who looks away with guilty eyes that swivel to the floor when looking at the beer in his hand and taking another nervous but quick swig.

"Well, honey, you better be going," the daughter says, standing when he comes out of the seat, smiling from the burning subsiding. She holds him and kisses him a little longer than usual, lightly sniffing before pulling away, and he knows he's busted when looking at his watch quickly when turning and rushing for the door.

At the Compound, the major finishes his tour in the control center.

"Attention!" a senior officer yells, seeing Major Fields approaching the central platform.

"Everyone gather around, please!" the major says, gazing over the large, filled room. "For those of you who are new or visiting, my name is Major Fields. I'm the Underground and Compound's Commanding Officer, and this is my longtime colleague and friend, Captain Carrington," he says, pointing and nodding to the captain, who smiles, waving. "We've been friends for some eleven years or more," he continues, looking around until spotting Tom. "There's one other familiar face out there," he says, finally making eye contact and waving when an officer motions Tom to the front.

"Folks, tomorrow will be a serious challenge for us all. You've put in some pervasive training over the last year or so, and tomorrow will be the time to put all that you've learned and trained for through the test. So here's to wishing you all the greatest of success and as always, remember our motto: Kill or be killed but don't be killed alone! If all goes as planned, after tomorrow night or the morning thereafter, the Cuban Camp will no longer exist," the major says, waving when ending his speech.

Tom nervously approaches the platform, looking at Tee, who frowns at him, turns, and walks out.

"Thanks for the disc, Major Fields; it's proven to be very valuable," Tom says confidently.

"Really? How so?" the major responds somewhat in a daze, smiling while opening an envelope a junior officer just handed him.

"Well, we now know the unknown man in the footage is an ex-Strike Force high-ranking official, a commanding officer maybe, from the tattoo extending slightly from under his sleeve."

"Tattoo? That's a good observation, Chief," the major says, briefly breaking his train of thought.

"Yes, sir, an academy graduate of '55, maybe earlier," Tom responds in deep thought, recalling the footage.

"How do you know that?" the captain asks, in deep thought and interest, with a curious stare.

"Because..., that's the year the Department of Defense slightly changed the ring's style and lettering."

"Great work Chief because none of my guys caught that either," the major says, giving him his undivided attention when looking at his senior intelligence officer, who looks off quickly and fades back out of view.

Tee flings the door open and swiftly runs up to the major. "Sir, this just came into intelligence from headquarters!"

"All right!" the major shouts, looking at the document with excitement. "We just received permission to launch an imminent attack on the Cuban Camp! Pass the word for an imminent attack at 2000 hours tomorrow," the major yells, looking at Tee somewhat proudly.

Tee retrieves the document and takes it over to the senior watch officer, who immediately passes the word and time over loudspeakers throughout both facilities.

"So what's the plan?" the captain asks with a confused stare.

"No offense, buddy, but due to the classification of this mission, I can only share bits and pieces as I see fit. Let's just say your men will accomplish their mission after all and hopefully get their revenge."

"Ok, but is there anything the ship can do to support the mission?"

"No, with almost a year's planning, we've got it down to the wire."

"Well, there has to be some way we can support this mission; how about stealth cruise missiles?"

"Great thinking, captain, but how long will it take for the ship to bear arms for such a strike?"

"Hmm..., I can't say just yet, but I'm sure a few calls will have to be made to Washington. Come to think of it..., we can get an answer even quicker if the Bear calls."

"Bear?"

"Yes, it's the secret entity's code name, I presume," the captain says, reaching for the phone. "Do I have satellite communications here?"

"Yes, it's automatically secure," Tee says, looking at Tom even more pissed when rolling her eyes.

Captain Carrington dials the ship's secure number and covers the mouthpiece to muffle the team's voices in the background.

"Hello. . ., Captain Pie-!"

"Captain Pierite, this is Captain Carrington!" he says, interrupting his greeting.

"Hey, great news: I got the message to your wife!"

"Great!" he says with a sigh of relief. "Has the call come in yet?"

"No..., well then again, there was a call when I was in the head (bathroom) a minute ago, but they were very impatient and hung up."

Captain Carrington explains his plans for missiles, and then dives into another unrelated conversation when informing the captain of what he thought about the team's elimination when the phone beeps twice. Captain Pierite clicks over without warning or hesitation. "Commanding Officer, USMSP R.L—" the commanding officer begins to say when interrupted abruptly by a deep voice.

"Never mind the salutations, Captain," the voice declares, pausing for seconds.

"Please hold on; I'm about to go secure," Captain Pierite says with eyes dead set on the flashing red phone panel.

Minutes pass.

"Ok, I show you're secure; is the Strike Force One captain or XO available?" the strange man asks.

"No sir, they're ashore, possibly identifying the three killed in action..., but may

I ask whose calling?"

"Admiral Tilton," he responds, quickly fabricating his name after cutting his eyes over at his favorite bottle of whiskey when his mind zooms with all kinds of uncertainties. He sits oppugning whether the mission is fully accomplished and successful.

"Greetings, Admiral..., wait a second, sir," the captain says, pausing and pretending to have been talking to someone when he eases up and opens and then shuts the door to make it seem like someone just had left. "I've just been told by my operations officer that the lieutenant and captain called on the high communications circuit. They left word that our Special Forces team was eliminated. They're requesting immediate missile support to take out the Underground and Compound, plus support the remainder of the mission!" he says, relaying Captain Carrington's deceptive plot.

"What! Hell..., that's great!" He pauses in a trance. "The missiles, that is...," he responds quickly to not confuse the two comments. "So..., how many missiles do they desire to put on the target?"

"About twelve, based on their detailed intelligence and reconnaissance assessments, indicating that the facility is heavily armored. Most of its structure is deeply embedded in the mountainside."

"My goodness..., that's a lot of ordnance!"

"So, do we have permission to launch, sir?"

"Hell, Captain! I don't have that kind of authority! Who do you think I am?"

"Oh, I'm sorry, sir, I thought this was the Command Center!" the captain says, looking at the phone's blank automatic tracer window.

"Well, it's not! I'll have to forward the request over for approval!"

"Thank you, sir. I'll wait for confirmation over the secure satellite high communications ready-strike down circuits."

"Very well, Captain; I'll forward your request immediately."

"Aye, aye, sir, and have a nice day!"

Captain Pierite clicks back over. "Hey, that was Admiral Tilton..., well, at least that's what he said his name is, but come to think of it, there's no Admiral Tilton active in the fleet. Well, anyway..., he bought off on the idea of the missile launch, so is it possible that you can give me the coordinates now so that I can pre-position my strike team and the vessel?"

"Perfect, Captain, wait while I have this officer relay the coordinates," Captain Carrington says, passing the phone to one of the senior intelligence officers after Major Fields nods, authorizing the transaction.

Major Fields leans in quickly, verifying the coordinates with eyes swarming over the map.

Captain Pierite reads the coordinates back for verification and then continues in conversation with Captain Carrington. Both captains continue into various topics until the ship's announcement system keys up.

The Strike officer inputs the coordinates into the secure system and transmits them to Washington's Command Center.

When Washington's Intelligence Officer, Admiral Michaels, receives the information, he's distracted by another urgent mission and fails to validate the strike coordinates but confidently approves them. He stands, twisting his long waxed mustache ends while looking around.

The ship's announcement system keys up again with a soft feminine voice filling her lungs. "The ship's in receipt of urgent missile tasking! The ship's in receipt of urgent missile tasking! The ship's in receipt of urgent missile tasking!" "The ship's in receipt of urgent missile tasking! she repeats, following protocol.

"Well, I'd better be going, Captain; that's my call to bear arms," Captain Pierite says, pulling his pen from his desk-mounted holder.

Three knocks come upon Captain Pierite's door, with it swiftly opening. The Strike Officer passes a sheet of paper to Captain Pierite with the missile's tasking and each missile's authorization attached while the Communications Officer looks on. "The strike team is standing by to put twelve STLF missiles on target, sir, simultaneously!" the Strike Officer says, backing away and standing beside the communications officer.

Captain Carrington overhears the numbers. "My goodness, that'll damn near demolish the place," Captain Carrington mumbles.

"Just following orders," Captain Pierite says, approving the task and orders when pressing the phone to his ear, dialing his password into the digital authenticator, and then passing it to the Strike Officer as the Operations Officer enters.

"Good hunting, skipper!" Captain Carrington says, ending the call and quickly turning, updating the major and his senior officers.

The major immediately notifies his superiors of the U.S. missile support and obtains approval to add the modifications instantly. He hangs up, reaching for the PA mic. "Attention..., this is the major! Due to security and to prevent any compromise of this mission, no one is to communicate outside the Compound or Underground tonight!"

The Compound and Underground go into lockdown, with everyone making preparations, receiving, and sending reports in the control room.

The PA system keys up again inside the Compound. "Please be advised..., Phase One is scratched due to the support of the U.S. vessel that will provide twelve surface-to-land missiles. I don't expect there will be much left when we roll in, but be sharp and ready should their major control room be more heavily armored than predicted!"

The following morning, the Compound and Underground personnel were up bright and early, eating, then training and brief most of the morning.

Everyone lounges around in the afternoon, waiting until around 1730 when they start muster and take head counts.

Over at the Cuban Camp, the watch team intercepts an unidentified transmission from the ship's radar. His team makes several attempts to reacquire the signal, but they cannot triangulate the location, but in anticipation of target acquisition, the Cuban watch officer authorizes training the big surface-to-sea guns seaward.

The ship immediately set silent mode on all communication circuits and radars when receiving a second lock-on from the Cuban satellite.

Captain Pierite and his senior officer sit in silence with the captain in deep thought when briefing that other land sensors could have detected the ship. He thinks harder and then backs away from the officers, giving the order to increase speed and head outside the line of demarcation.

At the Compound, around 1800, everyone quickly assembles in the loading area with feet continually shuffling all over the place.

One formation at a time, they begin boarding command vehicles, jeeps, and two-and-a-half-ton vehicles lined up in the long tunnel.

An engine revs high, increasing speed out of nowhere when groups begin backing away fast at the corner, seeing the stand-off command and control eighteen-wheeler pull around the corner. The Command and Control Center immediately establishes voice communications with the Underground and Compound watch teams while operators inside adjust and tweak the vehicle's satellite uplink and communications gear.

Ten huge monitors automatically energize, finally fine-tuning themselves when the major and ship's captain suddenly appears on separate large monitors, followed minutes later by the Underground and Compound's senior watch officers.

The next-to-last monitor to load is the ship's Missile Control Information Center, followed by a live, geographical display of the Cuban Campgrounds.

All other small satellites instantly link and display on smaller operator-monitored screens.

The troops patiently wait for the first star, which appears around 1837 hours when the steel doors open and moderate alarms sound.

Tom motions his men and other team members over when joining hands as Tom leads them into a lengthy, going-into-harm's-way prayer.

At the end of the prayer, Tom and Oggie added their special quotes, and other troops followed suit.

"That was cute, Tom!" Tee says, smiling and looking into his eyes. "My team definitely needs to implement this procedure as standard practice," Tee says, nodding to the guy who is second in command to her.

"Thank you!" Tom whispers, less tense from her smile and compliment.

With dimmed park lights, the trucks begin single-filing out.

Two jeeps and ten trucks closely follow each other, loaded with over two hundred troops.

The Command and Control vehicle follows about ten miles behind the convoy and monitors all hostile and friendly movements, including mobile, hostile vehicles and stationary rockets on the island and along the hillside. It manages to secretly jam all Cuban receivers, decreasing the Cubans' ability to collect data from any long-range intelligence resources.

Now, the long drive starts along the shoreline, heads up several steep hills, goes deep into the mountains, and lasts well over an hour without detection.

The convoy finally reaches the outer perimeter of the Cuban sensor surveillance area and travels a few more miles until two miles outside the Cuban's operational surveillance area. They proceed up a steep embankment when the Command and Control vehicle immediately turns off the main road, heading down a heavily wooded trail.

The eighteen-wheeler travels a few hundred yards deeper in the woods until finally appearing at the edge of the woods. It stops in an open field that appears on the satellite display as a huge, circular baseball field.

The Senior Officer checks the coordinates and then leans forward, pressing a console button, when the electronic skylight slowly opens, revealing bright stars against the black, velvet-looking sky. He presses another button, and a spear-like sound echoes through the woods when a camouflaged web lunges well over fifty feet in the air.

The thick webbed net hovers high and then finally starts to slowly drift to the earth, fully covering the vehicle until transparent to the naked eye.

All vehicles cut off their lights a few hundred feet from their final destination, and the senior commander authorizes the setup of the first fake security checkpoint.

With the first vehicle reloading its troops, the convoy advance again, setting up another fake checkpoint, and then advances up a hill ten minutes later, stopping at the base of another hill leading to the Cuban Headquarters and Camp's front gate.

At 2055, a classic black car with spinner rims lowers on hydraulics as it pulls up to the first checkpoint. The car slows fast and then stops as directed when two security guards approach with weapons drawn.

"Hey! What's going on here? Who are you guys?" the woman driver asks, half stoned out of her mind from previously snorting three or four lines of cocaine and drinking.

"Federal Island Reservist..., I need to see your driver's license, registration, and proof of insurance," the guard says, leaning slightly forward and looking at their beautiful faces. He leans deeper into the car with his face freshly coming up alongside the driver's beautiful face with the woman's fresh, frizzled hair running over his face as he takes a deep inhale of her enticing scent.

The female driver's perfume quickly mingles with liquor when rising deep in his nostrils.

The guard's playful index finger comes forward, going back and forth, insinuating naughtiness. "Hmmm..., I'm sorry, but I'm going to have to ask you to step out. It appears you're under the influence of alcohol and narcotics or something else," he says, looking down at the driver's beautiful curved hips in tight, faded fatigues. His eyes roam up to her 44D breasts before looking at the other beautiful women who appear to be either Puerto Rican or Colombian.

The beautiful girl behind the front passenger leans forward, smiling. "Umm..., do you need mine, too?" she asks, lifting her top and flashing huge breasts, before quickly pulling her top back down.

The sexy girl behind the driver leans back hard, pressing against the backrest. Without warning, she fires her 9MM on automatic from under the jacket in her lap.

The guard continually jerks with several rounds hitting his head, chest, and waist, with him looking like he's dancing and walking backward.

The other soldier falls to the ground when hit in the shoulder and neck by another woman before being able to aim.

The guards at the next checkpoint look down the hill, hearing and seeing gunfire with the exchange of more fire and muzzle flashes when bloody screams blare through the seriously second-wounded soldier's handheld walkie-talkie.

"You bitch!" the second guard shouts, clenching the talk button with one hand and his neck with the other.

The first guard clenches his throat tighter, lying in the road, trying to slow the bleeding, when another round hits him in the temple, dropping him.

The stoned woman in the front passenger seat rises against the headrest, taking aim and shooting the second guard in the leg.

The guard low-crawls to the side of the road, weak and almost unconscious, sending several more death cries that cause some in hearing distance to cringe. "Help! Intruders!" he screams into his bloody walkie-talkie.

Tires squeals, burning rubber for microseconds when the driver floors the gas pedal with her foot trembling when finally releasing the brakes and instantly bringing the car up to ninety, even one-hundred-plus miles per hour on the straightway.

"Help! Intruders!" the second soldier scream into his bloody walkie-talkie with his last breath before falling lifeless in the thick brush.

The woman in the passenger seat phones the Cuban Headquarters on auto-dial but gets no answer, or tone.

The two soldiers at the second checkpoint immediately switch their weapons to automatic when seeing the car distancing the scene at top speed, then slowing to make a sharp curve.

The front-seat passenger presses the phone tighter to her ear after hearing it ring a third time when accidentally terminating the call and swearing.

The car comes up to sixty miles per hour, clearing the sharp curve, and they see the second set of guards aiming in standing prone positions.

When the car straightens out, the driver floors it, bringing it in excess of ninety miles per hour again.

The woman in the passenger seat phones the Cuban Headquarters on auto-dial but gets no answer, so she auto-dials a friend at the Cuban Camp.

The hood rises from the engine's brute and supercharged power, with each woman firing, with the women in the middle leaning to fire, instantly dropping the guards before they can take cover.

The car makes it to the top of the hill, slowing to sixty again to clear another wide turn when coming into full view of the line of military two-and-a-half-ton trucks on the straight stretch of the road.

"Cuban Command Post!" the soft woman's voice finally answers.

"Oh shit!" the front-seat passenger shrieks as the other girls scream at the top of their lungs when seeing a truck's camouflage canvas drop down and the big guns train down at the car.

Instantly, the mini-tank-size gun barrel rapidly jerks from left to right and then drops, synchronizing with the car and quickly acquiring its target as they come closer in full view and continue closing even faster.

The female driver thinks quickly, executing a short stride of zig-zagging when the big guns lose their lock and move as if in slow mode when a soldier flips a switch leaving the gun dancing from side to side.

"Hello, Candi, Candi?" the girl inside the Cuban Camp screams.

The women scream even louder until the back of the truck lights up with automatic, silenced fire.

Several rounds from one M90 machine gun repeatedly fire, with the car taking the brunt of the rounds, slowing down rapidly, even though the driver floors the gas pedal.

The passenger and girl behind her instantly die as rounds take off heads, penetrating their chests.

More rounds swept through the car when the mini-close range weapon mounted to the roof lights off, hitting the other women but missing the driver, who intentionally tries swerving out of the line of fire when the barrel swings to the far right.

"Hello, Candi..., Sherry, Jillian..., Coa Coa!" the girl inside the Cuban Camp frantically screams, trying to think of the new girl's name. She presses the phone closer, trying to make out the muffled background noise the big gun made, which was still spinning after the last round left the barrel. The second M90 automatically fire, not missing a beat.

The front-seat passenger's arm dangles out the window and ejects the phone, which bounces off a boulder and then a cliff, heading for a long drop into the sea.

The last barrage of fire comes from troops taking aim and hitting the driver in the head and chest. One round to her temple causes her to veer against a stone wall and jackknife off the steep cliff.

The rear wheels spin even faster as the driver's deadweight foot presses down harder, the car whistling while gliding through the air for about half the length of a football field.

The passenger behind the driver jerks and comes to, screaming, until the car bounces off the cliff's lower ledge that sticks out slightly over the sea, bursting into flames and still dropping.

"Hello, Candi, Candi?" the girl inside the Cuban Camp screams a third time before the phone goes silent after plunging into the sea and slowly sinking.

Captain Pierite overhears the forward lookout reporting a fireball in the lower hillside. He stands listening to the second report that comes seconds later while on the bridge giving the OOD authorization to bring the ship out of silent mode in preparation for strike support.

Another lookout's report of the fireball's flame dying down comes seconds later when the car is fully submerged.

The young Cuban woman lieutenant runs to the Cuban Camp control room and slams the door open, running over and leaning over the operations control watch officer's desk, staring into his face, almost out of breath and confused. "Sir, there's something wrong! I just got a call, and it sounded like my friends..., I heard heavy gunfire in the background during her transmission and right before the phone died."

"So what? Call her back! Maybe they're at an arcade or somewhere playing games with you," he says in a deeply-rooted Cuban accent.

"You don't understand..., before the call, Candi said they were on their way back to post."

"Listen! It's not my job to babysit your girlfriends," he says, staring deeply into her eyes with a frown.

"Do you see those guards?" he asks, pointing at the large monitor that displays several troops diligently guarding the main entrance. "Do they look excited? Damn it, when they get excited, then I'll freakin' get excited!" he sarcastically says, looking around at other watch standers who either are working or being nosy.

"Ooh! You, asshole! I guess you're still pissed because Candi refused to go out with your lame ass! You damn punk!" she screams, slamming the door against the wall when exiting. She runs down the long corridor toward the headquarters office, entering a restricted area until reaching the corridor's entrance of the heavily guarded underground secret passage between the Cuban Headquarters and Cuban Camp, where two male guards stop her.

"Whoa, whoa, whoa! Where do you think you're going, little missy?" the taller guard asks with the palm of his hand extended to her chest, backing her up a few inches and not touching her.

"Let me through! I have urgent matters to relay to Headquarters!" she says, pressing forward until the tall guard's hand presses hard upon her collarbone; when she fights to get through until the short guard grabs her from behind.

The short guard secures her arms by her side and holds her tight, giggling and pressing hard against soft butt cheeks until her body's movement turns him on.

She fights and continually kicks to be free.

The tall guard's cigarette flickers up and down, giving her orders to calm down when he turns, taking a few steps away, reaching up and slightly turning the camera to take them out of view. He turns back to her, running long, callused fingers through her semi-damp hair, kissing her smooth cheek while his hands caress her body. He steps back, slinging his weapon over his shoulder when pressing against her.

The short guard guffaws like a crazy man until spitting out his cigarette.

"Stop it, you filthy-ass animals!" she screams, spitting in the tall man's face while still fighting to be free.

The tall guard freezes, pissed, and trembles with a slow, un-balling fist coming back slowly until sprung tight when slapping her with all the strength he can muster, then tearing open her fatigue top with buttons rolling over the carpeted floor.

She hacks up phlegm hard, spitting in his face a second time, and tries leaning forward to bite him, but he forces her forehead back with the palm of his hand. She shakes his hand away fast, screaming when spitting into his face a third time, when he sinks his hand around her neck, squeezing with all his might.

The tall guard's face turns fierce, and his eyes turn bloodshot red.

She tenses, mustering up all the strength within her, abruptly extending her knee upward, striking him in his groin, and causing him to fold and then drop to the floor with a vein in the middle of his forehead, moaning.

The short guard instantly loses his grip before gaining his balance.

She leans forward with great force, quickly slamming her head back and head-butting him, causing him to stagger with blood gushing out of the middle of his forehead. In stealth mode, she snatches the taller man's gun from his holster while he's still kneeling in severe pain.

"Drop it, drop it!" she says, aiming at the short man wiping his bloody face with one hand while struggling to draw his weapon until lowering it with one hand coming up high fast, then his other hand.

With both guards in the line of fire, she motions them to the maintenance closet and onto the floor, then shuts and locks the door, pressing the access button and opening the main corridor to the Headquarters building.

She takes off in a heavy, forward lean and sprints as fast as she can, advancing faster around the wide corner and picking up her pace.

With an attack order received from Major Fields, the Compound's trucks start their engines almost simultaneously and advance the last five miles toward the Cuban Camp.

The last truck clears the last curve, and Tom looks out over the cliff toward the sea in the moonlight and sees the USMSP R. L. Peterson steaming at bare steerage way.

Minutes later, the trucks come up to top speed, closing both Cuban checkpoints, which are in sight of each other, as well as the main gate at the end of the road.

Back in the States, Kelley is lying across the bed watching television when her phone rings.

Her father calls asking about the kids and Tom, plus checks to see if they are still coming when Kelley breaks down crying after talking with him for minutes and then breaks her silence about her ex-lover and kid's father, Jeff.

The Senior Cuban Watch Officer sits still pissed about his subordinate's rude behavior when lighting a Cuban cigar and leaning his chair back on its hind legs when the Cuban guards disperse without notice.

The guards continue running around and shooting while taking cover behind steel barriers, making several transmissions that fall on death ears while the signals are being blocked.

One guard switches frequency to VHF, and with one loud outburst over the speaker, the watch officer and his team's eyes widen from the sudden movements.

The Cuban Watch Officer falls flat on his back, scrambling across the floor until low-crawling to the console fast on his knees with his hands extended forward, sounding both the attack and emergency alarms.

The loud, long, hand-cranked, and electric alarms blare over the Cuban grounds.

Automatic big camouflaged big guns, masked by big thick bushes, begin stabilizing and slowly training around until aiming toward the convoy.

Several men jump from the forward trucks, setting up anti-tank missiles while the big guns slowly fire, lobbing giant shells while slowly aligning with the convoy.

One man from the Compound mounts his shoulder-held weapon while his partner plugs in the power pack, taking aim at one of the three big guns, taking one out, and then rearming to speedily take out the other two, which follow the same training and firing patterns.

In the secret, well-protected corridor between headquarters and the Cuban Camp, the man and woman guards lock and load their AK-47s.

With binoculars in hand, Tom sees the ship once more before it vanishes over the horizon with the silhouette of the United States flag gracefully waving while blowing mildly in the moderate winds.

In the secret corridor, the man and woman guards look at one another excited, hearing fast-moving footsteps moving even faster while beating against the thin, black rubber matting. They turn in disbelief, staring into the large monitor as they simultaneously bring their weapons to shoulder level. They catch sight of the girl approaching at top speed with a weapon in her hand when their eyes bulge with the male radioing the first two guards for confirmation and getting nothing.

"Halta (Stop)..., halta (stop)!" the woman guard screams in a broad British accent, taking a more direct aim until the girl's head is perfectly aligned in her crosshairs as she holds her breath.

"No, wait!" the young girl screams, hearing a loud pop when running at an even faster pace when finally brandishing the gun, stopping and staggering. She falls forward from multiple rounds that shred her body.

The male guard spits out his cigar, grasping hold of the podium and clenching his weapon tightly, then lean over, puking his guts out while holding his stomach. He looks away, gaining his composure, and then pukes again when looking over at the mangled, bloody body off to the side of the corridor.

Kelley continues in a mild conversation stateside until she fully breaks down. "Why, Daddy? Why?" she asks, enraged and screaming at the top of her lungs. "Why did you have to kill him?"

There is silence as her father sits with tears in his eyes, staring at the ceiling and absorbing his tears. "You know why..., just think about the things you shared with him about your uncle and me. Think about it! He was plotting to bring us down! Did you not know he was a damn reporter and intelligence agent?" he says with eyes excitedly wandering back and forth at the troops running by in the encased, soundproof corridor at the Cuban Camp.

"Yeah, yeah, but we promised to keep our lives secret, and he promised me, and I told you when you confronted me about this! So tell me why?" she asks in a rage, with tears running down her cheeks.

"Ok, fair enough," he says, wondering if it was right for him to break his silence and jeopardize everything he'd worked so hard for and for which he is still working. He grows outraged hearing her cry about the thing she allowed men to do to her in the States when suddenly she grows quiet. "I think you need to do something for me to make it right," she says, staring into space.

"Do something? Huh? Something like what? The last time I did something, you hated me for it, and to this day, you still hate me," he says, looking at the officer flagging him down through the window with his gun high over his head. He reached for a key, rushing over to his gun vault.

"Damn that..., you owe me this one time, so do something to make it right," she says again in a rage, crying harder.

On the battlefield, Tom instantly notices white spurts of lights flashing at microsecond intervals over the horizon where the ship faded when hearing a mild whistling sound growing loud and fast as the first and second large surface-to-land missiles whistle high overhead, slamming into the Cuban Camp and Cuban Headquarters.

The detonation grows so forceful that it shakes the huge trucks and causes parts of the road to crumble along its edges before cracking across the road in various sections.

The upper parts of both facilities disintegrate, with smoke heavily pouring out of the deep craters when there were second and even third orders of effect from the explosions after delayed warheads explode.

The ground shakes the trucks even heavier while creating ripples in the neat green sod landscaping and concrete, sometimes even splitting the soil several feet apart.

Kelley hears a loud blast and jumps up, sitting on the bed's edge when the phone goes dead. She makes several nervous attempts to call back but is unable to, receiving recorded messages that the lines are down.

The Underground's front trucks continue opening fire on the Cuban troops at the checkpoints and main gate while troops on the rear truck watch the horizon light up with more inbound missiles.

A bright light appears out of nowhere, illuminating the sky and looking like someone had cut on a bright strobe light.

Many of the Cuban troops, well hidden in dark places, stop shooting, nosily amazed at the bright fluorescent and multicolored lights, and soon fall to the ground, hit by automatic gunfire.

The light grows brighter and then starts to descend to earth slowly, until growing dim and then fades fifteen minutes later.

Tee leans from the side, sitting on the truck and staring at her lead, waiting for the signal to deploy the troops.

Tom counts the remainder of the detonations with a finger held up for each missile passing high or low overhead until one passes so low that it appears to have been coming straight in for the truck when he yells and drop with everyone on the truck ducking.

After the twelfth missile, Tee receives the signal and shouts. "GO! GO! GO!"

Tom jumps down and screams to the troops, waving them off: "GO! GO! GO!"

They bail out, single-file, and run toward the Cuban Headquarters, which looks like an old, deserted power plant, with eyes swarming over the building now engulfed in thick, black, gray, and blue smoke as fires continued billowing out.

With Tee and Tom's hand signals, the team runs like precision troops in a well-rehearsed and trained scenario until splitting up.

Some run toward the Headquarters, while others head for the Cuban Camp, instantly setting up perimeters and assuming lying prone positions when exchanging fire with more Cuban soldiers who attempt to exit the smoke-filled buildings and grounds.

Now, eighty or more Cuban soldiers die from the missile detonation alone, but the raging attacks from both forces continue nonstop.

After two hours or so, the smoke starts to clear around the buildings, but the craters continue heavily burning, with smoke continually pouring out.

The Underground and Compound teams and Tom's team advance inside the smoke-filled hallways, where they exchange fire for what seems like hours.

With heavier battles, it seems that the Cuban men and women have continually poured out of the woodwork; the more the teams kill, the more appear from underground tunnels.

Tom, Oggie, and Tony break off from the team they are with and stay close together. They cross the large grounds and come onto the grounds of the Cuban Headquarters, taking cover behind a few trees and seeing many heads running through the second-floor stained-glass window. They draw closer to the building and take cover in the thick bushes until backing up into a pile of polished metal.

Tom's hand extends forward, rubbing over the warm, old, primed, and gray bulk-steel gun barrel until taking out a couple of troops on the top of the building and some exiting the building. Tom's eyeball stays pressed tightly in the scope of his sniper rifle, scanning the building until finding two senior-ranking officers standing in what seems like a heated discussion.

Both men's hands begin pointing into each other's faces when Tom takes a steady aim at the taller officer, who appears to be a general officer.

With a few more steps closer to the window, the high-ranking officer stands with his chest stuck out, neatly brushing his hand over his thick plastered gold insignia on his shoulder boards and then the gold scrambled egg hat he just had donned. He appears to have screamed at the other officer when he brandishes his AK-47, loads the weapon, and turns to the window.

The loud AK sounds off, taking out three Compound troops approaching Tom and his men, who are well hidden.

With a tightly-held breath, Tom pops off one round, hitting the general in the middle of his forehead and knocking him backward.

A junior officer who just had run into the room rushes past the general, Kelley's father, and when several steps away, he runs back, looking down at him, then stares at his collar's emblem with its green eyes shining. He reaches, pressing the button on the back of the emblem, deactivating it when jumping up fast, hearing a door kicked in when firing several shots, and then taking off through a steel vault door.

In a flash, Tom and his men trot around the backside of the building and make several unsuccessful entry attempts until coming upon a padlocked door. Tom fires on the lock, shattering it and swinging the door open.

They proceed down a dim hallway filled with debris, listening and then creeping forward with their backs against the wall.

Three male Cuban paratroopers approach from around a corner, and their sudden movements force Strike Force One to unload, instantly dropping them to their deaths.

Tom and his men advance through the building until approaching a point in the hallway blocked by a collapsed overhead caused by missile destruction. With a quick assessment, they turn back and move down the hallway at an even faster pace with weapons vigilantly trained ahead.

Tom throws up a tightly-balled fist, motioning them to stop when they close in on an adjacent corridor, then ease up on the corner to make sure the corridor is clear before taking off again at a slow jog.

They advance halfway down the last, long corridor, where they hear a woman's voice that sounds like Tee's when coming to a slow trot until freezing in place and looking around, trying to figure out from where the scream is coming.

Tom advances, then stop with a tightly balled fist held high. "Tee..., is that you?" Tom shouts, recognizing her voice the second time when determining the direction.

They turn, taking off at a fast sprint when coming up to top speed.

"Tom, over here!" she yells, seeing them rush by the cracked open door. "I've been hit!" she loudly moans, crying.

They stop, turn, and slowly approach the entrance, securing the external entrance when Oggie stops and motions for Tom to cover him while he proceeds through what appears to be a bulk storeroom.

Tom backs against the wall with shoulder-strapped 9MMs in both hands and at waist level, scanning the entrance until nodding and signaling Oggie to enter.

With the three finally inside, they scan the room to find Tee's leg sticking out from behind a row of barrels as she wiggles and try to prop herself up against the chain link fence while remaining well hidden.

Tee whistles, motioning them to the back of the room, then grows quiet.

Tony covers the entrance as Tom and Oggie maneuver around various pallets of boxes, making their way closer to the center of the room.

Tom and Oggie freeze in place from time to time, listening for movement, but they don't hear or see anything.

Tom immediately sprints across the open bay, dropping down and rolling when machine gun fire loudly echoes throughout the room. His body and pained shoulder come to a dead stop against a cold, rusty barrel, where he positions next to Tee. "Are you alright? How many of them do you think are in here?" he nervously mutters, hearing the last round pass inches from his head.

"Four, five, maybe six," she says, holding her chest and gasping for air.

"Are you sure? Where?" he whispers, peeping around and then pulling his head in fast when seeing the barrel of a weapon projected against the far wall.

Tee points up toward the offices on the second deck and then to the lower-level back rooms when gasping for air again. She tightens her makeshift web-belt tourniquet on her upper thigh. "I'm so glad to see you guys," she whispers, profusely sweating and breathing harder.

"Do you have an extra clip?" Tom asks, feeling around her web belt.

"Only one," she weakly says, handing it to him while uncontrollably coughing and sounding like her lungs are slowly filling with blood.

"Are you going to be all right until we secure the perimeter?" he asks, lightly grinning to comfort her while patting her thigh.

"I don't know..., I really don't," she says, uncontrollably coughing again and quieting when hearing fast shuffling feet in the rafters.

"You just hang in there for me, the major, and your daughter!" Tom confidently says, gently patting her hand again, but this time to add a strong sense of security.

"Why should I? Did you change your mind about your loyalty to the major?" she asks, smiling, frowning in pain and straining when coughing up a little blood when trying to laugh. She strains more, tightening the belt and wiping blood from her mouth with her fatigue sleeve when staring at tom with weak, dimming eyes. "Tom," she coughs, wiping blood from her mouth again.

Do me one favor," she says, coughing up more blood. "Tell the major to take care of our baby and spend quality time with our precious little angel!"

"I won't have to because you can tell him yourself as soon as we get you out of here!"

"No, damn it! I'm serious! Tom! I'm not going to make it, and you know it, damn you!" she lightly screams, coughing up the first chunk of blood. "I'm so damn serious right now, Tom..., I'm not going to make it!" she screams, then whines, gritting her teeth when her mind refocuses on her daughter, mother, and the major.

Oggie jerks to one side, spotting a fast-moving shadow when exchanging fire above Tom and Tee's heads.

Tony replicates Oggie's movement, firing in the upper decks, hitting a man, and dropping him headfirst to the concrete floor.

Tom turns to help Tee sit up, placing a hand on the cold pavement and slightly slipping in something wet and warm. He pulls his hand to his face finding it covered in blood, and instantly freezes, hearing an unfamiliar sound of something scraping in a back-and-forth motion. Tom leans forward, peeping until finally identifying the direction when bending and looking at the other side of Tee. He squints, and something catches his attention, causing him to look past her in the corner a few feet away, finding two of Tee's men face down in a puddle of blood.

Now, what first sounded like metal scraping on concrete grows even louder when Tom trains his weapon further to the right, finding another one of Tee's bloody men looking as if he is shivering with one hand reaching out to him; the other clenched around his deeply slit throat.

The soldier and Tom stay eye-to-eye when he jerks a few more times with the barrel of his weapon still grinding back and forth against the concrete floor before finally freezing in place seconds later.

A tear swells in Tom's eye seeing the man jerk once more when taking his last breath.

Tom breaks his train of thought, regaining his thoughts when wiping tears from his cheeks with his other sleeve and refocusing on Tee to keep her grounded.

"Other than your leg, where else have you been hit?" he asks, wiping his bloody hand on the upper side of his pants leg.

"My ribs, possibly my spine," she replies, immediately biting her bottom lip to keep from screaming.

"Hang in there, damn you! Don't give up on me, Tee!" he snarls with teary eyes, pointing his index finger in her face.

Rounds spark from metal-rimmed barrels near Tom's head and ricochet off in different directions when Tom slumps down and immediately turns over, exchanging fire with Oggie and Tony.

Tom repositions closer to her when the second set of rounds spark near the barrels, with some rounds falling even closer to Tom's head and, this time, causing him to slump down and take even deeper cover. Tom looks around and then up quickly, spotting a shadow moving into open view, but loses sight of it when taking a quick glimpse over at Tee when she screams. He sits listening to Tee's heavy breathing while looking around again until hearing her gag and gurgle when her breathing grows harder.

"Look out, Chief!" Oggie screams, trying to find where the shadow against the wall is projecting.

Tom rolls to his side when a tall, dark-skinned Dominican-looking woman stands between two tall barrels on the second level, directly across from Tom and Tee.

The woman's head feverishly goes back and forth when without hesitation; she pops off several automatic rounds, with one penetrating Tee's temple.

Tee's head drops back without a sound when abruptly dropping forward, with the single round instantly killing her.

Without warning, more rounds come causing Tom to roll back over to his other side, barely missed by the second barrage of gunfire whistling past within microseconds.

Oggie quickly repositions, finally bringing the woman into view when his eyes take a precision stare. He freezes, holding his breath, releasing several direct rounds into her chest, forcing her lifeless body over the handrail and to the floor.

Tom sits up, leaning over towards Tee, with water filling his eyes while trying to maneuver closer to her and when within arm's length, he stares into her beautiful face for seconds. He extends a hand forward and moves her long hair from her face, kissing her cheek, then moves closer, with a hand at her eyebrows, closing her eyes and accidentally smearing blood across her face. He drops down in deep thought when getting his thoughts together when rolling to his stomach and low-crawling in view of Oggie and Tony, waving to let them know he is alright. His second motion follows, letting them know to cover him. At the same time, he repositions, and within seconds, he comes up on a corner, sticking his head up near a wooden crate, flinching from a single round whistling past and shattering the corner of the crate behind him.

Oggie exchanges fire with yet another woman well-hidden on the upper level but misses with four of the four untrained shots when shooting and ducking.

Tony maneuvers to the back of the room, taking an indirect aim when zooming in on the bottom of the grated rails where a woman's foot hangs out, slightly overexposed. He rocks off balance and then moves a few more feet closer, getting a better view, with Tony taking a more direct aim, firing a single shot, shattering her heel, then firing more rounds in her upper and lower body when she sprouts up, dropping backward.

The woman's weapon falls freely to the lower level, screaming a bone-chilling cry with her leg caught in the railing as her body sways back and forth until her leg snaps at the calf. She screams louder, dangling upside down for seconds, gasping for her last breath, yet screaming and squirming until trying to pull her sidearm from her shoulder holster with all that was in her.

Tom takes steady aim and slowly brings her into the crosshairs, giving her time and allowing her the pleasure of thinking she would work her way out of the predicament and survive.

Finally, she grips her weapon tightly in hand, screaming through the pain and wiggling around, trying to aim at Tom, but she's quieted when Tony's single shot to her head silences her.

Instantly, more gunfire rings out from the upper level, shattering the slightly-tinted glass windows on the second level.

Tom scans the upper level's walkway, motioning once more for Oggie and Tony to cover him as he advances toward the bottom of the ladder, and when well into position, Tom trains his weapon upward. He slowly advances upstairs; remaining close to the wall, then works his way over to the glass-encased office area until his head emerges near the window, where he takes a few steps forward.

Instantly, bullets penetrate a long row of windows, causing Tom to run forward and drop onto the metal grating. More bullets pass, shattering more windows until they hear voices when a door slams and bright lights energize.

There is total silence, with only the mild humming of the fluorescent tube lighting rising in their ears.

Tom stays down with his hands over his head until looking back and motioning Oggie to advance upward as he covers him.

From the top of the ladder, they check the whole storage room below, secure the first office, and walk back out with their weapons drawn.

Tom scans the upper level again, looking inside the next office, which is a dimly-lit room; jerking back when his eyes cast over the room, finding the top of someone's head near the corner. With his finger slipping in the trigger well, Tom quickly motions his intentions to Oggie, who positions himself in a corner to cover the room better.

Tony backs into a dark corner below and secures the ladder and main entrance.

Tom kneels at first, then low-crawls over to the main entrance before kneeling again in a prone position, cracking the door open and glancing inside; soon realizing it's the back of a woman's head. He quietly maneuvers to the second door, sticking his head in, and immediately recognizes its Nichelle when doing a double take. "Nichelle..., Nichelle..., are you alone? Is it safe?" he whispers, looking the room over. He makes eye contact with her again.

Nichelle nods 'yes,' mumbling through a flimsy taped mouth with stale tear traces streaking across her perfectly made-up face.

Tom inhales deeply, training his weapon around and expressly making his way over to her. He removes the tape, kissing and hugging her before motioning for her to be quiet when a sudden, unfamiliar noise causes Tom to jump and train his weapon toward the back room. He stays tense, listening for seconds before immediately figuring it to be an electric fan motor revving up to max speed.

Nichelle begins moaning a soft but frightening cry. "Thank goodness you found me, sweetie!"

Tom's eyes rove over the room once more until turning to walk back over and untie her.

"Wait, there's valuable information you may need over on that desk," she says, nodding at the desk he just had passed.

"Which desk?" he asks with eyes roving over her gorgeous body until finally noticing the Cuban commander's emblem pinned neatly on her collar and then the Cuban academy ring on her finger.

"Over to your right," she says, repeatedly motioning with her head while pretending to have her hands tied with her tightly gripped 9MM trembling until her finger slightly presses on the trigger.

Tom nervously looks in the direction where he last saw Oggie through the mirrored glass, winking before turning and placing his 9MM down.

Still, Oggie doesn't see him when turning to assess an unfamiliar sound in the upper level before looking back side of the room at Tom again.

Tom leans over the desk, looking at the bundle of photos scattered about, freezing in shock when staring into the faces of the men of Strike Force Two and his four men. He stares closer with tears in his eyes, seeing some of their heads decapitated, their bodies mutilated or burned. Tom gazes, noticing their frowns, some possibly while still alive, when visions flash in his mind, wondering how someone took some pictures even after Bobby, Johns', and the ensign's death, and this alone puzzles him.

A few teardrops fall onto the pictures, his vision blurring when a loud, fast screech comes from the chair, heavily sliding across the floor, bringing Tom out of the daze.

Nichelle swiftly springs upward, dashing forward and charging while screaming and drawing her 9MM from her back.

Glass instantly shatters with three semiautomatic rounds from Oggie's weapon, piercing her chest before she can align Tom with the muzzle.

Her body jerks with each precision round, entering at simultaneous intervals until she falls to the left just as Tom executes his famous roundhouse kick to her face.

Tom stares at her, lying there in agonizing pain, breathless and mangled, with her cheek pressing deep into the carpet when dropping to his knees. "Why, Nichelle? Why! Why didn't you kill me instead?" he screams with eyes full of tears.

"Believe me..., I tried, you bastard! I wanted to finish the job personally; my sister should have finished with you bitches!" she screams, coughing up blood. "I guess it was your lucky day, huh?"

Tom meditates on what she meant by his lucky day, not giving the cranberry juice any thought, but his mind instantly drifts back to the shoot-out in the mansion.

"Your sister? That stupid-ass trick tried to kill us for no reason!" Tom shouts.

"Screw you, mothe—" she says, unnoticeably deactivating the Bear's emblem on her collar with the light dimming then off when cringing while taking her last breath.

The entrance door flings open, and Tony speedily advances from the cubbyhole, coming up from behind the camouflaged woman. He trains his weapon at the back of her head until the barrel slightly moves her head forward.

She drops her weapon, allowing it to dangle on her shoulder strap, then freezes with hands high above her head until Tony lowers her arm, when she nervously turns and then smiles, seeing Tony with a finger pressed to his lips to quiet her.

Tony looks upstairs and whistles to Tom and Oggie.

"We've got the Cuban major in the Headquarters Control Center!" the woman shouts, running back to the main entrance to cover it while waiting for them.

The two make their way down quickly, with the three running out behind the woman, down the long hallway, and upstairs into the almost demolished large command and control room.

The Underground's Senior Officer has the major strung up with hands tied behind his back and swinging freely, upright from a rope extended from his webbed belt.

The major's face and his clothes are drenched in blood.

"Where's the disc?" the senior officer asks, walking up to him with his hands folded behind his back and his specially-made pistol tightly fisted.

"Damn you, punk ass bitches!" the drunk Cuban major shouts, wiggling to get free. His head drifts around the room to find the Cuban General, General Rice, with his face stale, still sitting in a chair with his boots pointing upward, dead from a single shot to the middle of his forehead.

"Wanna play, ah? Oh yeah..., you'll tell us or die with that little secret, pal."

"Then kill me now and stop freakin' wasting my damn time, you senseless-ass moron!" he screams with snot and saliva dripping.

"Where are the discs and chips, sir?" Tom screams out of nowhere, walking up and forcefully sucker-punching the major in his ribs with all he can muster.

"Ooh..., ho, ho, ho!" the major screams, jerking and bouncing around like a heavyweight boxing bag just hit by a professional boxer. "It's going to take more than that wussy-ass punch, Soldier!" he screams, hacking up a wad of saliva mixed with cold and spitting at Tom.

Tom frowns and then turns, walking away, wiping his face with his shirt sleeve until another male soldier hands him a few tissues from a box lying on a desk. His mind wanders and then refocuses when staring over at the general, whose face looks more like an older version of Kelley's son. In a trance, he walks closer, staring at him, but misses his name tag when another officer distracts him by grabbing him by the shoulder. Not giving it any thought, his eyes wander about the room over several documents thrown around when he notices several small preset fires going in the background in preparation for destroying all classified documents.

Tom stands with his back to Tony when he pulls out his nine-inch knife and rushes up to the Cuban major at a relatively fast pace. He places the knife to his throat. "Listen, bitch, my brother died in this hell-hole because of your bullshit, so I don't have any remorse for your sorry, lame ass! Look! I'm just about fed up with your senseless-ass bullshit! Now, tell us where the damn disc and chips are located!" Tony screams, frowning.

"Your brother, you don't say, huh? Well..., good enough for your punk-ass, shithead brother!" the Cuban major shouts in a slurred speech when spitting at Tony this time.

Tony wipes the overspray of bourbon scent from his face, staring with a mean and then terrified stare when backing up a few feet, laying his nine-inch knife on the desk. His hands go expressly to his back, feeling around for a bigger knife in the back of his waistband. "Ahh!" Tony screams, charging, grasping, and lifting the Cuban major in one arm while cutting the rope as they both freely fall forward.

Tony rides the major to the floor, slamming into the Cuban major's chest when his back slaps against the old hardwood floor hard. He swiftly climbs on top of him like a cougar on its prey when withdrawing his knees and coming up fast, half-straddling the major's body.

The rope around the major's hand begins unraveling. Upon registering it, he abruptly balls his fist before bracing himself when Tony administers two devastating blows to his face, slightly knocking him unconscious and onto his stomach.

The major's hand quickly reaches for his collar, pressing the button on the back of the bear emblem with the bear's eyes flickering then dark.

Tony snatches him back, reaching forward, grabbing him in the collar, and ripping the major's shirt open. His hands go high over his head, motioning the two Soldiers closest to him to hold the major down when spreading the major's arms open with one Soldier' boots pressing hard on his wrists. Tony grasps his knife, slowly lifting it high over his head again.

Tom finally comes out of his deep train of thought, finding the room growing quiet when looking into another officer's face and seeing him in awe. He comes up from behind several Soldiers who gather around, leaning over one of the men's shoulders, finding Tony with the knife high over his head. "No, Tony!" Tom shouts, diving forward and advancing only a few feet before being apprehended by two officers.

Tony drops the blade down fast, puncturing the major's chest cavity dead center with force so strong that some of the blade sticks to the floor when Tony screams, working the handle back and forth to free it until easing it out. He expressly drives it in again and then eases it out until slowly carving his brother's initials deep in the major's flesh.

The major heavily strains but keeps back from screaming in pain, trying to be tough before his enemies until, out of nowhere, he screams for as long and as loudly as he can, trembling. He burst into screams of excruciatingly painful and dreadful cries that dwindle to a slow, slobbering sniffling with many faces cringing and heads turning, unable to bare the sight.

"You still think it's good for my brother, no bitch?" Tony shouts over the major's loud screams when punching him in the face several more times.

"Damn your..., ooh!" the major screams when Tony thrusts the sharp blade deep into his heart and slowly twists it.

Tony pulls the blade out, pressing it to the major's throat, slowly rocking it until severing his main artery.

Blood squirts and then spray across Tony's neck and uniform as he stands, still straddling the major with one hand leaning against the table to support his weight.

The men release the major, and he clenches his neck, gagging and gurgling until taking his last breath.

The Underground's Senior Officer motions the troops to pick up the scattered documents and anything of mission value, and when motioning to release Tom, he drops forward in disbelief. "So tell me, sir, what do we do about the discs and chips, now?" Tom asks with eyes cut over at the dead major.

"It doesn't matter, Chief. We'll burn this mother down to the ground. Besides, Plan Charlie destroys their vital communications and satellite."

The senior officer retreats outside, and the next officer in command sounds the alarm, directing and motioning his platoon leaders to take head counts; that later shows a loss of about forty troops.

Everyone takes their time retrieving all of their comrades' dead bodies, placing them in black body bags, and loading them into the front two-and-a-half-ton truck while everyone embarks on their designated trucks. They also load the wounded in the second truck with the medics when engines rev up almost simultaneously when the last man sits down.

Buildings continued blazing with fresh fires and bombs set by the demolition team.

The bulk, heavy pre-charged C4 packets lay set with detonations within the hour.

The command and control trailer sits parked, with personnel working diligently to get the trailer secured for movement.

Out of nowhere, a group of teens come off their hiking trail along the highway and cut down the trail where the eighteen-wheeler sits in a grassy field. They unknowingly proceed past the quiet trailer when the teen closest trips over one of the transparent, camouflaged tent's weights.

The chubby kid goes face-first into the dirt, and his friends look back, bursting into laughter while continuing their journey. He springs up, dusting off just as the trailer is prepared to come out of hiding, when loudly firing off engines, making everyone freeze in their tracks.

They all stand frightened with their eyes bucked open, some looking through the woods while others are looking in the air, trying to figure out the origin of the loud noise.

Scared out of his wits, the last teen appears behind his friends in a flash.

The driver of the command vehicle feels very playful, wanting to get a good laugh out of the new female co-driver he's been flirting with, so he leaves the camouflage active. He finally receives orders to join the force, and steps on the gas pedal, temporarily dragging the camouflage weighted bags while bringing the vehicle up to top speed. He leans to one side, making a very wide turn in the huge field to ensure he wasn't throwing passengers around. He begins circling the kids and then comes up on the other side of them, still invisible, and the group freezes with eyes now attentively following the sound as if they can actually see the truck.

The driver straightens the trailer after the turn and picks up speed, barreling down on the kids until deactivating the camouflage, which sucks in the nets as if they never were there.

The big rig and trailer emerge out of thin air, sounding its loud, irritating horn and scaring them.

The kids scatter for their lives, a few dropping their backpacks, which are immediately pulverized when the huge tires smash them deep into the dirt, beyond recognition.

The driver overshoots his turn, fighting the steering wheel with all his might and swerving to miss a tree when safely aligning the vehicle to transverse back through the narrow wooded path.

Those in the mobile command room buckle in tight, gripping their consoles.

Those standing folks hold on tightly to hanging hand straps when heavily rocking back and forth.

The edge of the paved highway finally comes into view when the driver slows the rig and comes to a standstill at the path's edge. He patiently waits for the convoy to pass and then joins but remains ten miles behind per command policy and directives.

Inside the command trailer, victory dances are seen on the command and control vehicle's big screens after the Underground's major makes the damage assessment reports.

The convoy's lead vehicle stops as directed when several miles from the Cuban Camp, observing a moment of silence in honoring their fallen troops.

After a solid minute, the engines rev back up, and the convoy advances up a steep road.

The most senior truck leads the way through the hillside at a slower-than-normal pace when the convoy has completed well over half the drive.

The troops jump with eyes over against the mountainside, hearing several loud explosions when seeing bright fireworks lighting up the sky in the background where the Cuban Headquarters and Cuban Camp once stood.

Hours later, at Kelley's, the phone rings with her uncle in tears, trying to figure out how to tell her that her father is killed in what he perceives is an explosion, based on his informant. Kelley brakes down in tears, yearning to reunite with her father, and feels empty knowing he's gone.

They spend quite some time talking about her father, comforting one another until the conversation dwindles to just small talk, but before hanging up, he transitions into more personal business. He also requests that she fly to London to meet with him and close out all of her father's affairs, and she agrees.

When the convoy arrives at the Compound, everyone attends an after-action brief and departs.

CHAPTER EIGHT: THE CUBAN MASSACRE

Tom goes to the city and settles the rental car damages, plus rents another car. He arrives at Latisha's way later than expected, and he's surprised to see that she lives in such an extravagant, gated community versus what he'd expected based on what he'd seen of island housing. After going through tight security, Tom pulls into the driveway cutting off the headlights, noticing the lights in the front room out seconds later. He lifts the wine and flowers from the front seat and then looks back at the house. He approaches the door with his hand inside his jacket, on his gun, with wine and flowers behind his back, ringing the doorbell.

"Who is it?" a soft, mellow feminine voice answers with the door slowly opening.

He makes eye contact with Latisha, who falls in his arms before backing up, pulling the roses to her nose, inhaling a deep breath of them, and smiling.

"Thank you so much, sweetie..., you know..., you just missed my daughter."

"Really? Well, I was looking forward to meeting her."

"I'm sure there will be plenty of time before you leave." Latisha closes and locks the stained glass and wooden door, engaging the deadbolt, when turning and placing hands on her hips. She gives him a seductive stare.

"I thought that maybe we can do the breakfast buffet at a place I've heard folks on the island talk about," Tom says, kissing her neck right down to her collarbone.

"Hmm..., you mean the Centurion? Mmm..., ok, well, in that case, we still have time. Besides, we could chill for a few, so excuse me while I slip into something more comfortable," she says, winking and pulling away. Latisha adjusts the stereo volume to a whisper and exits through the hallway.

Tom settles in on the couch, resting his back on the armrest, staring at the ceiling when comfortable, recapturing the entire deadly operation, play-by-play.

Latisha reenters about ten minutes later, finding Tom deep in thought and not noticing she's standing there.

"Can I get you something to drink?" she asks, startling him.

"Yes..., the usual if you have it, please..., thank you."

Tom watches her tighten her sheer, red, Oriental silk robe against her body, with the material perfectly revealing her beautiful naked curves. He knows firsthand, from the way the robe drapes over her sexy body, that she had on neither bra nor panties, but for confirmation, his eyes browse over her hourglass shape as she stands near the fireplace lighting a few candles.

She lights the fireplace, and when the initial high flames reflect through her tall legs, he confirms his first thought of her having on nothing. He continues gazing between her long legs until he almost sees her perfectly-curved pelvis and what could have been perceived as lips between her wide-gapped thighs when staring longer and aroused.

She lifts the drinks, walks over, hands him his drink, and then leans forward, placing her glass on the table when her robe slightly falls open.

Tom can't help but admire her large, silver-dollar-sized areolas, which look as if they've been honey-dipped, lightly glazed in butter, and then browned to perfection. He takes a sip, slides over, and places his hand on her leg, gently stroking her soft thigh back and forth. "I just love silk..., so tell me..., how did you know red was my favorite color?" He kisses her soft lips until his tongue sinks deep in her slow opening, hot mouth with tongues playfully fighting back and forth until his lips run up and down the shaft of her finely-structured neck. He stops at her collarbone, kissing it over and over and sucking on it until getting a twitch and a smile from her when a chill runs down her spine.

She begins throbbing until crossing her legs and holding them tightly while slightly shifting away from him and shaking off the feeling before leaning closer again.

He extends his glass as a gesture to a toast when Latisha responds with glasses tightly touching when Latisha smiles. He stares at her until his mind drifts back to the shoot-out and Tee.

Latisha soon makes a comment that requires a response, but she doesn't get one. "Are you even listening to me?" She pauses. "Mmm..., how can you be when you're looking off in outer space and rubbing my thighs, which I must admit is making me so damn..., Ahh!"

Tom breaks his concentration, staring into her beautiful eyes. "I'm sorry, sweetness. It's just that I can't seem to break my thoughts of the special operations. Man, we lost so many Soldiers."

"What happened? You know you can tell me because I can keep a secret," she says with pretty glistening eyes and batting eyelashes.

"Really, umm..., then let's see if you can keep this one," he says, leaning into her and causing her to respond to his advances.

Latisha repositions her back against the thick pillows as he unravels her robe's straps with his lips, allowing the robe to open completely, revealing her naked, sunbaked, pecan-tanned body.

He comes up, draping over her, balancing on his hands and knees while his mouth applies tender kisses to her belly until he has her totally aroused, causing her to arch her back in pure pleasure as he slowly works his way to her belly button. He feels her raised pelvis pressing against his chest as he slides down further until her hand moves down, patting the bald curvature a few times as she spreads her legs wider.

Tom gets turned on by how her pelvis rotates as she twirls her hips in a slow, seductive grind until she moans, and he applies more small kisses, causing her to spread her legs wider. He buries his face deeper between her thighs, and she continually tries resisting her screams but can't, so she gently bites her bottom lip.

She eases a leg over his back, making herself readily accessible for him to kiss and suck even deeper when her hand releases his head and then grasps a fistful of his hair, guiding his head deeper into sheer pleasure. She arches her back, whining, and twirling her hips even slower while continually moaning for minutes.

Tom remains in one spot for well over twenty minutes or more, teasing, pleasing, and causing her to flinch, flex, and relax over and over again until her body trembles like a leaf.

Her thighs press hard and then harder together. "I'll be damn! Damn..., mmm..., ooh..., ooh, Tom," she continually moans for minutes and then quiets, holding back more before screaming as long and as loud as she can. "Mmm, ooh, shh..., I driivahundaaue! Damn..., mmm, ooh, I driivadamnhundaaue!" Latisha blurts out, stuttering some senseless, unspoken, and broken-Arab-sounding language with no meaning when g control. She grows breathless and tries screaming again but can't when a teardrop falls from the corner of both her eyes. "Mmm..., damn, babe, Mmm, damn, damn, damn," she playfully moans, pounding the pillow with each spoken damn. "Damn!" she seductively moans one last time, gasping for air yet begging for more.

Tom moves the coffee table back and eases to the floor, where he falls onto his back, kicking off his shoes and expressly squirming to remove his clothes when down to tight briefs, Latisha slithers completely out of her robe and off the couch.

She sits beside him, playfully stroking his thigh to get him aroused again, and then grabs him in a tight fist, feeling him flex in an attempt to tease as she grasps him and tries making the tip of her fingers touch the tip of her thumb. She meditates, kneeling and sliding her fingers inside the rim of his tight boxers, then gently pulls them down and starts to tease him when he springs upward, slightly grazing the bottom of her chin. She slithers down midway to his thighs.

Within minutes, Tom feels so woozy that his eyes cross a few times when he tries fighting off the increasingly pulsating feeling. He grows as still as metal but manages to hold back and gain control after a few seconds.

After some time, Latisha mounts him, guiding him centimeters from her, and then takes him like a true, professional rider until screaming. "No more, babeee..., no more!" she cries. "No more, you're too, too, too, too, too deep," she screams, slightly stuttering from him bucking.

He focuses too much on her sexy voice and releases quickly but quickly reloads from her feeling so good to have something new, hotter, and tighter, then about to lose it again when Latisha uncontrollably screams. "Not again! Tom! Ooh, man, this is so damn good, sweetie!"

He can feel her body temperature rising like an inferno when he moans to keep

Tainted Obsessions

his manly image but can't keep his toes from curling. "Mmm..., mmm..., mmm..., babe, ooh yeah," he moans, trying to be the quiet storm he proclaimed to be when deep in some sex. He's quick to reload a third time, minutes later when Latisha repositions on her knees.

She kisses him and then rolls over, curling up against him until cuddling in his strong arms with her cool, damp, black hair resting against his chest as she breathes harder until tears roll from her eyes. "No man has ever handled me like that. Damn..., you were definitely deep and it definitely felt like you were somewhere you shouldn't have been, babe. I've never felt it that deep before or felt that other entry open, but damn, it was the greatest ever," she says, lightly trembling at her thighs.

After a while, Latisha turns over and looks into his eyes in a daze smiling until her face becomes serious. "Do you still love her?"

"What kind of question is that, Latisha?"

"One, I want to be answered, do you?"

Tom continues avoiding the question but playfully tries changing the subject a few times until she grows quiet. He senses she's a little pissed, so he soon welcomes her closer in his arms, stroking her spine to relax and comfort her. A few French kisses clear her mind, followed by gentle strokes that eventually bring a smile when she cuddles closer.

The music pauses, and she hears his stomach growl a deep and long roar.

"Poor babe," she says, rubbing his hard abs while kissing his chest and running her tongue through coarse chest hairs. She stands seconds later, slithering back into her robe, then hands him his clothes and reaches for his hand, leading him through the sconce-lit hallway to the bedroom where they shower together and get dressed.

They arrive at the Centurion just before the buffet closes, and seeing how it's a lovely morning and a light breeze is coming off the ocean, Tom recommends eating outside to catch the milder breeze and break of day.

Back in the states, Kelley catches an early flight to London to meet with her uncle and arrives eight hours later, greeted by a limousine, chauffeur, and escort vehicles, presidential style. She arrives at the castle, where she's greeted by old, familiar faces and new, friendly staff members who escort her to her uncle's chambers.

After Tom and Latisha's candlelit breakfast, they take the scenic route back and arrive around 0600.

They get undressed and have follow-up sex in the king-size bed before a bright sunrise breaks through the thin, sheer curtains.

They practically slept half the morning away from pure exhaustion, but she awakens later and prepares a fruit dish, which they use to play the taste game while blindfolded, and then have more hot sex.

Later, they are awakened in the day's warmth from the bright sun's rays still penetrating through the seams of the sheer curtains. They get up, use the bathroom, and then cuddle more until falling back asleep.

Around 1400, Tom awakes but leaves Latisha in bed, still exhausted and in a deep sleep. He showers and then dresses so he can make it back to the Compound for the last phase of the operation's pre-briefing.

On the ship, Captain Carrington land and runs from the helicopter, rushing through passageways up to Captain Pierite's cabin to brief him on an excellent strike mission. In his briefing, he refrains from disclosing the Underground's intentions of launching missiles at the Cuban satellite because he wants to make sure there is no conflict of interest should the ship receive strike orders to launch missiles against outbound Bazumi missiles.

Later that evening, Latisha sits around the house anxiously awaiting Tom's call or visit, but neither comes, so she rests more. Not realizing how tired she is, she soon falls fast asleep on the couch with the phone near her head.

At 0730 the following morning, Tom meets with Tony and Oggie in the large, half-filled briefing room.

Within a couple of hours, the entire control room is full of staff, crew, and over forty new military recruits who walk around with freshly-issued uniforms: straight out of boot camp.

"Everyone, take your seats, please," the most senior officer says, staring into the large crowd before signaling to the male ensign to dim the overhead lights. The senior officer lifts the seal from the envelope, turning on his laser pointer when beginning his highly-classified presentation, which contains full-length pictures of General Rice, the Cuban major, co-leaders, and even still and motion pictures of Nichelle, profiled in full-dress military attire while being presented with a Medal of Valor.

Tom stares in deep thought, unable to break his thought of how much Kelley's son looks like the general and the fact that they have the same last name. For a quick second, he's close to bridging the gap between the two until easing from his seat when thinking he'd seen a woman who looks like Kelley's best friend, Tricia.

His mind quickly shifts to Nichelle, and he holds his head down in disbelief, reminiscing on the short but enjoyable moments with Nichelle when he becomes aroused. His mind refocuses on her involvement and desire to kill him and his men when his desires instantly fade.

For the remainder of the briefing, a female officer presents, and it pertains mainly to plans and procedures for taking out the Cuban satellites.

The bright lights soon come on, bringing Tom out of a deep trance.

"Finally," she concludes. "Memorial service for Tee will be in the Underground's chapel and our other fallen troops in the Compound's chapel immediately after that. The secretary will post family funerals and burials later..., so..., are there any questions?"

No one acknowledges, but personnel immediately stand and head for the Underground's homecoming service, scheduled for orchestration by Major Fields.

Tom walks into the huge auditorium, finding the major sitting on stage with his wife and Tee's daughter.

Before starting the main ceremony, the major proudly introduces their daughter during the presentation. He speaks highly of Tee's excellent and decorative services and then pins their daughter with Tee's Medal of Honor and Valor.

The major's wife sits gazing over at Joe from time to time, and whenever she catches his attention, she looks away with her nose turned up, acting as if she's a proud peacock, with her shoulders drawn back and her chest stuck out.

Joe sits smiling, and when feeling no one is looking, he winks at her.

Now, seeing how Tee is out of the picture, she feels she has major all to herself again.

After the joint troops' services end, Tom arrives at his room listening to soft music. He walks past the couch, discovering that someone has printed a briefing folder containing phone bills and slipped it under his bedroom door with most documents printed on Cuban bonded paper. He thumbs through the documents and notices that the phone transactions are from the Cuban Camp to Washington or vice versa in the months leading up to and during the covert operation. His fingers begin scrolling to the bottom of the bill, discovering that someone made calls as late as the same day they had stormed the Cuban Headquarters and Camp.

He eases the soft music down a few notches when the soft-ticking clock in the quiet room beside the bed grows louder until the phone rings, startling him.

Captain Carrington responds excitedly, congratulating Tom and his men on their part in Operation ELI, and asks about the package receipt.

They talk for over half an hour before the conversation tapers off.

"So what's the plan, sir? Will we rendezvous with the ship tonight or tomorrow?"

"No, no..., I left tickets with the major. The three of you can fly back to the States next week, so enjoy your little vacation. Hey..., give me a call at the office next week and update me on your status and plans for the remainder of the covert U.S. mission, 'cause I have to get to the bottom of this," he says, reclining on his back, in his bunk. He cuddles closer in the cozy sheets, his thick fingers running through Tamara's semi-wet, freshly washed, fragranced hair.

Without warning, the ship takes a hard left and then a sharp right turn while conducting its weekly submarine TACK-41 evasive maneuvers.

Tamara braces the side of the bulkhead (wall) with one hand when the vessel takes a sudden thirty-degree roll and maneuvers, then increases speed.

The call soon ends, and Tom heads over to Tony's and then Oggie's room, where the three talks for minutes and then walk off with Cynthia hot on their trail.

The four reach the control room, where Tom presses the buzzer, and the vault-type door flies open.

"Come on in, guys! I was just about to send someone to get you," the major says, looking over the shoulder of the Soldier who is still holding the door open.

"Afternoon, Major Fields!" Tom says, nervously walking up to him.

"Afternoon, Chief! So tell me..., you've been treating my little Lattia good, yeah?" the major whispers, leading Tom off to the side of the desk.

"Like a perfect gentleman," Tom says, a little tense, not knowing if the major knew he had intimate dealings with his daughter.

The blue screen blinks and stabilizes as everyone watches the Cuban satellite orbit track along its prescheduled flight path.

The major slightly reclines back in his high chair, lighting a Cuban cigar and watching the satellite as it zooms across the big screen from a distance. "Tracker! Set the speed ratio to 1:100,000,000, and zoom in on the bottom tip of the satellite," the major says, taking another puff and blowing an almost perfect doughnut-shaped smoke ring up in the air.

"Aye, sir, zooming at this time," the tracker shouts from across the room. He zooms in on the satellite's image until it is more precise and appears closer.

The major stands with his eyes widened in shock when the tracker focuses on something moving behind the Cuban satellite.

"Sir, it looks like two satellites tracking together," the watch officer yells, looking back over his shoulder.

In Washington, D.C., tension grows fast in the Washington Command Center as they maneuvered their satellite after receiving tasking from Admiral Kitts via Admiral Michaels, the intelligence officer on duty, to exploit all satellites in the vicinity of Grand Bazumi.

Excitement grows in the Washington Command Center. "Mr. Vee," Captain Fikes says. "Activate scanners and see if we can get information from the satellite out in front of us."

"Aye, sir!" Mr. Vee responds, manipulating the high-tech control panel.

In Bazumi, Major Fields kept his eyes frozen on both satellites. "Conduct a frequency scan, and come up on whatever frequency the Cuban satellite is on so we can override its operational controls. Determine what frequency the other satellite is on as well!" Major Fields excitedly yells.

Both command centers intercept the downlink to the Cuban satellite simultaneously, with more tension growing until the noise levels get out of control.

The operators from both centers worked diligently to collect as much communicable information and electronic data from the Cuban satellite and each other as possible.

"Chief Jones, increase the signal's reception," Captain Fikes yells, easing into his high chair. "Have intelligence provide as much data as possible on that other satellite, and tell me where the hell it came from!"

"Increase frequency reception!" the major screams, biting down hard on the cigar with a frown.

Washington continually tries deciphering the Cuban and other satellite's encryption devices until the Underground gains limited control, but they know it will take some time before having full control, the time they didn't have.

Tension grows even greater in both Command Centers.

The Cuban satellite continues operating in automatic tracker mode while opening its two side sensors and bottom microscopic lens. The satellite's lens slowly focuses and zooms in on the entire spectrum of the Bazumi Islands, as scheduled biweekly. However, the view is too close for the Command Center to figure out what they are actually viewing in the center of the targeted, red, illuminated box on the monitor, which is still flashing.

"Major..., I was able to break into the jamming mechanism!" the Underground's junior officer reports.

"Great! Activate jammers now!" Major Fields shouts victoriously.

The male junior officer activates the Undergrounds satellite's jammers, flipping the spring-loaded switch back and pressing the flashing red button on the console.

Instantly, four small cylinders discharge from both sides of their satellite, and immediately, a blast shift monitors in both Command Centers, causing small explosions when the canisters release small, metallic yet highly reflective strips of material into outer space.

The Washington Command Center and Underground's screens become slightly distorted and clear a little later, but they still are blurry as the telescopic lens unsuccessfully zooms in on portions of the damaged Cuban Camp for a fraction of a second.

The Washington Command Center's view worsens and then blacks out from the Underground's control of the electronic jammers, which totally degrades their reception.

"Check the coordinates! Mr. Vee, wasn't there an old power plant there a few days ago?" Captain Fikes asks.

"Checking now, sir," he responds, checking the map's coordinates and then looking over at the Cuban satellite's blank navigation display window. "I can't verify the coordinates because we've lost the link to the Cuban satellite. I'll need to re-link and get another image. For some reason, it's not powerful enough at this distance to look down. We need to maneuver closer and re-link with the Cuban satellite, but that could take some time," Mr. Vee acknowledges.

Major Fields slowly stands with a shit-eating grin. "Fire Control Officer, check the coordinates and prepare to conduct a laser strike at maximum power out!" he shouts.

"Aye, sir," he acknowledges, looking over the huge control panel.

"Sir, navigational coordinates are satisfactory! I'm ready to launch on your command!"

"Very well!" Major Fields boldly replies.

Loud alarms begin sounding on the Underground's lawn. Bright lights pulsate in unison and at two-second intervals. The twelve-foot Battle of Iwo Jima-like statue that's built on top of the missile doors slowly rolls back, revealing twelve, thirty-foot towers that flash a red, pulsating light in unison with the second set of alarms. Two of the twelve tower's lights turn yellow for seconds and then cycle to a bright, steady green before more alarms silence.

Captain Fikes stands looking over all of the red, flashing console buttons. "Damn it, Chief Jones! Call the transmitter room and tell them to give us more power out now!" Captain Fikes shouts in rage with his tightly-balled fist slamming into the top of the console.

The Underground's fire control officer flips back the missile launcher's spring-loaded clear protective cover and holds it open.

"Launch on my command: five, four, three, two, one, launch!" the major shouts, slamming his hand on top of the control console's ledge.

The Underground's fire control officer lightly presses the two red-flashing laser buttons and releases the protective covers when the loud spring-loaded clips smack against the console and sound off throughout the quiet, tense room.

A vibration comes with a heavy, thick gray smoke flashing outside the Underground from the bottom of the missile boxes. Missile doors instantaneously fly open, almost invisibly launching two VFLRF long-range missiles. Smoke trails extend upward through a few thin clouds until the booster is visible to the naked eye minutes later, plummeting back to earth into the danger drop zone, outlined in painted red stripes.

"The estimated time of impact is twenty minutes, sir!" a voice resonates.

"Very well!" the major says, reclining in his chair.

On the ship, all the sensors instantly alarm the air, surface search radar, and fire control equipment, with all registering missiles in flight.

The OOD rushes in, bringing the communications equipment out of maintenance, and establishes communications with Washington.

Chief Jones stands in the middle of the control room, staring into the flashing control panel. "Captain, the transmitter's maxed out!" Chief Jones finally shouts.

"Everyone, check your consoles! I need to get this intelligence data and verify these coordinates now!" the captain nervously screams.

Ten minutes pass, and the Washington Command Center's picture is still distorted, but console operators work diligently to get the system back up and operational.

"Captain, the transmitter room needs nine more minutes to do a double bypass, which should clear the picture! Our satellite should be where we need it to be by then," Chief Jones shyly says.

"Damn it, Chief! We don't have nine more freakin' minutes, so you tell them to hurry the hell up! This damn satellite's not going to wait on us, damn it!" Captain Fikes screams, staring into a distorted screen.

An intermittent radio transmission bleeds out of the overhead speakers in Washington's Command Center, but it's very garbled, and no one makes out the message or unit that transmitted it.

The voice transmission immediately repeated seconds later, slightly clear but still somewhat garbled and broken.

There is a third transmission, but the Command Center doesn't receive the last transmission because their communications gear is recycling again.

The ship makes several more attempts to reach Washington.

Communications to the Washington Command Center are lost when the technicians in the transmitter room take the communication circuits down while troubleshooting, as per the standard procedures during poor communications.

The ship's missile systems and other weaponry systems alarm above decks and swiftly jerk back and forth, then right to the left, searching and immediately acquiring their targets.

The newest class Fikes-Class submarine emergently surfaces without warning, shooting high in the air, almost out of the water, and plunging deep into the sea. It heavily sways for minutes before balancing out minutes later and immediately acquiring a lock on the missiles.

Now, the submarine had been directed into the area hours earlier after receiving training information to locate the USMSP R.L. Peterson as part of a targeting mission, which quickly turns real-world, per Admiral Michaels' orders.

Captain Fikes instantly receives an intelligence report that the submarine is out of the training area and stands shaking his head in disbelief while checking the coordinates, which he knows are not right but acknowledges, and knowing how nosy and nasty Admiral Michaels can get, he disregards questioning him.

Tension grows in the quiet missile launch room until, instantly, the active-lock buzzers sound through the room.

"Washington Command Center, this is the USMSP R.L Peterson; we're tracking two unknown outbound missiles from Bazumi..., request permission to intercept with surface-to-air missiles, over!"

Seconds later, the submarine makes the same report to the Washington Command Center.

The major sits puffing on his Cuban cigar, and after eighteen minutes, he electronically displays the two-minute digital counter on the large monitor.

The excitement in the control room grows tense as everyone at the Underground join in on the last ten seconds of the countdown. "Nine, eight, seven, six, five, four, three, two, one," roars the entire Underground's control room in a high pitch.

Azreay'l

The ship finally reaches the Command Center via a secure phone and relays the missile information.

In the middle of reporting, the Washington Command Center's satellite picture focuses on the Cuban Camp. It then vibrates from the blast of the two missiles simultaneously slamming into the Cuban satellite. The impact from the blast causes grave damage to the Washington satellite's telescopic lens, making it blink off and on until finally blacking out.

Everyone in the Underground continually shouts when hugging and shaking hands while dancing around after total victory.

Tony and Oggie start doing a few crazy-looking dances, which ends in Tony doing the Robot, Cabbage Patch, and finally, the Bump against Oggie a few times.

Washington Command Center's communications team angrily works diligently until their satellite finally stabilizes, but the screens are still distorted.

The door to the ship's missile room slams open. "Stand down all systems!" Captain Pierite screams with high-pitched missiles' lock buzzers de-energizing while still locked onto the Underground's satellite, which is in the background.

The drop zone coordinates of the satellite are immediately passed to the ship from the Underground, by the direction of Captain Pierite, with the OOD expediently maneuvering the ship out of harm's way. He plots the position of the satellite's entry into the earth's atmosphere on the chart and relays the information back to Washington.

The ship's turbines whistle a high, quick pitch, and a high tail feather of water shoots upward from the ship's rear as it increases speed. The ship maneuvers around other seagoing vessels, creating a huge circle, and begins launching flares from its torpedo-type canisters mounted on the forward, side, and aft decks. The USMSP R. L. Peterson continues tracking the satellite and recalculating the coordinates for the satellite drop zone as they sail further from the shoreline to remain outside the expected drop zone. The ship begins warning all surface vessels and aircraft to stand clear of the hazardous drop zone, which is illuminated with red flares over VHF and UHF radio waves,

Instantly, the submarine acknowledges its new orders just received and begins increasing speed and diving quickly, astern of the USMSP R. L. Peterson.

Within the hour, the fire-blazing satellite can be seen by the naked eye shooting across the sky like a fallen star until disappearing for seconds before blacking out.

A heavy vibration comes when a huge surge forms in the ocean and creates a fifty-story-high mushroom-shaped water cloud.

The deep ripples cause the ship to slowly rock from side to side for seconds as it increases speed to forty-five knots and levels out to a smooth ride.

The Underground's victory dinner is announced over the loudspeaker immediately after the battle damage assessment reports are given by the major.

Tom and his men attend the first hour or so before straying off, one by one.

On Tom's last night, Latisha's daughter Laquisha stays with friends and Latisha picks her up early the following morning while Tom stays packing.

Latisha returns half an hour later and rushes to the door, fumbling in her purse for her keys, smelling hickory smoked bacon, and with one last turn on the lock, the door flies open.

"Babe, you didn't have to cook..., I was going to do that as soon as I got back," she says, rushing to the kitchen door and making eye contact.

"Not a problem, sweetness. I love to be in the kitchen, so get used to it," Tom says, smiling while flipping over the last slab of hickory-smoked bacon, cracking a few eggs, and quickly stirring the grits that were beginning to stick to the bottom of the pot.

"It looks delicious!" Laquisha says, finally appearing at the door, looking, listening, and bashfully smiling.

"Finally, I get to meet you!" Tom happily says, meeting her halfway in the kitchen and giving her a big bear hug to bring a big smile upon her lovely face.

"Put your things away, dear, and get ready for breakfast," Tom says, smiling at Laquisha.

"What are you doing to my daughter, Tom? You've got her over here, and I've never seen her like this."

Laquisha walks out, totally embarrassed, and returns minutes later. She reaches into the cabinets and drawers, pulling out silverware and china to set the table.

When seated, Tom gives thanks for the meal, and they enjoy their little family-style breakfast in mild conversation until it dwindles to small talk.

Tom looks over at the clock, then his watch, and signals to Latisha that it's time to go. He loads his luggage in the trunk, climbs behind the wheel, and cranks up while Latisha locks the front door.

Laquisha climbs into the backseat and looks back at her mother as she approaches, grinning.

The three indulge in more, mild chitchat during the thirty-minute ride until a few minutes from the airport's exit.

Tom soon parks, unloading his luggage, then rushes inside to check in and register his weapons with authorities before coming back out.

The three finally walk inside and head for the boarding area, where they spot Oggie, Cynthia, and Tony.

Tom, Latisha, and Laquisha wave, then break off to go over and change Tom's seat from aisle to window.

Twenty minutes later, the attendant starts boarding the rear rows.

Tom looks into Latisha's eyes as they fill with tears that trail down her smooth cheeks.

Cynthia is also in tears but tries her best to pull it together.

Tom looks around to find Laquisha, slightly hidden behind a support beam with tears in her eyes.

The flight attendant soon asks the remaining passengers to board, but Latisha holds him tighter, not wanting to let go.

Tom hugs her tighter and instantly feels Laquisha's arms wrap around his waist from behind when he looks back into her watery eyes, using all his inner strength to keep his tears from falling.

Cynthia releases Oggie and looks over at Tom, Latisha, and Laquisha, who are still huddled. She walks over, putting her hand on Latisha's shoulder, slightly holding her while Tom kisses her and gently pulls away.

"I love you, babe, and I'm going to miss you guys," he says, turning and kissing Laquisha on the forehead before walking away and waving.

Minutes later, the women wait for the airplane to taxi away from the ramp and then come together at the huge window.

Within minutes, the plane lifts and disappears around the big building before becoming visible again as it passes the huge lobby window.

The women walk outside through a side door, waving as the plane makes its final pass and climbs higher into the thick, white clouds.

When they arrive at Norfolk International later in the evening, Tom reminds Tony and Oggie to stay low-key and not make or receive phone calls unless on their new Sky-Tel phones. He drops them off and registers at a hotel near the Norfolk Naval Base.

The following morning, Tom picks up Oggie around 0700 and arrives at Tony's ten minutes later, blowing the horn several times, but there's no response, so he waits a few minutes and then put the car in reverse and backs out.

"Hey, Chief!" Tony yells, running toward the car at top speed with his duffle bag draped over his shoulder.

The car stops, and they look around until spotting him at the rear of the trunk.

Tony opens the door, throws his things in, and climbs in the backseat, buckling up. "I had to walk my daughter to the sitter," he says, almost out of breath.

"So, when is the funeral?" Tom asks, looking over his shoulder again while backing out.

"Monday, but my parents are willing to postpone a day or so."

"No need, because we need to finish this job quickly. Out of respect for Bobby, we need to be there on time and not a second late," Tom says, looking at Tony through the rearview mirror before looking up. He fights the steering wheel hard to the right and swerves while backing out of a driveway. "I still haven't gotten word on when Robert's or Michael's services will be either, but I'm sure Captain Carrington is on top of it."

Tom takes back streets to the military installation, and when he approaches the back gate, he slows, and they show their IDs for access to the air station side of the base. With a few evasive turns to miss the road's directional cones, Tom makes a left and heads for the gymnasium.

He pulls in front of the building and stops when Tony and Oggie step out for drinks while he makes a call to Strike Force Headquarters.

"Strike Force One Headquarters, non-secure line, how may I direct your call, sir or ma'am?" the sad but fragile woman's voice asks, while staring at the photo on her desk of the whole team in smiles while dressed in their full dress-white uniforms.

"Yes, Mr. Wettsel, for Captain Carrington, please!" Tom says, heavily disguising his voice.

"Please hold, sir, while I transfer your call."

The background music plays and then promptly clicks over to silence.

"Strike Force One Headquarters, Captain Carrington!"

"Yes, sir, top of the morning, sir..., Chief Powells!"

"Morning, Chief..., how was your little vacation?" Captain Carrington asks, standing at his office door, waiting to receive a package from his secretary, who waves a courier's package overhead through the glass window.

"It was fine, sir, just a little shorter than expected," Tom says, putting the car in drive and pulling away when the last door slams shut.

Captain Carrington anxiously grasps the package, smirking and nodding to his secretary. He expressly locks the door, sneakily easing the blinds shut. "I see, so where are you now?" Captain Carrington asks in an over-delayed response when walking over to his desk and untwisting three sets of securing ties. He dumps the thick, brick-sized bundles of hundreds over the table, gazing over large, big-face bills until picking up the folded check and kissing it with a shitty grin.

"We're outside gate seven..., I thought I'd call rather than come near the office since we're supposed to be deceased in anticipation of this stateside covert operation." Tom says, easing to the stoplight with eyes wandering over a few Sailors, in formation and crossing.

Captain Carrington opens the medium-sized registered containers with his name typed on them. "I knew you would do the right thing, Chief," the captain says, sitting and leaning back in his chair and then leaning forward for the letter opener. He breaks the envelope's seal and allows the other sealed envelopes to fall freely onto the desk when pausing. "I already made reservations, but I didn't know if you guys would make the first flight, so I reserved seats on a second which leaves in three hours. I contacted a buddy who will meet you at the airport and get the weapons, blueprints, or anything else you might need. He will also get you inside the gates of the Washington Command Center if needed," he confidently says, stashing the medium-sized express mail packages with the loot inside the safe.

"Not a woman, I hope, because we've had just about more than we can take of these combative-ass women."

"No, no, no!" he cackles in his deep voice. "His name is Lieutenant Commander Villan, but he prefers Mr. Vee. His best friend, Captain Wright, was a casualty of this ordeal. I told him, you need to survey the premises for leads, so whatever you do; don't tell him it's a high-ranking official or that it's a hit because he'll probably flip his lid."

The captain ends the call and eases the blinds open, peeping over the office to find a few nosy individuals staring back when he walks off and sits working on an open computer file.

Tom and the guys arrive at the Norfolk International Airport an hour early so they would have time to get their bags processed and weapons checked in with the authorities.

Now, airport lines are long due to delayed flights, but they eventually board around 1300 and land at Baltimore-Washington International (BWI) shortly after that.

After receiving their belongings, they stand near the baggage claim area looking around until Tom spots a lieutenant commander in his dress uniform.

The officer sits with his back to Tom, stuffing his face with a burger and fries.

Tom finally slings his bag over his shoulder and cautiously approaches but stands a few feet behind the officer. "Excuse me..., Mr. Villan, Mr. Vee?" Tom asks, changing the bag to the other shoulder.

"No, Westernbaud," the fat officer responds, stress—testing the buttons on his tight uniform while extending his hand to the left to shake Tom's hand while still stuffing his face with more fries.

"Chief Powells!" a fragile male voice responds when a five-foot-eight, about two-hundred-pound, medium-build, stocky man approaches in civilian attire from behind.

Tom and Westernbaud turn, looking Mr. Vee over from head to toe.

"Mr. Villan!" Tom responds, turning and rudely leaving Westernbaud's hand extended open.

"Yes, sorry I'm late, but traffic this time of the day is a monster," he says, firmly shaking Tom's hand and then the guys'.

"No problem, sir!" Tom says, casting his eyes over Mr. Westernbaud's shoulder. "So, what's the plan?" Tom asks, taking a few steps toward the departure exit.

"I was hoping you could tell me. Ron..., I mean, Captain Carrington said you need some stuff, and I'm to take care of getting it for you guys," he says nervously. "So what is it you need?" he mutters, exiting through the double doors.

Tom goes into a mild trance as they walk across the crosswalk. His eyes roam in and about a few vacant and then occupied vehicles. Tom's mind happily fills with all sorts of new toys when he blurts out: "Automatic, silenced and suppressed, preferably a few 9MMs, M16s, or .357s, a few ten-inch-thick blades, a few machetes, and three pairs of night vision goggles, for starters. I'll think of some other things by the time we get to where we're going," Tom says, adjusting and tightening his bag on his shoulder.

"Geez, man! What do you plan to do, start a small war?" he asks, opening the driver's door of his brown, dull, primed jeep.

Oggie climbs in the backseat and notices a folded airline ticket stub, which he moves under the driver's seat with the tip of his boot before putting his bags between his legs.

"Did you have any luck getting the security badges?" Oggie asks.

"Hell, I knew it was something I forgot. My partner couldn't get the badges when asked, so the earliest will be later tonight, but...," he says, nervously looking over at Tom when interrupted.

"Oh, never mind, sir, just get the building's blueprints, and we'll handle everything else," Tom says, looking over his shoulder and winking at Oggie.

"You need blueprints? Yeah, I can handle that," he says nervously.

Twenty minutes later, Mr. Vee pulls into an old, run-down hotel's parking lot on a back street and parks.

A gray stretch limousine passes behind the jeep and slows near the end of the street.

The limousine driver's eyes wander through the rearview and side mirrors while three women and two men passengers look through the rear and side windows.

"Why are we stopping here?" Tom asks.

"So you can get a room."

"What? You've got to be shittin' me, right? Shiiiiiittttt (Shit)! I'm not sleeping in this sleazy-ass hellhole. Have you heard about the growing bedbug epidemic in cheesy hotels?" Tom asks, looking over his shoulder at Oggie and chuckling.

"Then what did you have in mind?"

"Ah, Ramekin Hotel, maybe nicer?" Tom says, looking back at Oggie again.

"The Ramekin or nicer? Hell! You're talking about a four-star hotel. There are probably too many people there to be sneaking in weapons!"

"Really? Then that's why they call it sneaking, but hey..., no worries, sir. I read just last week that half of the hotel is closed for renovations, so the place should be practically empty. You just take us to the Ramekin, and we'll handle the rest."

"All right, the Ramekin it is, and if it's packed, don't say I didn't tell you so," Mr. Vee confidently says, pulling away. He stops at the edge of the main road with eyes nervously wandering over the background through the rearview and then side mirrors until merging into moderate traffic. He vanishes around the corner of a skyscraper when the limousine swiftly turns and follows.

Within seconds, the limousine vanishes around the same building.

A tall Cuban woman stands from the tall grass alongside the hotel, waving toward different positions, around, inside, and on top of the dilapidated hotel.

Immediately, militantly-dressed personnel fades in from the tall weeds, doors, windows, and the roof, launching out on ropes. They speedily converge on the leader as if in a full dress rehearsal. As if coordinated, a mixed group of twenty men and women converge along the side of the hotel, either with drawn weapons or weapons well hidden.

A bus pulls alongside the hotel when an African-looking woman steps off, waving for everyone to load up.

Mr. Vee parks along the walkway of the Ramekin Hotel when sweat begins beading up on his forehead when wiping his forehead and nervously looks around.

The limousine slowly turns down a side street, stopping and pulling over about half a block away.

Tom rushes inside and registers with false identification and, minutes later, reappears unnoticed. "Well, sir, how soon can you get the blueprints and things we need?" Tom asks through the open window when opening the door and grabbing his things.

"Give me two or three hours. What room are you in?"

"Eight-zero-one," Tom responds, looking at the scribbled number on the electronic key's card holder.

"All right, I'll get your shopping list done as soon as possible."

The bus soon passes the limousine, pulls over, and heads down to the end of the street, where the flashers come on and then turn off.

Everyone on the bus begins opening their luggage and pulling out the same colored outfits.

The bus engine starts, and the driver makes a U-turn and then parks facing the back of the hotel, which has its lights out.

Tony and Oggie climb out and drape their bags over their backs.

Mr. Vee revs the engine and then speeds off, skidding wheels across the lightly-sanded asphalt.

Not wanting to draw any attention, the three entered through the stairwell on the side of the building.

The bus driver anxiously starts the engine when the bus jerks and stops with the driver sitting, looking at two state patrol cars that just had pulled into the gas station at the corner.

Inside the room, Tom, Oggie, and Tony check the room over thoroughly and then unpack with gear strewn over the room.

Tom turns on the television while Tony and Bobby continue unpacking. Tom orders steak and shrimp dinners from a local restaurant's delivery service when their gear is neatly laid out.

When the food arrives, Oggie opens the refrigerator and breaks out the miniature bottles of wine and twelve-ounce beers. He sets the wine on top of the counter and throws a beer to Tom and Tony.

After dinner, Tom pulls out the phone bill, spreading it over the bed when kneeling. "Hey, look Oggie!" Tom says, motioning him over. "It looks as if these calls were made simultaneously, daily. If we only had a face to match with the name," he says, staring at the long, frequent phone listings of two numbers alternating down each of the bills. "Captain Carrington said he goes by the name Bear," Tom says with eyes scrolling up and down the phone bill in deep analytical thought when his mind drifts to an old movie. "Hey, Tony, do you remember the guy you impersonated so well in the movie, Father Telley?"

"Yeah, what about it?"

"I need you to impersonate that guy with the Cuban accent when I dial this number in about an hour."

"All right, but what do I say?"

Tom coaches Tony on what he should try to obtain from the call, and Tony walks off while Tom continues looking over the bill with Oggie.

An hour passes, and Tony picks up his Sky-Tel and passes it to Tom.

Tom looks at his watch and then sits on the edge of the bed, dialing. The phone ring once and Tom passes it to Tony. "Just make sure they initiate securely so our identification codes don't show up," Tom says.

"Command Center, Specialist Smith, non-secure line. How may I direct this call, sir or ma'am?" the desk clerk asks in a soft and sexy voice, with the phone pressed tightly to her ear, listening to Tony's heavy breathing for seconds.

Tony's hand continually covers the mouthpiece until she slams the phone down.

"Some woman answered," Tony says, slowly hanging up.

Tom waits five minutes and then calls again, passing Tony the phone.

"Command Center, Specialist Smith, non-secure line. How may I direct your call, sir or ma'am?" she asks, listening to the heavy breathing again before hanging up.

"She answered again," Tony says, hanging up and sitting on the edge of the bed.

Tom waits ten minutes, staring at his watch and counting the last few seconds before passing the phone to Tony.

"Command Center, Specialist Smith, non-secure line. How may I direct this call, sir or ma'am?" she says, closely listening until pressing the phone tighter, hearing muffling sounds from the television when her face frowns. "Don't call here if you don't have anything to say!" she shouts, still waiting longer for a response that never comes.

"Is there a problem, Specialist Smith?" a deep male voice asks as he walks up from behind her.

"Yes, Admiral, someone's called three times with nothing to say. They act as if this is some kind of joke, and I'm just sick and tired of it!" she says, slamming the phone down.

"Well?" Tom asks, seeing Tony's face light up.

"Someone's there with her; I heard her say, admiral!"

"That's probably him! Let's give it twenty minutes this time." Tom says, taking a seat on the edge of the bed.

The desk clerk looks at her watch and then begins stuffing her things in her purse. She walks by the admiral's office and bids him a delightful evening.

The admiral wishes her a good evening in return and shuts off his computer, sitting in the dark with visions flashing through his head, then sits a little longer until yawning a few times. He looks back down at his watch when grabbing his briefcase, loading his things and then his 9MM from his bottom drawer.

Tom looks at his watch and then passes Tony the phone.

The admiral runs from his office to the receptionist's desk. "Command Center, Admiral Kitts, on a non-secure line. May I help you?" he asks, looking into the blank caller ID with a sneaky grin with eyes constantly locked on the control room's door.

"Yeah, man..., can you talk?" Tony whispers in an imitated, scratchy voice.

"What? Who is this?" the admiral asks, looking around when thinking he heard a door open.

"Don't worry about that, man. The question is, are you able to talk?"

"Listen, I don't have time for silly-ass games!" the admiral says, checking to ensure the office is empty, then looking at the closed office door across the hall and back at the control room door.

"Man, I don't have time to play your games either! I've got flash priority traffic to pass from the major."

"Wait..., wait..., can you go secure?" the admiral whispers.

"Wait, I'll try, but we've been having problems with these worthless phones I presume you supplied us with..., look..., I'll try to initiate, but how do I know you're the man I need to talk to?"

"I am, damn it, now just tell me what in the hell's going on down there. I haven't heard from you guys, our satellite's down, and your satellite is nowhere to be found!"

"Like I said, how do I know if you're the guy I'm supposed to be talking to? The major told me only to talk to the Lear!"

"It's Bear, not Lear; you damn idiot! Now tell me what the hell's going on and what's the message?"

"Wait, I still can't initiate, can you?" Tony asks.

"Yes, wait...," the admiral excitedly responds.

"Ok..., I show that you're secure now. Uh..., we had intruders penetrate the Cuban Camp, so we went into communications silence on all satellites and radio frequencies. By the way, the girls took care of the U.S. military team you sent down, and they thank you for that little extra bonus. Surely, killing them was a damn pleasure."

"Great, are they all dead? We saw that the Camp was destroyed, but what happened?" the admiral asks with a sinister smirk.

"Yes, the team is as dead as a doorknob. The Camp..., well, it's a decoy we recorded on our satellite downlink side when the U.S. and other unidentified satellite came too close for comfort," Tony says with a disgusted look.

"It's good to know the team is finished up because those guys knew too damn much about the last operation with Strike Force Two. They had to be eliminated before information leaked. Hell, there were just too many top officials' heads that would have rolled had they leaked information from that deceptive and deadly mission. Well, enough about that; just pass to the major that the White House called a day ago to inform me that the money is ready for transfer. I'll personally be picking it up from the U.S. Treasury Department in an hour or so. What about the disk? Are you still going to be able to carry out downloading the disk should they try changing their minds about the money at the last minute?"

"Yeah, we're good, but did they come up with the full amount?"

"Yeah, one-point-four billion as demanded, and in very large bills, might I add. I convinced them to let me deliver it versus electronically transferring it..., those suckers!" the admiral says, chuckling inside while pulling his other firearm from his handbag. He slips the weapon into the holster while sliding a box of ammunition inside his jacket pocket. He rattles on about nothing and then agrees on a meeting time and place before hanging up.

"Well?" Tom says. "What's with all the small talk?"

"This is all about money, man..., one-point-four billion, in mean greens! Hell..., killing us was just a prime opportunity during their deceptive and cunning scam. Someone wanted us wiped out so we wouldn't disclose information about the last operation with Strike Force Two. He mentioned something about many high-ranking officials losing their jobs, so I'm going to assume doing some hard time."

"So where's our 20:00, well, 20:30 hot spot?" Tom excitedly asks.

"He said an abandoned building at the end of the airport strip on top of the hill."

"Great work, Tony! He played right into our hands," Tom says.

"Yeah, my impersonation really paid off, huh? Speaking of nervous, this guy probably hasn't slept in a while. He was very concerned about the lack of communications with the Cuban Camp and their satellite."

"Well, tomorrow, we're about to change his restless nights to eternal rest after 2031. One minute is all I need to put this sorry-ass punk out of his misery," Tom says, slamming his balled fist tightly in his hand while in deep, meditative thoughts.

An hour later, Mr. Vee stands outside unloading boxes on the miniature dolly and finds the plane ticket stub extended from the bottom of the driver's seat. He reaches for it and holds it up to the light, thumbing through it until his eyes buck, and he takes deep breaths and then swallows hard. He nervously looks around and then folds the ticket and pushes it in the crease of the backseat until it falls behind the seat.

A sharp knock comes upon the door.

Oggie walks over; looking through the peephole, then opens the door and pulls it wide open so the long, medium-sized crates easily fit through the door.

"Here's everything, along with blueprints and badge templates," Mr. Vee says, lifting the architectural rolls from the top of the open crate.

"Thanks, sir," Tom says, nodding to Mr. Vee.

"Anything else?" Mr. Vee asks, wiping sweat from his forehead.

"Yes!" Tom says. "Could you pick us up tomorrow around 1930 and drop us off? I promise that will be the last thing we need."

"You mean for the hiyau..., I mean mission?" he said, in a broken tone, trying to cut off the word "hit" before it almost slipped out.

"Yeah," Tom says, deep in thought about what to do next.

"No way..., Captain Carrington promised me some action on this mission. I'll pick you up, but I'm 100% committed to this mission!" Mr. Vee says quickly, overusing the word "mission" to try and throw them off.

"All right, sir, we'll let you in, but don't expect to do much because there's not much to be done; it's all just reconnaissance."

"With all this artillery? Riiiggghhhttt (Right)..., reconnaissance my ass, but thanks, Chief," he says with a smirk. "Well, I'd better be going because dinner is calling," Mr. Vee says, nerdish-like with eye gazing through the thin curtains, spotting the bus's headlights. He nervously fumbles for the doorknob with sweaty fingers slipping off a few times, then clumsily pulls the door open and into the back of his heels.

"Thanks again, sir."

"Not a problem," Mr. Vee responds, slowly pulling the door shut and walking quickly to distance himself.

"Man, is this guy good or what? He's a nervous wreck for sure, but these guns..., damn..., nice! Look at them! Still in shipping cases, and they're practically new!" Tony says, gazing over the untouched weapons.

"He's right," Oggie says, walking up next to Tony. "Look at these knives: shiny, sharp, thick blades." Oggie pulls a sheet of paper from his pocket and runs it over the sharp blade, shredding the paper without effort.

"Damn, now that's sharp as all getup!" Tony smiles.

"Oggie, throw me the blueprints," Tom says, turning and reaching for the prints as they fly through the air.

Tom kneels and looks over the phone bill again and then back at the guys from time to time. He spreads out the blueprints and starts tracing the building's security system. "Tony, make sure the phone batteries are fully charged, and Oggie, lay out the weapons," Tom says, finally rolling the blueprints and phone bills together.

Mr. Vee rushes out through the hotel's double doors, sprinting and looking back while running up to the limousine. He exchanges words with the driver, who jumps out and waives the bus out of the vicinity.

Tom eases onto the bed and drifts in thoughts until finally registering that Mr. Vee was about to mention a hit but cut it short and played it down. His eyes scanned the room and then over at the crates when dropping the blueprint roll and walking up to Tony and Oggie. He lifts a cartridge and notices it is a little lighter in color than usual. He pulls out the first three bronze-tipped rounds and closely examines them, then the others, finding them red, blank, training rounds. Shit! I'll be damned, freakin' dummy rounds.

Oggie and Tony stand off to the side, looking at Tom's face as it transitions from confusion to anger, then rage.

Tom removes the 9MM from the case, noticing how clean it is. With the chamber open, he holds it to the light but doesn't see the light reflect through the barrel or chamber. He notices that the weapon is a little heavier. "Damn!" Tom shouts angrily. "That little freak! Hell, we've been had!" Tom yells, looking at Oggie and Tony, even more enraged.

"What, Chief?" Tony asks.

"Tony, step away from the crate!" Tom guides Tony by his arm behind him.

Tom's eyes roll over the crate while assuming a prone position, hurriedly low-crawling over and putting his ear to the crate. He listens for unusual sounds but hears nothing, so he pulls out his pocket knife and peels the corner of the crate back. Tom tilts the crate slightly to one side, seeing four long metal pins extending slowly downward and deep into the carpet. He lowers the crate when the soft, low tones and then soft double-beeps sound.

There comes a steady beep, about the decibel of a straight pin, dropped on a hardwood floor, when motioning for Oggie to turn off the television.

"Tony, pass me that knife!" Tom whispers, holding his hand wide open behind his back until he has a nice grip on the handle. Tom jams the blade into the side of the crate, breaking off the corner of the pallet. He peeps inside to find two medium-sized bottles attached to an activated digital timer that's counting down to two hours and fifty-five minutes. "Damn! It's a gas of some sort, maybe!"

"What! Just wait until I get my hands on that little bastard!" Tony says, balling his fists tightly.

"All right, we have two hours and some change before show time, fellas! We need to account for our inventory," Tom says, quietly pulling out the ammunition and weapons and throwing them on the couch.

Now, after all the weapons except one is reconfigured and the ammunition is counted, they realize they could be very short.

"We only lost a weapon and four hundred rounds, so we need to use what we have sparingly or abruptly run out," Tom says, knowing they would be short if an all-out shoot-out lasted over two minutes.

"Chief, this stuff's getting crazy! Is it ever going to end?" Tony asks in a daze, with eyes glued to the floor.

"I don't know, but I'm about to get paranoid and shoot anything moving!" Oggie responds somewhat in a trance while thinking about his girlfriend and her two kids.

"Come on, let's gear up! Put the extra propelling lines on your belts. We'll be ready should they come early," Tom says. "Better yet, let's take a quick tour and pick out a couple of good hiding spots around the hotel."

Tony passes out the black web belts while Oggie pulls out their blue-and-black camouflaged uniforms, black shirts with hoods, and black boots.

They pull out infrared goggles, test the batteries, and then put them back with the other gear.

Tom breaks out the ropes, hooks, toboggans, and securing straps. "Tony, I need you to find the maintenance room and secure the lights in the back of the hotel," Tom says, looking at his watch. "Make it quick, slick! It would be best if you carried your gun, and here's your bulletproof jacket," Tom says, throwing him the distinctive, black, all-weather jacket.

Tony grows impulsively excited when Oggie dons his night-vision goggles and steps onto the balcony.

They scan the woods and parking lot.

Tom's eyes stay glued in the tall weeds and then up in a tree until he finds himself looking into a possum's beady eyes and then at another set of eyes where the bus once was parked, soon realizing the second are the eyes of a stray dog.

Comforted, Oggie removes the night-vision gear.

Tom looks down at his watch, timing Tony with his stopwatch, while Oggie looks down when the back spotlights go dark.

"Seven minutes..., not bad, considering he had to find the maintenance room," Oggie joyfully says, looking down at his watch again.

"Yeah..., that wasn't bad, was it?" Tom acknowledges, resetting his stopwatch and gazing out into the dark field when the sound of crickets grows to a dull whisper.

Tony emerges minutes later. "Am I good or what?"

"Yeah, yeah, pipe down, buddy!" Tom says, staring at him with a concerned smile. Tom's mind speeds up, oppugning whether they have enough ammunition to sustain the battle.

"Make sure my outstanding work shows up on my next evaluation, Chief." Tony giggles.

Tom breaks his train of thought and looks over at Tony. "Listen..., if you don't put your jacket back on and get ready to get out of here, I'm going to be evaluating right now; but it will be on how long it'll take you to pull my steel-toed combat boot out of your butt!" Tom jokingly says, bursting into laughter.

Tony and Tom giggle.

Oggie joins in on the laughter for a second and then gets serious quickly, thinking about their jam when cutting his laugh short with his mind on his loved ones again.

Tom cuts the night lamp on, and they evenly separate their gear, man up, and drape their 9MM straps over their shoulders while positioning their weapons on their backs.

Tom turns out the night lamp, and they exit through the balcony door, slightly leaning against the mild wind that starts to blow briskly. "Oggie, anchor the hook here, and let's scale the wall," Tom says, pointing at the base of the ten-inch steel-beam support structure.

"Got it, Chief!" Oggie bends, securely wraps the anchor, and pulls it tightly to test it.

"Hey, I'll go first!" Tom says with one leg over the railing when bracing on the ledge and facing when lunging backward with hands releasing the tension line and dropping to the next level. He reaches the fifth floor, bracing himself when looking up to find Oggie on the ledge and Tony stepping onto the ledge. Tom twists in the air, and on the third twirl, he sees movement in a room out of his peripheral vision when locking himself in and stabilizing with feet pressed hard against the balcony's rail.

Tom quickly refocuses his sight, finding a three-hundred-pound, maybe heavier, naked woman bent over until standing with hands high above her head, swirling her hips around in circles. He squints, noticing she has on little pink pasties, a stretched thong, and pink high heels when she stands with her hands on her hips and spins around a few more times before starting in on her exotic dance.

Tom slightly leans to his left, catching sight of a seventy, maybe an eighty-year-old man sitting with hands tucked in his drawers.

The old man stares at the woman as if in a daze and then smiles for minutes, giggling and joyfully spanking his kneecap when taking a wig of his fifth of liquor a few times and then anxiously staring again, as if in a daze. He seems to be stoned while watching the woman perform a few more ridiculous-looking moves and then spin around and stop with her back to the old man.

Instantly, the old man takes another swig and slides his hand into his drawers again.

Several eyes stare through binoculars, watching the three maneuvers against the hotel.

One set of eyes watches them through a sniper-style rifle with the back of Tom's head in the crosshairs for seconds until a feminine hand lowers the rifle down to the other women's side.

Tom bursts into a burst of quiet laughter and then releases the tension, and without delay, drops quickly. He looks up quickly, finding Oggie and Tony closing in fast as they slightly twirl, still descending fast. Tom unlatches, and Oggie drops next to him within seconds and unlatches, with Tony following suit.

They release from their lines and immediately walk around in the dark, scanning the building's neat architecture and well-landscaped grounds.

"Post!" Tom whispers, kneeling and driving the big knife into the ground while supporting his weight on the wide handle. "We have about two hours or so before those bottles disperse, so we can throw them out here and let them ventilate quicker. You guys cover the roof; Tony, you cover the front; and Oggie, the back, using infrared as needed. I'll start inside, maybe on the elevator's roof. Tony, set a remote timer so the hall lights are off; hell, just black out the entire hotel once they're inside, and we can go to full infrared operations."

"Chief, there's one thing we haven't discussed," Tony expresses.

"Oh yeah..., and what's that bud?"

"The one-point-four billion!"

"What about it? No..., let me say this..., pull your head out of your four-corner contact. Listen..., do you think these guys will be stupid enough to bring that kind of money? Man, get with the program. They're coming for one thing: to fill three-body bags so they can get in their comfort zones with no worries. You see, you need to focus and, like, real quick, slick."

"Yeah, Tony, let's not forget the Bear is an ex-Strike Force officer and a commanding officer, more than likely," Oggie says.

"Give me a break! That old geezer can't step to this," Tony says, clowning when popping and locking like an old break-dancer.

The tall Jamaican woman who sits watching Tony's ridiculous dance bursts into a peal of great, silly laughter before passing the binoculars around in the limousine.

Within minutes, the limousine is filled with laughter and soon shakes from side to side, from heavier laughter when the limousine cranks up and slowly pulls away when another limousine comes in sight.

Tom and Oggie burst into deeper laughter until tears roll with them bent over in deeper laughter until Tom can finally catch his breath when trying to wipe the smirk off his face. "I wouldn't underestimate these guys so easily. I mean, hey..., they managed to plan a successful one-point-four-billion-dollar heist right from under the government's nose, and obviously, it worked. They also accomplished having an entire team wiped out and more than half of another," Tom says, with a more serious face.

Oggie's face grew stale. "No shit, we're lucky to be this far in this trap, so don't go slipping at the last minute, Tony. I plan to see my family again, but that depends on your performance," Oggie says, concerned and in deep meditation.

"It's time to put these guys to rest for the government and people's sake," Tom says, weighing deep thought as to the danger his family would be in if these men were to go free.

They tuck their weapons under their jackets and walk around to the side entrance, where Tony picks the lock, and they survey the inner architecture. They return to the room, placing the empty crate, with the bottles, on the balcony.

Tony and Oggie quickly exit, taking positions on the roof, but Tom remains in the room in deep meditation on a more detailed and effective plan until distracted by the balcony window fogging.

Tom stares at his watch and sees a reflection, realizing the gases have been released prematurely. "Our little bottles just activated," Tom reports through his mouthpiece.

Minutes later, Oggie sees and smells gas as it rises to the roof. "Wow, I'm a little light-headed already. I smell a light sulfuric scent and see vapors. Hey, I'm moving to the west corner until this stuff clears," Oggie says, with his vision slightly fading in and out.

"I guess they were anticipating killing us in our sleep because those bottles are pretty small but dispersed fast," Tom says. "Oggie, drop four ropes, one on each corner. I feel like a good workout on the ropes tonight," Tom says, gazing back at the completely fogged window.

"All right, Chief, consider it done."

"Tony, do you have anything out front yet?"

"No, Chief, it's quiet! Just a couple of people leaving and a lot of college cheerleaders getting off a school bus," Tony says, thoroughly analyzing the pretty, young-looking cheerleaders through his binoculars. He quickly refocuses on the thick-bootied blonde, built like a stallion with a long ponytail draped over her shoulder and cut just beneath her breast.

"How do you know they're college cheerleaders?" Tom asks, looking at the window again while pulling out his weapon and taking it off safety.

"Because they're all dressed in team short skirts, white/black cheerleader shoes, and besides, the name of the school is stamped all over the side of the bus," he responds. He releases the binoculars to the lanyard around his neck and, by microseconds, misses seeing the next-to-last woman's weapon, extended just below her short miniskirt. He looks behind him, hearing a generator kick in, missing the last girl, who loads her 9MM in plain view and tucks it in the waistband of her too-short miniskirt.

"How do you know they're not from the Cuban Camp?" Tom asks, slipping his gun back into the holster.

"Come on, Chief, we left that Cuban crap back in Bazumi!" Tony replies with a frown.

"Maybe you're right, but stay vigilant."

Tom looks over at the window finding it clearer, then waits for a while before cutting out the lights and pulling the curtains back. He barely slides the door open and lightly inhales, immediately light-headed when forcibly slamming the door shut and stumbling into the chair before falling to the floor. He begins jerking and slightly foaming at the mouth, somewhat paralyzed for minutes.

The women enter their room and, like precision soldiers, put their weapons together and change into military-style fatigues.

Ten minutes or so pass when Tom sluggishly climbs to his knees and braces the bed for support until flopping down on it, still dizzy.

"Chief, a black limousine just pulled up," Tony reports, pulling the binoculars back to his face.

"That gas is dangerous, guys!" Tom interrupts in a slurred speech while trying to focus his eyesight with fingers running over his eyelids in a circle.

"Why would you say that?" Oggie asks.

"Cause I'm buzzing like a biiiiaattch (bitch)! I was going to throw the bottle off the balcony, but screw that!" Tom says, sitting while still trying to adjust his vision. He places a hand over one eye at a time. "Man, I'm buzzing somethin' bad!"

"Are you alright?" Tony asks, releasing his binoculars to the lanyard again.

"Yeah, I'm coming around, but hey, anything on the limousine?" Tom asks.

"No, it's just sitting there..., wait..., the door's opening."

"Well?" Tom anxiously responds.

"It must be one of the girls' fathers or a relative."

"What? Wait; don't tell me..., he's wearing a damn team short miniskirt with cheerleader shoes too?" Tom says, shaking his head.

"Naw, he just went on the bus," Tony responds, anxiously pulling the binoculars up again.

"He's on the bus?"

"Never mind, he's just getting their luggage," Tony says, looking through the binoculars and lowering them, missing the sight of the man loading his weapon.

The man neatly tucks the gun back in his holster before grabbing the luggage and walking off.

The large suite fills with women and men who quickly remove their wigs.

Two lesbians still in heat from their foreplay in the back of the bus on the long ride over rush in from their hallway security patrols and head to the far side of the room, slowly undressing.

The tall female team leads look around in excitement. "Everyone hurry and change so we can conduct a quick brief! The first thing I want to do is secure this hotel, so no one escapes. Chop, chop! We brief in thirty minutes when the admiral gets here!" the tall African beauty yells with eyes nervously wandering over the room. She stands, strapping her extra gun onto her thigh, and lowers her fatigue top.

The noise in the room grows louder until the lead warns them to keep it down.

The two lesbians stand, not having even touched their weapons. Well hidden behind two tall, tropical-like plants, the Dominican woman, Kaye, winks and licks her tongue out and then twists her hips in a seductive dance. Her eyes browse over the room to make sure no one can see her and then over Kim Lee's five-foot-four-inch, one-hundred-twenty-pound hot Asian body.

Kaye, five-foot-eight, one-hundred-forty pounds, and a muscular chick, seductively twist her hips from side to side, stretching her cheerleader skirt over her curvaceous hips and pulling it halfway to her knees. She accidentally slides her thong down, pulling it up quickly, noticing a man leaning back, and looking. She moves further out of his view, fully cupping her panty-stretched pelvis in her hand and playfully winking while blowing kisses at Kim Lee.

Kim Lee giggles, then blow kisses back until peeping around the tall, leafy plant to make sure no one is looking when sliding her hand over her raised, panty-covered pelvis. In a playful but heated mood, Kim covers her pelvis again, quickly humping her hands a few times to get Kaye's undivided attention. She grew pissed, finding Kaye distracted while talking to another girl.

Damn, Kaye thought, almost out loud, when gazing over and immediately breaking her conversation off with her mouth slightly open. She stays in somewhat of a trance with eyes buck, seeing Kim slip a fingernail inside the rim of her panties and then lick her fingers.

Kim Lee keeps teasing before winking and motioning Kaye to meet her in the bathroom.

Kaye slides her hand into her bag, fumbling around for seconds until pulling out her eleven-inch strap-on and miniature-sized finger vibrator, which she shields and secretly slides into her pants pocket. Before she reaches the bathroom door, another woman rushes inside and slams the door shut. Kaye motions for Kim Lee to wait, then turns and leans against the wall. She hears the toilet flush and faces the door, tapping her foot to pretend she's anxious to go next.

The door speedily flies open, and Kaye motions to Kim Lee, slip inside, and shut the door.

Kaye rushes to the sink and pulls out the eleven-inch toy, strapping it on tight. She pulls the straps a little tighter with eyes immediately looking back at the door as she speedily pulls her fatigues back up.

Kim Lee vigilantly looks around, observing everyone who is focused totally on hurriedly gearing up. She walks to the door, looks around once more, and then slips inside, keeping her back against the door with her index finger pressed hard against the lock. She twists the knob to ensure the door is locked and stares at Kaye with lustful eyes. She slips her top up and cups her breast with her index finger firmly extending underneath it, almost touching the nipple.

Kaye pulls her hair over her shoulder, and then turns in the heat of passion and rushes into Kim Lee. Her hard body presses against Kim's as she forces her harder against the door. Her tongue sinks deep into Kim Lee's mouth when her waistband comes midway her upper thigh, and the strap-on pops up, bobbing up and down a few times until settling in the five o'clock position.

While smiling and seductively licking her lips, Kim Lee looks down, surprised and overly heated.

"Mmm...," she moans, staring back into Kaye's eyes.

Kim Lee freezes in deep thought, then spits in both hands, grasping the cool, thick rubber. She continually strokes it until it is somewhat warm to the touch. With both hands at the waistband of her pants, she slips her fatigues down, pulling them off, but leaving on her G-string.

Kaye turns and guides Kim Lee so her back is to the sink's counter, then lifts her onto it with her hand pressing under her armpits.

Kim Lee's soft cheeks tense as she eases onto the coolness of the marble top, but she warms up to it quite well.

Kaye guides her back against the mirror, pulls Kim's knees upward, and slightly pushes her feet back against her cheeks while Kim Lee spreads her legs wider.

Kim Lee's hand extends to the faucet, turning the knob until the water trickles and then adjusting the temperature until it is hot and warm. She splashes warm, cupped hands of water over her stomach a few times until a steady stream of water slowly rolls between her thighs, slightly wetting the rim of her G-string.

Kaye runs coarse and lightly callused hands over Kim Lee's thighs continually until Kim Lee trembles. She grips her toy tight in her balled fist and raises it to the counter, allowing the tip barely to rest on Kim's raised pelvis.

Minutes later, Kim Lee slightly pushes Kaye back when feeling Kaye's finger running along the rim of her panties at the thigh and slightly tugging. Kim Lee is tensed and about to scream. "Damn! No..., I can't, babe; it's too big!" Kim Lee quietly pouts and uncontrollably giggles until it abruptly tapers off. She begins to slide off the sink's counter when Kaye's hand gently forces her back. Kim caresses a bra-covered breast and playfully leans into Kaye while continually trying to ease off the sink.

Kaye backs up more to allow Kim room to stand and then flips her, bending her over the sink's counter. With a fistful of the hard, flexible rubber, she glides it over and around Kim's G-string-covered pelvis until she closes her eyes and moans in heat. Kaye stops briefly, waits for Kim to open her eyes, and then motions for her to be quiet. Kaye's hand instantly covered Kim Lee's mouth, muffling her moans, which turn into a light scream.

Kim Lee slightly pushes her away, forcing the firm rubber from between her thighs.

Horny as all get up, Kaye begs and almost cries in a whisper. "Babe, no, no, why did you push me away? Mmm, ooh, babe, damn, please, let me in so I can bust..., please!" Kaye pouts and continually begs. "Why are you teasing? I've waited so long for this," Kaye whispers with tears in her eyes while staring deeply into the mirror into Kim Lee's pretty baby face. Kaye's horny hips continually move back and forth like a humping addict.

Before Kim can stand, Kaye's hand rests on her back, forcefully pushing her forward, into and over the sink counter. She quickly remounts her again and humps her like a maniac until one finger slides alongside Kim Lee's thigh in an attempt to slide her G-string to one side.

"Kaye, Kaye, damn Kaye, no babe! Babe, no, oh hells no!" Kim Lee whispers in a mild scream.

Now, Kaye is so anxious and tense that Kim can tell she is about to lose control when a sharp knock comes upon the door. Kaye's so heated and excited that she can't stop humping, he backs away fast and drives forward hard with the rubber tip slamming into the front of the sink, and she humps harder until Kim Lee falls back into her, causing her to stumble back a few feet.

Next comes a few heavy pounds.

Kim Lee swiftly turns, slapping Kaye's face to break her concentration. Kaye's face freezes in confusion when she looks into the mirror at her hips still humping and then down at her tightly closed fist. She finally registers the last knock when rushing, taking off the strap-on and hiding it under a towel.

"Hey, is anyone in there?" the soft-spoken woman's voice yells.

"Yeah, we're almost dressed, and we'll only be out a sec," Kaye says, grabbing a towel and wiping water from the sink and floor. She hands Kim Lee the damp towel and grabs her things.

They dress quickly, and Kaye hides her toys.

They immediately look each other over, checking to make sure they look presentable.

Kim Lee looks in the mirror and pretends to have problems with her bra strap.

Kaye cuts her eyes back and then opens the door, with a short African woman rushing inside.

The African woman jumps up and down until almost dancing on alternate feet to get her fatigues to unfasten and past her hips. She freezes, curiously looking at them while speedily squatting on the toilet, then looks with a disgusted frown when letting off a loud fart and a whirlwind stream of piss followed by a few more giggle-jerking farts. Instantly, the woman's face turns red, and her lips poke out when bursting into a burst of loud laughter. Kaye rushes out, shaking her head, pissed.

"Yah stankin' trifling trick!" Kim Lee shouts, clamping her nose while breathlessly pushing the door open and quickly shutting it.

"Stankin'?" she yells. Hell, I'm not the one who has this bathroom smelling like freakin' poo-poo. Yah, two nasty hussies should be ashamed!" the African girl shouts at the top of her voice, pissed.

The room grows quiet as everyone looks over to find Kaye and Kim scurrying over to the far side of the room when light whispers emerge, and soon mild conversations start again.

CHAPTER NINE:
A TRAITOR'S WAY

A great deal of time had passes since the man taking bags inside from the bus has reappeared when instantly, the electronic doors open.

The man walks back onto the bus, but this time he is onboard a lot longer.

Tom's mind goes into overdrive. "Tony, didn't you say the car was a limousine?" Tom asks, remembering the various limousines Nichelle and others on the island had gotten in and out of. "Hmm..., why is it that the boss is doing all the heavy labor while the chauffeur sits on his lazy tail? Ok..., listen..., I want you to put one round through the passenger-side window, now!" Tom says confidently.

"Are you serious?"

"It's just a window, right? You're damn skippy. I'm serious!"

Tony takes precision aim and a deep breath and squeezes off one silenced round, shattering the window.

The limousine's transmission loudly thumps as the driver slams the car into drive. He revs the engine, and the tires burn deep rubber marks across the asphalt.

"Man, this guy just peeled the hell out of here!" Tony pulls his binoculars to his eyes, following the limousine and continually providing updates.

Minutes pass. "Hey, the limousine's pulling over and turning around at the end of the street." A few more seconds pass. "Now, it's just parked with flashers on."

"All right, they're here, gentlemen, and they're easy to identify because they're wearing cheerleader uniforms, remember?"

"Oh, man!" Tony responds. "Not this crazy-ass mess again!"

Tom dials the hotel, and the attendant answers on the third ring. "Yes, sir, I just dropped my fiancée off at your hotel for a cheerleader's conference. I can't remember which room she asked me to call before picking her up later, so can you be so kind as to provide that information?"

"What? Now, sir, you should know I can't give out personal information."

"Heck, man, I'm halfway across town now! Could you just help me out, just this once?" Tom says in a frustrated tone.

"All right, just this one time. Give me your fiancée name?"

"Lisa Smith, but the room's not in her name!"

"Then how would I know which room she's in, sir?"

"Like I said, I just dropped her off with her cheerleader friends; it's about twenty or more of them from the bus, remember?"

"Oh yeah! Those cheerleaders," he says, fumbling through paper copies of room rosters.

The stairwell's door quietly swings open and then slowly closes but remains cracked open. "Yes, Suite 605, but please don't tell anyone I provided this information," he says, looking out the front window when he thought he heard a door open.

The stairwell door continues to stay cracked open.

"No problem. Thanks, mister, and have a lovely afternoon!"

Tom adjusts his headset. "Oggie, Tony, our guests are in 605. Oggie, there are roughly forty rooms per side, so give me an estimated alignment to the fifth column of windows on the backside," Tom says, immediately remembering the hotel's numbering system.

The beautifully-built Jamaican woman with a very dark complexion and black hair with blonde streaks stands, replaying the desk clerk's words in her mind. She finally registers that he has given out their room number and frowns with her finger pressed tightly on the trigger while slipping through the door and easing from around the thick, marbled pillar. She tiptoes up behind the desk clerk, unnoticed. Her handgun with laser scope comes to eye level as she trains the crosshairs at the back of the attendant's head. Her finger presses even harder on the trigger until she can barely feel the slightest movement in her finger.

The elevator bell rings, and a tall, buff, young German girl runs out with her weapon pointed in a sweeping motion and then sharply over at the desk clerk's body.

The clerk stands still, looking down over the guest roster, briefly gazing up and down, and then doing a double take. His eyes grow wide as he freezes with slow-rising hands high over his head, with tears quickly swelling in his eyes when begging for his life. He takes a few steps back and jumps forward, feeling something cool pressed against his skull, and, in fear, surprisingly raises his hands higher.

"Don't move an inch," the girl behind him harshly mutters while pushing the barrel deeper into the back of his skull, forcing his head to tilt forward slightly.

The beautifully-built Jamaican woman's strong hand slaps against his shoulder, and she moves him away from the main entrance and window. "This jerk just gave out our damn room number! Get upstairs quick and tell everyone they know we're here!" the Jamaican woman screams with the attendant feeling warm spit splatter on the back of his freshly-cut, high-top-fade shaven neck.

The German girl drops her aim and runs for the elevator door, but it closes before she can reach it, with feet slapping into the shiny, marbled floor as she slows and turns back for the stairwell.

The roof's door quietly cracks open, in intervals, until it opens just enough for the slender, fatigue-clad body to pass through.

The slender female's weapon quickly and quietly comes to eye level as she aligns the front and back guides to a perfect firing solution. She slowly advances, taking over ten soft steps forward, then one more, and stops. "Drop it!" she whispers with the cold barrel pressing into the back of Oggie's skull.

Oggie's gun drops, dangling on his shoulder strap. His eyes roam to the right and left while slowly raising his hands over his head. His tongue eases out and hooks his mouthpiece, bringing it close to his lips. He holds the transmitter at the edge of his lips and seals it while clearing his throat real hard, and the amplified noise causes Tom and Tony to yank their headsets off slightly.

Tony turns his head with breaking speed, easing the headset back over his ears when looking in Oggie's direction.

"I got you..., drop on the count of one!" Tony whispers through his mouthpiece. He eases around and snaps his head to one side, instantly aligning the woman's head into the crosshairs. He takes one soft step, moving slightly to the right to prevent Oggie from being in the line of fire. "Three, two, one...!" he spits out without delay.

"Turn—" the woman begins to say when her body falls forward and into Oggie's back. Her body slumps into him until he steps to the side, dropping her to the rough gravel roof with the back of her head spread open.

"What?" Tom asks, confused by a delayed response.

"Damn, Tony, did you have to be so gruesome?" Oggie whispers, wiping blood splatter from the side of his face, back of his head, and neck.

"What, what is it?" Tom asks again.

"I'm not taking any chances, man. That's one for me!" Tony says, smiling while trampling over Tom's last transmission.

"They know we're up here, Chief," Oggie says, pulling out a handkerchief and wiping the side of his blood-splattered face.

"Great!" Tom replies. "I'm going down for a look. Oggie, cover me over the side," Tom says, quickly maneuvering.

In the stairwell, the German chick had just made it to the third floor, where she freezes. Her eyes scan over the heavy construction gear blocking the stairwell. The yellow warning signs dazzle her as she quickly reads a few and then lunges forward, climbing over the gear toward the door like a jaguar. Her tight, gloved hands grab the door handle to find it locked.

Tony had just dropped to the deck on the roof, hearing a squeak from the roof's door. He low crawls into a prone position, covering the roof's entrance.

"The ropes are in place, Chief," Oggie says, dropping two more.

Tom takes a deep breath and holds it while sliding the door back and hastening through it. He immediately goes airborne over the railing and, with a death-defying leap, lunges from the balcony with his hands spread wide and then closes them quickly as he grasps the ropes. He swings out and then back, sliding to the next level, where his back slams into the concrete wall. He locks himself in position and then twirls around until walking the ropes over against the building. He grabs the second rope, then the third, making his way alongside the building, seven stories high. Securing himself with the third rope, he disconnects the first and second ropes, dropping to the room he perceives is 605.

His eyes instantly grow wide, capturing all of the sharp movement in the room when hanging there, watching for seconds, and then bracing his foot on the handrail, staring deeper through the sheer curtains. He eyes them, locking, loading, and chambering rounds while the last two chicks hurriedly lock and load and sling weapons over their shoulders.

Tom switches to automatic, and when looking through the scope, the door swings open.

The German-looking chick runs inside, waving and screaming at the top of her lungs, and Tom hears her muffled, deathly screams bringing her head into the crosshairs.

With a deep breath, Tom's head snaps to one side when eyes adjust to the scope as she becomes clearer in the crosshairs. Tom unloads the entire forty-round clip through the balcony's glass door; the first round dead center in her forehead, when spraying from left to right until there is clicking.

Several people drop from being hit just once or twice, but others drop and roll and then low-crawl to the other side of the partition.

Tom ducks, immediately hearing gunfire and seeing sparks ping from the steel hand railing as they precision walk over to where he is positioned. Instantly, he presses the tension release, dropping quickly and continually twirling around quickly until his boots press hard into the soft ground when taking a stance and bracing, hearing the window in front of him shatter. His hand drops, and he snatches the knife from his hip, cutting the rope and sprinting along the back of the hotel until veering hard toward tall weeds and woods at top speed.

Out of nowhere, a high pitch, muffled helicopter blade sound rises in his ears when suddenly, red, silenced, automatic tracer rounds whistle close on his trail, cutting down some tall weeds and thin trees.

On the roof, before Tony makes it to the door, another weapon slowly extends through the crack of the roof's door, and he charges, dropkicking the door and crushing the person's arm.

A woman's voice loudly sounds off in a dreadful cry until Oggie fires three rounds into her chest, forcing her backward. Her movement causes the door to retract and then open as she tumbles down the concrete steps.

Tony and Oggie ease the door open with very attentive eyes, scanning the stairwell with weapons drawn at eye level. They cautiously advance with their eyes on the Colombian-looking woman wiggling around and jerking while taking a few more gasps of air. She jerks hard, managing to flip fast with her face pressed against the corner of the metal and concrete steps with blood dripping from metal deck grate to metal deck grate until taking her last breath.

They stand nervously; listening and watching until her eyes quickly grow stale, then proceed to the sixth level.

Oggie cracks the metal door open and trains his weapon into the hallway.

In the back of the hotel, Tom stands in darkness, looking up at the giant oak tree before throwing a rope around one of its thick branches. He pulls himself up, repositioning, and when finally in position, and with a precision-trained weapon pointed at the balcony, he takes a shot at a woman standing with her weapon trained toward the pitch-dark woods. Red tracer rounds fired back at Tom on automatic when she takes cover, screaming. She quickly reloads, retaking aim, firing closer and almost accurately at Tom when looking through infrared goggles. She leans forward like a true professional, taking a steady aim when slipping her finger into the trigger well.

Tom blinks with her in the crosshairs, firing one shot, and she expressly folds over the railing, dropping from the fifth floor onto concrete. He maneuvers more and assumes a prone position on a more substantial branch while scanning the perimeter again. He finds a male figure easing out of the back exit and picking up speed as he runs into the far end of the woods.

Tom squints, then squints again, recognizing Mr. Vee as he slows down, creeping deep into the tall weeds, training his sniper rifle in a 180-degree radius. He patiently waits for Mr. Vee to get closer and slithers to one side of the sturdy oak tree's branch with eyes locked on him until he's almost under the tree.

Mr. Vee takes a few more calculated steps, looking around until he is directly under the tree when Tom drops, knocking him to the ground with his weapon flying forward and into the tall weeds.

Tom speedily recovers to his feet, swinging his strapped 9MM behind his back when the quarter-lit moon pierces through thick clouds, shedding more light into the field. Tom rocks back and forth in a karate stance, staring into Mr. Vee's face as he shakes his head to regain consciousness.

A woman runs out onto the balcony, looking over the grounds until finding slight movement in the field. Her rifle snaps to eye level as she tries to acquire Tom in the crosshairs, but Mr. Vee remains frozen in position and in the way, in fear, looking up at Tom and afraid to make a fast move.

For microseconds, the woman's finger stays slightly on the trigger while taking deep breaths and holding it in until losing sight of Tom when the two begin slowly going in circles in karate stances.

"Come on, you traitor! I can't believe you would be stupid enough to come back," Tom says, kicking Mr. Vee in the stomach and causing him to roll over and slowly crawl. "I'm going to rip you a new one!" Tom moves into a different karate stance, kicking at Mr. Vee, but misses when Mr. Vee performs his infamous, swift roll-and-duck tactic.

The woman patiently waits for another perfect potshot, but they're now behind another tree, so she maneuvers from side to side but still can't see them.

Mr. Vee vigorously comes to his knees, diving near Tom's legs, when he's double-kicked in his ribs.

Tom draws his knife from his hip, wobbling before balancing on his feet. "Get up!" Tom shouts, kicking Mr. Vee's weapon further away and stepping on it while backing up. "I said get up, you cowardly-ass bastard!"

While staring at Tom under-eyed, Mr. Vee slowly stands, holding his ribs.

"For my life, I can't believe you would stoop as low as these guys for the sake of money!"

"Hell, man!" He says, sounding stoned off liquor. "For a third of what they offered, I'd kill my beloved mother," Mr. Vee thoughtfully responds, backing away with bloodshot eyes.

"Oh yeah? Well, it's too bad you'll never live to see the money, more or less spend it or betray your mother, for that fact," Tom says, diving into him, dropping him and rolling in the taller damp grass.

The two go at it for minutes, alternating who is on top until Tom barely ends on top and forcefully stays there.

Now, with both in sight; the woman lifts her binoculars and tries refocusing her sight through the scope but can't see them, just the tall weeds rocking back and forth.

Instantly, the moon fades behind thick clouds again.

"Shit!" she shouts, dropping the binoculars on her neck lanyard when reaching for her gun and taking a firm stance, aiming and waiting.

Tom places the knife on Mr. Vee's neck, bending over more until pressing it against his main artery.

Mr. Vee fights with all he has to push the blade away, but Tom strains more, keeping pressure applied with anxious eyes locked on the blade until finally seeing blood squirt out, then squirt harder with each timed breath.

Without warning, the moon shines through the opening of another cloud, and Tom sees a thick, long trail of blood riding along the knife's edge.

Tom instantly feels Mr. Vee rapidly losing his strength and continues slightly rocking the blade more profoundly until hearing the blade scrape the bone.

Finally, Tom tilts the blade upward, accidentally missing Mr. Vee's main artery by inches, when with all his strength, he punches Mr. Vee in his face, knocking him out cold.

The woman grows impatient, unable to get a clear shot, so she slings her weapon over her shoulder and runs, almost invisibly lunging from the balcony into the ropes, grasping one tightly with leather gloves. She slides down, her body slowly twirling to get a better view of Tom, and he catches movement in his peripheral vision when leaning forward and grabbing Mr. Vee's weapon from the grass. He stealthily repositions, leans back, takes aim, and shoots the woman in the back twice, the third round causing her to scream for minutes before he retakes a steady aim. He tenses, holding his breath, shooting the rope, severing it, and dropping her four stories, lifelessly.

Tom jerks and twists, forcing Mr. Vee's mouth open when cramming a handful of crabgrass inside. He rolls Mr. Vee over, tying the rope to his belt loop, and then throws the excess rope over the branch, straining to lift Mr. Vee's deadweight by his feet until he begins to move again. With a single blow, Tom knocks Mr. Vee out cold again, then secures the line and pulls him upright; securing him again so he looks as if he's standing. With the excess rope, Tom rigs Mr. Vee's empty rifle to his body, pointing the rifle toward the hotel. "Ok, guys, Mr. Vee's done, but don't count him out of the game just yet!" Tom says, bending forward to catch his breath.

Tom immediately hears the back door slam against the building and drops to the ground, low-crawling to taller grass. He freezes in a prone position, promptly maneuvering toward the hotel with eyes gazing through the darkness, watching the tall, black-clothed woman's figure train her weapon as Mr. Vee had done.

Mr. Vee stays lightly slumped over and still supported by the ropes, continually growing weaker, and then continually murmuring in a low tone until nodding off as if drunk when finally gagging a few times while trying to spit.

The dark, silhouetted body continually advances toward Tom and Mr. Vee.

The woman's gloved hand slowly removes the camouflaged hoodie, and she freely shakes her long hair out until she is freezing in her tracks when nervously jerking and pointing her weapon at the silhouette, not knowing its Mr. Vee. She slowly reaches with a sturdier aim, activating the white halogen bulb, handheld flashlight, which pierces through darkness onto the somewhat mangled body, taking fearful baby steps toward it.

Out of nowhere, Tom makes a bone-chilling owl screech, muffling the sound when firing off one silenced round into Mr. Vee's leg, causing him to yell a painful yet garbled cry.

Mr. Vee's eyes fly open and dim quickly when staring into the bright white light. His face slightly transforms from the bright light mixed with his agonizing pains.

The woman screams, seeing the transformation of his monster-looking, bloody face, and drops the light, silently firing on automatic until the clip is empty with the spinning barrel still mildly spinning fast.

Mr. Vee's lifeless body slumps forward against the ropes, ripped into shreds.

The woman's finger nervously stays pressed on the specially-made weapon's trigger, with the empty barrel slowly spinning with a light fading whistling sound.

Mr. Vee takes one last death-defying jerk with his mouth dropping open. At once, his head slumps over, the gun finally drops from his body unnoticed, and the nozzle hitting the tree's above-ground, raised root brings the woman to instant fear. She struggles, instantly brandishing another gun from her back waistband, training it on him with eyes froze on the silhouette when reaching for the flashlight. She shines the light, aiming once more, when coming closer, with her weapon at his bullet-riddled face, suddenly realizing its Mr. Vee. She gags, slumping forward and feeling sick to her stomach. Her hand immediately drapes over her mouth with her jaws puffed out until she can no longer hold it when vomiting.

"Drop it, drop it!" Tom whispers, fading out of pure darkness with his 9MM aimed at her face.

She freezes and then turns slowly, grasping for the trigger well, falling backward while discharging automatic rounds from her weapon, some sparking off the back of the hotel. With the gun in an upward motion, she screams her last breath as the last silenced round from Tom's weapon penetrates her chest. She collapses, jerks, wiggles, and gasps for air for seconds until her eyes are rolling in her head.

"Where are you, guys? Mr. Vee is out, and so are two other women. I can't account for the room, but I'm sure I got about ten or fifteen of them," Tom says, taking their weapons and looking around until easing out to the edge of the woods.

There is total silence for minutes, with eyes peeking out a cracked door, watching three camouflaged people exit a stairwell.

"Sixth floor," Oggie whispers, still peeping through the slightly-cracked-open door. He leans back with eyes swarming over the number 605, just to the right of the door and across the hall.

Tony and Oggie slowly step out and rush over to the door, slowly churning on the knob, then walking inside and scanning the room with weapons drawn at eye level.

Suddenly, they hear a woman's voice lowly crying, with the cry rising higher until hearing a clip slapped boldly in a weapon. The bathroom door abruptly swings open when kicked by a sexy Mexican woman rushing into the room, frozen in her tracks and surprised to find them there.

"Drop it!" Oggie quickly maneuvers the aim from her chest to her head.

"Drop it, slowly, and now!" Tony shouts, aiming at her chest.

She nervously backs up slowly. "OK! OK!" she acknowledges in a beautiful accent while leaning forward, lowering the weapon, but inching her fingers in the trigger well when muffled shots ring out with her weapon fired into the floor, unknowingly taking out a few more militant women in the lower room. Her barrel aimlessly flies upward until Tony and Oggie's 9MM rounds penetrate her chest and face, forcing her backward.

Tony flies backward and leans back against the wall, a bit sick from the sight of her bloody, mangled face, and in a flash, he looks over at Oggie, who smiles.

"Hey..., any sign of the Bear?" Tom whispers through his mouthpiece.

"Nothing..., no sign yet," Oggie acknowledges in a laughing whisper.

Tom assesses the environment, keying up his mic. "I'm in the main lobby, working my way up the ladder well," Tom says, looking over to find the desk clerk's brains splattered against the wall. His eyes scroll about, finding the phone distribution panel broken up with wires sparking. Tom exits through a side door and climbs the stairwell to the second floor to find three dead hotel workers and four other slain bodies he perceives as guests. When he reaches the third floor, he sees the construction, so he heads back through the last exit.

"Room 605 is all clear!" Oggie reports, looking over at Tony, still wiping vomit from his mouth with a towel from the bed.

Three quick, single shots flow into the room from the hallway, followed by a barrage of fire, leaving Tony and Oggie dropping and taking cover.

There is total silence for minutes, but they aim, low-crawling over dead bodies toward the door, and before securing the door, a silver smoke canister bounces off the slightly-cracked-open door, rolling into the middle of the room. Their eyes widen as they advance faster, low-crawling over another dead body.

Oggie takes the tip of his gun, pushing the partially-busted door close.

A light hissing sound grows when the canister slowly begins spinning around, with bubbles forming on top of its silver, flat lid.

"Gas!" Oggie screams.

They exchange fire from both sides of the door, penetrating larger and smaller holes in the wall and door until shredding it into pieces.

Tony speedily stands, covering the shoe-polish-sized canister with a blanket when leaping over more slain bodies, dropping the canister in the toilet.

Dense gases bubble faster, creating a heavy, foam-like substance below the bowl's water line, with foam rapidly filling the basin and well above the regular water line. Tony stands holding his breath while trying to flush the canister, but it jams in the toilet's mouth. Gases grow more potent, so he snatches a towel from the rack, cramming as much as he can inside, but the sulfuric-like odor grows even stronger until he feels lightheaded.

Tony backs up and out quickly, slamming the bathroom door shut, and drops, barely missed by silenced rounds fired into the room when his mouth flies open, and he lets off a deep breath of air.

Another canister drops to the floor, spinning and dispersing faster than the first when Tony and Oggie come up fast, exchanging fire while advancing on the door and further from the canister until stumbling into each other. They immediately lose their balance and collapse together, still having enough strength to maintain consciousness.

"Balcony!" Oggie shouts, embracing and balancing against Tony.

They stumble, running toward the balcony before losing consciousness as their bodies fall lifelessly through the broken glass door.

Tom tries reaching them several times, but there's no response, so he sprints faster, opening the hallway door to the sixth floor, where shots riddle the door with a few whistling by his head when he tenses. He stands with his back to the wall listening and waiting for the perfect entry, and at the end of the next barrage of fire,

Tom dives toward an adjacent parlor.

Shots ring out as he rolls a few feet before hitting his shoulder on the table's edge. "Ahh!" Tom screams in agonizing pain, with his shoulder feeling somewhat dislocated.

Now the shooter is sure he'd gotten a fatal hit but waits and quietly listens, nervously twisting on his long, waxed mustache ends.

Tom stays quiet for a long spell pretending to be dead, then begins quietly low-crawling to the edge of the long hallway, firing a couple of rounds when standing and taking cover behind a giant statue. With a long, concentrated, and targeted aim, Tom scopes in on a man's kneecap, which slightly sticks out near a colossal pillar at the corner of the adjoining hallway, when a single, silenced round hits the shooter in the leg, somewhat crippling him.

"Ooh!" the tall man screams, grabbing his leg and limping down the long hallway, firing several more un-aimed rounds back over his shoulder.

"Tony, Oggie! Tony, Oggie!" Tom screams, kneeling and leaning forward to catch a glimpse of the limping man as he exits through the stairwell at the far end of the hallway. He hears the door slam shut and looks both ways, then run to the room, grasping the doorknob, only to find it locked. He twisted hard until peeping through the shredded door. His eyes rove over the semi-smoky room, spotting gas fumes rising and mingling with cool air from the air conditioner.

The slight hint of sulfur makes him light-headed, so he backs up and calls to them again, but from afar, when jumping, hearing the stairwell door open and abruptly shut, when backing against the wall behind a stone pillar.

Not seeing anyone, Tom pushes off and runs as fast as possible with his 9MM trained ahead. "Tony, Oggie, come in! Tony, Oggie!" Tom screams again when slowing near the exit and presses his back against the wall, taking over. He opens the door, finds a blood trail leading downstairs, stands listening for seconds, and then advances cautiously. He comes upon corners where he stops, training his weapon, and then slowly advances again.

Tom makes it to the ground floor, where he follows the trail out the back door, where it fades into the darkness with hotel transformers lightly growing in his ear. He advances, finding another trail of blood and moving faster until hearing someone yelling, but from a slight distance.

He freezes with wandering eyes until confirming the direction of the voice when his hand slips behind his back, pulling out the backup .22 and taking it off safety, then placing it back in the back of his waistband. He surveys the area, then pushes off from the wall and runs across the dark grounds in a stealth zigzag pattern toward the front of the hotel. Just before the lit area, he drops like a deadweight, assuming a prone position and briefly assessing his surroundings until spotting a tall male figure limping along the lit side of the hotel. He sees the man's weapon tightly gripped with his other hand waving high over his head.

"I'm here!" the tall, built man screams when his free hand weakly falls to his side, and he slightly bends over, putting more pressure on the wounded leg with the weapon still rising high over his head.

Tom remains undetected when taking off at top speed, running several yards behind the unidentified man and lunging, dropkicking him in the back, bringing him hands first to the rough pavement skinning his hands, and leaving blood smears.

The blunt force causes the man's weapon to hit the ground and expend a few rounds before sliding several feet away.

The man rolls over, shocked to find Tom standing over him with his weapon drawn at shoulder level when nervously twisting his long waxed mustache ends when moving his hand to his side, cringing in pain.

Tom's frowning face stares eye-to-eye with the man, with sweat dropping from his forehead.

"It's over, Bear!" Tom screams, looking down at Admiral Michaels, blood splattered shiny name tag. "Look at you! You're a damn disgrace to your fraternity and country!" Tom yells, spitting in his face.

"Spare me, please," he cries heavily. "I beg of you!" the admiral screams, clutching his deep wound until gritting his teeth as a wad of spit clings to his cheek.

"Spare you? Right! I don't think so, but I'll tell you what I'll do, something that should've been done long ago!"

"I can make you a very wealthy man!" the admiral yells, gritting his teeth tighter until finally wiping the spit away.

"Money?" Tom asks. "Hell! Great men are dead because of your senseless-ass greed and bullshit!"

Tom bends over, grabs the admiral by the collar, lifts him a few feet off the ground, and stares deep into his face with his war-torn face.

Unknowingly, a body slowly stands on the bus's steps with a weapon aimed at the admiral's head and then over his heart. The weapon slowly moves to the right, realigning with Tom's head dead center in the crosshairs.

"I had no choice, damn it! It was Lieutenant Smith's idea to eliminate you and your men because he was afraid a federal investigation would lead to his and others' arrests," the admiral yells with one hand on the ground to support his body weight, then expressly holds his hand over his face, blocking Tom's spring-loaded fist.

"What? Strike Force One has served this country well, always modeling policies and guidelines with honor, courage, and commitment. Hell! These guys had real lives and loving families! You fool! You've broken the Strike Force Code to protect our own, and I'm here to execute the best interests of the Code and the United States!" Tom screams, forcefully shoving him back down to the concrete and still staring intensely into his eyes.

"I was forced into it, Chief!" he cries. "You have to believe me! The Cubans threatened to kill my family and me!" the admiral screams, faking his cry while lying. He keeps his face covered, but now with both hands.

Tom looks around in pity as if about to buy into the lie when looking back down at him with a mean stare. "Well, you would've been better off dying in their hands. At least you would have died with honors!" Tom shouts in rage when visions of his men's deaths flash before his eyes. "What gives you the right to judge us?" Tom screams, staring at his tattoo and ring while reaching down and grabbing him deep in his collar again. With brute strength, Tom jerks him up and draws back a tight fist, hitting him in the face several times before he can respond when the bus door window shatters; a silenced round missed Tom's throat by centimeters when the second nip him at the collarbone.

"Oh shit!" Tom shouts, grabbing the pained area and falling toward the admiral when his stomach takes a direct hit from the admiral's foot when he rolls Tom high over his body, slamming him hard into the asphalt on his back with him sliding him several feet, with his headset sliding even further.

"What took you so long?" the admiral screams with fiery eyes. "Were you waiting for him to kill me so you could keep all the money for yourself?" the admiral angrily screams when looking up at Captain Carrington, who stands with a cigar in his mouth, one eyelid closed to deflect the strong, burning cigar smoke.

"Hell no! Actually, I was waiting to see if you would spill your guts and rat me out like you did the lieutenant," he says, leaning over and extending his hand to the admiral, who springs up as if never wounded.

"Now look at you, Chief," the admiral screams, snappily standing while finally showing pain again. He supports his limp weight on the captain's shoulder, and the captain stumbles a bit. "You could have very easily had a new life, you dumb ass, but noooo!" he said, leaning over and spitting at Tom. "Bear! Bear?" he yells out at the peak of his frail voice. "The Bear's not a person, you damn idiot! You can never kill the Bear, you fool! The Bear is a leadership position, so killing me would have done nothing but automatically transfer that leadership to the next in command. You've managed to screw up this whole two-point-eight-billion-dollar operation. However, I must admit it was rather clever of you and the Underground to utilize U.S. assets to destroy the Cuban Camp. Those Underground jerks were contract hire hits, not the Cubans," the admiral says with a smirk.

The captain swallows hard because when debriefing the admiral in their initial undercover meeting after he returned stateside, he never told the admiral the missiles were his idea.

"It was a simple exchange of monies, the teams for the Underground. A sweet little deal between the Cubans and us, I might add," the admiral adds with an even bolder smirk.

"So this is how it goes down, huh, Captain?" Tom says, straining through the pain. He tries moving a little, but his body is slightly numb, and his back aches.

"So it goes, Chief, so it goes," the captain says, closing one eye again when the cigar smoke burns. "You see, the admiral here offered me the deal of a lifetime upon my arrival to the States. Yeah, a deal too sweet to turn down, especially with retirement just around the corner and all," he says, pointing his gun in Tom's face.

A slight hint of cognac rises from Captain Carrington's drunken breath.

Tom coughs. "So, pretending to be under duress was a crock of shit! Damn, how could I have been so damn blind to buy off on that lame-ass bullshit?" Tom yells, enraged, eyes drifting over the ground to locate his weapon.

"Oh no, the lieutenant was a good guy, acting under strict orders to keep a tight watch on the captain, poor ole' soul, but he failed in his mission. He was only supposed to keep the captain under strict surveillance and not let anyone communicate with him due to the captain's stronghold with influential people onboard and back in the States," the admiral says.

"I see..., so he was just another man loyal to the country, huh?" Tom says sarcastically.

"Yes, very loyal! He was so loyal that he'd kill when told and without question, although this mission gave him lots of fake intelligence. With the promise of promotion, we had to make it all seem as though he was doing his job," the admiral cheerfully says, cringing through the pain.

Captain Carrington smiles, looking at the admiral. "Yeah, not to mention that he was in love with you," Captain Carrington says with a smirk.

The admiral takes a deep whiff, finally confirming the slight smell of cognac, and finally sees cocaine dust on his mustache. "Enough of the jokes," the admiral says. "Kill this bastard, you damn addict, you damn drunkard..., you alcoholic!" the admiral shouts with a mean stare while pointing at Tom.

Out of nowhere, a bright beam of light draws the admiral's attention to the edge of the building, spotting the limousine's signal lights still flash when joyfully waving both hands high over his head to get the limousine driver's attention.

Per the admiral's directions for the driver to stay in the limousine no matter what, the driver stares, tense, and anxiously fights, not breaking his commander's order, when immediately, the flashers go off.

The car pulls away slowly and then slightly turns to the left and maneuvers around the side of the hotel through the parking lot. The limousine's lights disappear for a quick second before a reflection of the lights shines along the side of the bus.

"So, another wasted, good man! You suckers are all the same: out to screw over anyone to get to the top!" Tom says, slowly sliding back a few feet while stretching one hand over for his weapon and stopping when finally remembering that the pained area is his spare .22.

The admiral limps back over to the captain and puts his hand on his shoulder, balancing his weight while frowning in pain.

"Forget it, Chief!" Captain Carrington says, pressing his size-thirteen shoes dead in the center of Tom's chest and causing the admiral to limp closer. "You're finished here, son! It has been nice," the captain says, slipping his finger into the trigger well.

"Goodbye, my dear frie—," the captain begins to say when the admiral's voice screams above the captain's, demanding he kills Tom that instant when finally registering the distant, single pop.

With an instant headache, the captain freezes with a confused look, with blood gushing from the hole in the middle of his forehead, down between his eyes, around his lips, and onto Tom's chest as he slightly leans forward, trembling to balance.

The admiral stares at Tom and points again, not noticing the blood. "Shoot this bastard, now!" the admiral screams, pissed when looking up at Captain Carrington after feeling his body tense again but heavier.

Frozen in a stance, Tony pumps yet another silenced round dead in the center of the captain's chest, forcing him to stumble backward a few feet yet stand in a long stagger.

Glass faintly shatters almost simultaneously when Oggie fires in a kneeling prone position from the dark.

The admiral finally registers it all and does a double take, seeing the captain's frown again. His eyes stare at the blood gushing out of the hole when jerking his deadweight from the captain, knocking the gun from his hand. He dives expressly toward the gun, which tumbles across the asphalt.

Tony's third round pierces the captain's chest again, and the fourth tear apart his spine with his coked-up body, no longer able to withstand the pain when he falls lifelessly.

The fifth round strikes the admiral dead center in his chest while he's still in free fall for the weapon.

The admiral lets off a loud, deathly cry and fights with all the strength he can muster to remain in the push-up position and then tries to stand again. He goes into disbelief with only the money on his mind when he collapses with the weapon in hand.

"Don't even think about it! Drop it!" Tony shouts, hurriedly advancing and pointing his weapon at the admiral's face with the Bear frozen in place with hands shielding him from the gun.

The Bear slowly releases his grip while growing weak quickly from losing more blood. With his eyes rolling back in his head, his eyes grow weak as he fights to roll over onto his stomach, take the pressure off his pained chest, and free his airway. His hand instantly slips to his collar, pressing the button on the back of the bear-shaped emblem with the emblem's eyes flickering before black.

Before the limo driver's side door is visible, the limousine comes to a slow creep, veering off into the curve and abruptly stopping with the headlights rocking back and forth. The fluctuation of the lights against the bus causes Tom and Tony to look back.

Tony kicks the admiral's gun away, places his feet in his upper shoulder blade, and pulls out the thick, long, sharp blade. "This is for my brother!" Tony screams, lifting him with a fistful of hair. His hand moves at stealthy speed, slitting the admiral's throat from ear to ear and causing him to bleed like a hog.

The admiral's body trembles for minutes until released when his body falls deadweight.

Tony cries loudly and slowly stands, then drops down, lifting and snapping the admiral's neck before forcefully dropping his head to the asphalt.

There comes a slight sound from the limousine's door slamming.

Tom comes to his feet and limps a few feet over to the edge of the building, squinting until bringing the limousine in full view.

"How bad were you hit?" Tony asks, ripping Tom's shirt collar open. "Man, you're lucky; it only nipped your flesh," Tony says, applying more pressure to the wound to stop the bleeding.

"It feels like it shattered the freakin' bone," Tom responds, in excruciating pain when more pressure is applied. "Hey, the admiral mentioned something about the Bear transferring positions to another leader so we could never kill the Bear; I wonder what he meant by that or how they implemented that process," Tom says, staring down at the ground puzzle while looking at the gold emblem of a golden bear on the admiral's and captain's collars. He stared at it for seconds until noticing the lighted bear's eyes only on Captain Carrington's collar.

The limousine advances at a very slow pace with flashers back on.

Tom grabs Tony's gun, but Tony lowers it by Tom's side.

The limousine slowly pulls up, and the driver's window comes slowly down with them hearing Oggie's crazy laugh. "Fleet Sailors!" Oggie playfully yells in a loud voice that echoes between the two hotels.

Tom climbs in the backseat and Tony in the front.

Oggie swerves around the side of the building so he and Tony can run in and get their identification, bags, and things.

At the hotel across the street, two women front-desk attendants just had walked onto the quiet porch to take a cigarette break. They go into a deep conversation, and one bends past the pillar, noticing a strange car's headlight go out.

The hotel attendant backs slightly behind the pillar, spotting a long-haired woman getting out and running to the front corner of the Ramekin Hotel with a big rifle-type weapon in hand.

The tall, long hair woman comes up on the two bodies fast, kneeling and checking the admiral's and then the captain's pulse. Her eyes wander over both when creeping back over to Captain Carrington, pushing the button on the back of the bear emblem, before taking off in a fast sprint toward the hotel.

The attendant shoves her coworker, getting her attention, and she too takes cover close behind the stone pillar, with eyes deeply set on the woman until she vanishes around the side of the building. The two women peep near the spot where the woman knelt, wondering what she might have been doing, and then go back to their conversation.

The tall, armed woman's eyes swarmed over the limousine's parking lights while taking her time, creeping up on the back while parked near the hotel's rear exit.

The two nosey attendants look again when the first to spot the limousine points to it, and their eyes float alongside the building again.

"Girl, this is not looking good! What if they are about to rob the place?" the shorter attendant says, backing up quickly and running inside to call the police.

The tall, older attendant runs across the street, coming up on the grassy part of the driveway near high bushes and missing seeing the two slain bodies. She peeps around the building and then jerks back when spotting the tall woman taking slow steps toward the back of the limousine. She cuts her eyes over her shoulder when hearing footsteps approaching minutes later and waves to her nosy coworker, who beats feet over to where she's kneeling and well hidden.

The fast-moving coworker slows down, and she pulls her down alongside the side of the hotel.

They peep around the corner together, watching as the woman slows, then stops and looks over her shoulder with her weapon trained toward the two women, who draw their heads back fast. They stay with their backs to the concrete building for minutes until finally peeping again to find the woman looking to the right and then back toward them when quickly retaking cover. They wait a few seconds and then inch over, peeping back along the hotel's side, senselessly giggling in fear.

Inch by inch, Tricia slowly moves in on the limousine, looking around diligently until she is inches from the bumper, where she sees the back of Tom's head. Her fingers ease into the trigger well, bringing Tom's head into the crosshairs just as Tony and Oggie rush through the open door, their boots mildly slamming in the soft grass.

"Oh shit!" Tony sounds off in a bloodcurdling scream, startling her and causing Tom to slump down when the cannon boom sounds, shattering the back window.

A loud thump comes to the trunk when Tricia falls forward from the automatic gunfire from Tony and Oggie, who are standing off to the side yet behind her.

Oggie's hand comes upon her shoulder expressly, snatching her back when she slithers off and down but manages to get her hand up to her collar, pressing the button on the bear before taking her last breath.

They jump in the limousine, and Oggie revs the engine.

Tony jumps out and reaches back for her latest model weapon, throwing the new cannon-style gun in the front seat and slamming his door.

The two attendants hear distant sirens and keep peeping; feeling secure in knowing law enforcement is just up the street.

Oggie steps down on the accelerator, backing over the dead body and stopping the limousine when the bumper is inches from the hotel's wall.

Sirens sound even closer when Oggie slams his foot hard on the accelerator, running over the body again while slinging the limousine around until it fishtails while heading toward the front of the building.

Seeing headlights barreling down on them, the two women back away quickly.

The limousine shoots out, and Tony's head shoots from left to right, spotting two heads popping out with eyes bucked wide.

The two run toward their hotel at top speed, and in a flash, the front driver's-side hubcap rolls away from the limousine and seems to be chasing the two women, who run even faster with eyes peeled over their shoulders, screaming.

Tony instantly notices they are hotel workers and playfully and quickly discharges a few automatic shots from the cannon gun in the air, with the women taking a last-minute dive into the hotel's flower bed.

The two tumble after a few rolls, then quickly low-crawls behind the pillars, bruised and scared, turning fast with eyes following the limousine as it speeds out of the area.

The women's hearts continually pound at top speed with eyes pierced on the limousine for a second when it swerves around another corner toward the main street and peels rubber again.

Within minutes, Oggie cuts down another side road and veers into the mild traffic flow, increasing speed, before reaching the exit. He quickly comes up on the over path, catching a glimpse of the blue lights flashing as two police cruisers rapidly close in on the hotel.

Thirty minutes later, Oggie cruises into a somewhat rural-looking community and pulls into a vacant business parking lot, anxiously climbing out with Tom and Tony in tow. He pops the trunk immediately, and their eyes grow wide, finding two thick suitcases.

Tom leans toward the first case, cautiously popping both locks, and then opens it slowly.

They are speechless, staring at hundreds of millions in large, crisp bills until their mouths drop open when opening the second suitcase.

"We're rich!" Tony shouts without hesitation, jumping up and down while holding onto Oggie's shoulder. He releases Oggie and commences his favorite dances, the Cabbage Patch and then the Smurf, to get a good laugh out of them.

"Well, not exactly, because we have to return it!" Tom says, trying to keep a straight face and hold his laugh after seeing Tony's face grow stale when winking at Oggie.

"He's right, Tony..., the government will hunt us down if they don't get all of it back, plus, they'll think we're part of this scam!" Oggie says, feeding fuel to Tom's expeditiously executed prank.

"So what?" Tony responds. "We can leave the country before they figure it out. For all they know, we're dead anyway, right?"

"Is that the kind of life you want for yourself and your family? Do you want to constantly be on the run and have to look over your shoulder the rest of your life?" Tom asks, fighting back the smile and laughter.

Tony gives it some serious thought. "Maybe you're right," he says, pissed.

Oggie reaches into his vest pocket and pulls out a mini first-aid kit, backing Tom to the back door and onto the seat, attending to Tom's wound.

Tom climbs in the front seat and begins pressing the preset phone number designated to ring at the White House when Oggie finishes patching him up.

Tony climbs in, and Oggie pulls away just as a woman answers.

"White House Operator, two-six!"

"Yes, the President, please," Tom says, leaning back to ease the pain.

"You've got to be kidding me, right? Did you say the President?" She asks, listening to the low-level rap music in the background.

"Yes, why? Is there something wrong with that?"

"Why..., duh! You don't just call the White House asking for the President of the United States as if he's your homie or something," she says, thinking it was just another late-night prankster.

"Listen, little lady..., I've had a hard night, not to mention my dog just died, and my wife just left me!" Tom jokingly screams. "Now, if you don't get off your sweet little ass and have the President call me in twenty minutes, then maybe you can explain how you hung up on someone who called concerning the return of billions in stolen money back to the government!"

She instantly flies forward, spilling a sip of hot chocolate on the desk, and instantly wipes it up. "What's the number again, sir?" she asks anxiously.

"Four-five-nine, two-two-one-nine," he says, reading the number off the front panel of the dash near the phone's receiver.

"I'm so sorry, Admiral Michaels," the operator responds, finally looking at his name and number in the phone's LED. "I apologize for my behavior, sir; it's just that I get so many pranks time of night."

"Not my problem, but I'll be waiting," Tom says, terminating the call.

Thirty minutes later, the phone rings.

"Hello, Michaels?"

"No, sir, is this the President?"

"Yes, but to whom am I speaking?" He asks, with a cast of about five security officers sitting at the table and the Secretary of Defense standing by his side.

"Good morning, sir, Chief Powells, Strike Force One."

"Chief, who?" the President responds.

"With all due respect, sir, that's not important. I'm calling in reference to the large sum of money, possibly billions, supposedly to be transported by Admiral Michaels."

"Ohhhh..., that money! So where is he? Put him on!"

"Well, I'm afraid I can't do that, sir, because he's dead, as well as Captain Carrington, the commanding officer of Strike Force One. These two, along with Lieutenant Commander Villan from the Command Center, were behind this whole deceptive plot to get this money from the government. They killed Strike Force Two and half of my men," Tom says, adjusting his position again for comfort.

"Well, that's sad to hear, son. What about the opposing force in Bazumi, the Underground and Compound, or was it..., the War Fighters?"

"No, sir, all deception, obviously, but it was the Cuban Camp and Cuban Headquarters to blame. We destroyed the Cuban forces and all their troops, sir. There's nothing left, not even their satellite, thanks to the support of the Underground and Compound operating out of the Bazumi Islands and the USMSP R. L. Peterson." Tom goes into minor details and tells the President about the exchange of money between the Cubans, Admiral Michaels, better known as the Bear, and then his men, the best he knows how. He also makes mention of the admiral's comment about not being able to kill the Bear and makes it known that he didn't fully know what it meant or the setup of the chain of command or operation.

"So Michaels was the leader, huh? Well, I'll be damned!"

"Sir, I want you to ensure they're buried without honors because they're a disgrace to our country."

"I agree, Chief, and I'll see to it, but where's the money?"

"Right here, locked in the trunk of Admiral Michaels's limousine. My men and I are exhausted from this ordeal and don't care to be involved in some long, drawn-out investigation or hearings. Sir..., to be honest, we wouldn't even know where to begin on this mess, especially since there are so many loopholes in this deceptive plot and mission. With your permission, sir, we'd like to leave the money in the limo at the airport after, say, 5 a.m.?" Tom says, looking at his watch, which reads 3:45.

"I do sympathize." The President of the United States hesitates for a few seconds, thinking deeply. "Very well, Chief..., so you say the entire one-point-four billion is intact?" the President asks.

"I don't know for sure, sir, and I haven't bothered to count it, but it's packed in large suitcases and spread over the trunk. Now, keep in mind, there were a few Cubans that may have managed to get away stateside, near Western Branch Road," Tom says, creating an alibi for the missing money by linking the money to the Cubans, the dead bodies, and the crime scene.

The President almost burst out loud in laughter at Tom's lie to account for any missing money.

Others at the table are in silent tears but refrain from their outburst when seeing the President with his index finger to his lips to silence them.

There are a series of low-tone clicks during the conversation that go unnoticed.

A Cuban woman sits in the deep basement of the Cuban Headquarters Intelligence Room, checking through all frequencies of the Sky-Tel phones and Admiral Michaels' secure phone, in accordance with the Cuban Camp's operation orders, daily and throughout the day. The female intelligence interceptor operator anxiously sits, listening.

"I see; well, you and your men have done a great job, Chief," the President says with a smile, still trying to hold his laugh. "Your country and families will be proud of you and your men. Well, thank you very much for returning the money, son. You know, it's not every day someone turns in money, not to mention over a billion, which they could have very easily walked away with, so I do respect you and your men for your honesty and commitment. Have a good day; this is your Commander-in-Chief, out!"

Tom smiles instantly, feeling proud of having spoken to his President, so there is an unintentional delay when hanging up when hearing a foreign voice before the call ends.

The Cuban woman forgets to hang up the last of the Sky-Tel phones issued to the Cubans during the initiation of the planned attacks in Bazumi.

Tom stares at the phone's headset, shaking his head in disbelief as he plays with the thought of having a tapped phone when a late joke comes to mind. "My president?" Tom says, terminating the call. "Hell, I didn't vote for your ass!" Tom chuckles, sneering until wiping the smile from his face when Tony and Oggie look back with mean stares.

"Ha, ha, ha, ha," Tom giggled again. "I was only kidding, fellas!"

Oggie drives a few more miles, turning off at the airport exit, and then slows at the crossroad, staring at the long-term parking sign when veering off into short-term parking.

Tom reaches deep into his bag and passes Tony the bank cards for electronically purchasing their tickets.

Tom and Oggie count off seven million in large bills, leaving the remainder strewn over the trunk.

They head inside, check their weapons in and sit in the boarding area for twenty minutes when the attendant begins boarding the flight at 0445. Upon taking their seats, they see the highway leading to the airport lit up with blue and red lights.

Out of nowhere, other law enforcement vehicles, metro police, S.W.A.T., and helicopters swarmed the area. The Special Forces slowly advance on the limousine, with the three eagerly watching several dogs jump from the K-9 truck.

After a quick, thorough search, the explosive team backs away; a gentleman gets out of a black stretch-SUV government limousine, dressed in a long trench coat, and looks like the President of the United States, but they're not sure due to the distance.

The plane taxis down the runway, and they soon lose sight of the emergency response lights.

Back in Norfolk, Virginia, an hour later, before separating, Tom discusses his plan for the disbursement of the funds to include their four fallen brothers' families. He recruits Tony and Oggie to help move his personal belongings from Kelley's to storage and a few things to the barracks the next day.

Early the following morning, they meet up at Kelley's place. Not sure how long Kelley was gone or when she was due back, they rush through the house, packing as quickly as possible.

Tom grabs a few things from the office, unknowingly moving some of Kelley's things that connect her back to her dark past.

Within a month, Tom is waiting to close on a new four-bedroom house on the beach, which he purchased for around four hundred thousand.

Nearly three months later, Tom receives a late call from Latisha's daughter, who informs him of her mother's frequent crying and mentions overhearing her mother and aunt talking about a new baby.

Tom's first thoughts are to fly down and surprise Latisha, but instead, he assures Laquisha that everything will be fine. He tells her not to tell her mother they had talked because he wants to see how Latisha would handle breaking the exciting news.

Now, Latisha calls days later, about the same time she calls daily, and engages in mild chatter while Tom is at work. They talk about several things that bring them to tears of laughter before she starts listening more than talking. She stands before a full-length mirror, placing her hand over her stomach, gently sliding her hand under the maternity top, and rubbing her warm belly. A few tears instantly fall to her cheeks when she calls into question whether Tom would think she's tried to trap him with her pregnancy. She stays quiet a little longer until he hears her sniffling. "We need to talk," she says, tensing.

"Wait..., what? We have been talking; what do you mean?"

"Tom..., I'm pregnant!"

"What? Man, that screwed up because I thought it was just you and..., "

"Tom!" she replies, interrupting him.

"But now I can see I wasn't the only one, I mean...," he goes on, jokingly.

"Tom!" she shouts again, interrupting his continuous babbling.

"How could you do this to us?" Tom asks in a slightly raised, fake tone.

"Would you just shut up and let me finish!" she angrily screams.

"All right, but you know that...," he continues.

"You're the daddy!"

Tom covers the mouthpiece and pulls the phone from his face, chuckling.

There is silence as Latisha presses the phone closer when Tom brings the phone back to his ear, smiling.

"Tom!"

"Yeah?" he whispers with a deep grin.

"Well, are you going to say something?"

"What do you want me to say?"

"Damn you, Tom! Here I'm, pregnant with our child, and all you can ask me is what I want you to say. You're lucky I'm not standing there because I would jump on you and kick your butt!"

Tom bursts into laughter, thinking how much he misses and loves her when he suddenly remembers the meeting he has to prepare. "Hey, babe, I don't mean to cut you short, but I have a briefing to prepare for, and afterward, I have to call a few people and brag about the greatest news ever," he says, smiling.

"Ok, babe..., Tom, you've made my day, babe. I'm the happiest and luckiest woman in the universe to have such a great man to father my child," she says with tears rolling down her cheeks.

"Ahh..., Latisha, that's the sweetest thing I've ever heard, babe, and you say it with so much meaning and class," he says, laughing.

"Stop it!" she pouts, wiping her tears.

"I'll give you a call later, babe..., I miss you."

"I'm in love with you, Tom..., I miss you, bye babe!" she says, hesitantly listening for his response when easing onto the bed's edge.

"Love you! Bye-bye!"

She sits, looking into the mirror for minutes until rubbing her warm belly again. Her hand moves from the top of her belly, working its way around to the middle. Her hands sometimes caressed the bottom of her belly in a circular motion. She repeatedly rubs her belly until noticing her breasts growing firmer.

Deeply focused and feeling sexy, she kicks her slippers from her feet, reclining onto her back when reaching for the radio next to the bed, tuning it to a contemporary channel and stretching out. Her soft hands grasp and bring a breast upward in each hand, massaging them in a circular motion. Her hips begin slowly and seductively twirling, with her perfectly round cheeks tense from the pleasure, grasping some of the loosely-fitted maternity skirts with each inward thrust before letting go. After minutes of gentle thrusts, she slightly pulls her feet back until her knees rise high, slipping her skirt to her upper thighs and parting her legs.

She playfully pats the curvature of her fat pelvis a few times vigorously, stroking it as she runs fingers along the lining of her thigh's opening a few times. Her mind drifts to Tom for minutes before moaning and calling his name. "Damn..., Mmm..., ooh!" she moans until lightly and uncontrollably giggling. "Damn...,

Mmm! Babe, don't you know this is the best you've ever had? I mean, you have to know because I'm the first to conceive your baby," she says, acting childish while rubbing the curvature of her pelvis again.

The phone rings, startling her.

Two hours later, in the States, Tom is well into his brief with his temporary Commanding Officer, Captain T. Farrington. Afterward, he calls his mother to tell her the great news, and then Martha who answers in tears.

"Martha! Martha! Are you all right, Martha?"

"I'm fine, Tom, but its Kelley. She's in the hospital again. Kelley walked in on Jeff and some girl again."

"Oh, Martha, I don't understand why she's chasing that no-good loser anyway!"

Martha stays quiet for a few seconds. "Well, let me finish. Anyway, Kelley lost her mind and wanted to fight the girl, but Jeff beat Kelley badly, even worse than before. The hospital considered putting her on life support the first day, but she's recovering rather well now."

"Can you please tell me which hospital and room she's in?"

"Morgan General, Room 710."

"All right, Martha, I'll swing by and check on her later, but where's Jeff now?"

"He's in jail, the one not far from the house, and under a thirty-thousand-dollar bond, so I don't see him posting that anytime soon."

"Well, take care, and tell the kids I'll stop by tomorrow and spend some time with them," he says, listening to her cry until she hangs up.

When the office is empty, Tom phones Oggie and confides in him about the things Kelley is going through, and in conversation, he mentions Jeff's name and the location before hanging up.

Tom sits in the dim room, meditating on Kelley until finally breaking his concentration. He picks up the phone, calling the hospital's information desk and the lady patches him through but does not pick up on it being the seventh floor - the psychiatric ward.

"Hello?" Kelley's deeply meditative and sorrowful voice answers when her mind goes into overdrive to ensure any questions of abuse are directed at Jeff while covering up her most recent self-inflicted wounds and any recent, fictitious fights over Jeff's women.

"Hi! It's Tom..., how are you?"

"Tom? I'm all right, I guess, babe. I knew Martha would call you."

"Well, not really..., actually, I called her to see how everyone was doing."

"Yeah, everyone except me, right?" she replies with tears in her eyes.

"No, Kelley, especially you."

"Please, Tom, spare me the bullshit! You don't have to say things to make me feel better. Hey, look..., I realize I messed up the best thing I ever had in my whole life."

"Look, I didn't call for this, Kelley; I called to see how you're doing, so let's just put that comment behind us for now?"

"It's hard, babe," she whines, wiping away endless trails of tears. "I mean, you gave us everything, and I let that jerk mess it up," she says, crying even harder.

"Kelley, Kelley, Kelley..., you should know by now that we learn from our mistakes. The things we go through in life are lessons, and we must go through them because sometimes things are inevitable, but we learn to pick up the shattered pieces and move on."

"I know, huh..., and it seems as though you've done quite well at that..., moving on, that is, but what about the kids?"

"Kelley, just hang tight and give them time. They're old enough to know you're not perfect. We taught them well," he says, easing back in the chair with a tear rolling down his cheek.

"All they talk about is 'Daddy' this and 'Daddy' that. Hell, they haven't even seen you since you've been back," she says, angrily raising her voice.

"It was best for the time being, but I'll see them tomorrow, but as far as we go, I needed time to get myself together before seeing you."

"Get yourself together? What is that supposed to mean?"

"You know, time to get over the love I have for you and time to get over what we lost," he says, with tears immediately filling his eyes.

"Get over me? I thought you had done that already since you refused my calls and visits since returning. Oh, and another thing? You know, that was some cowardly shit..., getting your things while I was out of the country."

"I had to do it that way to keep from making a dumbass mistake."

"Oh yeah, and what dumb mistake is that, Tom?"

"Trying to rekindle something no longer there."

"Not there for who? Me or you?"

"Definitely you! You see, Kelley, I never stopped loving you, and I'll always have a place in my heart for you because you were my best friend and first true love."

A gut-wrenching feeling comes over her when she leans forward with a balled fist to her stomach. "Then why can't we work together and get through this?" she asks. "You were the one who always said love could conquer all," she says, wiping tears from bloodshot, darkened, ringed eyes with her cotton gown.

"Well, it's not that easy, Kelley, and you know it. When this mess initially surfaced, I felt like I wanted to die. I mean, the pain was just so awful. The only reason I kept my sanity is because of the mission, but had I been stateside, I don't think I could have dealt with it as such," he says, wiping a tear from his cheek.

Kelley feels sick to her stomach, churning her fist tighter until she is on the edge of puking.

"Tom, I'm still in love with you, babe. I just got caught up, ok?" she says, feeling like she is about to throw up again while meditating in more profound thoughts.

"Oh please, Kelley, this isn't the right time for that lame-ass excuse."

Deep in meditation, she's stunned to hear him curse so easily because she's never heard him curse or swear in general conversation the whole time she's known him.

"I promise I'll make it better, babe. I'll never let you down again, please..., please..., please, can we just try one more time?" she cries.

Tom is quiet for some time, pondering when thinking a little longer until thinking of Latisha.

"So, how was your visit? Did you have a great time with your father?" he asks, putting off answering her question.

"He's dead, but I had to go over and assist my uncle in handling his personal affairs and the disbursement of his will."

Tom puts on his thinking cap. "Really? I'm so sorry to hear about your father. What happened?" he asks, thinking about the Cuban general and the timing of his death.

"I really don't care to talk about it right now," she says, "Maybe later."

He sits in deep thought until he visualizes the man who looks just like her son. "Well, I really wish you two would have had a chance to bond," Tom says, sitting up and wondering how much her father might have left her and the kids in his will.

"Understand, but I'm at peace with it all now. As bad as I hate to say this, I just hope he made peace with God before leaving," she says when she thinks of her past lover and best friend from London when thinking about her friend's execution. A tear rolls down her cheek, and she is quiet until breaking her concentration. "Well, enough of that, back to my question: Please, can we just try one more time?" she suddenly cries.

Tom stays quiet for a little longer when his mind fills with thoughts of him making love to her and fades into her being nude and making love with Jeff. His mind instantly shifts to Jeff beating her and her liking it. "Kelley, I just can't! I mean, I just can't," he says, wiping a single tear from the corner of his eye.

She holds the phone in her lap, trembling while crying hard and then harder.

Tom presses the phone tighter to his ear, listening until her cry tapers off to a whisper.

The phone clicks, and the dial tone grows louder.

She sits, staring into the mirror puzzle until she breaks her concentration when her eyes browse over the room and onto Martha's gift basket, containing candy with a thin but sharp aluminum wrapping. She sits listening for the nurse while creeping over near the sink, staring into the mirror again, when drawn into somewhat of a trance, looking over several other items in the basket.

She tears open a wrapper and drops candy to the floor, turning the wrapper sideways and gently running it over the veins at her wrist. She begins pressing it harder and rubbing it faster, but it is too flimsy to break the skin, but her wrist turns bright red from the constant pressure and friction and burns, though still unable to break the skin. She looked around for something else in the basket that she could use to transform into a sharper object.

She stares a little longer, empties four wrappers, drops more candy, and collapses the wrappers together. She takes small steps toward the door and slips the wrappers into the tightest corner of the door and deep into the seam of the door's jam. With the door almost closed, she leans into it with her back, applying light pressure until hearing the wrapper stretch and the door seal come together.

The irritating sound of the yawning plastic brings the nurse out of her train of thought.

Kelley stands crying and lightly chanting, then crying more until her voice grows louder with her cry.

The door instantly flings open, and the attentive nurse rushes in, looking around in excitement. "Ma'am, what are you doing?" she asks, forcing Kelley from the door and fighting her way inside while looking at the plastic wrapper lodged in the door seam.

Kelley feels shamed, lowering her head, when thinking up a quick lie. "I accidentally spilled the candy by accident. I'm sorry; I'll clean it up," Kelley says with a tear rolling down her cheek.

Seeing Kelley depressed, the nurse walks up and guides her back to the bed. "Never mind, you just get back in bed and get some rest," the nurse says, lifting Kelley's leg from the floor.

The nurse tucks in the sheets alongside the railing, and then proceeds to the door, looking back at Kelley one last time. She begins cleaning the mess scattered over the floor when noticing something of a yellowish-purple color in the door jam. She looks back at Kelley and removes the small, thick, metal-like object from the door's jam. The nurse thoroughly looks the room over to make sure there's nothing else with which she can harm herself.

After hours of rest, Kelley wakes from a loud, ringing phone. She lies there for seconds before gaining her composure, still very depressed, but finally, she reaches over. "Hello? Hello?" she answers.

"How are you, dear?" her uncle asks when Kelley breaks down crying.

Kelley tries to remain rigid, seeing how that's how her uncle and father had raised her during the time she lived with them in London.

Their conversation lasts well over thirty minutes when she breaks down and tells him of the abuse she's endured at Jeff's hands.

Her heart fills with great anger when meditating on Tom, to the point where she wants Jeff to pay for all he has taken her through.

Her uncle sits intensely, listening and tenses from time to time, jotting down key things that cause him to cringe. His fists balled tightly as his anger grew deeper.

Now, when she'd gotten out all the things about Jeff, Tom's name drifts into the conversation, but things about Tom are more pleasant until she tells him about things confirmed or relayed to her from reliable sources, things that not even Tom knew she knew.

Her uncle sits listening until becoming even more intense when his mind shifts to Jeff and the things he's done to her when his balled, tight fist slams against the desk's edge. His teeth bite down, clenching his cigar as his anger grows deeper.

"Enough! This Jeff character! This bastard! I'll kill this bastard," he screams, quieting when she refrains from saying anything else.

She sits in silence, thinking about her ex being executed by them, though he never confirmed which, so he quickly changes the conversation and tries cheering her up again.

Now, when her uncle hangs up, he calls in a few associates, inquiring about a few returned favors. After the third call, he acquires the help of a friend who is his brother's best friend. In a rage, and for his brother's sake, her uncle requests that Jeff pay dearly but doesn't want Jeff killed because he knows his niece would never forgive him for having her kids' father taken out, so he thinks of something even more sinister.

The following morning, Jeff receives a call in jail, an alarming death threat concerning his mother. Irresponsible as usual, Jeff takes the threat as a joke thinking it is Tom trying to rid him of Kelley. In a rage, Jeff makes very slanderous remarks, pissing off the man who's broken, cursing English words turn to more of a deeply-rooted Russian accent.

The man screams in Jeff's ear, bringing him to fear when speaking more in a pissed-off German accent, with the only understandable words being 'mother' and 'murder before the phone dies.

Jeff slowly hangs up and meditates for a while before finally taking the threat seriously. He slowly walks out of line and quickly turns, trying to jump in line again to call his mother and warn her, but he starts a commotion that causes him to have an escort back to his cell.

The following day, in the afternoon, Tom goes shopping and then heads over to Martha's.

Martha hears the truck's door slam and runs to the door. She opens the screen door and steps onto the top step with a smile, waving. "My, aren't we classy!" Martha says, watching Tom slip on his suit jacket. Her eyes meandered over the new black-and-chrome extended-version SUV.

Within seconds, Brandon burst through the door, leaping off the top step, hitting the ground, and running into Tom's arms. "I missed you so much, Daddy," Brandon yells with tears of joy.

"I missed you too, little man," Tom excitedly yells, lifting and kissing him on the cheek before placing him back on his feet.

Tom reaches out for Ashley, who just had run up, leaning over, hugging, and kissing her, while Martha looks on with uncontrollable tears.

The kids stand admiring the new truck until opening the door and climbing inside.

"What about my kiss?" Martha shyly asks, wiping her teary face with her hand when Tom approaches the top step.

"You know you get a big one, Martha," he says, embracing her and kissing one moist cheek and then the other. Tom leads Martha to the truck, where he shows her and the kids the vehicle's slick new features.

Amused, Martha sits in the front passenger seat in a daze until finally breaking her concentration. "Let's go inside so I can start dinner. Come on, kids!" she says, stepping onto the running board.

Tom enjoys the meal and the kids and hangs around until around 9 p.m., well after the kids are sound asleep. He walks out with Martha and leads her to the back of the truck, opening the rear cargo area and removing the black leather tarp when the back interior light lights up the cargo hold.

Martha's eyes grow wide, gazing over the shiny, wrapped gifts.

Tom reaches forward. "Here, these are for you and the kids, and these are for Kelley," he says, pointing at separate piles of boxes and then picking up a medium-sized box.

"Thank you, but you shouldn't have," she says, pulling the package to her chest with a smirk.

"It's a token of my love because you've always treated me like a son since I've known you. I'm really sorry things turned out the way they have, but Kelley will always be my friend, and you'll always be my second mother."

Martha lets off a bright smile. "It's nice of you to speak so highly of me," she says, kissing his cheek when cologne rushes deep into her nostrils.

Tom helps Martha carry the gifts inside, unloads them on the couch, then reaches deep into his pocket.

"Please give these to Kelley," he says, passing her the spare car key. "Tell her the balance is paid in full, so she can arrange a date to go over and have the title switched. The balance on the mortgage is paid in full as well, so she should receive papers from the mortgage company in about a month or two."

"My goodness, Tom, you are truly blessed. What did you do, hit the lottery? No man would think of a woman the way you have of Kelley during all this mess."

Tom smiles. "Deep in my heart, Martha, I love Kelley so much that it hurts, but I know now that it can never be."

"I understand, son; well, anyways, I guess I do."

"Here's five thousand," he continues, pulling out a cashier's check. "I want you and the kids to take a cruise or getaway this summer."

"Are you sure this isn't going to put you in a financial bind?"

"Oh no!" he guffaws. "There's plenty where this came from, and I don't have to want anything, well, at least for a while. So now, the best for last," he continues, pausing for a second and smiling.

"What is it?" she asks anxiously.

"Great news," he says in excitement when grasping her hands. "I have a kid on the way!"

"Oh, Tom!" she glistens. "When? Who? I'm so happy for you! Where?" she asks, puzzled and marveling as to whether he was the unfaithful one in the relationship the entire time.

"She's from the Bazumi Islands, but I just found out yesterday. Well, that's when she finally got up enough nerve to tell me."

"I know she's a beautiful woman because you have great taste in women. So, tell me, when I will get to meet this woman?" she asks, mainly thinking about how Kelley would take the bad news.

"Well, if possible, I'd like to keep it our secret…, well, until I tell Kelley."

She smiles. "My lips are sealed…, scout's honor, though you know I'm no scout!" she laughs, raising her fingers but playfully crossing her other fingers behind her back, jokingly when showing them in deeper laughter.

"Thanks, Martha," he says, kissing her hand.

Martha walks him back out and stands on the top step until he backs out and pulls away.

The phone rings, and she waves again, turning for the door, but it stops ringing before she can reach it.

Kelley calls again minutes later, and Martha tells her about everything they had done and then mentions everything as Tom asked.

"Oh, Martha, what have I done!" she screams, falling back on the bed in tears.

Over at Oggie's house, he sits searching in the papers for the assault charges brought up on Jeff and can't find them, so he calls around to several police stations and finds the housing Jeff.

He closely listens to the bailiff and discovers that Jeff is finishing up his time for non-support when devising a swift plan and swinging by to pick up Tony. Not wanting to expose the plan, he kept Tony in suspense as to where they were going and what he had planned.

Tom is about thirty-five minutes from his house when his Bluetooth activates. "Tom!" he answers, turning the radio down.

"Feel like hanging out tonight?" Oggie asks, passing a car on the bridge.

"Why not?"

"Well, meet me and Tony at Lee's Field, say around midnight."

"Ok, I'll bring the liquor," Tom says, looking at his watch.

Jeff stands in the police station, collecting his valuables and waiting for his discharge. He signs the papers stating that he would appear on his scheduled court date, then approaches the watch captain's desk, explaining the call concerning his mother, and is immediately allowed to use the phone. Jeff calls his mother, and he doesn't get an answer on his first few attempts. After the fourth try, he reaches her and is relieved when anxiously giving her the details of the call, when warning her to lock her door, and report the incident to her servicing police station.

CHAPTER TEN: A REVENGEFUL QUEST

Tony and Oggie pull along the curb in the dark near the police department.

Oggie dives into a general conversation to keep Tony unfocused on why they are there.

Tony becomes curious when Oggie steps out of the jeep. "Hey, Oggie, why are we here?" Tony finally asks, climbing out with eyes following Oggie over the top of the jeep.

"Patience, my dear son..., patience!" Oggie mumbles, slowly climbing back in and looking back.

The well-suited bondsman walks out and looks around, then over to where Oggie is parked waving.

"Now him..., that was a bondsman," Oggie says, waving back. "Now, that cat!" Oggie says, pointing to the guy who just had walked onto the porch and was now standing on the top step. "That's Kelley's kids' father."

"You're a damn genius, Oggie. Let's kick his ass right here in front of the police station," Tony says, climbing back inside.

"No..., no..., Chief gets first dibs on this one, so no guns or knives, right?" Oggie replies with a serious look.

"Do I have to answer?"

"Give it to me, Tony," he responds, holding his hand out.

"Man!" Tony says, handing him a handgun and then hesitating whether he will hand Oggie the knife.

"Is there anything else?"

"All right! All right!" he says, digging deep in his pockets and handing him two metal spikes and a switchblade.

"Are you sure there's nothing else?"

"That's it!" Tony says, wiping away his frown while staring back at Jeff, who is making his way up the street in the opposite direction, kicking a can.

"Are you sure?"

"I said that's it, now come on! He's getting away."

Oggie cranks up and speedily turns around, trailing behind Jeff until reaching the bus stop, where he pulls alongside the curb.

"What's up, man?" Tony asks, leaning toward Oggie while changing the radio station. "Are you waiting for the bus?"

"Naw, I'm busted, so no money for that. Hell, I just got out of the fucking slammer!" Jeff says in a nasty tone.

"Need a ride?" Tony asks, adjusting the channel and then turning the volume down.

"Yeah, I could use a lift so I can go and put my foot knee-deep in this girl's tail. So, where are you guys heading?"

"Just joyriding for now, but man, you sure look like you need to unwind."

"For sho (sure); I sure could use a cold one," Jeff says, running his fingers through his semi-permed-looking hair and pretending he hasn't seen the cooler in the back seat nor the folded beer boxes on the floor extending from under the seat.

"Hell, you're in the right place at the right time, main (man). You can go handle your business with ole' girl later. We're meeting a friend who's bringing the serious stuff. Hey, you're welcome to the ice-cold beers, dude," Oggie says, pointing over his shoulder and looking away with a smile.

They introduce themselves, and Jeff jumps in the back, popping the top off a cold bottle and taking the first one straight to the head in almost two swallows.

Within seconds, Jeff is rattling on for minutes, degrading Kelley and talking about how he's never going to pay child support.

Oggie drives out to a rustic area near the Churchland community and turns onto a dark, paved street, where they continue for about a mile.

The streetlights soon fade in the background, and the road turns pitch-black and becomes heavily graveled.

A distant streetlight is soon seen ahead as they gaze through the dark until it brightens and lights up the corner of the deserted-looking baseball field.

Oggie pulls under the streetlight, turns off the engine and music, and climbs out.

Tony and Oggie grab the cooler and place it on the picnic table.

They sit on the table's top, kicking back with another cold beer.

"Looks as if someone's been here already," Oggie says, pointing at the empty beer and liquor bottles strewn over the ground.

"Well, there's plenty of beer to go around, so drink up," Tony says with curious eyes cut over at Oggie until mischievously sneering.

Oggie smiles and then walks over, nudging Tony when seeing headlights approaching from afar when walking to the jeep and cranking up the tunes.

Tom's watch beeps when about fifty yards away. He switches his high beams to fog and stops a few feet from Jeff, who is so drunk that he doesn't even realize the car is even there.

Oggie turns up the volume a few more notches, and by now, Jeff is wasted and begins dancing around to his favorite song, which he sings at the top of his drunken voice.

Jeff goes on in his own little world until turning and jumping, somewhat startled when finding Tom's car when playing it off and clumsily continuing with his silly looking dance.

Tom remembers Jeff's face from a picture he'd seen when first meeting Kelley.

Jeff begins dancing slowly in a drunken sway to the slow jam when his arms shoot out as if he's dancing with a partner, until kicking up dust. He swirls around a few times, then stops, confusingly looking at the license tags until pointing again, hee-hawing.

"What's so funny?" Tony asks.

"It's Tom! Hey Tom," Jeff says, singing, waving, and dancing around in a circle but stumbling across a majority of the words, worse than before. Jeff thinks back to where he had seen Tom for a split second, but Tom's new hairstyle and increased muscular build sort of throws him off.

"What's up, fellas?" Tom says, looking at Tony and then Oggie and winking while shutting the door.

"Not much," Oggie says, nodding in Jeff's direction.

"Hey, Jeff, come on over," Tony says, motioning to him with a beer bottle in his tight fist.

"I want you to meet my friend, Tonto."

"Tonto? Hell, his tags spell T-O-M, Tom!" Jeff blurts out with his hand held out to shake Tom's.

"No, no, no, Tom stands for Tom Thumb! That's my code name," Tom responds, frowning and tightening his fists when his nostrils begin continually flaring from being so hyped.

Jeff leans forward with his hand out again, and Tom turns and walks away.

"Ok, Tom Thumb, can I get a handshake or what?" Jeff asks with his hand still extended fully while watching the back of Tom's head as he continues over to Tony and Oggie.

"Just how I like 'em, dumb and pissy-ass drunk," Tom says, whispering and winking to Oggie while approaching. "He won't feel the real pain until sometime tomorrow," Tom laughs, and Tony titters.

"Hey Jeff, tell my friend all that wild and crazy stuff you were saying about your kids' mother on the way over! That crap really turns him on," Tony says, pumping up Jeff's pathetic ego.

"Oh yeah?" he says, clutching another ice-cold beer and chugging it down in three swallows when starting in on his slanderous remarks. Jeff repeats everything as if rehearsed and doesn't miss a single word, though his slurred speech is heavy.

Tom patiently waited until after all his degrading remarks about Kelley. "Wow, sounds like a real woman you've got there, partner!" Tom says, neatly tucking his shirt inside the rim of his trousers.

"Real woman? Who? What woman are you freakin' talking about? You can't even be talking about that trick! She's not even a woman..., she's a damn killing machine, but she knows better than to screw with me! I don't give a damn about her or her damn child support! If she thinks I'm going to take care of those damn snotty-nose bastards, she'd better think again," Jeff confidently says, reaching for yet another cold beer. "Hell, as mad as I am right now, every time they pull damn money from my pay from now on, it will warrant me putting my foot in her stankin' tail. Shit! I've got arrears up the yin-yang! Huh, I bet that'll get her attention and force her to stop them from pulling money out of my paycheck, huh? What you think, Tony?" Jeff says, giggling and waiting for a response from Tony, which never comes.

Tony just shakes his head and, seconds later, guffaws in a dry spell.

"Well, Jeff..., tell me something..., this ass whipping, do you think it hurt her?" Tom asks, tightening his fists down at his side when briskly walking over and up to him.

"Hurt? Ah, man, that was long ago, and it only happened once, but I whipped her so freakin' bad back then that her dead ancestors felt it," he says, bursting into loud laughter at his own senseless comment. "Don't you get it? Sometimes you have to catch them off guard to get the upper hand, especially when they are a trained killer."

Tony and Oggie burst into laughter, knowing he is talking out of his head and knowing Tom is about to tear him a new one.

"What ancestors?" Tom asks, not catching on to the fact that the fights happened long ago. He removes a long-neck beer bottle from the ice chest and turns up the beer, draining it in two and a half swallows.

"Hell, at least three generations," Jeff responds in a drunken delay when bending to his knees, bursting into silly laughter.

"Do you love her? No! What I should've asked was, have you ever loved her?"

"Love?" He laughs ridiculously. "Hellz no! Are you crazy as hell, or what? She is and will always be something I can hit and stand up in at the drop of a hat."

"Wow! So you have no feelings at all for a woman who gave birth to your two beautiful children? None at all, huh?"

"What part of nada are you not feeling, dude? I said nada, and I meant not a dang drop!" he confidently responds, trying to act tough while looking at Tony and Oggie. His index fingers begin slowly going in circles around his head when pointing at Tom while his back is turned, sneering at Tony and Oggie.

In a daze, Tom turns back to Jeff. "I see, well back to that ass-whipping..., can you tell me if it was even as bad as this?" Tom yells, breaking the twenty-two-ounce long-neck across Jeff's nose.

"Fuck, what the hell!" Jeff screams. "Shit!" he screams, grabbing his lips when Tom retracts his fist from a devastating hit and the staggering blow that follows suit with blood splattering over Jeff's white shirt. He grabs his face, staring at his bloody hands and screaming even louder.

"Come on! I'm going to teach you a little something about respect for a real woman," Tom screams, looking at his sore knuckles before shaking off the sting.

"Respect? What in the fuck is wrong with you, man? Are you crazy?" Jeff cries, instantly feeling more sober than drunk when wiping blood from his face with his sleeve and backing away fast.

"Man, my ass, its Mr. Tom to you..., punk!"

"As in Kelley's...," Jeff starts to say. "Damn!" he screams, grabbing his lips after Tom retracts his fist after two more quick and forceful directly-connecting punches.

By now, Jeff feels as if he is totally sober when trying to run, but Tom clips him and then dropkicks him in the back, forcing him face-first into the tall grass.

Jeff continually rolls a few times before stopping with his hands pressing hard into the grass and finally bracing himself with his arms.

Tom rushes up and reaches down, punching him in the face and giving him four to five hard whacks. "Who's the trick now? Who's the damn trick now? Damn you!" Tom screams, grabbing Jeff in the collar and repeatedly dropping his upper body to the grass.

Jeff balls up, crying like a newborn baby.

"Oggie, give me a cold one. I've got a long night ahead," Tom says, rolling up his long shirt sleeves.

Before Oggie can reach him, he points over Tom's shoulder toward Jeff, finding him grabbing an empty beer bottle from the ground and balancing on the one hand, trying to stand.

Tom looks to his left and catches sight of Jeff's shadow with the beer bottle high overhead when Jeff takes off at a slow, then fast pace.

Jeff comes up on Tom while he still intentionally has his back turned.

Tom's eyes eagerly follow his shadow until he's several feet away, and then energetically lifts his leg, nailing Jeff in the head with a roundhouse kick with the bottle flying upward, and Tom manages to catch it and break it across Jeff's head. "You little weasel! You can't even take me face-to-face like a real man, huh? Oh, you can't fight a man, but you can beat up on a damn woman! You damn coward!" Tom shouts. He opens the beer Oggie hands him and pours it over Jeff's head.

"Beat up on a woman? What the hell are you talking about? I ain't beat up on no woman. Man, please let me go! I'll do anything you ask! Hell, I'll never see Kelley ever again!" he screams and then cries in severe pain.

"Pal, when I'm finished with you, you'll never want to see Kelley and that child support? Oh yeah, you'll pay, and you better not be late," Tom says, dropkicking Jeff in the chest while he's kneeling to stand.

"No, please, no!" Jeff cries, falling hard and flat on his back.

"Get a little rest because when you move, that tells me you're ready for more of this," Tom says, heading over to Tony and Oggie.

"Chief, he moved his leg!" Tony yells, bursting into laughter.

"What?" Tom says, running up to Jeff, kicking him in the seat of his pants, and causing him to crawl a few feet and curl in a fetal position.

Jeff balls up to block Tom's foot the fourth time.

"What generation is that, third or fourth?"

"I don't know!" Jeff cries, coughing and spitting up a little blood.

"So which generation felt that..., huh? How about this?" Tom asks, pulling his middle finger back so far that the bone snaps with Jeff screaming a loud, dreadful cry, leaving Tony and Oggie cringing.

"What generation would you say that was, punk?" Tom screams, his voice slightly echoing over the field.

"Sixth, seventh..., oh goodness, please help me! I'll pay for the support! I'll pay the support!" Jeff cries out loud, sadly reaching in Tony and Oggie's direction for mercy when they begin feeling bad for setting Jeff up, looking away.

Their eyes drift to the ground, no longer able to look into his watery eyes and swollen face.

Jeff reaches for them several times, but they sadly look away.

Tom finally turns Jeff on his back and immediately feels sorry for him and has pity after seeing his bloody and swollen face. He walks to the jeep and grabs a rag from the back, pouring beer over his hand to clean up the blood. "Let's get the hell out of here. This cowardly-ass dude can't endure a whippin' of this magnitude until morning. Besides, he's no challenge. This punk has had it; he's washed up," Tom says, shaking off the pained cut on his knuckle.

Tony winks at Tom and then Oggie, walking over to the passenger seat, reaching under the seat, grasping a knife by the handle, and taking off at top speed.

"Tony, no!" Oggie and Tom scream, almost in laughter.

"Tony, he's not worth it!" Tom screams, faking while maneuvering to intercept Tony in a grip and grab.

At stealth speed, Tony ducks right and then left, evading Tom in a wild and silly scream when slipping to the ground, whisking Jeff up in his arms, and holding him in a full headlock. He pressed the knife hard against his neck without warning. "Say your last words before I put your ass to sleep..., say them!" Tony screams, shouting in rage while taunting him.

Jeff cries louder and begins begging for his life.

"Tony, no!" Tom yells, slowly removing Tony's knife-totting hand from Jeff's throat until Tony releases his grip, climbing to his feet, senselessly giggling.

Tom leans down and into Jeff. "Let me make myself clear," Tom says, jerking Jeff by the collar and slightly lifting him. "If you mention our names, you're a dead man! The first of the month, Kelley gets her child support, and you'll never see your kids until you learn to conduct yourself as a real man. If I find out you've been within three miles of her or caused her harm, we'll come back like thieves in the night. We'll have no mercy on you, like tonight, but ten times worst. No matter where you are, we'll find you, understand me?"

"Yes! Yes!" Jeff cries in a low voice as blood and tears mingle, rolling down his face.

Tom makes Jeff repeat what he said, and halfway through his slurred repeat, Tom interrupts. "Close enough!" He snatches Jeff's cell phone from his hip, dialing 911, fearing Jeff bleeding to death after leaving. "I should leave you here to die, but I'll be generous for Kelley and the kids' sake," Tom says, looking down at him in disgust.

After Tony and Oggie load the cooler, Tom jumps in his car and pulls alongside Oggie's door. "Hey, don't think you're getting off that easy..., we still have a fresh bottle of Sekif's Cognac to polish off," Tom says, holding the gallon-sized decorative bottle over his head. "My place?"

"We'll follow you," Oggie says with eyes cut back over at Jeff, sneering.

"Thanks for the treat," Tom says, nodding at Jeff, who is low-crawling toward the taller weeds and trees.

"Anytime," Oggie and Tony say almost simultaneously when they acknowledge with smiles.

Near the city, they pass the ambulance and police, speeding to the scene with flashing lights and blaring sirens.

The medical response vehicles arrive with two officers and medics searching the grounds for minutes before finding Jeff in a wooded area, halfway passed out. They move him to an open area on a stretcher and try rendering assistance, but it takes a while because they have no clue what Jeff is saying. They take turns asking what happened or where he was hurt since he kept pointing all over his body. While the medics work on bandaging him up the best, they know how the officers ask several minutes of repeated questions, unable to understand he was saying there was a mugging.

Jeff tells them he was able to call for help before the muggers took his phone.

The cops are not quick not to buy his story, nor did they care after finding his phone in the grass a few feet away and running his name in the system to find he has several domestic violence charges.

Outside the police station, Jeff's mother steps out with wandering eyes while standing, pondering. She realizes there is nothing the police can do to protect her when refusing to go home, so she goes to a friend's house and hangs out for hours. She keeps drinking liquor and talking until she is somewhat wasted and tired, and the drinks have her feeling herself. She becomes full of talk and bold, pumping down the pint-sized bottle of liquid courage. Pretty soon, she feels the call is a hoax, so she asks her friend and her friend's son to drive her home.

When they arrive, her friend and her friend's son go inside and walk through the house to comfort her.

Satisfied, Jeff's mother walks them to the front door, where they hug, and she thanks the woman's son.

The car's headlights energize, lighting the front of the house and doorway.

Jeff's mother stands rocking from side to side while watching the headlights until the car slowly backs out of the driveway with lights fading down and away from the house.

The dim porch light poorly lights the front porch until a few feet on each side of the house is fading into darkness when a medium-built, buff man fades in from the darkness alongside the house.

The shady-looking character pulls his phone from his pocket, dialing to inform his boss that he is in position for the execution of the plan. He whispers in deep conversation with his boss, and before being put on hold, he watches Jeff's mother stagger from room to room.

They walk in unison until they are in the back room, where she undresses and stands, looking in the mirror and singing slurred. Finally, she slips into the bathroom and dresses into her sleeping clothes. She stumbles to the bed and falls to her knees, praying before slowly pulling herself to her feet.

In London, Kelley's uncle receives the call of the imminent plan being in place and ready to be executed when feeling sorrowful, knowing the murderous actions would draw his niece further from him. He sits listening to the detailed plan, and his heart is immediately softened, when in a hesitant thought for minutes until he calls off the plan.

Jeff's mother lies in bed, almost passed out, when the gun trains down, and her head comes off the sights of the AK-47.

The man fades into darkness, accidentally backing up onto the paw of the neighbor's cat, which screams a deathly cry.

The neighbor, an old man, leans from his bed, pulling back the curtains and shining his wife's flashlight out between the dark houses, when the killer's head vanishes as if he was never there.

The following day, Tom and the kids surprise Kelley, picking her up from the hospital, though she's expecting Martha.

Tom hides the flowers and stuffed animals until close and then surprisingly presents them.

The kids have big smiles on their faces.

Tom backs off after a hug and looks at her beautifully made-up face with her looks like a million bucks.

Later that evening, Tom, Kelley, and the kids go to their favorite Japanese restaurant, and it's like old times.

Afterward, they go over to Tom's house, where they play board games as if a family again and deep in her plot to stay overnight.

Kelley is keen on keeping the kids excited and awake until the next-to-last game, which mellows everyone out. When Kelley yawned a few times, she ran her fingers through her hair. She looks at Tom with dimmed eyes and convinces him to let them sleep over since it is so late.

After the kids are asleep, Kelley suddenly gets her second wind. She entices

Tom to share a bottle of wine, which leads to a deep conversation. From time to time, Kelley tries redirecting his thoughts to their shattered dreams and soon realizes that he is intentionally avoiding her lead, so Kelley slides closer. With her hands gently upon his thigh, she seductively comes on to him, thinking he's drunk, but he keeps refusing her advances when she quiets for minutes and then bursts into tears.

Tom keeps playing hard to get and then gives in to her and pulls her deep into his arms. "You'll be fine, babe," he says, holding her tightly until his eyes close, taking a deep breath of her. "We'll always be the best of friends."

"But I need more, Tom. You're all I have, babe."

"No, you have the best darn kids any mother could ask for; besides, I must go on with my life and new family."

"What? What fucking new family?" Kelley screams, hurt by those words finally coming from the man she so loves when continually licking tears from her sexy, full lips.

His mind transitions in disbelief that she cursed. "I met a great woman who was there for me when I was going through this ordeal with you." He goes on to tell her everything about Latisha but refrains from telling her it was during his mission. Finally, saving the news about the baby for last, he has no choice but to hold her tight when she goes into an even more resounding cry.

Well over a half-hour later, she finally calms down; he leads her to the bedroom, where they climb onto the bed, fully clothed, and cuddle. Kelley cries throughout the night and doesn't get any sleep because she knows it will be her last night with him.

When Tom passes out, she massages him and gets him somewhat excited.

"No, Kelley, no babe, I can't do this," he says, turning over and falling back asleep.

Tears pour nonstop, with Kelley jerking with each inhale when she tries even harder to stop crying, but occasionally and inadvertently wakes Tom from shivering in a heavier cry.

Before sunrise, she falls into a deep sleep in his warm, strong arms.

Before his alarm sounds, Tom is awakened and cuts it off, quietly gathering his things and showering downstairs.

Kelley awakens hours later, sitting in bed, listening and looking for him until looking over at the clock and realizing he's already left for work. She walks through the house straightening thing and then wakes the kids and have them get dressed. Kelley strays into Tom's study, flipping through his personal belongings and then his Rolodex, removing a card and anxiously dialing a number. The phone rings a few times when she slowly begins swirling the chair around, with one foot slightly pushing off each time.

"Hi, babe!" Latisha answers in joy.

"Hi, Latisha, this is Kelley."

"Kelley?"

"Tom's ex..., now, please hear me out, please!"

"Ok..., I'm listening," she responds with attitude while staring at the caller I.D. again.

"I found your number in Tom's Rolodex."

"His Rolodex? Where the hell is Tom, and what are you—?" she begins to ask angrily before being interrupted.

"Listen, please," Kelley says, crying in a light voice. "Tom told me everything, so I'm calling to congratulate you on the baby and for finding one of the finest men put on this earth. I don't know what Tom told you about me, but it doesn't matter. I know I've hurt him, and I know now that he'll never forgive me, but of all things, I want to see him happy, so I need to ask a favor."

"Please stop crying, Kelley; I feel so sorry for you," she says, wiping a tear from her cheek. "You're right; I know deep in my heart Tom's a great man, but what do you want from me?"

"Well, I have a substantial amount of money in an account that Tom put away for the kids and me during the beginning of his last mission. I don't know what you and Tom have planned, but it would mean the world to me if you could come here for a month or so. I mean..., I'll pay all your expenses, but I want it to be a surprise. Please don't tell him, please!"

Latisha pauses in deep interest, and her heart races in excitement. "I would be delighted, but I have to make arrangements for my family business and my daughter with my sister," she says, hesitating more and still smiling. "All right, Kelley, I'll do it!"

"As I said, I'll pay all expenses, even the money you'll lose from your salary."

"Oh, Kelley, this means so much," Latisha says, wiping her tears.

"It means so much to me as well. Well, it means the world to me," Kelley says, slightly slumping over and pressing her stomach with her hand when feeling sick from talking with her. She manages to play the conversation to almost nothing and then ends the call abruptly with an excuse of having something about to burn on the stove when slamming the phone down and rushing to the bathroom, throwing up several times.

An unmarked car pulls up outside Tom's neighbor's house.

The driver and passenger cautiously watch Tom's house and the other houses.

Seeing Kelley come out with the kids, the two people in the unmarked car look away and then shadow Kelley from a distance.

Kelley makes it home, and the strange car pulls up and parks across the street.

The two people sit for hours until the kids walk out and head for the school bus stop.

When the bus rounds the curve, they wait another twenty minutes, continually staring around her and the neighboring houses.

Kelley's nosy old neighbor, who is great friends with Martha, comes up alongside her house, still bent over and picking up weeds here and there. She eases into the front yard unnoticed and draws her knees in the flowerbed, hearing the car crank up, making a U-turn, and quickly pulls into Kelley's driveway.

Two women swiftly exit the vehicle and cautiously look around while walking it up to Kelley's porch fast.

The tall woman's black-gloved hand knocks on the door several times, but there's no answer, so she turns the knob, finding it locked.

The shorter woman's gloved hand slides deep inside her purse, gripping a miniature, toy-size pistol with a specially-made silencer.

Kelley's nosy neighbor unknowingly stands from her flower bed with eyes meandering over the two strange women for minutes before taking a few steps to the edge of her yard. "May I help you? I'm Kelley's neighbor. She's in there, but maybe she's asleep. What can I do for you?" she asks, leaning on the sun-dried hoe's handle, supporting her weight.

The short woman brings her purse to her face as if looking for something; when releasing the weapon when the tall woman looks into her face and then turns to the neighbor.

"We're with Kelley's insurance company, and we were in the area and decided to drop by to see how her new policy is working out," the tall woman says, looking around and then back at her accomplice, who turns and walks back to the car. The tall woman draws closer to the fence, indulges in yard talk for a few more seconds, and then bids Kelley's neighbor a good day.

Kelley's neighbor stands staring at the tall woman until she climbs in the driver's seat, and when the car backs out, Kelley's neighbor gazes over the license plate, memorizing tags. She drops the hoe and rushes for her front door.

The two women notice the woman's sudden movement when the car slows in front of her house and then pulls over to the curb, where it sits for minutes. The women watch the old woman through the glass storm door as she scribbles.

The short woman's hand slips inside her purse again, her other hand grasping the door handle when the driver throws the car in gear.

They pull away and then pull over again a few houses down.

Alongside Kelley's backyard, a garbage truck pulls up to collect more garbage.

Kelley looks up, pinning the last pair of jeans on the clothesline, and turns to find her nosy neighbor at her kitchen window with a confused look painted on her face. Kelley smiles, waves to her, and then reaches down to pick a piece of paper, and before she can turn back to the door, the neighbor loudly bangs on the window again, trying to get her attention. The garbage truck pulls off, and Kelley hears the woman's last bang against the glass when she looks up to see the curtains swaying back and forth.

Thinking her neighbor wants to gossip, Kelley rushes for the front door, where she opens the door and sits inside on the stairs for minutes. Kelley patiently waits as accustomed, expecting her neighbor to walk through the door any minute, but after some time, Kelley hears two car doors slam, followed by tires squealing. She sits longer until she finally stands and walks to the door, looks up and down the street, walks out onto her front porch, and looks over at her neighbor's door, finding it shut. She takes a few steps off the porch when her phone rings, distracting her.

Later in the evening, Kelley calls Latisha back to confirm there were no problems with the money transfer and to get her flight itinerary.

Two days later, around 10:00 a.m., Kelley and Martha meet Latisha at the airport.

At first, Kelley is speechless yet constantly staring at Latisha's radiant beauty.

They take her to lunch and then go shopping for a pretty maternity dress before resuming window shopping. They stop at the market and select a thick, juicy steak, shrimp, lobster tail, and veggies for Tom's dinner.

When they arrive at the house, Kelley uses Tom's spare key from under the doormat where she left it, and when Latisha sees Kelley pull out the key, she and Martha look at each other mysteriously.

The two grow suspicious about how she knew where the key is, but Latisha suddenly forgets about it when Martha distracts her, indulging in a more pleasant conversation.

Kelley calls Tom's job and asks the receptionist to inform her when Tom leaves, then tell her the surprise and ask the receptionist to keep the secret in confidence.

Since there's not much time to prepare the meal alone, Martha and Kelley pitch in and help prepare the meal the way Tom likes it.

While listening to most of the conversation led by Kelley, Martha becomes very curious as to why Kelley is telling Latisha all about Tom's personal business.

The conversation initially has Martha on edge, but when Kelley looks over to see Martha's face, she changes the conversation to something more pleasant. From time to time, Martha would look over and catch Kelley staring at Latisha and her swollen belly with a hateful demeanor, which she quickly cleans up when feeling she's under a microscope. It becomes obvious to Martha that Kelley is very jealous of Latisha's beauty and energy. Minutes later, Martha is once again uncomfortable with Kelley's actions and starts to feel she has more hatred than joy in seeing Tom happy.

Once dinner is almost ready, Kelley's phone rings.

"Hi, Kelley; Tom just left. I'm so excited!" the receptionist says, pulling her things from her desk. She shut down her computer in hopes of getting an invite to what she perceived as an open dinner party.

"Thanks!" Kelley says, rudely hanging up.

The receptionist thinks the signal was dropped, so she immediately calls back, but Kelley places the phone on vibrate and refuses to answer.

Kelley calculates the time it takes for Tom to get there, and with little time to spare, Martha and Kelley walk over, hug Latisha, and say their goodbyes.

They step off the porch, and Latisha stands at the door, waiting until they are halfway down the sidewalk before shutting it.

She walks to the kitchen, immediately seeing them through the picture window, then turns and tends to the food for minutes. She then turns once more, finding them still sitting in the car, and tears run down Latisha's cheeks seeing Martha leaning over and hugging Kelley to comfort her.

When Latisha turns to tend to the food and looks once more, she hears the car crank up and sees it slowly pulling away. She turns and removes the chilled bottle of Sekif and a non-alcoholic beverage from the freezer, then stirs the shrimp simmering in the medium glass pot one last time. She looks back minutes later and spots movement in the yard out of her peripheral vision when slightly pulling the curtains back to find Tom walking up, dressed in his white combination cap, choker-white uniform, and white shoes.

Immediately, her hand drapes over her heart when she gasps for air in sheer ecstasy and then slowly catches her breath, inhaling and exhaling while backing into the dining room.

Tom walks in and throws his cover on the couch with the too-familiar aroma of Kelley's favorite "getting sexy for you" meal rising in his nostrils. He peeps around the living room, dining room, and inside the kitchen, looking for Kelley and the kids, and then leans over the stove gazing at the hearty meal. He removes the cover from the pot, deeply inhaling the mingled flavors when Latisha surprisingly steps out from behind the door.

Tom's mouth drops open, rushing over and engulfing her with a tight embrace and long French kiss. He takes a few steps back, rubbing her swollen tummy until his head comes upon her belly, pressing his ear against it, listening to the little heartbeat when the phone rings.

"Hello?" he answers.

"Surprise, babe! Surprise, Tom!" the two cheerful voices simultaneously yell.

"Thank you, Kelley and Martha. Only the two of you could have brought so much joy to my heart this day," he says, feeling a little uncomfortable from his comment yet smiling at Latisha, whose eyes are filling with tears.

His words and excitement bring a gut-wrenching feeling to Kelley's stomach, but she instantly plays it down by straightening her face when finding Martha standing in the other room, staring back at her with a less-than-cheerful smile.

"It's the best I can do, Tom," Kelley cries in a soft, weakening voice.

"Thanks again for the locket and diamond, Tom. I love it," Martha says when finally smiling again.

"Yes, thank you, Tom," Kelley mutters, deeply thinking about how empty her heart feels.

"You're both welcome."

"We'll all get together one day before Latisha leaves if it's all right with you, Tom," Kelley says, saddened when taking a deep swallow.

"Hey, sounds great," he responds, feeling sorry for Kelley yet pulling Latisha in his arms while she's reaching to turn the stove off.

"Bye! Bye-bye!" they say simultaneously before hanging up.

Tom holds the phone and keeps quietly kissing Latisha before hanging up.

Latisha continues cooking while they continue their conversation, filled with the details of the mission. He discusses his newfound wealth amidst a well-candlelit room. Deep in conversation, she is keen to finagle her way around and lead him to questions, and her tone finally gears toward a slight hint of interrogation about Kelley being at the house and the key being under the mat.

Tom gets speechless, and then assures her she has nothing to worry about until they are into jokes with a playful spirit before retiring from dinner. Tom brings her back to her playful mood when commenting on previous phone jokes about a pregnant woman's warmth.

They clean up and turn in early because Tom can't stay away from the thoughts of having that extra heat he's never experienced.

After Kelley sees the kids in their rooms, she drifts into her bedroom and sits on the bed, in the dark, for hours. She cries until slightly banging the back of her head against the headboard. In a deeper cry, she falls over, balling up in a fetal position, crying harder until relaxing on her side. She feels totally numb when it finally hits her: Tom is totally out of her life, and the possibility of reconciliation is over. She meditates for over half an hour longer, and then sits up, sliding her feet into her slippers when quietly exiting the room.

Kelley walks down the dimly-lit hallway, looking in the kids' room when passing to make sure they're still asleep. Halfway down the dark stairway, she stumbles over a metal toy, forcing it loudly down the wooden steps. "Shit!" she shouts, unknowingly waking her daughter when bracing the handrail and holding on tight. Her heart races fast from almost losing her balance when an ache grows at her toenail as the toy continually makes several more loud bangs down the steps before resting against the throw rug near the front door.

Kelley makes it to the kitchen and sits, taking more time to relax, then sits a little longer, waiting for her heartbeat to become regular again when slowly standing. She opens the refrigerator, removes the orange juice carafe, takes a swig, and then walks over to the sink. In a daze, she stares through the kitchen window until noticing her reflection fade in from the dark window when a reflection of the light shines through the cracked-open refrigerator door. She stares in the window for minutes in deep thought until breaking her concentration and looks down, finding a sharp butcher knife submerged in the dishwater with a few other dishes scattered.

She instantly goes into deep thoughts of killing herself and ending it right then and there. She takes another swig, slowly bringing the carafe from her lips, holding it at chest level, and meditating more when her body grows numb, thinking of Tom lying in bed and holding Latisha. Her eyes slowly drift to the knife, hearing continual chanting voices as she slides her hand into the cool water and picks up the knife. She stares at the blade as if obsessed with it and then turns it on both sides. Her eyes run up and down the sharpness of the blade from different angles until relaxed and in an even deeper trance when the carafe falls freely to the stone-tiled floor, shattering into little pieces.

The juice and glass fling up against the front and side of her feet and legs with eyes still pierced on the shiny blade without blinking.

Instantly, bright, white lights bring her out of the trance, and she jumps and stares into the window, making eye contact, yet still in a daze.

"Mommy..., Mommy, what happened?" her daughter cries with her finger still on the light switch. She stays in the doorway staring at the back of her mother's head for seconds.

Finally, she breaks the second trance, registering that her daughter is there when slowly turning to her and staring into her daughter's face when her hand loosens the knife, dropping it back into the water.

Her daughter hears something bang against the bottom of the sink, so she rushes over with wandering eyes.

"Watch your foot, babe; there's glass down there," she says, shielding her daughter, but not before her little eyes find the knife slightly rocking back and forth just beneath the thin suds.

Kelley's heart falls to her stomach, and gentle tears rush down her face as she turns and embraces her daughter, who grasps Kelley really tight around the waist, comforting her.

"Everything will be all right, Mommy. I promise everything will be all right!" Ashley repeats to comfort Kelley while looking past her mother and over at the slightly cracked open refrigerator.

"I know, babe. I'm just missing Daddy right now. I mean, I really, really miss him. You can return to bed, sweetie, while Mommy finishes the dishes and cleans up this mess."

"No, I want to stay with you, Mommy. I can't sleep. Can I sleep with you?"

Now, to assure her daughter that everything is ok, Kelley allows her to wait while she cleans up and puts the dishes in the dishwasher, and when done, they hold hands and walk to Kelley's bedroom. They climb beneath the sheets, cuddling until falling fast asleep.

Kelley arises early the following morning, carrying her daughter to her bed.

She starts going through her things, getting her house in order, then piddles around in her closet for a while. She finally pulls out a black box hidden deep in her closet, opens it, and thumbs through documents with several documents strewn over the bed. She thumbs through her things a little longer until pulling out several photos when heading into the living room. She lights the fireplace and waits thirty minutes for the flames to rise higher, then throws all types of documents linking her to the dark side of her life, one item at a time. Tears heavily fill her eyes, soaking the top of her satin blouse.

The following day, Saturday, Tom and Latisha mainly lounge around, watching television and videos.

Later, they indulge in a classy little Italian restaurant for dinner and then go for a long walk on the beach, returning later, exhausted.

After Latisha freshens up, she slips into a sexy maternity nighty and joins Tom in the living room with the baby name book they had picked up earlier.

Tom sits with his back against the arm of the chair when Latisha eases onto the couch, backing up into him until he puts his arms around her.

They cuddle and begin thumbing through the book together until dusk when she becomes thirsty. They flip through a few more pages, and satisfied with the names they agreed on, Tom flips on the television and stretches his hand alongside the couch, lifting another book from the book rack. He thumbs through the last novel Kelley had purchased, reading the introduction.

Tom thumbs through a few more pages, still watching television and slowly yet accidentally flipping past recently-purchased airline tickets to Washington, DC, and Bazumi. He flips to the back, reads the back cover, and then slides it back into the book rack. He waits for Latisha to stand and then turns off the television before going into the kitchen to pour her a warm glass of milk and returns, placing the glass next to her on the end table. He eases into the chair next to her while she opens the baby book again and looks up a few more names that had come to mind.

She scrolls through a few more pages, puts the book on the end table, and cuddles next to him. "Umm..., I sure could use some more of that gentle loving like last night," she says, sneering and running her soft, manicured nails along the long axis of his thigh, instantly arousing him.

"Then let me see what I can do," he playfully says, leaning over and then into her, causing her to respond when she repositions her back against the couch and a few pillows.

Tom kisses from her soft lips down to her material-covered belly, and then moves down where he can feel her raised pelvis pressing hard through the material and against his chest when dropping and caressing her with his mouth, trying not to wet the material. He instantly feels her hips moving in a circular motion until her moans grow louder and then taper off as he repositions.

She spread her legs widely, playfully burying his face deep in her luscious thighs.

Tom begins teasing her and turning her on for minutes.

Latisha manages to resist her screams when biting her bottom lip when turned on by tense foreplay, until quickly overheated and totally aroused. She holds back her scream for minutes and then screams at the top of her lungs until giggling. At the peak of passion, she is breathless when trying to scream again but can't when a teardrop falls onto her cheek and slowly transitions along the smooth curvature of her lovely face. "Mmm, damn, babe, Mmm, damn, damn, damn," she moans, pounding her fist hard against the back of the couch; when her voice becomes muffled when her soft, thick thighs clench both his ears. "Damn!" she seductively moans, gasping for air and yet begging for more.

Tom eases to the floor, smiling when seeing her trembling uncontrollably.

She tries shaking off her continuous tingling and throbbing sensation, but it's useless.

"Stop it! It's not funny, babe!" she pouts.

Tom eases onto his knees, unzipping his trousers, and before he can reach down, she grabs a handful of him wrapped in his briefs. In an attempt to tease her, he moves her hand, but she reaches again, leaning forward with all her might.

Their hands go back and forth in a playful tug of war for minutes, and the room instantly fills with laughter until she thrusts forward fast, and a loud slap comes when she accidentally thrusts deep into the family jewels.

Tom drops forward in severe pain with a thick vein rising in his forehead, and he becomes lightheaded.

"Oh, babe..., babe..., I'm so sorry, sweetie!" she shouts, sitting up quickly and staring into his face, transforming into the severest of pains.

Tom's eyes water and then appear to have crossed for a second when fighting to shake off the worst pain, with tear after tear falling.

Latisha stands, caressing the back of his head until rubbing his shoulders and back while he remains bent over, still on his knees.

Finally, the pain subsides a little, and he manages to climb back onto the couch and zip his pants.

They sit in a quiet room for minutes until Tom bites his lip for seconds, trying to hold back his laughter. His stomach gently jiggles and then hardens when bursting into great laughter, which brings her out of sadness.

Within seconds, she leans into him and joins in the laughter until their laughter trickles into a giggle and then slowly subsides.

Something captures Tom's attention when looking through the blinds, catching a set of car taillights passing the house slowly. He gazes at the door for seconds before getting up to put the glass back in the screen door and shutting it before walking into the kitchen.

After a few minutes, Latisha heads upstairs to the restroom to brush her teeth, and afterward, she pulls out her head scarf from her beauty bag.

Another car pulls up front with the lights off when the door opens and gently eases shut.

Soft footsteps creep onto Tom's porch.

A gloved hand lifts the doormat, removes the spare key, and walks back to the car parked in front of the neighbor's house.

The three cocaine-filled woman's eyes make constant contact, each sniffing as if in a sniffing contest.

The girl in the backseat, who never has been high before, eases into the middle of the seat, hallucinating after taking another hit of cocaine. She passes the tray back to the front-seat passenger, who slides it back into the glove compartment.

The rear door opens, and the medium-built woman steps out with her eyes going back and forth as if expecting something to land magically on her face any minute. She climbs in the driver's seat and stares over at the passenger.

The original driver, a taller woman, who is still standing at the driver's door, leans into the window, looking over at the front-seat passenger, nodding and smiling before winking. "This will be quick! Meet me here in half an hour," the original driver says, walking to the trunk, where she stashes four weapons in her jacket-style black holster and then walks back to the driver's door.

The woman behind the steering wheel leans out the window, looking back toward the house.

The front passenger pulls out the long, narrow, white china tray from the glove compartment, again loaded with cocaine.

The three converge on the tray in the driver's lap, taking in one long line apiece and then softly giggling and softly chuckling, but more stoned.

The tall woman walks up the paved walkway, looking back to find the car still parked, and shakes her head in disbelief. Her feet continually softly pound the pavement until picking up her stride and quietly creeping up on Tom's porch. Her bloodshot eyes appear through Tom's sheer curtains, scanning the room at breathtaking speeds until spotting Latisha walking out of one room and returning seconds later.

Tom stands in the kitchen with his fingers anxiously and continually taps against the countertop until pressing a few microwave button keys. His eyes dance around in a circle as the flat popcorn bag makes its continual rounds. He thinks he hears a beep from the alarm but isn't sure, with the loud microwave's fan blowing on high, but knowing recalling locking the door, he ignores the warning and waits for the untimed popcorn to finish.

Tom gets curious about the time to spare, taking a few steps into the living room, looking around, and then gazing at the door. His eyes quickly wander toward the top of the stairs before rushing over to activate the alarm. His feet shuffle across the floor toward the kitchen, but as soon as he vanishes into the kitchen, a door slams shut and Latisha screams at the top of her voice, and something loud smashes against the door.

Tom nervously jumps and dashes through the door, calling out to Latisha twice while sprinting across the living room to the top of the stairs at lightning speed. His hands press hard on the door while turning the knob, and he thrusts forward, sliding in his tracks with the door slamming into the side of the tub and retracting shut. Tom freezes with eyes locked on the tall woman with the gun barrel pressed tightly against Latisha's temple.

The tall, elderly woman's bulged eyes stare deep into his, not blinking when heavily sniffing and jerking her head to one side a few times until whisking her long hair from over her eyes.

"Calm down! There has to be a way we can settle this," Tom says, very slowly advancing a few inches.

"Don't take another step, or your little whore here gets it," she says, sniffing more frequently until thick-looking snot drools and then vanishes each time she sniffs, hard.

"What do you want? Anything, just name it, but please don't hurt her, please," he begs.

"Please don't hurt her, please!" the woman repeats in a stoned yet perfectly mocking voice, like that of a witch. "Shut up! You pathetic little shit! There's one thing I can't stand, and that is a whiny-ass man!" she says, jumping at him in a punk fashion.

Tom jumps back like a chump but remains calm while taking a few hard swallows, and then a few steps back to ease the tension. Instantly, perspiration engulfs his body when he notices a slight movement in the woman's trigger finger whenever she adjusts the angle of the gun.

Tears continually roll down Latisha's face while she holds her hands high over her head, trembling with eyes moving with the suggestive motion that she is about to do something, but he has no clue what.

The pungent smell of burning popcorn grows stronger by the second.

"What is it you want? Anything, just name it," he says again. "If it is money, I have plenty," he says, reaching for his wallet to extoll his wealth.

"What I want, you've taken, and I can never get it back! Money? Ha! Boy, please! I have more money than you can shake a freakin' stick at!" she sniffs even harder in a stoned state.

"Then look..., maybe there's some mix-up," he says, slightly remembering where he'd seen her after hearing her voice a second time.

"So, you do remember me from the elevator, ey?" she asks, feverishly releasing Latisha and holding her hair in a pinned-up fashion to reveal her true hair color. "Oh yeah, I have the right house and the right damn man," she says, snatching Latisha into her arms again. "Your damn girly here was just in the wrong place at the wrong time, or was she? You tramp and hoe wrecker!" she says, pressing the barrel tighter to Latisha's temple until it leaves a slight indentation.

"You killed my husband, Major Davis, and my daughters, Nichelle and Nadine. I'm here for revenge, three for three," she says, sliding her hand around Latisha's neck and aiming the barrel at her belly. "Let's see, which shall I take first? Maybe the baby, like you took my firstborn," she says, heavily sniffing again.

The loud smoke detectors begin beeping in unison and blaring in their ears.

"Get on your knees!" the woman screams over the alarms with the gun pointed at him.

Tom slowly kneels with his hands raised well above his head. His eyes stare deep into the woman's face, finally recognizing Nichelle's and Nadine's facial features, which he had never recognized before.

Latisha's eyes roll once more when her head slams backward as fast as she can move it, head-butting the woman. Her arms abruptly whisk down at lightning speed, knocking the gun from the woman's hand as she runs into Tom's arms.

Tom's eyes follow the gun, which falls behind the woman and slides into the corner near the toilet.

The woman struggles to maintain her balance, moving fast yet disoriented when falling back onto the toilet's reservoir and fighting to draw another weapon while half-repositioned.

Tom hurriedly guides Latisha to the door when the woman, still half-sprawled over the toilet, accidentally fires two unbalanced rounds into the ceiling.

The next barrage of fire pierces the door as Latisha passes through it, and the last one nips Tom's shoulder blade but barely breaks the skin.

Tom holds Latisha tight, carefully rushing her downstairs and easing her into the laundry room, throwing a hand full of clothing and bedspreads from the floor over her and then backing out. He gazes over his shoulder, and his ears stay very receptive when sliding the door shut, freezing in place, and listening.

In an instant, he maneuvers to the back of the house and quietly stands in view of both the kitchen and hallway, where he hears the steps and handrails squeak as she slowly makes her way down the stairs. She comes down slowly, bent over the railing, training her weapon around until making it to the bottom step, which squeaks even louder.

In her peripheral vision, she spots Tom through a living room mirror in alignment with the hall mirror when he blinks, and she vanishes right before his eyes, coming up on the dining room side of the house at top speed to regain sight of him.

Tom runs past the second alarm pad, pressing the police, fire, and ambulance buttons simultaneously when slowing and turning with his back to the wall, listening and looking until sliding in front of his study with his hand on the knob. He slips inside, but when the door is close to being shut, it squeaks, and loud shots ring out with a few rounds shattering the door's wooden framed edge, ripping the corner of the door to shreds.

In stealth mode, she comes up on the door and stands listening to the loud alarm blaring over her head until she slams the gun's barrel against it, silencing one of the eight.

Tom nervously lifts a key from the corner of the desk, anxiously guiding it toward the lock of his wall-mounted weapons display while looking over his shoulder, frozen in place, and then looking again to realign it when he notices the doorknob slowly turning. He quickly pushes the key forward and accidentally drops it behind the heavy, low-cut wall unit. He lifts his black-belt karate statue in a flash, smashing the glass, and clutches three five-spiked stars.

He pulls two knives from his ninja set, crams as much as he can in his waistband, and draws tense when lowering himself behind the oak table and focusing on the door until it slowly opens. Sweat profusely drips from his face while patiently waiting, and he soon spots her muscular stocking-covered leg leaning inside.

In total silence, the sound of the clock grows in their ears.

More perspiration builds on his face when he sees her slither inside and shut the door.

She looks the room over and then eases up on the office desk finding the chair settling down from being brushed against in passing.

Tom leans further down, holding the three stars between each finger, so they don't touch.

Out of nowhere come several loud knocks and yells, which causes her to look back but instantly refocus when Tom jumps up immediately and as if in slow motion, with three stars simultaneously whistling through the air.

One star penetrates her temple, staggering her; one goes to her jugular vein, making her wobble worse, and the last she blocks, but it splits her hand open with the gun freely falling from her tight grip and landing on top of the low wall unit, spinning until sliding behind it onto the floor.

There comes a loud crash forcing the front door open from top to bottom with firefighters and police officers rushing in and standing on top of the door, which lightly rocks back and forth against the doorknob. They stand curiously, looking around before swarming throughout the house.

A woman, the on-scene officer, and another officer come running inside within seconds.

Tom stares in disbelief, watching the stoned-out woman shake off the pain as if unaffected when slowly pulling the stars from her hand, jugular and temple, sneering.

She wobbles more, feeling a little faint, but the cocaine instantly numbs the feeling as her hand reaches along her waist for her long, thick blade. Her face transforms into pure evil, something sadistic, when she lets off a loud scream, frightening the response team when charging Tom with full force.

She pounces several feet away, stopped by the long oak table that Tom pushes up on two legs, when her face slaps hard against the furniture and her body lifelessly slides down the long axis of the table.

A leather boot fleetly rises to the study's door and thrusts against the door with brute force, knocking the door against the wall and driving the doorknob into the sheetrock.

Tom jumps and ducks.

"Freeze!" the two male officers scream feverishly, training weapons about the room and zooming in on Tom, who slowly raises his hands. "Get on your knees!"

Tom kneels with hands to the back of his head when shots ring out when the woman springs up without warning in stealth mode with the knife high over Tom's head.

After the fifth round to her upper body, she falls back and rolls to the floor, grasping her collar and pushing the bear emblem's button in the back with the bear's eyes fluctuating before black.

Latisha emerges from behind the male officers with the on-scene officer, who taps them on the shoulder and motions for them to lower their weapons.

Paramedics rush in minutes later and too late, so they dispatch to the coroner's office.

The firefighters place the microwave on the front porch and set up oxygen generators, ventilating the house with loud, high-velocity fans blowing.

The on-scene officer leads Tom and Latisha out through the semi-smoky hallway while other officers canvass inside and around the yard.

Tom embraces Latisha, wiping her tears as they come through the living room, and when they reach the front door, a fireman directs them to the ambulance, where they wait while the paramedic sets up the examination gear and table at the side door.

The police officers assist with getting the nosey neighbors back to their houses and one officer walks up and even frightens the neighbors, telling them to lock their doors and not open them for anyone.

Minutes later, two of the four officers and the firefighters leave on another dispatch.

Two officers and one paramedic wait inside for the detective and coroner.

Latisha is paranoid and shaken up, still very attentive to her surroundings, and turns, hearing a distant car door slam.

Through the darkness emerges a small, built woman is walking briskly across the neighbor's driveway, standing out of place and suited in a long trench-like coat, sort of like the one the tall lady wore. The woman smiles, waving while strutting onto the sidewalk, where her heels click even faster and louder when picking up her pace.

Latisha's eyes follow her and feel at ease seeing the woman's smile and friendly gesture when closer, but she's unsure as to whether the woman is a neighbor or not when turning and listening to the paramedic's instructions, so she knows how to care for Tom's wound properly. Her eyes drift from the bandage to the woman again, who looks like she's coming directly toward them.

A little uneasy and thinking back on the trench coat, Latisha touches Tom's back, getting his attention, but he's overly focused on the paramedic's detailed directions.

Latisha's head quickly moves from left to right between Tom and the woman who is less than forty feet away when her big smile becomes a mean and vicious frown. She briefly halts in her cocaine hallucination and lets off a high-pitched scream.

Tom looks around to see where the scream came from when instantly, she brandishes a twelve-gauge, double-barrel, sawed-off pump. Stoned, she drops back as if she's falling backward when cocking the weapon and pulling with a moderate click.

The click makes Tom and Latisha jump.

The stoned woman looks down, surprised, finally remembering the gun wasn't loaded, when leaning back, swiftly and almost transparently loading two slugs like a true professional. She holds the stock and snaps the barrel in alignment, and the too-familiar sound sends a chill down Tom's spine and causes the paramedic to look in the rear window, thinking he saw someone sprint past.

Tom pulls Latisha next to the ambulance and downward until she's slightly slumped over.

The woman leans back and fires a round, spraying the side of the ambulance with beads sinking deep into the paramedic's chest, slamming him inside against the far wall and splattering blood all over the inside.

The two officers duck, backing against the wall fast and confused, when barely hearing the muffled gunshots over the loud fans.

One officer moves slowly toward the living room with his back pressed flush against the wall.

The other officer replicates his partner's movement while calling for backup.

The two come up to the front door, and the first officer cautiously disconnects the fans and then backs up against the wall.

Tom and Latisha come up on the other side of the ambulance, still bent over, when another shot rings out, bursting the side window just as they pass with shattered glass dropping onto them. They remain bent over, yet still moving quickly until taking cover behind a large oak tree in the neighbor's yard.

"Didn't think you were going to get away with killing my baby's daddy, did you, Tom? Not to mention fathering this foreign bitch's baby when my child has no father!" the too-familiar feminine voice screams.

"What? What are you talking about?" Tom screams.

"Captain Carrington..., you bastard!"

"What kind of whacked-out people are you?"

"Whacked? Bitch, I wasn't so whacked when you were banging this out on the ship, and trying to stand up in it, was I?" she yells, grabbing her crotch like a man. "Oh yeah, you were damn good, but sex is nothing without love!" she screams, stoned out of her mind.

Now to the ensign, things appear to have been in a slow spin when she hallucinates that there are three Grand Reaper figures standing off to the side, pointing her to Tom and Latisha. A smile grows on her pretty face, which changes to horror in a flash.

Latisha slightly pulls away; furious, knowing Tom had sex with her but refocuses when slugs slam into the tree, with some whizzing by them.

"This shit is crazy!"

"No, what's crazy is you took what belongs to my baby and me. My baby is fatherless now because of you! You bastard!" she screams in a painful voice.

"You never said anything about having a child with him."

"We were planning on getting married next summer, you fucker!" Her eyes fill with tears, and her hands abruptly fumble over the weapon, reloading and then pumping off two more rounds. She nervously reloads again and clicks the weapon back to the ready position bringing it to eye level.

The police officers look out the front window, trying to assess the situation fully.

Dispatchers try making contact with them after they turn down their radios.

"The captain is already married, you dumb ass! Did you think he would marry your lame ass just because you are stupid enough to get pregnant? Now just calm down and think about what you're doing, Tamara!" Tom yells, finally recalling her name before nervously peeping around the tree.

The officers manage to sneak onto the lawn unnoticed. "Freeze!" they shout almost instantaneously.

Tamara slowly lowers her weapon and seems to comply until, in a stride, advancing on Tom and Latisha. She takes a blind aim back at the officers, still advancing toward Tom and Latisha, when shots ring out, one hitting her in the back and the other in her leg with screams.

"No!" Tom screams, peeping around the tree and whisking Latisha closer when seeing the tip of her gun's barrel.

One more round comes from the short officer, then another, causing Tamara to stumble headfirst while her finger is still lodged in the trigger well when the gun discharges, blowing her brains across the neighbor's lawn.

The second paramedic springs from the porch, rushing up from behind the officers, fearfully looking around. His eyes wander over to the back of the ambulance, seeing it splattered with blood.

Tom remains kneeled with Latisha still slumped against the tree. He reaches up, wiping her teary eyes through his teary eyes, and then stares at her, shaking his head in disappointment.

The faint sound of a distant car door slamming gets Latisha's attention immediately. Her eyes and head train in all directions until her eyes drift through the darkness to see if she can find where the sound is coming from, with the officers and the paramedic looking around, puzzled, as well.

With one last snort of cocaine from her long fingernail, an unnoticed feminine figure comes from the same place as Tamara, but she's wiser, cutting alongside a house and sweeping across the neighbors' back lawns at an even faster pace. She comes up alongside Tom's next-door neighbor's house and pierces out of darkness, well hidden from the officers, but when she peeps out, Latisha gets a good look at her.

Latisha's mouth speechlessly falls open, rapidly taking shelter behind the tree and pulling Tom closer while trying to talk, but in fear and shock, nothing comes forth. She cries hard, trying to speak, but starts hyperventilating.

Tom looks around and then puts his hands over her mouth to control her breathing. He holds her and looks around the tree with teary eyes, noticing a weapon extended over the head of a dark, silhouetted, feminine figure alongside his neighbor's house.

The paramedic looks around and then over to the ambulance for his assistant, only to find his leg hanging out of the door.

The two officers and paramedics instantly turn when hearing heels briefly click loudly across the narrow concrete driveway.

Tom's vision clears a little. "Behind you!" Tom screams, seeing the blurred, dark silhouette when two shots ring out almost instantaneously from a sawed-off shotgun, dropping the two officers and paramedic.

"Come on out, bitch!" the too-familiar voice loudly resonates.

"K-K-Kelley!" Latisha fearfully stutters.

Kelley feverishly reloads; aiming for the tree they are hiding behind and sniffing hard.

"Kelley! What do you think you're doing, Kelley? Hell, think about what you've gotten yourself into here!" Tom screams, peeping out and seeing the three bodies sprawled across the lawn. "Kelley, get out of here now, and we can make this right!" he screams, feeling sorry for her.

Kelley stands sweating profusely and sniffling like a prize racing horse. "Think? Fuck, I've had plenty of time to do some damn thinking. Hell, your captain let me in on the money and was too anxious to tell me all about this cheap-ass tramp..., well, tramps, you were screwing on your mission since there seems to be many," Kelley screams, sniffing harder until a thin trail of blood runs down over her top lip. She wipes her runny nose with her sleeve. "Yeah, and the nice, old Cuban woman you just killed was grateful enough to tell me about all those other damn women you were screwing on the damn island, including her daughter! Tamara also told me about your little sex drill on the ship. So, you know what? You're not even half the man I thought you were! You're nothing but a damn male whore! You sure are one to talk loyalty and quick to degrade me to Martha about Jeff, huh?" she screams, somewhat relaxed when her voice rises, and she feels relaxed enough to lower the gun down to her side. "How the hell you gonna try and hold me to one standard when you knew all the time you were on some grand fuck-fest! Yeah, you thought your shit didn't stink, but it sure as hell does now! How in the hell can you have the damn nerve to just stroll back into the States with a brand new piece of ass and a damn baby? What was I supposed to do, just take all this bullshit lying down?" she shouts, careening back and forth from standing too long in one spot, new to the feeling when the ground begins to spin.

Several neighbors' curtains swing back and forth.

Kelley stays quiet, waking in circles and trying to adjust to the first time high that is out of the world.

In the house next to Tom's, two heads stay low, yet they try to assess the situation with the wife on the phone with the 911 operator, giving by-the-second updates.

Other law enforcement vehicles are held off a block away, still trying to establish communications with the two officers for a tactical-situation report.

Tom's neighbor's wife runs from window to window, looking for the officers who the dispatcher says are on sight but can't see them.

The SWAT team is on alert and manning up at the station.

Tom thinks quickly about getting her talking so he knows her position. "You mean you bought off on all those damn foolish lies, Kelley? Captain Carrington was dirty as hell..., and those women..., all lies!" Tom yells to confuse Latisha, and it is confirmed to have when she wipes her eyes and kisses his hand. "He was feeding you bullshit to get you caught up in this mess to hurt me! Damn all those lies, Kelley! The fact remains; I can't believe you would destroy your life like this. What about the kids?"

"Ha! You are the damn liar! I was there in Bazumi, and I was there in Washington. I saved your life several times when you were in the crosshairs because I loved you! My life? Damn, my life! You were my life, damn it! Kids? Ha! What kids? I have nothing to live for now because they hate me because you left us," she screams, taking aim ahead.

Tom shakes his head with the missions and near deaths flashing in his mind fast when Latisha looks up.

"She's lying. She has never been to Bazumi or D.C., for that fact, she doesn't even know where Bazumi is," he whispers, trying to convince Latisha when he hears her heavily breathing after Kelley confirms that she saw things and knows for sure about the other women he had screwed.

Tom tries reasoning with Kelley for seconds until she advances rashly on them.

When she reaches the officers and paramedic, she trains the shotgun on him and then the officers, nervously kicking them to make sure they are dead. She nervously aims at the tall officer when a shot rings out from her hallucinating that he had jumped up, blowing out his back. She pulls the trigger again, blowing his brains out, thinking she saw him on his knees with his weapon drawn.

With an even slower reload from being so stoned, she stands in a supportive stance, firing twice at the tree that Tom and Latisha are behind when Latisha screams, hearing buckshot sinking deep into the tree and flying by when embracing Tom tighter.

Kelley fumbles around in her coat pocket until finally pulling out two more rounds, reloading even slower when hallucinating from the drugs and thinking she saw demons pointing her to the opposite side of the tree. She sniffs a few times loudly to stop her nose from running while slightly rocking back and forth until slapping the barrel into alignment again and firing two more shots at the tree. Kelley staggers heavily from side to side, finally feeling the full effects of the drugs when bringing the shotgun to eye level, aiming when Tom and Latisha's heads pierce slightly from each side of the tree and vigorously retracts. With full force, Kelley takes off screaming like a lunatic, rushing toward the tree and coming into plain view, causing them to back up while staying close to it.

They beg and plead for their lives until Tom is heard crying more than Latisha while hiding behind her, yet pulling her back in his arms while continually backing away.

"Got your asses now!" Kelley screams with the shotgun aimed at them as they fade in and out of view from Tom, continually pulling Latisha back around the tree and out of view.

Kelley comes closer, staggering and forcing them backward until her back is to Tom's house again. She runs faster, bringing them both in sight when pressing hard on the trigger with a loud click, then screams when their hearts drop.

Tom's mind draws blank until he pulls Latisha backward around the tree, and they turn, sprinting for another large tree with him, keeping his eyes in line with the last tree and maneuvering her to remain well hidden.

Kelley fumbles in her pocket and staggers a few times while looking down and reloading, and then finally looks up and to the side of the tree, finding them distancing themselves. She takes a stance, aiming with her finger still in the trigger well, and presses just as they vanish behind another thick oak tree.

"Freeze!" the slightly-wounded short officer screams, low-crawling a few inches and grasping his weapon when training it at her back before she turns, hallucinating there are several officers with their guns drawn.

Kelley's heart races fast, turning from the hallucinated officers at a fast pace toward Tom and Latisha when a shot ring out, with her hallucinating many with one to her spine, staggering her, but she feels no pain.

Tom screams when the second round to her upper chest near her heart causes her to let off a dreadful cry with stoned laughter, but the last round slows her, shattering her kneecap and causing her to fumble to the ground.

The officer comes to his knee, then to his feet, wobbling, limping, and quickly reloading.

Tom inhales a deep breath. "No!" He lets off another scream as he falls to his knees and brings Latisha downward, yet manages to brace her fall to protect the baby.

Kelley springs up on both feet three times but drops each time when hit.

Latisha swiftly crawls to her feet and stands behind Tom, supporting him with her hands on his shoulders.

Tom swiftly stands and holds Latisha in his arms, guiding her over to Kelley with receptive ears and eyes to any strange sounds or movement, cautiously expecting another surprise at any moment.

Kelley's body trembles like a leaf, eyes faint while taking deep and short sips of air.

"Why, Kelley? Why?" Tom asks in tears.

Kelley low-crawls at almost a snail's pace a few more inches, reaching for the gun until the officer stumbles over and puts his foot on it. She rolls over and looks up, coughing up more blood, then struggles, flopping onto her belly when feeling the deep, burning wounds. With all her strength, Kelley rolls over once more and slowly over again, covered in blood. She coughs up more blood while lifting her head and gasping for more air. "Because..., I..., Love..., You..., and..., I...,," she says, unnoticeably easing her hand to her collar, pressing the button on the back of the bear emblem as she takes her last breath. The bear's eyes turn black as her head lifelessly falls to the ground.

A trail of her blood expressly forms in a puddle and trails along the embankment toward the street.

Tom's eyes fixate on something gold on the back of her folded-back collar when his head curiously cocks to one side when flipping her collar back to find the too-familiar golden bear emblem. He stares at the emblem for minutes, puzzled over it, and then removes it and another pendant he had brought her, holding it tightly in his hand with his free hand closing her stale eyes. Tears continually fall until his sight is somewhat blurry. His mind is totally puzzled as to how Kelley could have gotten involved so deeply in such a short time while slipping his hand in his pocket when the short officer limps over with his hand held out.

"I need what you just removed from her as evidence," he says, looking into Tom's eyes under-eyed.

Tom fumbles around in his pocket and, slipping him the pendant he had brought, keeping the bear emblem.

"It's just something I gave her long ago," he says, looking at Latisha, who looks at him in a daze and with an unsure stare, knowing he is lying by not turning over the second pendant.

The neighbor whose lawn they are on nervously clears the top step, and his wife suddenly appears behind him. She ran over to help the short, bloody officer who had fallen to his knees in severe and unbearable pain.

Distant sirens close in fast, with five cop cruisers swarming the dimly-lit street and canvassing the whole block.

The coroner and detective show up within minutes.

Soon, the whole street fills with blue-and-red lights, including the SWAT team that emerges up the hill from behind trees.

Two officers rush over and assist the wounded officer and then check the other officer's pulse, lying face down in a pool of blood.

Other officers converge and check on the severely wounded paramedic before going to the ambulance and finding a dead body inside.

Tom and Latisha stand, looking around until a new officer rushes up and drapes them with a blanket. He rushes them out of the crime scene and walks them over, near the street's edge, beside his cruiser.

With everyone cared for, bagged, and tagged, the officers secure the scene and assist the other officers in fully taping off the crime scene.

A second coroner's vehicle arrives, and they begin loading the slain officer and paramedic's bodies. When the door slams shut, a heavy hand bangs on the door, and the driver looks out of the side mirror while flipping the flashing red lights off and following an officer's direction as he maneuvers close around other parked first-responder vehicles.

The other van follows closely.

Another ambulance pulls up at the end of the road and stops, waiting for a car to pass. The ambulance dips to one side a little, and the bay's interior lights briefly come on and then turn off. The driver looks in the side mirror and then moves forward, looking ahead to find an officer waving them forward.

Out of nowhere comes a moderate to loud tone that turns into bells and loud chimes that grow louder.

Tom wipes his tears with his hand and stops, staring back at Kelley with teary eyes, feeling sorry for his actions on the mission and, most of all, the initial call to Kelley, which started the snowball effect that he felt eventually destroyed her life. He is heavily despondent until refocusing when finally feeling a slight vibration at his hip when reaching for the pager and squinting to read the message: 'DISCONNECTED.'

He clenches the pager, slamming it to the pavement with all his strength, and pulls Latisha closer.

With one last look at Kelley, he pulls Latisha closer and limps over to the ambulance that had just pulled up.

The officer reaches for the door, and it flung wide open with shots ringing out with Tom and Latisha dropping down and off to the side of the ambulance.

The officer staggers backward a few feet, holding his throat until dropping to the ground.

A long-haired Cuban woman quickly trains her specially-made gun around for Tom and Latisha when a barrage of gunfire stormed the back of the ambulance, dropping the woman back into the ambulance and halfway onto the bloody stretcher with two SWAT team members sitting in the tree, still combing the area with precision aims. Their eyes wandered over the blue-and red-light-filled street, observing everyone frozen in place until slowly standing after hearing, "All clear!"

The end…, hope you enjoyed it!

Fair winds and following seas!
Azreay'l - Cheers!

Terminology

Aft—most rear point of the ship
Bearing—direction
Bow—the most forward point of the ship
Brow—a ladder attached to a platform or bridged from ship to land
Bulkhead—a wall, temporary wall, or partition
Bunk—bed
Cabin—captain's sleeping quarters
Closet point of Approach (CPA)—closet point at which two objects will come together
Faded—disappeared
Fantail—most rear point of the ship's external weather deck
Head—a bathroom
Headgear—a hat
Junior Officer of the Deck (JOOD)—assistant to the OOD
Lifelines—safety lines; to prevent personnel from falling overboard
Lollygagging—playing around or horse playing
Messenger of the Watch (MOOW)—junior enlisted person in a security role
Officer of the Deck—responsible to the captain and ship's safety at sea
Platform—a stand; for boarding a vessel while docked pier side
Port—left or left side
Quarterdeck—vessel's main entrance
Quarters—where people sleep
Racks—coffin-type stacked beds
Senior Supply Specialist (SSS)—one who deals with supply duties
Special Forces Training (SFT)—training for special weapons and tactics
Specialist of the Watch (SOOW)—senior enlisted person in a ship's security role
Stand on vessel—vessel's right to continue on heading; on a collision course
Starboard—right or right side
Trawlers—small, silenced underwater boat engines
Wardroom—where officers and dignitaries dine
Watch-standing (working/security guarding)—various duties performed

www.ingramcontent.com/pod-product-compliance
Lightning Source LLC
LaVergne TN
LVHW091708070526
838199LV00050B/2307